The Hindi-Bindi Club

The Hindi-Bindi Club

MONICA PRADHAN

BLOOMSBURY

First published in Great Britain 2007
This paperback edition published 2008

Map by Jeffrey L. Ward
Book design by Jennifer Daddio

Bloomsbury Publishing Plc,
36 Soho Square,
London W1D 3QY

Bloomsbury Publishing, London, New York and Berlin

www.bloomsbury.com

A CIP catalogue record for this book
is available from the British Library

Paperback ISBN 978 0 7475 9276 1
10 9 8 7 6 5 4 3 2 1

Export paperback ISBN 978 0 7475 9491 8
10 9 8 7 6 5 4 3 2 1

Printed in Great Britain by Clays Ltd, St Ives plc

All papers used by Bloomsbury Publishing are natural, recyclable products made from wood grown in well-managed forests. The manufacturing processes conform to the environmental regulations of the country of origin.

For

ASHOK HARISCHANDRA PRADHAN
and
RAJANI YASHWANT KHARKAR

for your blood, sweat, and tears, your
courage, sacrifice, and sense of adventure
in leaving the world you knew behind,
and starting over in a foreign land,
with only two suitcases to your name.
From the bottom of my heart,
I thank you for my life.

And for

MORSE SALVATORE CALTABIANO
and
THERESA SALVAGE CALTABIANO

for raising a hero for me to marry,
and welcoming me into your family
with open arms from Day One.

And for

JIM,

a dream come true.

Truth in her dress finds facts too tight.
In fiction she moves with ease.

RABINDRANATH TAGORE
STRAY BIRDS, CXL

The Daughters

KIRAN DESHPANDE

(KEY–run)

PREITY CHAWLA LINDSTROM

(PREE–thee)

RANI McGUINESS TOMASHOT

(RAH–nee)

The Mothers

MEENAL DESHPANDE

(ME–null)

SAROJ CHAWLA

(Suh–ROWJ)

UMA BASU McGUINESS

(OU–mah)

Contents

Part One–The New World

Part Two–The Old World

Part Three—Passing the Torch

Part Four—No Place Like Home[s]

Part Five—East Meets West

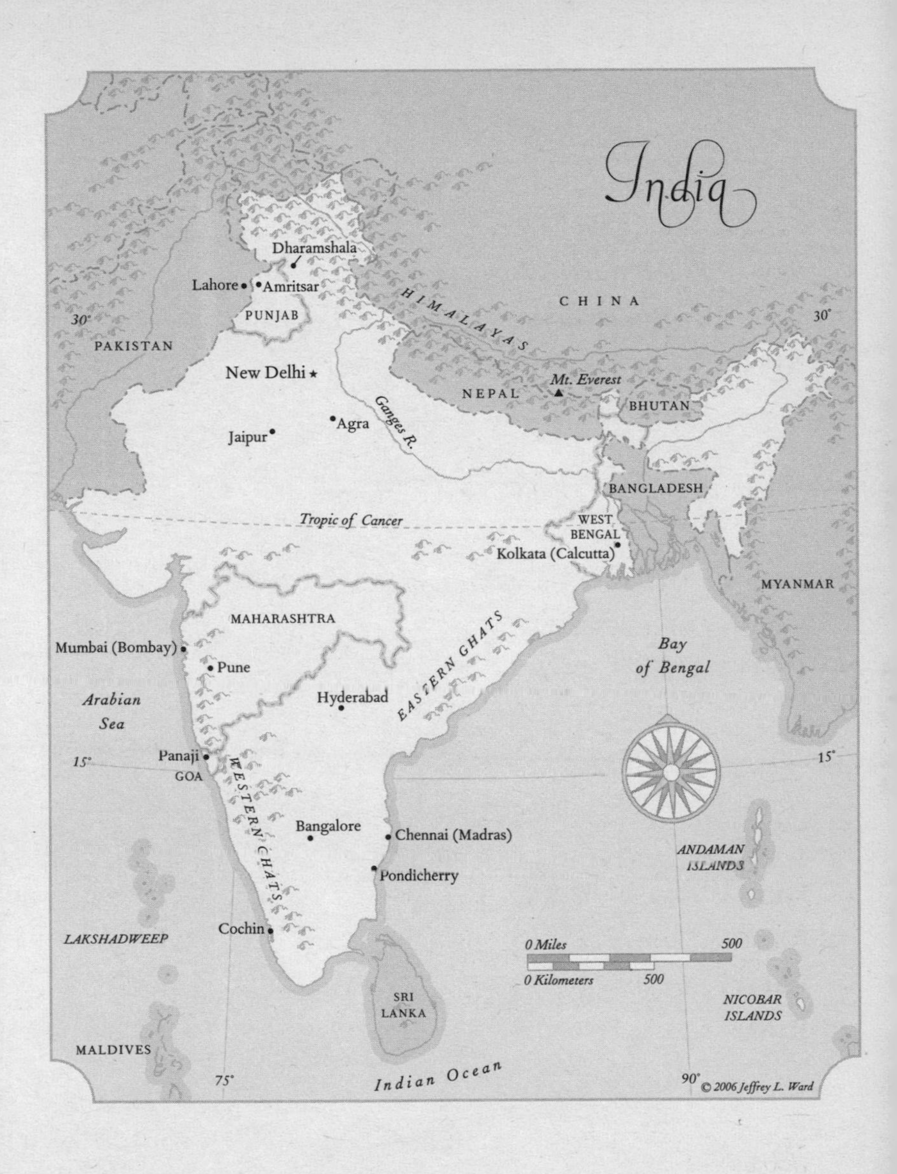
India
Dharamshala
Lahore
Amritsar
PUNJAB
30°
PAKISTAN
HIMALAYAS
CHINA
30°
New Delhi
Mt. Everest
NEPAL
BHUTAN
Agra
Jaipur
Ganges R.
BANGLADESH
Tropic of Cancer
WEST
BENGAL
Kolkata (Calcutta)
MYANMAR
MAHARASHTRA
EASTERN GHATS
Mumbai (Bombay)
Pune
Bay
of Bengal
Arabian
Sea
Hyderabad
Panaji
15°
GOA
15°
WESTERN GHATS
Bangalore
Chennai (Madras)
ANDAMAN
ISLANDS
Pondicherry
Cochin
LAKSHADWEEP
0 Miles
500
0 Kilometers
500
SRI
LANKA
NICOBAR
ISLANDS
MALDIVES
75°
Indian Ocean
90°
© 2006 Jeffrey L. Ward

PART ONE

The New World

Kiran Deshpande: Where Are You From?

I have lanced many boils, but none
pained like my own.
INDIAN ADAGE

I'm never sure what people want to know when they ask me: "Where are you from?"

The question doesn't offend me, as I'm curious about people myself. I'm fascinated by the origins of family trees, the land and seas over which seeds migrate, cross-pollinate, and germinate anew.

In my thirty-two years, I've traveled to all fifty United States, lived in ten of them, in every American time zone, most since I left home for college at seventeen and never moved back. A modern gypsy, I've developed an ear for accents. I'm charmed by different cadences. It's a game for me to place them, to listen for the fish out of water.

"Is that Texas I hear?" I ask with a smile—always a

smile, the universal ambassador of goodwill—of a lady in Juno, Alaska.

I *never* ask that slippery little devil, you know the one: "Where are you from?"

Sometimes, I envy people who can answer this deceptively simple question in two words or less. "Jersey" or "Chicago," "New Orleans" or "Southern Cal." People who've lived most of their lives in a single state, sometimes even a single town. People whose physical appearance or last name is unremarkable.

I don't fall into any of these categories.

When I get this question—not an everyday occurrence, but I get it more than most—I'm never certain what information the person seeks. Is it the origin of my own mid-Atlantic accent? My heritage? My married name (read off a credit card, a check, or a name tag)?

To cover the bases, I supply all three. Probably overkill, but I figure the desired answer's somewhere in here: "My parents emigrated from India in the 1960s when my father went to medical school at Harvard. I was born in Cambridge but grew up outside of Washington, D.C. My husband's last name is Italian."

If I answer with a genuine smile, I almost always receive one in response, which strengthens my belief in karma.

A guy once told me I looked like Disney's Princess Jasmine, except my boobs weren't big enough. For the first four years of our marriage, I assumed he exaggerated on both counts.

Princess Jasmine is prettier than I am, but she isn't bigger than a B-cup, thankyouverymuch.

In retrospect, as I reflect on his statement (something I do less as time goes on), I wonder if he meant my boobs weren't big enough *for him*. This would be a logical conclusion after coming home early to find his face sandwiched between a pair of D-cups. *Silicon* D-cups, which is my professional opinion as a practicing physician, not just another ex-wife whose husband screwed around on her.

I am wondering about this today as I appreciate the latest and greatest "water bra" in the Victoria's Secret dressing room. It's the first week of December, and I'm almost finished with my holiday shopping, so I'm splurging on a few things for myself. The water bra has a lovely effect, I must admit as I turn from side to side. I take it off and decide I look great, with or without the bra. I'm young. I'm healthy. My body is well toned. Nothing sags.

So why am I crying?

A tissue box sits on a ledge, as if my meltdown is not an isolated phenomenon in these dressing rooms. I thank whomever for the forethought and mop my face.

Why are you crying? I ask the woman in the mirror. *You have everything going for you.*

Yes, but where will it go from here? the woman replies. *And with whom?*

I turn my back because I can't bear to look at her anymore, but I can't leave either. Not like this. Once I was stuck in a stairwell after I lost a patient. I couldn't come out until I regained control, couldn't risk the family seeing me that way.

They count on me to be strong when they're weak. But who's strong for me when I'm weak?

The woman in the mirror mocks me because she still looks so young, yet for the first time, I feel the acceleration of time. It doesn't seem so long ago I turned twenty-two, med school and marriage my dreams. Now here I am a decade later, a doctor, married and divorced. I've crossed thirty, and I'm afraid if I blink, I'll be staring at forty, looking back on today.

"It seems like just yesterday I fell apart in the Victoria's Secret dressing room," I'll say as I recollect the days when I had perky breasts.

Stark reality presses against me, a cold stethoscope on my bare skin. I cringe and shiver, hug my arms, rub my goose bumps. The truth is I am terrified. Of squandering my precious time on this earth. Of wasting what's left of my youth. Of turning the big Four-O and looking back with regrets.

I'm a *family* doctor. Every day, I see *families*. I want a family, too.

I'm healthy and vibrant *now*, but with each passing year, my eggs age. I'm tired of wandering. Tired of my gypsy existence as a traveling doc, temporarily filling in where there's a need. Tired of running away from the fact my foolish heart betrayed me as much as Anthony's cheating.

I yank two more tissues from the box and discover they're the last ones. Isn't that life? One day the tissues run out.

So what's your strategy with the tissues you have, Kiran?

I don't want to freeze my eggs. I don't want to visit a sperm bank. I don't want to be a single parent, if I have any choice in the matter. I want a nuclear family. I want to put down roots, to let my seeds germinate, to watch them bloom and flourish. Not one day, if and when I ever fall in love again, but *now*. While I still have my youth, damn it.

I glance over my shoulder at the puffy-eyed woman in the mirror. Slowly, I turn and face her. There is a solution, if she's willing to keep an open mind, to think with her head this time, instead of her heart. I take a deep breath, hold it, and nod. And right there in the Victoria's Secret dressing room, in my yuppie-chick equivalent of a midlife crisis, I allow myself to contemplate something I always deemed impossible, dismissed as cold, archaic, *backward*. The mate-seeking process that served my parents, most of their Indian-immigrant friends, and generations of ancestors for centuries.

An arranged marriage.

Leaving the shopping carnival of Georgetown Park, I stand at the intersection of M Street and Wisconsin Avenue and wait for the WALK signal. You'd think I'd be done with malls, but no. When I got my driver's license at sixteen, Georgetown was *the* place to hang out, and for me, it's never lost its appeal. I love the shops and restaurants, the international and academic atmosphere, the colonial architecture. Whenever I'm back in town, I make a pit stop here on my way home. It grounds me.

I walk up the brick sidewalk to 33rd and Q. It's been five years since my last visit, but my ritual's unchanged. If I can get a space, I parallel park near my dream house, a Tudor that resembles a gingerbread house, its fence and gate laced with a jungle of ivy, trimmed to reveal the pointed tips of cast-iron rungs as straight as spears. When I graduated from high school, in addition to throwing a penny in the mall fountain and making a wish, I put a note in the mailbox on Q Street asking the owners to please call me when they wanted to sell the house. I hoped by the time they were ready, I would be, too. I'm still waiting.

With my purchases—a red poinsettia in green foil and white roses with sprigs of fern—ensconced in the passenger seat of my Saab, I take Key Bridge across the muddy Potomac and cruise down the G.W. Parkway toward the 'burbs. I'm tempted to stop—and stall some more—at one of the scenic overlooks (make-out hot spots). Instead, I crack the windows, crank the heat, blare the Goo Goo Dolls to calm my nerves, and force myself to keep going.

I'm *so* not looking forward to this. As if it isn't hard enough coming home with my tail between my legs, the thought of approaching my parents with my brainstorm makes it that much worse. I already know what's in store. The Mother of All Lectures. The Granddaddy of *I-told-you-so*s. A lifetime of smugness. Vindication they were right and I was wrong in my decision to marry Anthony... If only I'd listened to them... *Blah blah blah*...

No matter how old I get or how much respect I garner from the rest of the world, to my parents, I'm still an exasperating, recalcitrant child whose ear requires constant twisting. And in their world, I feel reduced to one. Which is why I avoid them as much as possible, and why I feel like a runaway coming home.

In my hometown of Potomac, Maryland, I almost run a stop sign that wasn't there five years ago. I slam on the brakes. The seatbelt pins me. I lunge my right arm out to catch the poinsettia before it takes a header. Too late. The plant sails off the seat, smashes into the glove compartment, and skitters under the dash, dumping black soil all over the cream floor mat and filling the air with the scent of damp earth.

Do you believe in omens?

I try not to as I drive through town, inventorying the new superimposed over the familiar. Widened roads. Bulldozed trees. New traffic lights at the intersections of new neighborhoods. A parade of 5,000-square-feet-plus homes squashed together on tiny, impeccably manicured plots. Luxury townhouses offer a smart alternative for those who can't afford sticker prices over one million dollars but want the amenities. Lots of dinky old homes, squatters on primo acreage, have been demolished, replaced with monoliths. I imagine the former owners cashed out and headed south. Gone, too, is the mom-and-pop service station where I dropped off my car for repairs, billed to my father's account, and a mechanic gave me a lift home in a tow truck. A twelve-pump Mobil with touchless carwash now gleams in its place.

Still, while much has changed, much remains the same. The salmon brick building of my high school. The golden arches of Mickey D's where we snacked after school and sports events, our home away from home. The 7-Eleven where we tried (no dice) to buy California wine coolers. The white picket fence of Shady Creek Stables where I learned to ride on a gentle mare named Shokie who had a penchant for carrots I tucked into my pockets for her. These and other landmarks greet me like old friends.

As I anticipate each twist and turn of the winding two-lane road that takes me home, I feel a strange mix of connection and detachment. Home isn't home anymore. I don't live here. I'm a visitor. A near stranger to my folks. Even more than when we cohabitated. They converted my old bedroom into a guestroom a while back, I heard. I wonder which of my photos they keep on display, if any, and where they stashed the ones they removed—like my wedding pictures.

How appropriate is it that the great philosophers the Goo Goo Dolls should choose this moment to sing my theme song, "Iris"? I join them and belt out the lyrics.

A mile away, I kill the music and raise the windows. As I pull into the driveway, my fingers tighten around the steering wheel, my muscles stiffen like the onset of rigor mortis, and I ask myself for the millionth time if it's really worth the grief. I'm sorely tempted to sneak around back and climb the trellis to the second-story roof outside my bedroom window where my friends and I used to steal away in high school and puff Marlboro Lights. (I quit cold turkey my sophomore year in college—during finals, which I don't recommend—but if there was a cigarette in my car right now, I sure as hell wouldn't waste it.) I wipe my clammy hands on my jeans and pop a stick of gum into my mouth.

Okay, Kiran. You're a big girl. You almost went into emergency medicine. You handle drug overdoses, spinal taps, emergency C-sections, and broken bones with nerves of steel. Surely, you can face—

Tap-tap-tap! Raps on my driver's-side window startle me mid-affirmation.

"Kiran! Is that you?"

My memory banks struggle to match the familiar, boisterous voice with the woman beaming at me. I press a button and lower the glass. It's the chunky gold pendant that dangles from long strings of tiny black-and-gold beads on her *mangal sutra*—Hindu wedding necklace—that cinches what should have been obvious.

"Saroj Auntie! I didn't recognize you at first!" What's different? "Your hair! What a cool new do," I blurt, as if I've been M.I.A. for five weeks instead of five years, then sheepishly add, "Or, uh, is it just new to me?"

One of my mother's oldest and dearest friends, Saroj Chawla, has known me since birth. "Why, thank you." With a hand, she props up the mop of curls, cropped into a chin-length bob that suits her buoyant personality. "It *is* a new do. To go with my new body." She grins and steps back, unbuttons her full-length, camel-colored coat, and whips it open like a flasher. I realize she has shrunk several dress sizes, shape-shifting from plump to voluptuous. "I lost fifty pounds on the South Beach diet."

My jaw drops. "No way."

She laughs. "Yes, way."

Somehow, "South Beach" and "Indian" have never gone together in my mind. What's Indian food with no rice, bread, potato—? I nearly gasp. "No *samosas*?"

"Not in the beginning. Now, everything in moderation."

"Whew. Thank goodness."

My favorite Indian appetizer, the triangular potato-and-pea-stuffed pastry is one of Saroj Auntie's specialties. Not only is she a culinary genius but, luckily for the rest of us, she owns one of the premier catering services in the D.C. Metro Area, possibly the eastern seaboard. She started it back in the Boston Days. That's how they refer to them, those early years in the States when my father and her husband were poor grad students on academic scholarships, my father at

Harvard and Sandeep Uncle at M.I.T. My dad says, "We were poor, but we didn't know we were poor, so we were happy." From their stipends, they supported their new brides and sent what savings they could to family in India, where every dollar made a significant contribution toward groceries, health care, clothing, education, rent, or utilities.

As the story goes, every day Saroj Auntie packed Sandeep Uncle's lunch in *tiffins*—round, stackable stainless steel containers holding different dishes. Indian Gourmet to Go. Before long, Saroj Auntie garnered a reputation as an excellent cook, and as word spread, others began asking for lunch *tiffins* and offering to pay.

Sandeep Uncle was dead set against his wife doing anything that could be construed as work for hire, a huge bruise to his ingrained masculine caveman-hunter-gatherer-protector-should-provide-for-woman pride, but Saroj Auntie appealed to his sense of manners and hospitality. She convinced him it was far worse to refuse requests for her cooking. Such refusal reflected poorly on them, and indeed on Indian culture, in the cases of Americans who expressed interest. As immigrants, they were India's cultural ambassadors, after all. And since it was unrealistic to foot the bill for the ever-growing number of requests, what choice did they have but to accept payment?

With much grumbling, Sandeep Uncle caved in. As her business grew, he continued to grumble, especially since *his* professional success grew as well, but Saroj Auntie persisted, and won.

I congratulate her on her latest victory and climb out of the car. She gives me her customary big squishy hug, mashing me against her ample chest, but despite all the I'm-Okay-

You're-Okay motions, I can't shake the niggling embarrassment of a patient in a hospital gown, her bare bottom showing out the back slit. Even if Saroj Auntie doesn't know the sordid details of my falling out with my parents (mum's the word with dirty family secrets), being one of Mom's best friends, she knows enough. And she knows that *I* know she knows, even if neither of us openly acknowledges it.

The December air is sweet and invigorating, cold enough for our breath to steam but not for our teeth to chatter. I pull on my leather jacket, leaving it unzipped, and we linger to catch up a bit before going inside. She updates me on the Chawla clan, and I give her the highlights of my upcoming assignment in Georgia. Belatedly, I register the B.M.W., Mercedes, Lexus, and Volvo S.U.V. parked around the cul-de-sac and wonder if my mother's having *all* her Indian friends over. Uh-oh...

"Is the—" I catch myself before I say "Hindi-Bindi Club," the age-old nickname we offspring gave our mothers' gatherings when we were little. "Are all of my aunties getting together tonight?"

"Yes, yes, everyone's coming, but we didn't know *you* were home. Or, no one told me." She plants one hand on her hip, the same endearing gesture I remember since childhood. "Do I have to scold your mom?"

The thought makes me smile. A wry smile. I doubt anyone's ever scolded my mother. They would have no reason. Unlike me, she's never misbehaved in her life, to my knowledge, and I'd be shocked if anyone told me otherwise. "No, Auntie. Mom doesn't know. It's a surprise visit."

"Oh." A slight pinch around her eyes. A wince? Before I

can be sure, it's gone. "Oh! What a *wonderful* surprise!" She claps.

Okay, I'm nervous again, my performance anxiety compounded by the awaiting audience. I'm not sure if it's better or worse to have the aunties witness my homecoming, not sure how I'll be received by my mother, let alone the Hindi-Bindi Club en masse. I expect I'll be the proverbial pink elephant in the room.

Saroj Auntie sighs. "Too bad Preity isn't flying in sooner, and staying longer. But she'll be here the day after Christmas, with hubby and the little ones."

"Mom mentioned that." *Woo-hoo. Indian Barbie and Corporate Ken, home for the holidays. Could this possibly get any better?* I force up the corners of my mouth. "Can't wait."

Taking my hand between hers, Saroj Auntie gives me a there-there pat-pat. "You kids scattered all over the map, didn't you? Preity in Minneapolis. Rani in San Francisco." She names others who have left the area. "So hard to keep in touch with your busy lives, isn't it? I'll give you Preity's email. Drop her a note later tonight. Let her know you're home. She'll be so excited."

Ah, the forced kinship of the second generation. I smile and nod, like we all learned to do. Make the appropriate noises. Shift my weight from one foot to the other. Pray Saroj Auntie doesn't come up with the brilliant idea to *call* Preity tonight and put me on the phone—put us on the spot—like the old days.

There's an assumption—or is it an expectation?—among some Indian-immigrant parents that because *they* are so tight with each other, *their children* are likewise best buds. Or should be. In my experience, not speaking for anyone else, that isn't the case. Foisted on each other because of our parents and shared heritage, we're friendly acquaintances more than friends, per se. Cousins, not siblings.

"Come. Come," Saroj Auntie says. "I've monopolized you long enough. Your parents will be so happy to have you back."

Maybe, maybe not, I think as I airlift the sole surviving roses and sling my purse over my shoulder. I've never been an angel like her Perfect Preity. Just ask my parents, who live to compare me with such exemplary role models. "Why can't you be more like so-and-so?" *So-and-so* was most often *Preity Chawla*. The only reason I wouldn't call her a Mama's Girl is the fact she's a Daddy's Girl, too.

Rani, on the other hand, was just as close to her parents without the nauseating perfection. She was my saving grace, a foil to Miss Goody Two-Shoes, especially during her goth stage. WiBBy, I called her. Weirdo in Black. I could always counter Preity's shining example with Rani's, though this seldom appeased my mother, who attributed all of Rani's transgressions, as she saw them, to having an American father. "This is what happens when we compromise our values," she would say, though never directly to Uma Auntie, the one who committed the alleged compromising in marrying Patrick Uncle. Theirs was a "love match." Gasp!

Uma and Patrick McGuiness date back to the Boston Days, too. Uma Auntie did her Ph.D. at Boston College, where she was best friends and housemates with Patrick Uncle's sister, Colleen. Colleen's family lived in nearby Charlestown, and they adopted Uma Auntie. She and Patrick Uncle got to know each other over time, very slowly, very innocently, because traditional Indian thought dictated: Good

Indian girls don't date, nor do they choose their own husbands. And a well-bred, upper-caste Hindu girl choosing to marry out of caste, out of religion, out of country? *Baap ré*. Loose translation: *Oh, Lordy.*

It was the double move, India to Boston, then Boston to D.C., that cemented the friendships of our parents. And for the mothers especially, having daughters within a year of each other. First came Preity (naturally), then me, then Rani. Growing up, we had a weekly playgroup. After we started grade school, our moms ditched us and lunched on their own. Always, our families gathered every month or two for a weekend shindig, and, often, we celebrated major holidays together. The "Indian friends circle" included others too, but our three families—Deshpandes, Chawlas, and McGuinesses—formed the core, a hub with spokes.

"Are Rani and her husband going to be here?" I ask. "Mom didn't know, last we spoke. Something about a gallery exhibit?"

"Right, right," Saroj Auntie says. "There was some mix-up with dates and whatnot, but they worked it out. Uma Auntie and Patrick Uncle are flying out there, then everyone's flying back here together in time for the holidays."

"Good," I say. *A buffer between Preity and me.*

I was thrilled to learn from my mom that Rani's recently gained commercial success with her modern adaptations of Warli art, a primitive Indian village style that resembles ancient hieroglyphics. Her husband's kind of an odd duck, but then Rani's always been on the eccentric side herself. He's great for her, I hear. *A good catch,* my mother says, a marked change of tune, making me wonder if she means it as a passive-aggressive dig: *Even Rani, of all people, married better than you.*

I remember when Rani first brought her then-boyfriend home from college for the holidays, something none of us ever dared: introducing a boyfriend/girlfriend to the Indian friends circle. The aunties and uncles still hadn't recovered from her turning down Stanford for Berkeley (blamed on the American-heathen influence of Patrick Uncle, naturally) when she announced to a kitchen full of bug-eyed aunties, "He's a computer geek, but he's my geek, and I'm crazy about him." Judging from their reactions, you would have thought she said, "That's right! He's great in the sack!" Never have I seen a group of women more in need of an economy-sized bottle of Valium. (Note: I wasn't around to see my mom tell the aunties about Anthony and me.)

Together Saroj Auntie and I walk toward the arched entryway and walnut double doors. To the west, the cherry lollipop of the setting sun glows between the pine trees. My father planted the row of trees along the property line the summer before I went to college, each a wimpy Charlie Brown Christmas tree look-alike. Now, treetops soar above our two-story house, limbs intertwine, needles blanket the grassless ground, and the brisk scent of a forest perfumes the winter air.

So many years in the blink of an eye.

"Will you stay until the New Year?" Saroj Auntie asks as I ring the doorbell. I have a key, but it doesn't feel right to use it.

"I'm not sure yet." Depends on how long I can stand the whiplash between past and present, especially since my older brother Vivek won't be here. He and his wife Anisha opted to spend this round of holidays with her family in Houston since they were here with his for Thanksgiving. Vivek is my parents' favorite, by a long shot, which I would resent, except he's my favorite family member, too.

"If I knew you were coming home, I would have brought your favorite *samosas*."

"Oh, Auntie. Did you have to tell me? Now I'm craving them."

She winks. "I'll drop off a care package."

My scowl turns upside-down, and my inner child emerges with a high-pitched "Thank you." Just as I hug her, my mother opens the door.

My smile freezes. My entire face feels encased in a plaster cast. *The prodigal daughter returns* pops to mind but stops short of my mouth, for once.

The first thing I notice is that her hair is shorter, too. Short-short. And sassy. Very *unlike* her personality.

Saroj Auntie squeezes my shoulder. "Special delivery for Yashwant and Meenal Deshpande," she says in a singsong voice. "Will you accept your parcel, madam?"

Lamely, I thrust out the roses, hoping she'll see them for what they are, an olive branch. My hands keep steady—from my training—but inside I'm shaking, evidenced in my voice. "I-I was just in the neighborhood . . ."

My mother's wide eyes mist, and her chin dimples like an orange peel.

My gut clenches in apprehension. *Don't cry, Mom. Please don't cry.* I can't handle her tears. Never could. Growing up, the rare times I witnessed a single teardrop, I didn't even have to know the cause to blubber right there on the spot.

Blinking, she takes my peace offering only to hand it off

to Saroj Auntie, then locks her willowy arms around me in a tight embrace. She feels different somehow, I can't pinpoint why, but she smells the same. Of clove shampoo and Johnson's baby powder. Of warm cooking spices and sandalwood incense. Of *her*. Of *home*. And just like that, I remember every childhood injury she nursed, every boo-boo she kissed, every time she *was* there for me when I needed her. Blocking out the times she wasn't, I close my eyes and hug her back.

She loves me, even if it doesn't feel like it most of the time, even if I don't live up to her unrelenting expectations. My mother loves me, and I love her.

Whatever else happens, I must not forget this moment.

Just because people don't love you the way you want, doesn't mean they don't love you the best they can.

Nine aunties turn out, a great showing for a weeknight, everyone comments. Though they're as sweet and solicitous as ever to me on the surface, I catch their furrowed brows, their anxious glances between my mother and me. They seem to hover over her. More than just lending a helping hand. Protective. Worker bees guarding their queen.

Do they think she needs protection *from me*?

At the thought, I feel small, hurt, *guilty*. In their eyes, I'm the bad guy. The Bad Daughter. Outnumbered, I shrink from the crowd.

It's my mother who rescues me, coming to stand beside me, the most popular girl in school befriending the outcast on the playground. Taking me under her wing, she rubs a hand over my back, eyes sparkling, nose wrinkling with her contagious smile.

"It's so good to have you home," she says, loud enough for everyone to hear.

"Thanks, Mom." My voice comes out hoarse, strained. *I'm sorry it took so long,* I want to say to her, but not with nine pairs of ears listening.

We stand like that a moment longer, an island in the Sea of Aunties, then she gives my arm a squeeze and asks, "Will you get the good silver, please?"

I nod, thankful for a task. From the china cabinet, I fetch eleven settings of heavy sterling plates, bowls, and cups, each engraved with MEENAL DESHPANDE and my parents' wedding date. I stack them on a side counter in the kitchen while Saroj Auntie uses hot mitts to remove items from the double ovens, placing them on the granite island per my mother's instructions.

"Smells wonderful, Meenal," she says, lead vocalist in an echoing, appreciative chorus. You know it's the truth when it comes from Saroj Auntie. Never one to give false compliments just to be polite, she has no qualms voicing a negative opinion, however unpopular. She can be blunt to the point of rude and flamboyant to the point of tacky, but she's so charismatic you can't help but love her. And she's right about the incredible aroma. . . .

Of course, we'll have to air out the house, but if you've ever tasted Indian food, you know it's worth it. Surveying the buffet, I forget all about *samosas*. Two appetizers. Three entrées. Four veggie dishes. A thick, hearty stew of *daal*—lentils. Picture-perfect, separated grains of buttery-nutty basmati rice—*basmati* means "queen of fragrance." A tower of round, light-brown *chappatis*—soft, thin whole wheat griddle bread.

I'm psyched to see my favorite chicken curry, garnished

with fresh coriander leaves that smack of lemon-pepper and ginger. I remember the first time my mother sent me on an errand to the supermarket: It was for coriander. She was in the midst of cooking dinner when she realized she'd forgotten it. "In the produce section," she said. I looked but couldn't find it. No cell phones then, I came home with parsley, which she said was "coriander's brother" in appearance, but unfortunately, not in taste or smell. Next time we went together, she took me to the elusive herb. Red rubber bands secured crisp green stems into bouquets of flat, fan-shaped leaves. We looked up at the sign: *cilantro*.

"Still your favorite?" she asks, beside me again.

I nod and wait until Saroj Auntie's out of earshot, then confess under my breath, "No one's as good as yours. *No one's.*"

She, too, lowers her voice. "Good, then I'll leave the world at least one specialty." She tells me she's written this recipe plus a few others *with measurements*, so I, with my meager time and more meager skill, can prepare them, should the impulse ever grab me one of these days. I brace for a comment about how Preity has a career, a husband, two children and still whips up a sumptuous home-cooked meal every night, but she either misses her cue or lets it go. "I haven't made it in a while," she says, "so you'll have to tell me if it's the same as you remember."

I sample a bite and fan my open mouth. "Hot. Hot. Hot."

"*Garam* or *thikhat?*" She asks me to differentiate between temperature-hot and spicy-hot.

"*Garam.*" I fan some more. Swallow. Give the thumbs-up.

She smiles and hands me a water pitcher. "Spring water, please."

I take a gallon from the fridge. "Where's Dad tonight?"

"On call," she says, which means he won't be home. Yes! Finally, a break!

My father's a cardiovascular surgeon. When he's on call, he's either at the hospital or the apartment he keeps nearby, since every second can mean the difference between life and death. Unlike my mom, my dad didn't have a privileged middle-class upbringing in their hometown of Mumbai—think: New York City and Hollywood combined—but what he lacked in privilege he made up in highly disciplined academic pursuit and a lifelong rigorous work ethic.

He grew up in a two-room apartment—*room,* not bedroom—the eldest of six kids. Everyone but my dad slept in one room; he slept on the balcony. In a city where rich and poor and everyone in between live side by side, he learned early on that education was the passport to a better life. With that goal, he rose every morning before dawn to study and prepare for school. His parents never had to nag him; he was self-motivated and competitive by nature. He made a practice of "standing first" in his class, scoring the highest marks, and earned merit scholarships.

When he was twenty, he lost his father to an unexpected heart attack, the reason he went into cardiovascular surgery. Overnight, he became the head of the family and sole financial supporter. "I came to this country with two suitcases and seven mouths to feed," he says. Over and over and over. (With his rags-to-riches life, he stands first in "uphill both ways" lectures.)

At the sink, my mother is snipping off the ends of the rose stems and arranging the flowers in a tall crystal vase with pale green sea glass at the bottom. She lowers her nose to sniff the closed buds and smiles, making my heart feel full.

Uma Auntie sashays into the kitchen double-fisted, the slender neck of a wine bottle in each hand. With her height—five foot seven—and moss green eyes, she's easy to spot in a crowd of petite, brown-eyed Indian women. A professor at George Washington University, she has this commanding presence, sharp intellect, and engaging rhetoric that make you sit up straight and pay rapt attention.

She dresses in a style I think of as "academic chic." Today she's paired a cream ribbed turtleneck with a navy wool blazer and clipped her hair at the nape with a tortoise-shell barrette. While Mom and Saroj Auntie shortened their hairstyles (I still can't get over my mom's pixie cut), Uma Auntie lengthened hers, so it falls an inch below her shoulders. In the middle parting of her hair, she sprinkled *sindoor*—red vermilion powder—which signifies she's married.

"Meenal? Wine for you?" Uma Auntie asks.

"No, thank you."

"Saroj? Red or white?"

Saroj Auntie eyes the choices, a Riesling and a Zinfandel. "Red, please."

"Kiran?"

I look at my mother. Even after I turned twenty-one, she still instructed me—and only me, not Vivek—to abstain from alcohol in the company of Indian friends. She coached me to refuse any offers with: "No, thank you. I don't drink."

That was before I married an aspiring rock star—complete with a shoulder-length PONYTAIL, small gold loop EAR-RING, and TATTOO of a cross over his heart—whom I met at a club in SoHo that fateful summer after I graduated from Princeton, before I started medical school at Columbia.

Yes, I know. Where's that copy of *Smart Women, Foolish Choices* when you need it? Not that it would have changed the outcome.

Until a drop-dead gorgeous man writes you beautiful poetry, plays Beethoven's *Moonlight* Sonata on a baby grand piano for you by candlelight, and serenades you with love songs in the shower, I don't expect you can fully empathize with my (hard) fall from grace.

Since I've caused her enough grief, it doesn't kill me to wait for some sign from my mother—parental permission—before replying to the booze question. It's the little things, Vivek advises me to concede. Small signs of deference go a long way.

My mom inclines her head. *Go ahead if you want.*

I want. I extend a wineglass by the stem. "White, please."

We form an assembly line and load our plates to take into the dining room. I serve myself as my mother taught, using my left hand and spooning each dish into its proper place. Meat at ten o'clock. Lentils at eleven. Condiments like chutney, lemon, mango pickle, and a pinch of salt disperse across the outermost twelve region, cold veggies and yogurt due south. Warm veggies nestle between one and three. Rice or *chappati* at six.

Fried fish, which we don't have, would take the nine o'clock spot but can shift inside (next door to meat and lentils) when dessert snags nine, a rarity at our house where "desserts are rewards, not side dishes," my mother insists. That is, unless *her* mother visits from Mumbai. According to my traditional *aji*—maternal grandmother—a properly served, well-balanced meal includes all six *rasas* (tastes): sweet, sour, salty, spicy, bitter, and astringent.

Dinner conversation starts with compliments to the chef, then segues to family gossip, books and movies, and current events. No one uses a fork, knife, or spoon. We eat with the fingertips of our right hand, keeping the left hand clean for serving, passing, and holding drinks. I tear off a piece of *chappati*—the only food-touching act that permits left-handed assistance—and envelop a piece of chicken, creating a bite-sized morsel. I'm competent at the fine art of Eating With One's Hand but lack the elegance, the finesse of the aunties in the same way I can stitch up a patient, but I'm no plastic surgeon.

The lemony chicken melts in my mouth. The gravy has just enough kick to give me sniffles. Ordinarily, I'm not a big fan of green beans or eggplant or cabbage, but Indian *bhajis*—cooked veggie dishes—are so well seasoned, even ho-hum veggies become quite yummy. I like to occasionally dip my bites in sour cream or alternate with *koshimbir*—raw veggies like tomato or cucumber in a refreshing yogurt or sour cream. This cools down the spicy-hot factor and cleanses the palate.

When I get close to finishing an Indian meal, I'm anal-retentive about my *chappati* and my complementary dishes ending together. I don't like to eat one without the other; it's just not the same. Ditto hamburgers and French fries. The optimal apportionment occupies my subconscious, and the aunties take this opportunity to inquire about my well-being (read: examine me, a mutant specimen under the microscope).

Auntie 1: Isn't it scary going to new towns all alone, not knowing anyone?

Me: No, it's fun meeting new people, and re-creating myself.

Auntie 2: But isn't it dangerous, a young woman by herself?

Me: I'm very careful, and I've taken self-defense classes.

Auntie 3: You must be getting lonely, *nuh*?

Me: Sometimes, but my work keeps me busy.

Auntie 4: What do you do outside of work?

Me: Sleep.

Auntie 5: I have a niece in Georgia, the daughter of a good friend of my brother's wife in Bangalore. They were classmates in college. You should call her. Get together sometimes. I'll give you her number.

Me: (Polite smile)

I explain that I'm nearing the end of my contracted stint, and when I'm done, the government will repay my student loans. I leave out the part about having these loans because my father cut me off—financially and emotionally—after I married against his wishes. (He didn't bless my marriage or my divorce. "What did you expect?" he asked, bewildered. "*Hya* American rock star*anchi lafdi nehamich astat, hen saglyanach mahtyeh.*" These American rock stars always have affairs, everyone knows that.)

I know the aunties are dying to know about my (nonexistent) love life, but dating, like every other taboo subject, requires discussion in furtive whispers behind my back.

"So I hear you've started movie nights and a reading group," I say and manage to wiggle out of the hot seat, at least for the time being.

Their movie nights feature Hindi films/Bollywood musicals, and the book group focuses on novelists of the Indian diaspora. Someone is invariably insulted by the depiction of Indians, or Americans, or Indian-Americans, or Non-Resident Indians in any given film, making for lively debate.

"What nonsense," says one auntie about the character in a popular crossover film. "N.R.I.s are nothing like that."

"Don't take everything so seriously," says another. "It's all in good fun."

"Bashing one's heritage is not my definition of good fun."

"Satirical humor exaggerates a kernel of truth," says Uma Auntie.

Some aunties huff and shake their heads; others nod.

The auntie who brought up this topic says, "I don't find perpetuating stereotypes and gross inaccuracies amusing."

From across the table, I spot the devilish gleam in Saroj Auntie's eye. "And you've never laughed at a *Sardarji* joke, or *told one*, have you?" she says, deadpan.

Ooooh, good one, Saroj Auntie! (Before modern political correctness kicked in, bashing this minority subculture was a long-revered national Indian pastime.) After some sputtering and guilty silences, everyone laughs.

My mother asks what book they're reading next. From what I can tell, the book-selection process involves as much discussion as the actual book.

"Please. Not her again," one auntie says. "Too crazy." She proposes an alternate, an international bestseller, but another auntie waves her hand in protest.

"No, no. She isn't an expatriate. And she's more of a political activist than a novelist."

"She's brilliant, that's what she is," says Uma Auntie, who teaches South Asian literature. "I don't always agree with her, but what a mind. What a mind. . . ."

"My mind is tired," says Saroj Auntie. "Why don't we read something fun for a change?" She suggests another author. "Her prose is like music. Lyrical. Lush. Evocative."

My mother winces. "Too Mills and Boon. Not realistic."

"*I* find M and B realistic," says Uma Auntie with a grin.

My mother springs from her chair like a jack-in-the-box. "Can I get anyone anything? More *chappati*?"

"Sit, sit. We can serve ourselves," the aunties protest, but she ignores them and retreats to the kitchen.

"I'll help." Since I'm out of *chappati,* I abandon my last few bites of green beans and go after my mother.

She stands with her head bent, her left hand gripping the counter. Tucked into the corner alcove in front of her resides the foot-high wooden *mandir*—shrine. Or as Patrick Uncle calls it, "the Hindu hut." Photos of my deceased paternal grandparents and white-bearded saint Sai Baba flank the *mandir.* Inside sit rose-petal-laden sterling idols: Ganpati, also known as Ganesh, god of beginnings and remover of obstacles; Krishna, god of love; Lakshmi, goddess of wealth and beauty; and Saraswati, goddess of wisdom. (Hindus believe in only one supreme God but acknowledge different names, forms, interpretations, paths to the divine.)

"Mom? What's wrong?"

Startled, she straightens and whirls to face me. "Nothing. Nothing. Just a little tired."

"Hawa gayli?" I ask and earn a smile of pride and pleasure that I remember this expression that means running out of steam.

She nods. *"Ho."*

"Understandably. You've outdone yourself. What can I do?"

"Eat. Please eat more. You're too skinny."

"I am not." I lift the hem of my sweater and show her my stomach. "See? I'm *fit.*"

"A fit little sparrow." She pokes my belly with her index finger. "Take half a *chappati,* so you can finish your *bhaji.*"

Our eyes meet, and emotion tightens my throat. How is it my mother can know me so well at times, yet other times not know me at all? She breaks away first, turning to the faucet to wash her hands. The din of aunties fades into the background like a hush falling over an audience. The world shrinks to encapsulate just the two of us. My mother and me, together on the same stage for the first time in five years. Together, yet each of us alone in our separate spotlights. Even the air seems to hold its breath, quivering in anticipation.

"*You* need to eat more," I say, my voice thick. "I didn't see any chicken curry on *your* plate."

"I'm a vegetarian."

"Since when?"

"Since . . ." She purses her lips, as if trying to recall. "Sometime last spring."

I frown. "You never mentioned it."

"Didn't I?" She lifts a shoulder in a delicate shrug. "I meant to." She tears a paper towel off the roll and dries her hands. "It's hard to say everything over the phone, isn't it?" At her weary smile, my heart constricts. I note her increased wrinkles, darker circles around her eyes, looser skin. She's shorter now, the slightest hunch in her posture.

I'm not the only one who's aging.

I swallow. Once. Twice. "Are you taking your vitamins? Getting enough protein? Calcium? Magnesium?"

"Yes, Kiran. I'm a professional doctor's wife."

Is that humor or irony? I can't read her expression, and the inability makes me sad. I don't like the distance between us. I don't *want* it anymore. This "separate lives" thing has run its course.

"Mom?"

"Hmmm?" She heats a *tawa*—griddle pan—for the *chappatis.*

"I . . . Here, let me do that. A culinary task I actually know how to do."

"That's okay—"

"Really, I don't mind." I wash and dry my hands, nudge her away from the stove, and take her place. I expect her to say something to the effect of there's hope for me in the kitchen yet, but she just squeezes my arm and thanks me.

Who is this pod person, and what have the aliens done with my real mom?

I laugh to myself, thinking she must be wondering the same thing about me.

One at a time, I flip the *chappatis* that she places on the *tawa,* counting each flip the way she taught. One, two, three, done. Watching her bustle around the kitchen, I want to say more, but I don't know what. I want to reach out, but I don't know how to break the ice that froze in layers over too many years. I'm afraid—of falling in, of needing help, of dying unassisted.

From behind me, my mother says softly, "I've missed you."

Tears spring to my eyes. I blink and bob my head up and down. "I've missed you, too, Mom. I hope you know . . ."

"I know," she says, and for the moment, it's enough.

It's a start.

When we finish, I take the plate of hot-hot *chappatis* into the dining room, returning to our program, already in progress:

"We're running out of authors," an auntie says.

"It's a short list," laments another.

"Why is that, do you think?"

I pipe up, "Because Indian parents offer their children two career choices: doctor or engineer." It's a joke; no one laughs. I sip from my wineglass. "Never mind."

I'm aware that I may drink wine and sit at the big table, but I'm not one of them. They will always be my mother's peers, not mine. They are the seniors; I am the junior. I will never completely get them, nor will they entirely fathom me. So I sit back and attempt to do as instructed all my life (with limited success): keep my mouth shut, listen to my elders, and try to learn something.

The aunties are in their late fifties to late sixties, both pilgrims and Indians, born in that Far East land of spices for which Columbus set sail and erroneously thought he discovered. Instead, they wouldn't arrive on American shores for hundreds more years, their sizable waves post-1965, a direct result of new, highly selective U.S. immigration laws.

"You mean *all* Indian men aren't doctors or engineers?" I once said in passing to Sandeep Uncle.

He was the one who first explained this phenomenon to me. "That was all they *allowed* into the country from India at our time. My elder brother stood first in his college. Brilliant man. Lawyer. Thrice he applied to come here, but Immigration said no. Finally, he went to Canada."

That's also why Indian parents *highly encouraged* their sons to become doctors or engineers—the professions that offered the best shot at economic success. And the American children born to those Indian-immigrant doctors and engineers? Care to venture a guess what that next generation was *highly encouraged* to become?

You got it.

My parents thought they were progressive for giving Vivek and me the option of choosing *what type* of doctor or engineer. (For the record, I became a physician *despite* my parents, not *because* of them. But let's just keep that between us, okay?)

Most of the Hindi-Bindi Club's founding mothers emigrated during those first big waves that India called her brain drain. Now they reign as matriarchs of the Indian-immigrant community, keepers of tales of the pioneer days before cell phones, before the Internet, before you could buy basmati rice in the supermarket.

From their animated conversations, I note that some (my mom) still have thick Indian accents, some (Uma Auntie) hardly a trace of Indian, and some (Saroj Auntie) an Indian-American *khitchadi*—smorgasbord. The aunties speak in rapid-fire English peppered with a liberal dose of Hindi, which I don't understand aside from a smattering of nouns here and there but sometimes decipher from context, tone, and body language.

My mom told me that when she first arrived in the States in her early twenties, her command of English, already strong from her convent school education, improved dramatically, but among the many things she missed about India was Hindi. "It's such a sweet language," she said, "with so many expressions that can't adequately translate to English."

In our Indian friends circle, most American-born types like myself are bilingual, but our second language differs according to Indian subculture—Indian states are like European countries, each with its own language and culture. (Imagine if New York, Mississippi, North Dakota, and California *really* had their own languages and didn't just *sound* that way!) Educated city-folk speak, at minimum, three languages: the two official national languages of English and Hindi, plus the regional language of their ancestral state, their *mother tongue*.

The mother tongue is the most common second language in Indian-American homes. In our home, you'll hear Marathi. In Saroj Auntie's, Punjabi. In Uma Auntie's, Bengali, which she and Rani speak, while Patrick Uncle's repertoire is on par with a dog's. "Let's go." "Sit." "Enough." "Stop." "Very nice."

When Indians of differing subcultures get together, they often flit in and out of English and Hindi with equal ease. To those of us who don't understand Hindi, they shut us out of what sounds to our ears like a secret, special language. Thus our nickname for our mothers, the Hindi-Bindi Club: They spoke in Hindi and sometimes wore *bindis*.

In my ninth-grade world history class, we spent half an hour on India. I learned about poor people in villages, something new for me. I also learned the "dot on the forehead" was a "third eye." This was also new to me—before the days of Third Eye Blind—and it conjured images of the cantina in *Star Wars*. (A little trivia: *Yoda* is the ancient Sanskrit word for warrior; *jedi* is the modern Hindi word. Yoda = ancient warrior; Jedi = modern warrior.)

I went home and consulted the expert in residence. "Mom? Tell me again, what's the significance of the *bindi*? I thought traditionally it meant a Hindu woman was married, and nowadays it can be pure fashion, like putting on jewelry or makeup. Plus, in religious *pujas,* it's like a blessing. Did I miss something? What's the deal with this third eye?"

"Everything you said is correct," my mother said. "The third eye is also correct. It symbolizes the capacity of human consciousness to see beyond the obvious, to perceive beyond what is visible and tangible, to tap the inner source within each of us that is the spring of divine energy and power. That is the metaphysical meaning."

"Oh. But it can also be *just* a fashion statement, right? With no deep meaning? Cuz my teacher didn't mention that part, or the married bit."

"Yes, Kiran."

My mother wears a *bindi* tonight, a peel-and-stick-on type in the shape of a dainty emerald teardrop that matches her cashmere sweater set. *Bindis,* along with *saris,* were also on her Miss List when she first came to America. That is, she missed wearing them without people whispering and rubber-necking. "In India," she said, "when men stare at women, it's rude and annoying, but a common, unfortunate part of the culture. Here, where staring is *not* part of the culture, and people are expected to show better manners, I feel singled out like some circus attraction."

Times are different now. Forty years later, the sight of an Indian woman in a city is not so rare. Still, my mother cherishes these get-togethers with the aunties who understand her in a way her American-born friends—and children—never will, where she can use Hindi expressions without translating, wear a *sari* and a *bindi* should the mood strike, and not feel like a foreigner.

Even after spending her entire adult life in America and becoming a naturalized citizen, she still says, in her Indian lilt, "I can never forget where I come from, the culture of my heritage. It will *always* be part of me, those first colorful threads woven into the tapestry of my life."

When the aunties start packing up to leave, Uma Auntie pulls me aside. She links her arm with mine and says, "Can I steal you away for a few minutes?"

"Uh, sure. Where to?"

"Somewhere private. Upstairs?"

In my former bedroom, Uma Auntie closes the door behind us. I have to admit that after my initial resentment, I like what my mother's done with the room. It's very inviting. A queen-sized mahogany sleigh bed with a fluffy white down comforter and throw pillows galore. Side tables with sleek candlestick lamps. On a shelf, there's a cute procession of five multitiered sandalwood elephants, arranged in descending height.

"Tonight couldn't have been easy for you," Uma Auntie says.

I give a nervous laugh, not sure where this is going. "No. No, it wasn't."

"Even Mother Teresa had her critics," she says. "That's what I've always told myself. No matter what you do, someone, somewhere is going to find fault. And each of us must decide whose opinion matters to us, and whose doesn't. Because God knows, you can't please everyone. It's futile to try. Come. Sit." Joining her, I perch on the edge of the bed, angling to face her. "I wanted to call you so many times, but I always stopped myself for one reason or another. It wasn't my place. Your mom wouldn't like my interference. I promised..." She shakes her head.

"It's okay," I say.

"No, but it will be. Now that you're home." She smiles. "Words cannot express how relieved I am that you're back, that you chose to come home on your own. I'm proud of you, Kiran. I have a *very good* idea how difficult these years have been on you. I, of all people, can relate. If Patrick Uncle's and my marriage hadn't survived..." She expels a breath, puffing out her cheeks. "That's why, of all your aunties, I'm the one who's butting in. For perspective only I can give you."

"Okay..."

From downstairs come the sounds of muffled ruckus. Loud farewells. The front door banging closed. Uma Auntie's green-eyed gaze holds mine with single-minded focus. "As displeased as your parents may get with you," she says, "as strained as your relationship may be with them, as tough as you think they are on you... even at worst, you still have it light-years better than I did with my father."

I swallow hard. Never has Uma Auntie talked about her parents. Rani told me years ago the topic was strictly off-limits, which I understood to mean a skeleton in the family closet. Curious, I asked my mom, but even she didn't know.

"Your parents did not, and would not, ever, under any circumstances disown you," Uma Auntie says quietly. "They didn't... banish you... from their lives."

I stop breathing. "Yours...?"

She gives a tremulous smile. "After Patrick Uncle and I married, *Baba* said I was dead to him. I thought he would come around in time. Certainly when Rani was born... He didn't."

"Uma Auntie. I'm so sorry."

"Me, too," she says. "Because I never could fix things with my father while he was alive, and then it was too late. It isn't too late for you, Kiran. Your parents have been waiting, *praying* for you to come home. We all have. Don't leave without working things out. Or you'll risk regretting it the rest of your life."

FROM: "Kiran Deshpande"
<Kiran.Deshpande@yahoo.com>
TO: Preity Lindstrom; Rani Tomashot
SENT: December 9, 20XX 11:17 PM
SUBJECT: A blast from the past . . .

Howdy, strangers! Long time, no see/talk. Thought I'd drop you a quick line to say: I'm home! :)

My mom had the Hindi-Bindi Club over for dinner tonight, soooooo you're sure to get an earful from YOUR moms.

Ho-ho-ho and see you soon,
Kiran

Meenal's Chicken Curry

SERVES 4

MARINADE:

1 pound boneless, skinless chicken breast, washed and cubed

2 teaspoons fresh garlic, peeled and minced or 1 teaspoon garlic powder

2 teaspoons fresh ginger root, peeled and grated or 1 teaspoon ginger powder

½ teaspoon cayenne powder (adjust to taste)

½ teaspoon coriander powder

1 teaspoon salt (adjust to taste)

*¼ teaspoon turmeric powder**

1. In a large glass bowl, mix together all ingredients.
2. Cover with plastic wrap and refrigerate for at least 1 hour, up to 24 hours maximum.

GRAVY:

2 tablespoons canola oil

1 bay leaf

1-inch cinnamon stick

4 whole cloves

2 cups yellow onion, finely chopped

½ cup tomato, chopped

3 cups water, divided ¼, ¼, ½, 1, and 1

½ teaspoon black pepper

¼ teaspoon cayenne powder (adjust to taste)

1 teaspoon coriander powder

½ teaspoon cumin powder

*¼ teaspoon turmeric powder**

¾ cup fresh coriander (cilantro), chopped and divided ½, ¼

*1 teaspoon garam masala**

½ teaspoon lemon juice

lemon wedges

1. Premeasure ingredients into small bowls and line them up in order of usage.
2. In a wok or deep 12-inch skillet, heat oil over medium heat. Add bay leaf, cinnamon, and cloves. Sauté 2 minutes. Add onion. Sauté until golden brown, then stir in tomato. Reduce heat to medium-low, cover, and simmer 5 minutes, stirring occasionally.
3. Now you'll thicken the gravy. Stir in ¼ cup water, cover, and simmer 3 minutes, then add another ¼ cup water.
4. Stir in black pepper, cayenne (if desired), coriander powder, cumin powder, and turmeric. Cover and simmer another 5 minutes, stirring occasionally.
5. Add ½ cup water. Cover and simmer until water evaporates, stirring occasionally. Repeat with 1 cup water.
6. After water evaporates, stir in the marinated chicken, ½ cup fresh coriander, and garam masala.
7. Increase heat to medium. Cover and simmer until chicken is tender, 10–15 minutes.
8. Add remaining 1 cup water and lemon juice. Reduce heat to medium-low. Cover and simmer until gravy thickens.
9. Remove from heat. Remove bay leaf, cloves, and cinnamon stick. Pour into serving bowl. Garnish with remaining fresh coriander. Serve with lemon wedges on the side.
10. Eat with *chappatis*, or poured over rice.

* Mom's Tips:

- ✔ Turmeric is bright yellow and stains counters, clothes, plastic, etc. Be very careful when handling and clean spills immediately.
- ✔ For store-bought garam masala, I like the "Kitchen King" brand.
- ✔ Never, ever, under any circumstances buy "curry powder."

Tomato Koshimbir

SERVES 4

2 cups tomato, chopped

1 cup yellow onion, chopped

¾ cup fresh coriander (cilantro), chopped and divided ½, ¼

¼ cup sour cream or plain yogurt

2 teaspoons sugar

½ teaspoon salt

1. In a bowl, combine all ingredients except ¼ cup fresh coriander. Mix well.
2. You can serve immediately or chill for up to 1 hour.
3. Before serving, garnish with remaining fresh coriander.

Preity Chawla Lindstrom: The Other Side of the World

Hearts are deeper than the ocean—
who knows their secrets?
PUNJABI PROVERB

"Once upon a time long, long ago, in a land far, far away," I read the same bedtime story my four-year-old daughter Lina and three-year-old son Jack have requested every night this week. If I omit a single word, they will catch me, correct me. They have it all memorized. We three are piled in Lina's pink-lace canopy bed. Downstairs, my husband Eric wraps up kitchen duty—I cook, he cleans, a division of domestic labor that works for both of us—and not for the first time, I give thanks for my blessings.

"Again, Mommy. Read it again," Lina says.

"Pleeeease," Jack says, preempting my prompt for the magic word.

"One more time, then lights out," I say. "Deal?"

"Deal!"

"Okay, here we go... Once upon a time long, long ago, in a land far, far away..." When I reach The End for the second time, Jack's sacked out, but Lina's still rearing to go. Eric appears at the door, ready to provide backup.

No reneging tonight, kiddo. Mommy and Daddy have Big Plans. Eric tucks Lina in and carries Jack to his room, where he does the same. We wait until they're *both* down for the count.

"Double-check," I whisper. "Triple-check." Our Lina's a sneaky one, always coming into our bedroom, claiming to want a drink of water, or go potty, never mind that she just did.

Eric peeks into Lina's room again and gives the thumbs-up.

Stifling our laughter like naughty kids, we sneak downstairs and into the garage.

"Man, the lengths you go to when you're parents," Eric says.

"Tell me about it." I stop, bump into him. "Keys. Do you have the keys?"

He waggles his eyebrows and jingles them.

"You are *such* a stud."

He laughs and kisses me.

"What was the first present you remember asking Santa for?" I ask.

"Lincoln Logs. You?"

"Guess."

"Aw, don't make me—"

"Come on, guess!"

"Ummmm... A musical jewelry box."

"Nope."

"A tea set."

"Nope."

"Gimme a hint, wife."

"A hint, husband? Well..." I pat the trunk of my car. "You might try looking in here."

"Oh, yeah?" He pops open the trunk and scans the kids' goodies that we're retrieving to wrap and rehide. "Hmmmm..." His gaze zeroes on a target. A slow grin. "A globe."

"Ding, ding, ding. We have a winner."

Eric chuckles and shakes his head. "The things I do for love."

"And sexual favors."

"That, too."

It takes a few trips to transport Santa's loot inside. We sprawl on the floor by our Christmas tree and, from time to time, tiptoe upstairs to check on the kids. Still snug in bed? Yep. Eric passes Jack's globe to me, so I can do the honors.

Oh, how I loved my globe, I remember as I wrap this one. I was four when Santa gave it to me. "Gifted me," as my dad would say. He showed me where we lived and the places he and Mom were born and raised. ("Born and brought up.")

"This is America," Dad said. "We are here, just outside the capital, Washington, D.C." Then he spun the globe clear around to the Other Side. He pointed to a peninsula similar to the shape of Texas—an analogy I'd make several years later—located above the Indian Ocean and below China. "This is India. Mommy and I lived just outside *that* capital, New Delhi."

I was fascinated. Everything about geography intrigued me. Countries and capitals. Land and seas. Especially the notion of the earth being round—people living on the Other Side. My day their night, my night their day. The fact we looked up at the same sun, moon, and stars. And perhaps most mind-boggling of all: the possibility that thousands of miles beneath *my* feet walked *other people's* feet!

Questions sprouted left and right in the fertile terrain of my mind. Why didn't people fall off Earth the way my Fisher-Price people fell off the globe? If you dug a tunnel straight down into the ground, would you come up on the Other Side like a rabbit? (I attempted to answer this one myself and started digging a hole in the backyard, but after hitting rock after rock, I concluded any passage to India would require a bigger shovel.) And if the "rest of our family" lived on the flip side—grandparents, aunts, uncles, and cousins—did I have a brother or sister over there, too?

I was four. I mentioned that, right?

Well, that was twenty-nine years ago. Today I have my own preschoolers. Lina isn't the least bit interested in globes. Hers sits atop the lavender bookcase in her room, serving the dual purpose of bookend and dust-catcher. She can't dress it up, invite it to tea parties, or really play with it in any way—geography games don't meet her definition of fun. It's Jack who takes after me in this regard. He is the dreamer, the explorer, always wanting to know how things work. I've seen how he covets his big sister's globe, which Lina refuses to relinquish. That sharing concept? Let's just say we're still working on it.

Between the two of them, I have my own homegrown, informal focus group. I'm a brand manager for a toy company, and my kids are chockful of strong, opposing opinions. The only thing on which they agree is books. Both love fairy tales, myths, and legends, as do I. I smile as I tie a ribbon around the newest additions to our library.

After Eric and I finish our tour of wrap-and-hide duty, we walk hand-in-hand to our room. This is my favorite time of all. The time when I snuggle into bed beside my husband and drift off to sleep with the knowledge I love and am loved beyond measure.

It's been that way from the start for Eric and me. We met in graduate business school at Northwestern. He said something brilliant during the first week of marketing class. We sat in concentric, horseshoe-shaped rows, me in front, him in back. I turned to see who'd spoken and caught his eye. I smiled. *Good one.* He smiled back. *Thanks.* When he dropped his gaze to his notebook, writing something on the page, a tinge of pink flushed his cheeks, instantly endearing him to me. Smart, cute, and shy.

"I'm going out with that guy," I whispered to my friend.

She glanced over her shoulder. "Okay, I'll take the one next to him."

She didn't. I did. We still joke about it.

That Friday, at Happy Hour, I invited Eric to dinner at my place. I grilled New York strip steaks, baby red potatoes with dill and lemon butter, and summer squash. Afterward, we did our homework together and watched *Forrest Gump* as a reward. He told me later it was the best first date of his life, and he was so buzzed from our goodnight kiss, he wasn't sure he should drive.

We were both at a point in our lives where we'd test-driven enough models to know what we wanted, and very soon, we found everything we were looking for in each other.

Eric proposed during finals. We married a year later. We both found jobs that excited us in Minneapolis. Minnesota is Eric's home state. It's a place I never imagined I would live, but after discovering this unexpected jewel, I never want to leave.

People sometimes ask if we, or our parents, had any issues with our religious differences. The answer is no. No problems whatsoever.

I wish this was always the case. I'm glad no one asks that question, because buried down deep is a blemish I've covered up, a memory that still prickles at my conscience every so often of another time, another place.

Once upon a time long, long ago, in a land far, far away . . .

An odd thing happens in the middle of the night. Out of nowhere, I remember a children's book. Not bought in a store, mass produced, but one of a kind, given to me.

Gifted me . . .

A finger of panic plucks me upright by the collar. At once, I'm wide awake. Where did I put it? I have an inkling, but it's been so long. Is it still there? *Please, tell me I haven't lost it.* I glance at the red glow of the digital clock on the bedside table. It's two in the morning, but I can't wait until a decent hour. I'm compelled to find the book *right now,* reassure myself it's safe. I ease out of bed, careful not to wake Eric, and pad downstairs, my sock-feet silent through the house.

It's because I'm thinking of India again. . . . Ever since that email from Kiran.

My heart leaps as I find the book, swathed in two yards

of achingly familiar, deep violet silk. I touch the delicate gold-embroidered border. It's the *duppatta* that matched my favorite, figure-flattering *salwar-kameez*. I bought the pants-tunic-scarf ensemble on my last trip to India. I was eighteen. Two trips preceded that, one when I was an infant, another when I was in kindergarten, for a grand total of three months of my life.

My parents aren't immigrants who often pilgrimage to the Old Country. It takes too long and costs too much with airfare $1K+ a pop. But more than anything, it's too upsetting for my mother to be there, and for my father to leave, so they prefer flying our relatives here and sparing themselves the grief.

My own nostalgia abated as I grew up, pursued my studies, and focused on the ground beneath my own feet, securing a toehold and forging my own place on this round earth. But there was a time when I could think of little else, when I yearned to return, like Peter Pan's Wendy remembering Neverland.

Now in the still of a winter night, I sit cross-legged in front of the gas fireplace in the study, my time capsule in my lap. I draw a breath and unravel my cherished gift. From its protective silk cocoon, a book emerges. Handcrafted. Bound with emerald green thread. I gaze in wonder, transfixed under its spell. I half expect the book to open on its own, flap its pages, and take to the air like an enchanted butterfly.

The years have yellowed the edges and stiffened the paper, so it makes a crinkly sound when I turn the page; otherwise, it appears well preserved. My fingers itch to touch the beautiful, flowing script and meticulous illustrations of a coastal west Indian town, but I don't risk smudging the black ink. There's something mystical about words on a page, their enduring legacy, their power to warp time and space, rouse long-dormant memories, so they feel as fresh as yesterday....

The crash and hiss of the Arabian Sea breaking against the rocks. Lanky coconut palms and lush green paddy fields swaying in tropical breezes. White sand, as soft and fine as powdered sugar between my toes. The stains of red soil and red curries. The layered *bebinca,* at least a thousand calories and seven kinds of sin in every sweet spoonful. Cashew *feni,* a pungent moonshine that went down like liquid fire, made me want to skinny-dip in the Arctic, and reeked from my pores. Most of all, I remember the heady rush of first love.

The book is his creation.

"People die," he said one night as we lay on the beach under a blanket of twinkling stars and a crescent moon, talking about life and the ramifications of existing in this universe. "But their stories live forever."

I read each line of his book, and the space between, some over and over, some with a catch of breath, and some with my eyes closed, for I, like my children, have memorized it all. And as with them, I too want the favored tale replayed, to savor anew.

When I've read from start to finish three times, I put down the book and turn out the light. I go to the two-story, arched window, where I tip back my head and peer up into the night sky. It's snowing and overcast, so I can't see the moon or the stars, but I know they're there, just as I know that thousands of miles underneath my feet walk other people's feet.

I touch the cold windowpane. Steam circles my fingertips. *I'm thinking of you. Do you ever think of me? Is that twenty-*

year-old young man still alive somewhere inside you? Does he remember me, as the eighteen-year-old inside me remembers you?

In the lamplight, snowflakes descend from the heavens like angel wings. As I stare, hypnotized, the winter wonderland of Minnesota blurs. A magic carpet materializes in my mind's eye. I smile a secret smile and imagine myself unlatching the window and unhooking the screen, climbing onto the flying carpet in my blue-and-green plaid flannel pajamas and hitching a ride to the Other Side of the World.

The Other Side of the World...

"We should split up," Riya-*didi* said. "The shops close at noon." Riya wasn't actually my cousin, but my cousins' cousin. Still, she told me I could call her *didi*—older sister—which gave me a warm, fuzzy feeling of connection I never had in my eighteen years at home.

My immediate family exemplified the stereotypical American suburban demographic in many ways, including but not limited to: two kids, one of each flavor; a black Labrador Retriever named Ash; a soccer dad and a mom who carpooled us from one activity to another in her Volvo station wagon.

Here you might expect me to launch into stereotypical differences such as our house smelling like curry and incense instead of chocolate chip cookies or apple pie (yes, sometimes); or my parents prohibiting drinking or dating (no, never... okay, *once*, but it was the exception); or the facts we were not white, not Christian, and therefore not in the "cool" majority (not an issue in our cosmopolitan D.C. suburb of McLean, Virginia).

No, in my family, those things didn't matter all that much. Certainly, they didn't alienate us. What did was more subtle: Unlike most American families, we didn't have relatives outside our tiny nucleus residing in the country. No extended family. And that more than anything else made us feel, at times, we didn't yet belong.

My parents' close-knit Indian-immigrant community provided wonderful surrogates. Outsiders usually assumed we *were* related. But it wasn't the same. In India, I felt the difference. Felt what was missing.

That year marked the fiftieth wedding anniversary of Dad's parents, *Dadaji* and *Dadiji,* an occasion mandating our attendance. Most of our large extended family had migrated from New Delhi to the west coast metropolis of Bombay, now Mumbai. (Half a century after independence from British rule, many cities reverted to Indian names. Bombay's *Mumbai,* Calcutta's *Kolkata,* Madras is *Chennai.* But then, it was Bombay.)

My parents, my thirteen-year-old brother Tarun, and I flew around the globe to join in the festivities: a winter holiday on the sun-kissed beaches of Goa, a popular tourist state south of Bombay. I had just finished my first semester at the University of Virginia, and my brain was so fried from finals and end-of-term papers that I crashed and slept for most of the twenty-four-hour journey. In doing so, I was the only one to escape jet lag.

While the others adjusted to the time change, like night owls snoozing through daylight hours, I basked in the attention our relatives lavished on me-me-me. *Dadiji,* known for her Dr. Jekyll/Mr. Hyde–like transformations between sweet granny and tyrant mother-in-law, spoiled me with a grandmother's copious affection. Riya-*didi,* four years my senior, assumed the role of cultural ambassador/translator, let me wear one of her breezy cotton *salwar-kameezes,* and took me out and about with her.

Though Westernized Indians strolled the streets in jeans, long skirts, and dresses—the same styles worn in the States—I found that oh so boring, reveling instead in their traditional garb. I didn't have the grace to pull off the midriff-baring *sari,* but the *salwar-kameez* suited me perfectly. How fun to play dress-up in such finery! I had to get my own; I burned through most of my pocket money on clothes. My mother cautioned me not to buy too many, as they'd go to waste when we came home. She was right—I haven't worn one since.

"Why do shops close early today?" I remember asking Riya that first day. I thought maybe it was like the early closing elementary schools had on Mondays.

"Not just today," Riya said. "Every day. Noon to five is siesta time. The Portuguese influence. It's everywhere."

My lack of knowledge made me feel awkward. During finals, Mom had sent a Goa travel guide in a care package with homemade oatmeal cookies, crunchy Granny Smith apples, and a tub of peanut butter, but I hadn't found a spare moment to crack the spine yet. I knew the bare bones, that Goa was a Portuguese colony for four centuries, until the early 1960s. "Am I flaunting my ignorance?" I asked and confessed about the unread book.

Riya laughed. "No, you're cute. It's fun to see the world through your eyes. And some things are more exciting to learn from real life, not books." She pointed out a card shop. "You go in there. I'm going next door. We'll meet outside."

I looked at my watch. Riya wasn't wearing one. "Wait, it's only eleven-thirty. We have half an hour." We didn't have so many things on our errand list to warrant splitting up. Maybe she wanted to be alone? Some kind of embarrassing purchase? My mind leapt to feminine hygiene or birth control. She looked too innocent for the latter, but in my first semester, I'd learned a thing or two about the "appearance" of innocence. And innocence lost. I was about to remind her I was in college now, a woman of the world, when she laughed again.

"Trust me," she said. "It'll take half an hour."

"For postcards and sweets?"

"You'll see."

"But...but..." I raised and lowered myself on my toes with the separation anxiety I had at age seven when my mom dropped me at ballet class. "What if I need a Hindi speaker?"

"Everyone speaks English," Riya said over her shoulder.

I knew this. Still, I liked having backup. The accents—mine and theirs—could prove tricky.

In the store, I selected a dozen postcards and got in line to pay from my stash of colorful Indian rupees that looked like play money from a board game. With only two people in front of me, I thought I'd be out in a breeze. I didn't count on them *shooting* the breeze. For ten minutes each. And counting!

I shuffled through my postcards, arranging and rearranging, reading and rereading the blurbs. My foot started tapping on its own. I barely resisted the urge to clear my throat. Not that it would have helped. Neither the owner nor the customers seemed in any rush. I contemplated starting my cards. At this rate, I could put a good dent in the stack before I left the shop.

Dear Jen, namaste *from the other side of the world. I'm writing this, not out on the beach sipping fresh baby coconut water through a straw as I should be, but standing in a line that's slower than molasses. . . .*

I glanced at my watch for the umpteenth time. At a low chuckle behind me, I turned.

It was his smile I noticed first, his twin dimples sweet, boyish, disarming. It was his eyes that lured me. Ink black. Intense. Soulful. In his hands, he held a sketchpad and a set of colored pencils. I guessed his age between mine and Riya's.

"First time in Goa?" he asked. At my nod, his smile stretched out, deepening the dimples and propping up the apples of his cheeks, so the skin beside his eyes crinkled. "The pace takes some adjustment. A watch serves the same function as a bangle. Ornamental."

"Yes." I thought of Riya's naked wrist. "I'm learning."

His eyebrows knit together. "You're . . . a foreigner?"

I smiled, pleased he hadn't figured it out until I opened my mouth. "I can dress the part, but the accent gives me away." We chatted a while. I learned his name was Arsallan, his family was from Bombay, and they usually spent their holidays at a beach or a scenic "hill station." I gave him the skinny on my family.

"Ah. So you're type of an Indian export," he said.

"Type of," I repeated, amused as always by different usages of the same English language. "Are you an artist?" I gestured to the sketchpad and pencils.

"By profession, no. I'm in medical college. This"—he held up the supplies—"is strictly time-pass. To amuse my nieces and nephews. You can hear them from here. . . . '*Chachu,*

Chachu, draw me a picture.' '*Chachu, Chachu,* tell us a story.' '*Chachu, Chachu,* let's fly kites.' "

"How many are there?"

"Twelve."

"An even dozen."

"No, more of an *odd* dozen." He grinned.

Riya entered as I was—finally!—paying for my purchases. I introduced her and Arsallan. "He's from Bombay, too," I said. It turned out they had mutual friends at each other's college. Six degrees of separation and all that.

Arsallan asked if we had plans later that night and invited us to a beach party. It was a casual invite, one of those "hey, swing by if you can" deals. But when he tossed those carefree words into the air, a feather of excitement tickled my stomach. I liked the idea our paths might cross again.

And they did indeed cross. At the party that night, and for at least a few hours almost every day afterward.

Mostly we walked, for miles along the seashore, leaving our footprints in the sand and watching the tide wash them away.

Too soon to make sense, I felt an uncanny familiarity with him, a connection that grew the more time we spent together. He didn't feel like a new friend. It was as if we had met a long time ago, in another time, another place, and were just picking up where we'd left off.

"Have we done this before?" I asked one day.

"Yes, we walked here yesterday."

I shook my head. "Before yesterday. Before I came here. Somewhere else. Sometime else."

He stopped, crooked his head, held my gaze. "So it's not just me."

I shrugged. "I can't explain it."

He smiled, his eyes warm on my face. "You don't have to. Whatever it is, we share the feeling."

Off the top of his head, he spun countless yarns about our past lives together. Tales that stretched from the pink palaces and desert sands of Rajasthan to the great pyramids of ancient Egypt, full of magic and adventure to rival *The Arabian Nights*.

We didn't touch, didn't even hold hands as we walked. Yet I felt him, close to me. I felt his heart.

The Vikings and Packers are playing at Green Bay, and I'm trying not to cut my finger as I chop vegetables for dinner and peek at the mini-television on the counter. I'm distracted not just by the game, my mind in the past, my knife in the present.

I'm dying to call my mother, to tell her about Arsallan's book, but I can no more tell her now than I could fifteen years ago. My eyes sting, and I know it's more than onion vapors.

Just because we choose not to talk about something doesn't make it go away.

I stir the Goan shrimp curry, stick my nose over the pot and sniff, taste the coconut gravy. Something's missing, but I can't figure out what. *Mom would know.* I glance at the phone. Should I? Shouldn't I? No. Better not. The way I'm feeling, I don't trust myself not to snap, say something in the heat of the moment and live to regret it. We'll be there soon enough, the day after Christmas. I take another whiff, another taste, and ponder. The missing ingredient flits on the edge of my senses. An elusive lightning bug, *now you see me, now you don't. Catch me if you can.* I take up the challenge, *I'll catch you, little bugger...*

Every other weekend, I cook Indian. At our house, it's a special treat, even for me, whereas when I was growing up, Tarun and I begged for the rare decadence of Kraft macaroni and cheese. My kids—all three of them—love to eat with their fingers. Any excuse to play with their food.

I dole out golden brown *samosas* onto four plates. I use my mom's recipe for the potato filling, minus green peas, which none of us like. For convenience, I cheat and substitute store-bought refrigerated dough for the pastry and bake instead of fry.

My mom has conniptions over how I Americanize her recipes. You've never seen someone micromanage to the degree my mother does. And in the kitchen especially, *oh baby, watch out!* As she'll be the first to instruct, there are right and wrong ways to do everything, and I mean *everything*. Chopping, stirring, standing, serving, cleaning. Probably even breathing. "You can't call *that* a *samosa*," she says. "It's a Hot Pocket."

Whatever. It's my kitchen. I can do what I want to.

Today I made one spicy batch for the adults to dip in mint-cilantro chutney or tamarind-and-brown-sugar chutney and another mild batch for the kids to dunk in ketchup. From the freezer, I fetch two frosted mugs and pour chilled Taj Mahal beer—strictly an export, not available in India.

"Peanut, take this to Daddy, please," I say to Lina, my sous chef in training. Will I become like my mother and micromanage my daughter one day? I vow *no way, never,* even as I instruct, "Careful. Walk slowly. Don't skip, or you'll spill." Lina's such a bubbly child, she constantly skips, rarely walks, given free will.

"Ah. This is the life," Eric says from the den, where he's sprawled on the couch in front of his new wide-screen television. He did the grocery run, so he's earned full couch-potato rights.

"Ah. This is the life," Jack echoes as he pushes his dump truck around the floor.

"Ah. This is the life," Lina says, skipping back into the kitchen.

I laugh and, just like that, the missing ingredient occurs to me. "Um, Eric? How much do you love me?"

"Enough to go back out and get whatever you forgot, if it can wait until halftime."

"That's love." I smile and lean back against the counter. Tipping back my beer bottle, I take a long sip. Life is good.

Don't open Pandora's Box.

One intercepted phone call in Goa, and it was over.

"Who's calling?" my mother asked. When her eyes widened, the hairs on my arms rose in foreboding. She looked directly at me. "Preity isn't available right now. I'll tell her you called." She hung up. "Arsallan Khan. A friend of yours?"

I nodded.

"*Just* a friend." A statement she wanted me to confirm, rather than a question.

I couldn't lie. I shook my head.

"Preity," she shot the two syllables of my name rapid-fire

like two bullets. "Khan is a Muslim name. He is a *Mussalman*."

"I know."

"You know?" She set her jaw in a firm line. "How can you know and be more than friends?" She paced, cheeks red, breath labored. "You know, but you obviously don't understand. You *can't* understand the scars of Partition." She shook her head, pain in her eyes. "It's *my* fault. That's what everyone will say. Your father and I shouldn't have raised our children in America. We sold out on our heritage."

I ached for my mom when she talked this way. "That's not true—"

"See how you talk back! That would never happen in India. Children don't contradict their parents!"

I couldn't defend myself—more backtalk—so I stood there with my gaze lowered as she delivered another of her lectures, her duty as a good Indian parent: tough love.

"You learned trivial details of American history, but not even the most vital of Indian," she said. "Your schools didn't teach you *one single thing* about *our* holocaust, *our* wars, *our* independence, *our* leaders. *Far* more important the leaders of tomorrow can name Columbus' three ships, your state bird, tree, and flower. *That* will help avert the next hostage crisis, or hijacking, or nuclear attack of *your* generation."

She was right that, up until then, everything Indian of relevance, consequence—everything critical to understanding problems facing the modern world—I learned from my parents. From their homeschooling. Even the significance of Gandhi.

When the movie *Gandhi* hit theaters, my parents took me opening day. They cried through most of it, even parts that didn't strike *me* as particularly emotional. Later, I learned their tears were as much, if not more, for the epic bloodshed that *followed* a nobly won independence.

For me, India's independence wasn't just a history lesson, pages in some dull, dry textbook. My parents, my family, lived it. Partition isn't *a* story. It's *their* story:

In 1947, after almost two centuries of British rule, India won independence, the triumph of a monumental freedom movement—*nonviolent* activism—led by Mohandas Gandhi, who came to be known as Mahatma, meaning "great soul" in Sanskrit. "I'm willing to die for this cause," Gandhi said, "but for no cause am I willing to kill." And Albert Einstein said about him, "I believe Gandhi's views were the most enlightened of all the political men in our time. We should strive to do things in his spirit: not to use violence in fighting for our cause, but by nonparticipation in anything you believe is evil."

At the stroke of midnight, August 15, 1947, the British Raj turned over the keys to the kingdom, returning the stolen "jewel in the crown" to her rightful owners. Buffed and polished, yes, but bashed into pieces.

Partitioned.

Hacking off chunks of the northwest and northeast created two countries. Democratic, secular India in the middle, flanked on either side by Islamic Pakistan, "land of the pure," a victory for the Muslim League. *The theory:* a separate homeland for the Muslim minority, should they wish to leave Hindu-majority India. *The reality:* the most colossal human migration and exchange of population in history. Unprecedented carnage.

How did it happen? Who was to blame? Ask five different people and you'll get five different answers. According to my parents and other family who survived to tell, fanatic leaders and militia groups played on communal fears and suspicions, and people of differing religions who'd managed to coexist in peace for centuries turned and raged against each other. For millions who suddenly found themselves on "the wrong side of the tracks," remaining in their homes wasn't an option. Driven by hope of a better future, or fear of peril, they got the hell out of Dodge.

In the Punjab, my family's ancestral state in the northwest, the dividing line carved by the British boundary commission onto a map, akin to a butcher's knife slitting the throat of a Hindu's sacred cow or a Muslim's sacrificial goat, rendered ten million people homeless. Among them, my mother's family.

Forced to flee their beloved Lahore, "the Paris of India," they were among millions of Hindus and Sikhs who migrated east. Simultaneously, millions of Muslims migrated west.

Along the way . . .

As my mother recounted to me in Goa, in excruciating detail, "One million deaths. Twenty thousand *reported* rapes. Almost a quarter million people declared missing." Then, as if all that wasn't horrific enough, her voice cracked, splintering my heart, *"Nanaji. Naniji."* More personal, more painful than aggregate statistics: my great-grandparents, our casualties.

My stomach felt queasy, and I had to sit. Intellectually, I'd absorbed the history. I'd learned that when you seized a family's ancestral land, forced people from their homes, tortured and murdered their innocents, or coerced religious conversions, there were ramifications. Lifelong, often multi-generational ramifications. The breeding of hatred. The quest for justice, or revenge, depending on your point of view.

Importantly, my parents wanted me to understand *Partition* was the root of modern-day tensions between nuclear-armed rivals India and Pakistan. Disputes over territory in Kashmir were ongoing aftershocks. And the problems of distant lands, like stones thrown in a pond, could one day, out of the clear blue sky, ripple to virgin shores with devastating results.

Gandhi said, "An eye for an eye will leave the whole world blind," but my mother, who revered the man, would be among the first to point out neither he nor I had her family's experience.

If Gandhi couldn't change her mind, what chance did I have?

Before I spoke, I chose my words carefully, knowing what an ultrasensitive topic this was, with reason. "I know there were atrocities I can't begin to imagine. You're right, I'll never completely comprehend Partition because I didn't live through it, or grow up surrounded by families who did. But Mom," I said gently, "communal animosity . . . it's like the Hatfields and the McCoys, passing down legacies of hate and prejudice to future generations, *innocent* generations. It's not right. It wasn't then. It isn't now."

"Oh, Preity." My mother heaved a weary breath. "If only life was that simple. Good and bad. Right and wrong. Friend and foe. You still see the world through rose-tinted glasses. Your lenses haven't cracked yet."

"Every major religion—well, except Buddhism—every

major religion has violent extremists. Hindus, Muslims, Sikhs, Jews, Christians—"

"Some more than others."

"Even so, it doesn't mean everyone is. Most aren't, and I refuse to punish people for crimes they didn't commit."

"Humph." She flicked her gaze to the ceiling where a fan revolved in lazy circles, its pace slow like everything else in Goa. "If we'd raised you here, it would be different. I could forbid you from seeing this boy, and you'd obey my wishes without question, without argument." She raised an eyebrow to punctuate: "*Grown-up* or not."

I bit my lip to keep from smiling.

"Good Indian girls don't date, you know."

"Actually, they do these days. Riya-*didi* says—"

"Riya-*didi* is not your mother," she snapped. "*I* raised you. *I* am responsible for you. *I* am the one who looks bad when people talk, if you cause a scandal. Your actions reflect on *me*."

I lowered my head. "I'm sorry, Mom."

"I am, too." She sat beside me, squeezed me so tightly I couldn't breathe, and pressed a series of kisses to my temple. "My *beta*." She prattled nonsense Punjabi terms of endearment. "I love you *sooo* much. You know that, don't you?"

"Umm-hmm."

"Good." She let up on the bear hug. "I forbid you from seeing him again."

"*What?*" I leapt from the couch and pivoted on my heel.

"You heard me."

"But you can't—! I'm in *college*. I'm legally an adult. You can't *ground* me!"

She crossed her arms, stuck out her chin. "I just did."

"Arsallan deserves an explanation," I said to Riya-*didi*. I had told her only that my mom flipped out and forbade me from seeing him. Riya seemed to understand without my elaboration. "I can't just drop off the face of the planet without a word."

"I don't know . . . If your mum finds out . . ."

She didn't need to finish. I didn't want to contemplate what would happen if my mother learned I betrayed her trust and went to see Arsallan, even if it was to say good-bye. I wished I had his room number. I tried to return his call, but there were too many Khans registered at his hotel, so many the operator flat out refused to connect me with even one random room.

"Will you go? Please, *Didi*. Please find him for me?"

She wrinkled her nose, clearly uncomfortable with the idea, but nodded. "Better me than you. But I don't know what to say."

"I'll write a letter. If you could just give it to him and get me his contact information . . . ?" At her nod, I hugged her.

The letter took seven crumpled drafts, because I kept tap-dancing around the truth. I was too ashamed. I didn't want to divulge the ugly words that echoed in my head.

My mother is prejudiced.

My mother is prejudiced.

My mother is prejudiced.

Finally, I opted for the lie: My family schedule had grown too busy for me to see him during the final days of our holiday. I apologized, expressed my deepest regrets that I couldn't say good-bye in person, thanked him for his friendship, told him I would never forget him and the wonderful times we shared, and closed with: "Please keep in touch. Love, Preity." I gave my college dorm address.

Riya scoped his hotel lobby for hours, but he never showed. Nor did she spot him at our favorite *chai* shop or any of the other places we'd frequented. "Sorry," she said. "I'll try to find his address and post your letter when I get back home."

Then, the day before we departed, I received a package at the front desk: Arsallan's handcrafted storybook. I searched for a letter or a note or his contact information, but came up empty.

I tore up my first letter and wrote another, better one, in which I poured out my eighteen-year-old heart. I thanked him for being so wonderful and told him I would cherish his gift forever. I tried to keep my tears from falling on the paper, but one hit the lower left corner and blurred two of the stars I drew beside a crescent moon. I wrote: "Always remember, we look up at the same sun, moon, and stars. Always remember, someone on the other side of the world wishes for you all the best. From my heart to yours, my love always, Preity."

To this day, I don't know if my letter reached Arsallan. Riya turned out to be a poor correspondent. She never answered my letters, and Arsallan never contacted me. This was before email. Before cheap international long-distance phone rates. The silence hurt, uncertainty plagued me, and the absence of my newly found-and-lost family and friends felt like a cruel joke. For months, my heart felt weighted by rocks, drowned at the bottom of a cold, murky sea. But life went on, as it always does, the currents dragging you along, whether you want to go with the flow or not.

In time, new people entered and exited, new experiences made my heart soar and sink again. As daily dramas unfolded, *today*s morphed into *yesterday*s with increasing velocity. Current events took center stage and pushed history further back into memory. I thought of my holiday in Goa less and less, but I never forgot.

I have never forgotten.

FROM: "Preity Lindstrom" <ToyGirl@comcast.net>

TO: Kiran Deshpande; Rani Tomashot

SENT: December 10, 20XX 09:25 AM

SUBJECT: RE: A blast from the past . . .

Kiran, good to hear from you. Welcome home. And yes, I did hear it through the Hindi-Bindi Grapevine.

;-) Said grapevine has kept me informed of happenings in both of your lives over the years . . . BTW, Rani, I hear congrats are in order! A =solo= exhibit. YAY FOR YOU!!!

It's been way too long since the three of us were in the same place at the same time. We're overdue for a play date. ;-)

Preity

Preity's Goan Shrimp Curry

SERVES 4–6

SHRIMP:

1½ pounds large shrimp, uncooked, peeled and deveined

1 teaspoon cayenne powder (adjust to preference)

½ teaspoon turmeric powder

1. Grab a pair of disposable kitchen gloves so your hands won't stink.
2. In a colander, rinse shrimp under cold running water. Drain and transfer thawed shrimp to large glass bowl.
3. Sprinkle with cayenne and turmeric. Use your hands to evenly coat. Cover with plastic wrap and refrigerate 30 minutes.

GRAVY:

1-inch piece of tamarind (from slab)

1 cup hot water

2 tablespoons canola oil

2 medium yellow onions, thinly sliced

5 curry leaves * (kadhi patta)

2 cloves garlic, minced

2 tablespoons fresh ginger root, peeled and chopped

1 fresh green chili pepper, * *finely chopped (adjust to preference)*

1 teaspoon coriander powder

1 teaspoon cumin powder

1 14-ounce can coconut milk

½ teaspoon salt (adjust to taste)

1 teaspoon sugar (adjust to taste)

fresh coconut slivers (optional)

1. In a small glass bowl, soak the tamarind in hot water. Set aside.
2. In a wok or deep 12-inch skillet, heat oil over medium-

high heat. Add onion and stir-fry until translucent, about 2–3 minutes.

3. Reduce heat to medium. Add curry leaves, garlic, ginger, and chili. Sauté for 1 minute.
4. Add coriander and cumin. Sauté for 2 minutes.
5. Add coconut milk and bring to a boil over medium-high heat.
6. Reduce heat to low, partially cover, and simmer to thicken gravy, about 10–15 minutes.
7. When tamarind is soft, mash through wire strainer. Reserve pulp and juices. Discard solids.
8. Add shrimp, tamarind, salt, and sugar to the gravy. Simmer uncovered until shrimp turns pink, about 2–5 minutes.
9. Remove from heat. Remove curry leaves. Garnish with fresh coconut slivers. Serve with plain, boiled rice.*

* *Preity's Tips:*

✔ Wear disposable kitchen gloves when handling seafood and chopping chilies.

✔ For kids and wimps, stir plain nonfat yogurt into their servings to cool down the firepower.

✔ If you can't find curry leaves, omit. This dish is still darn good without them!

Rani McGuiness Tomashot: The Land of Opportunity

He who does not climb will not fall either.

INDIAN PROVERB

I want to die. The alarm clock's going off, and I already hit the snooze button twice. I grope to silence it, haul myself upright, plant my feet on the hardwood floor. *Aag-doom! Baag-doom!* I remember my mother singing to me when I was little, a Bengali wake-up nursery rhyme.

Aag-doom! Baag-doom! Horses away!
Gongs, drums, cymbals play!
Crash! Boom! The noisy band
Marches off to Orange Land.
On parrot's wing, a golden ray
Uncle Sun's wedding day.
Let's go to market, me and you

For paan *and* betel *nut to chew.*
A betel *worm slips out of sight*
Mother, daughter have a fight.
Saffron flowers bloom anew
Fresh, sweet pumpkin stew
Little one, up with you!

I groan in protest and crash over like a felled tree—timber!—my head at the foot of the bed. My husband Bryan burrows his head under his pillow. He can't bear to watch my struggles to wake up. Too pathetic, too heart-wrenching, he says. He'd rather let me sleep in peace. But that isn't an option today. I have places to go, things to do, people . . . ugh . . . people to schmooze.

With a whimper or three, I drag my lead-weighted carcass out of bed and stumble to the bathroom. A little before seven, dressed in my running gear, I shuffle down the hall to stretch and notice an envelope someone slid under the door. At the contents, my heart stirs awake. Ooohing and aaahing, I flip through the latest photos of Anjali—nicknamed Anju—the three-year-old girl the couple across the hall is adopting from an orphanage in Kolkata, my mother's birthplace. They call it an orphanage, though it's mostly girls, not orphaned but abandoned and rescued from the streets . . . or worse.

"She's precious," I say to the proud parent-to-be warming up in the hallway between our condos. My running buddy George has already stretched and jogs in place waiting for me. Though I've told him before, I can't say it enough. "You're doing an amazing thing. Saving a life. You're good people, George. And Anju's one lucky girl to have you."

George just grins and says as always, "Thanks, but we're the lucky ones." I wait while he drops the envelope on the mahogany table in his foyer. Closing the door behind him, he asks, "Are you excited or nervous about tonight?"

"Yes," I say and raise an index finger to my lips then tap my watch. Neither of us a morning person, we have a No-Talking-Until-We-Cross-the-Golden-Gate-Bridge rule. My head's already pounding from the mental exertion of our minor exchange, and George's can't be far behind.

He nods, and without another word, we're off.

We run down Laguna Street, across Lombard and Bay, then west along the marina, past the early-morning windsurfers, and to the foot of the world's most beautiful bridge. At our early hour, we often find the Golden Gate shrouded in an eerie mist, as if an otherworldly phantom bridge, but this morning, the Artist has painted a clear panorama.

We yield at the ramp for cyclists descending from the west side, then trek up the east side. To our left, the vast Pacific ripples and splashes with crashing whitecaps. We keep an eye out for whales; one time last month we spotted a tail. To our right stretches the city skyline and the lone Coit Tower that juts from the top of Telegraph Hill like an enthusiastic thumbs-up on the peninsula.

Beneath my feet, the springy suspension bridge quivers like a trampoline in strong winds. The bouncing used to scare me so much I had to turn back before the first pillar. It took a while before I could cross to the other side, thanks in large part to George's coaching and patience.

We run the length of the bridge, past the ever-present scaffolding (they're constantly painting the bridge orange), and pause long enough for me to blow my nose and George to guzzle some water.

"You okay?" he asks.

I nod, and we retrace our steps. Impressive for a former asthmatic, I always think.

When I was ten, on our one and only family trip to India, I developed childhood asthma. At first, we assumed it was the pollution, but when we came home, the symptoms didn't go away. For years, I woke up gasping for breath in the dead of night. Worse, I was relegated to last-pick in gym class. Luckily, I grew out of it and kissed my last inhaler good-bye in college.

"You're coming, right?" I say to George. "Both of you?"

"Hell, yeah. We wouldn't miss your big night."

"Thanks. It means a lot to me. I still can't believe any of this is really happening. *My* work appreciated, exhibited *solo* at a kick-ass gallery, sold for real money."

"Kudos at last."

"That wasn't my motivation, but I did secretly dream of it. And now that my dream's come true . . ." I know what I'm supposed to say. "Now that it's reality . . ." I turn my gaze to the ocean.

"What?" George asks.

I shrug. "What you said. I'm excited and nervous. But enough about me. I get to hog the spotlight tonight." I smile. "Tell me, how are your parenting classes—?"

"No. Don't change the subject. And for God's sake, *don't* give me that fake cocktail party smile."

I smack his arm with the back of my hand. "Have I told you recently how much you annoy me?"

"Uh-huh. Gonna 'fess up or what?"

"Why do you know me so well? We haven't known each other *that* long." It's only been a year since Bryan and I sold our mini-mansion in Pacific Heights and bought the two-bedroom condo.

"Occupational hazard."

I smile, for real this time. "Wish I had a counselor like you when I was in high school." Luckily, I had great parents. Whom I miss terribly, especially during the holidays. I don't know how my mom managed to leave her entire family and move halfway around the world, while I rue being separated by a continent.

"Is it Bryan?" George asks.

"No. Yes. I don't know. Maybe." I pace my words with my breathing, another skill that took some time to master. "He's supported me every step of the way. This is his victory as much as mine. But I feel so guilty. I can't enjoy it with a clear conscience. How can I be happy when he's so miserable? I mean, he's happy for *me*, but *he's* not happy. It breaks my heart. Every day, I have the luxury of pursuing my passion, while my husband schleps off to a job he hates."

"Job still sucks, huh?"

"Big time, and it's not just the pay cut. . . . It was never *just* about making money for him. He can't stand not utilizing his full potential. He's an entrepreneur, a visionary."

"A leader, not a follower."

"Exactly. He's still grieving—maybe he's *always* going to grieve—for the company and the employees and the shareholders. It was his baby, and a huge part of him died with it. He knows he needs to move on, but he can't. He needs another dream, and until he finds it..." We turn a corner. My voice breaks. "He's so lost... And I can't help him. I can't reach him. Nothing I do or say makes any difference."

I want to cry but not there. My nose will run even more, and I don't have enough tissues on me. And where's my fucking runner's high, anyway? It usually kicks in halfway across the bridge, but lately it's eluded me. No matter how far I run or how hard I drive my body, I can't break through the magic barrier. This is the reason I run, for nature's miracle pill. *Where is it?*

"You said it, babe," George says beside me. "He's grieving. Grief takes time. Keep applying that balm, but quit expecting overnight results. And the last thing you want to do is crawl into Bryan's pit of despair with him. That won't help anyone."

"I know it," I say. "I know. It's just... hard."

"Well, there *is* something you could do. Doesn't sound like you're doing it—"

"What?"

"Let yourself be happy. Don't force it, but don't fight it, either. There's no reason to feel guilty. Bryan isn't jealous or resentful. He's genuinely happy for you. And you know what? Your pleasure's the closest thing he's got to his own right now. So don't cheat him out of it."

I cast George a sidelong glance. "I never thought of it that way." After a moment, I add, "That was some sleight of hand. You redirected my guilt to fuel the opposite outcome." I smile. "When you're good, you're good. You're good, George."

"I know." He flashes a cheesy grin. "That's why they pay me the little bucks."

"Oh, man. I knew I forgot something. Tell me you brought some of those little bucks with you because I forgot. Again."

"Gotcha covered, pal."

"Thanks. For everything."

We run to the Starbucks on Union, where we get four lattes to go (for us and our spouses), then walk the remaining blocks home. George's door opens just as we return.

"Wow," I say. "Who *is* that sharp-dressed man?"

Said sharp-dressed man chuckles. "Morning, Rani."

"Morning, Walker. Love the power suit."

"Thank you. See you tonight."

"Tonight." As George hands him a latte, I wave goodbye and go inside.

"Tonight, tonight, won't be just any night..." In his rich baritone, Bryan belts out the show tune from *West Side Story,* and I chime in with my off-key-from-fighting-a-cold soprano.

As he twirls me around the kitchen, I remember when we used to be silly like this all the time. It was what I loved most about Bryan. He wasn't afraid to be a complete and total dork. He took pride in it, embraced who he was. He had such courage and conviction, such strength of character. But when his dream shattered, so did his confidence. And with it, his joie de vivre, as the French call it, or *masti* as Saroj Auntie says. Passion for life. How I want to give it back to him.

Restore the gleam in his eyes. Rekindle his excitement. Resuscitate his *masti.*

"Pick you up at five," he says, grabbing his laptop bag.

We met the first day of our freshman year at Berkeley. We lived on the same dorm floor, though we didn't date until two years later. For two years, he watched my parade of boyfriends, if you can even call them that, since their average shelf life was two to four weeks. It seemed all the good guys were taken, already in relationships, as Bryan was with his girlfriend, who was two years younger and still in high school. That left the available market glutted with the commitment-phobic, just-want-to-get-laid crowd.

I looked around and thought: I'm the only virgin I know on this campus. Virgins were an endangered species. All of my friends were sexually active, which is not to say "sleeping *around*," though that certainly happened, too. Most committed, monogamous relationships, which was what I wanted, involved sex. So did flings, which accounted for the lifespan of my romantic interests. The guys I hooked up with seemed to view sex as a *prerequisite* for a relationship, bass-ackwards in my book. On this, I agreed one hundred percent with my mother: Why buy the cow if the milk's free?

Now before you pat me on the back, or the head, you should know I can't credit my "fine moral upbringing" or my "superior, wholesome values" for the fact I held onto my prized virginity until the ripe age of twenty. Don't think for a second it was any valiant struggle. It wasn't. The truth is, I was a loser magnet, which made it easy to keep my legs closed—a no-brainer—until Bryan.

"There's no high school girlfriend," he told me one day.

"You broke up?"

He shook his head. "I made her up."

"Why—?"

"Because I'm a geek, and I have no life. It was easier—"

"No. *Why* are you telling me this? Why not take the story to its natural conclusion and say you and Imaginary Girl parted ways?"

"Oh. Well. That would be because I'm in love with you. Madly. Deeply. Passionately. Irrevocably. Pathetically, I suppose, if you tell me I don't stand a chance..."

When I picked my jaw up off the floor, doves flew, conch shells blew, and the Gates of Paradise swung wide open.

I adore my husband. With every breath I take. Every fiber of my being. Ever more, every day. For ten years, we've grown together. I hope we never grow apart, but lately I worry about it. We're both in a holding pattern, wondering where our lives are going. What's next for us as individuals, and as a couple? I look at my childhood friends Kiran and Preity. One I haven't seen in years, now divorced. One happily married with children.

What direction will Bryan and I take?

At our front door, I lay my hand on his freshly shaven jaw, nuzzle my face to his neck, and breathe in his clean scent. "I love you, Bry," I say. Such inadequate words for what I feel.

"Love you, too." He pecks my lips, but I rise onto my toes, wind my arms around his neck, and deepen the kiss. He pulls away and lifts his head with a groan. "Save that thought. Gotta run, catch the yuppie bus."

"Have a good day," I say.

"You, too. Good luck."

After he leaves, emptiness swells inside me. A big black

hole that threatens to swallow me whole. I want to crawl back into bed and pull the covers over my head.

No no no. I shake my head. *Snap out of it.*

Every artist wishes for a life like mine. An opportunity like mine. No financial pressures. Ample time and resources. I'm damn lucky. I need to make the most of my gifts, put my blessings to good use. March into my studio and kick ass.

Determined, I shower and change, whip up a chocolate-banana soy milk smoothie and go to my studio in the spare bedroom. The morning light is perfect. I burn a stick of sandalwood incense and put on some mood music. Enigma's "L.S.D." plays first. *Love Sensuality Devotion.* The room reverberates with an intoxicating blend of New Age music, a club beat, and Gregorian and Native American chants. I absorb the atmosphere, hips swaying to the rhythm, and try to work.

Try and try. And keep making a mess. And more mess.

It's okay, I tell myself, trying to shake it off. You're warming up. It'll come.

But it doesn't. It hasn't. Not for days. Weeks. Months.

I was so jazzed when I started my Goddess series, modern renditions of mythic females. But my first taste of commercial success has turned me into a constipated artist. For the first time in my life, I can't gag the gremlins, haranguing voices in my head that constantly critique my work.

"You think that's art?"

"Will anyone like this?"

"Too much like the last one."

"Too different."

"Sloppy, Rani. Sloppy."

It's so draining. Not that my art has always provided a bliss hit—it is *hard,* after all—but lately, it never does. Lately, I dread it. I'm secretly afraid that somewhere on the Road to Success, I lost my own passion. Bryan lost his on his fall down. Did I lose mine on my rise up?

Jack fell down and broke his crown, and Jill came tumbling after.

No no no. My passion can't be lost; it's simply misplaced. I'll find it again. I have to.

I take a break and go to the kitchen. I'm tempted to open the refrigerator and pull up a chair (it beats turning on the oven and sticking my head inside), but I resist. I gather the ingredients for the chocolate *sandesh* truffles I'm bringing to accompany the chocolate-dipped strawberries and champagne the gallery has arranged. You gotta have protein, right? You'd never guess it, but these little babies are made with fresh, homemade cheese called *chhana* that looks, but doesn't taste, similar to cottage cheese or ricotta.

A celebratory sweet, *sandesh* means "good news" in Bengali. The "s" in Bengali is pronounced "sh," and an "a" is often "o." There's other tricky stuff that will make your eyes cross, so let's stick with this abridged *Hooked On Phonics* lesson and take my word that Bengalis have their reasons for pronouncing *sandesh* as *shawn-dhaysh.*

I tweaked Mom's family recipe for my own taste. The *sandesh* I had when we visited Kolkata commemorated my cousins passing their exams. Sweetened with newly harvested paundra sugarcane, shaped like conch shells, and packed in rice for freshness. I subtracted those steps and added chocolate—I find anything and everything tastes better dipped in, or slathered with, chocolate.

Making *chhana,* I try to think happy, pleasant thoughts, but a gnawing desperation claws at me. What if I can't do it? What if I can't produce what's expected of me?

Art is my life's purpose. Without it... I shake my head. I don't want to go there.

I concentrate on the *sandesh.* I roll the truffles in cocoa powder and crushed pistachios. Drizzle on melted chocolate. Make another smoothie. Add a splash of rum. Then a more generous splash. Go to my studio. Try to work again. Create stuff only my mother could love. Return to the kitchen. Do a shot. Get toasted. Still, nothing worth keeping. Flop onto the love seat. Fling an arm over my eyes.

I want my mommy.

When I was little, I was my mother's shadow. An only child, I was the center of her world, and she was mine. I followed her everywhere. If she shut me out of the bathroom, I sat outside the door and cried, whined, or wiggled my fingers under the crack until she came out. Every week she took me on field trips to the park, the library, the grocery store, and the fresh fish market.

I loved to watch her prepare Bengali food. When she cooked, she removed her rings and set them on the windowsill in a bowl of salt water. On her left hand, she wore her wedding band—gold with seven channel-set diamonds. On her right, she wore a white sapphire on her middle finger and a red coral called a *paula* on her ring finger. When preparing a large quantity, she sat on the kitchen floor and impaled such legumes as cauliflower, potatoes, and eggplant over a *bonti*—a contraption with a curved upright blade that served as an old-fashioned, manual food processor. Different dishes required different shapes.

"When I'm a grown-up, I'll chop all the vegetables, Mommy," I said, puffing out my chest.

"Okay, but until then, you glue your bottom on that stool." She positioned my stool at a safe distance, and I wasn't allowed to get up until she put the serrated knife away, out of my reach.

She let me stand on a chair at the counter when she rolled wheat dough into perfect rounds for *luchis*—puffy fried bread. She would give me a little ball to knead and flatten with my mini rolling pin, which was better than Play-Doh because I could eat it, though I never got the hang of shaping my dough into a neat circle. The odd shapes I created made my mother laugh and say, "If you hope to marry a Bengali, we'll have to work on this."

Fish was the singlemost recurring item on my mother's menu. Fish in a sweet mustard sauce was her specialty. She never ate or prepared beef. She said that for her, eating a cow was like eating a dog or a horse. "If one day you move to another country where people, given plenty of options, choose to eat dog burgers and horse steaks, could you learn to do it?"

No, I couldn't. And neither could she.

If not for my father and me needing a bit more variety, she would have served fish every day, every meal, even for breakfast, she loved it that much. Sometimes when Dad or I complimented her on a particular fish dish, she would say,

"One day we will visit Calcutta, and you will taste *hilsa,* the best fish in the world."

My father would pat her hand, hug her, or kiss her cheek. "We will, honey. We will."

We didn't go to Calcutta until I was ten because, after my mother eloped with my father, her father said she was dead to him, and as long as he was alive, she should never come back. She returned—just once—at the request of my aunt, Anandita-*mashi,* when my grandfather was on his deathbed.

Over the years, my mother had regularly written letters home, which my grandfather refused to read or hear, but Anandita-*mashi* saved them and read each blue aerogramme to him as he lay dying. When he heard my mother's words, he cried. And when he learned from Anandita-*mashi* it was my mother and her American husband who'd secretly subsidized their upper-middle-class lifestyle all along—not his deadbeat nephew as everyone had led him to believe—my grandfather finally asked to see her.

When she arrived at his bedside, he told her he had endured social disapproval to allow her—young, unmarried, and alone—to pursue her dream of higher studies in America. *His* father had overruled him and granted my mother permission. In return, she proved all of his fears correct. She shamed him by marrying my father, and no amount of black money—dirty money—could ever erase my grandfather's suffering. In Indian culture, a child's duty to a parent superceded all else, and she dishonored him and tarnished the family name. For that, he would never forgive her. The last words he spoke to her quoted an Indian proverb: "I gave her a staff for her support, and she used it to break my head." He died the next day.

My father said it was lucky timing, because he might have killed the old man.

I didn't learn any of this until much later in life. It still haunts my mother and enrages my father.

We never went back again, though my mother still writes—and sends money—to her family. (My parents provide complete financial support for Anandita-*mashi*, whom no one would marry because of her "defect" of epilepsy.)

Both of my parents came from large families, and sometimes, when I was lonely, when no kids could play with me, I would ask for a brother or sister. My Indian friends Kiran and Preity both had brothers, and I wanted one, too. My father would grab me and tickle me and say, "Why, when God gave us a perfect little girl?" Whenever he said this, my mother's eyes would soften, and I could see her love for him written all over her face.

The truth is I was a difficult pregnancy and delivery. My mother suffered two miscarriages before me, and after me, she couldn't have more children. In India, this would have been the Kiss of Death. Social ostracizing. As my mother explained it, the only fate worse than not producing sons was being barren. But none of that mattered to my dad. To him, our family was perfect. *Rani* means "queen."

Most of the time, I was plenty happy not to have to share. My parents or my stuff.

My mother stayed home with me until I went to kindergarten, then she worked part-time, so she was always home when I got out of school. This was great until I was a teenager and started to develop my own strong identity. No longer docile, I often disagreed with my overprotective mother. To her, disagreement and debate were often interpreted as disrespect and back talk "answering back," which frustrated both of us to no end and sometimes escalated into shouting matches.

One awful day in my hormonal, angst-ridden trauma-drama, I screamed, "In *this* country, we have freedom of speech! I have the right to express my opinion even if it's contrary to yours! Why can't you be like other mothers? I hate you! I hate my life! I wish I'd never been born!" I stormed to my room and slammed the door. Then I locked it, because I knew, right away, I was in Big Shit Trouble. With my mother *and* with my father, once she told him. Even in ambiguous disputes—which clearly this wasn't—they always sided together against me.

Half an hour later, when The Knock sounded, I was shaking. Whatever punishment was headed my way, it was sure to be bad.

"Rani, open the door," my mother said.

I didn't answer.

After a minute, the door opened, and my mother stood there, a bobby pin in her hand. She'd been crying, which made me cry worse than if she'd beaten me with her *chappal*—leather sandal—which she never did but occasionally threatened. "I-I'm sorry. I-I shouldn't have said those things."

"No, you shouldn't have," she said in a small voice. "My parents would have thrown me onto the streets to beg if I ever spoke to them that way."

"I'm sorry. I was disrespectful."

"Yes, and you were very hurtful."

I cried harder. "*I* was hurt, too!"

She crossed her arms and sat on the edge of my bed. "I

know you're hurting, Rani. I know this is a hard time. For you. For all of us. But I want to get some things straight."

I dropped my gaze and braced myself.

She leaned over and took my chin in her hand, so I would look at her. Meeting my eyes directly, she said, "Whether you like it or not, *I* am the mother this time. *You* are the daughter. One day, you'll have the freedom you crave. You won't have to ask my permission or explain yourself to me, and I can only hope you'll make the right decisions. If you're rash and follow your impulses without any thought to the consequences, you can hurt others and yourself badly. With freedom comes responsibility. Remember that."

I nodded.

"Remember this, too . . . No matter what happens, now or then, no matter how bad it gets, I will always be your mother, you will always be my daughter, and I will always love you. You are *the* most precious thing in my life, and I thank God you were born in this life, to me."

I stared at her in disbelief. How could she say such nice things to me when I'd just been so ugly? I didn't deserve her kindness. But when she opened her arms, I didn't question or hesitate. I launched myself against her, hugging her hard.

She hugged me back and said, "Even if we disagree, even if we fight, even if we hurt each other, we have to promise to make up, no matter how hard it is. I will never turn my back on you. I don't ever, *ever* want to lose you. I know I'm not like other mothers. American moms *or* Indian moms—"

"No, you're *better*! You're the greatest mom in the world! I love you, Mom!" We stayed like that for a long time, crying and rocking. I kept saying, "I'm sorry. I'm *so* sorry."

And she said to me the words her father withheld from her, "You're forgiven."

FROM: "Uma Basu" <ubasu@gwu.edu>

TO: Rani Tomashot

SENT: December 10, 20XX 11:44 AM

SUBJECT: Break a Leg!

Dearest Boo-Boo,

Hi, sweetie! How are you? I'm thinking of you on your special day! Dad and I wish we could be there for opening night, but we're with you in spirit -- and eagerly anticipating our VIP passes next week!

Exams have started, and campus is a stress factory. Dad landed safely in Germany. I will try to call you later this PM, but I know you have lots to do, and in case we don't connect: Have a wonderful time. Break a leg!

Love,

Mom & Dad

At the gallery—a chic converted warehouse with soaring ceilings, exposed rafters, and gleaming pine floors—I walk around in a daze. It's so unreal. Wall-to-wall bodies. All these strangers have come to see *my* work, meet *me*. Before I'm introduced, Bryan and I mill through the crowd eavesdropping on conversations, watching people tilt their heads this way and that as they scrutinize my paintings, murmur appreciation.

"They're eating my *sandesh*," I say to Bryan.

"They're hungry," he teases, and I elbow him.

Bryan wears a gray silk suit and a seafoam green shirt that brings out the flecks of green in his hazel eyes. I wear a light bronze, embroidered *ghagara-choli*—a flowing full-length skirt; a fitted, belly-revealing, short-sleeved blouse; and a long, gauzy scarf I drape behind my back and over my arms. I kept my jewelry simple. No necklace, as I've never liked having anything around my neck—scarves, turtlenecks, or jewelry. Still, I feel like a glamorous movie star with my few pieces. Teardrop emeralds dot my earlobes. A solitary iron bangle called a *loha* that belonged to my maternal grandmother hangs around my wrist. In my nose, I wear a small diamond stud.

When I was a teen, I dressed in goth attire—all black—and resembled a vampire. My mother cried when she saw my jet black dyed hair and multiple piercings. "Why does a beautiful girl do this to herself?" she asked. "Explain it to me so I understand."

I told her for me, it was like the gargoyles I collected. They looked evil, but their purpose was to ward off evil. "I don't have time for pretentious, judgmental people, so if they refuse to talk to me because of how I look, then it's worth it."

Today, one diamond stud does the trick.

"I'm the product of an Irish-Italian Catholic father from

Boston and an Indian Hindu mother from Calcutta," I say to my captive audience. "This multicultural heritage has greatly influenced my art. Growing up, I never felt *different* unless someone brought it to my attention. I never felt I had to choose, 'Am I this, or that?' I felt, and my parents reinforced, 'I'm both.' In my family, this was perfectly natural, normal."

My knees are trembling. I rehearsed in front of the mirror, then again with Bryan. *Is it too hokey? Are you sure? Because it's me, it's really me. From my heart...*

"It's easy to see differences among people, especially if they look, talk, eat, dress, worship differently. But there's more to every person than any peel-and-stick-on label. Despite the most blatant differences, there's almost always commonality if you look beyond the surface. At our core, human beings from all walks of life have more in common than not. My art attempts to show the synergy of cultural fusion—the notion that one plus one equals something greater than two—and the universal bonds that link us all together as one race, the human race."

Thunderous applause.

It's the most singular night of my life. The top of the mountain. Afterward, I think: There's nowhere to go but down.

As I lay awake under the weight of my sleeping husband's arm, the feeling grows, hollows out my insides like a melon baller carving a cantaloupe.

I reflect on all the immigrants who came to this foreign land, the Land of Opportunity, with nothing more than a dream. The American Dream.

The challenge isn't just in attaining, but in holding on. Keeping the dream. Or getting a new one.

I don't know that I have their courage.... To start over. To rebuild. To climb mountain after mountain.

How did the Hindi-Bindi Club do it?

FROM: "Rani Tomashot"
<RaniTomashot@hotmail.com>
TO: Kiran Deshpande; Preity Lindstrom
SENT: December 12, 20XX 09:23 AM
SUBJECT: RE: A blast from the past...

Hello, chickies!

Sorry for late reply. Chaotic stretch. SO GREAT to hear from you both -- looking forward to our playdate! I predict we'll pick up where we left off, like always. For better or worse. :P

See you soon!

XOXOXO,
Rani

Rani's Chocolate Sandesh Truffles

2 DOZEN

½ cup unsweetened cocoa powder

25 pistachios, finely crushed

16 ounces chhana *(fresh cheese recipe follows)*

½ cup sweetened cocoa powder

10 green cardamom pods, seeds only, crushed

6–8 ounces chocolate

1. Line a baking sheet with wax paper or baking parchment. Set aside.
2. Place unsweetened cocoa powder and crushed pistachios on two small plates. Set aside.
3. In a nonstick saucepan over low heat, stir *chhana* and sweetened cocoa powder into a whipped cream cheese consistency.
4. When mixture leaves sides of saucepan, remove from heat. Stir in cardamom.
5. Using a small cookie scoop, drop 1-inch truffle rounds onto the baking sheet. Allow to cool to room temperature.
6. For each truffle: Roll between palms to make uniform ball, gently roll in cocoa and/or pistachios, replace on baking sheet.
7. Melt chocolate over low heat; drizzle over truffles.
8. Serve at room temperature in decorative foil candy cups.

Chhana

[Fresh Cheese]

16 OUNCES

12 cups whole milk

¾ cup white vinegar

1. Spray a large Dutch oven with nonstick cooking spray.
2. Over medium-high heat, bring milk to a boil, stirring often to prevent sticking, scorching, and skin from forming on the surface.
3. Reduce heat to low, stirring constantly. One tablespoon at a time, stir in vinegar to "break" the curds and whey.
4. Remove from heat and let stand 15 minutes.
5. In the sink, line a colander with three cheesecloth layers. Pour in the cheese mixture.
6. Gather edges of cheesecloth to form a "hobo's sack." Twist, squeezing out excess liquid (whey). Plop a heavy can or gallon of liquid on top of the sack, wringing out even more. Allow cheese (curds) to drain for 20–30 minutes.
7. Remove cheesecloth. Discard liquid. Cheese should be soft and doughy.
8. Knead on a dry surface for 10 minutes.*

* Rani's Tips:

- ✔ For best results, use immediately.
- ✔ For next-best results, tightly wrap in plastic and refrigerate for 2 days, tops.
- ✔ After 3 days, don't say I didn't warn you.

PART TWO

The Old World

Meenal Deshpande: What Is Best?

The same stream of life that runs through
my veins night and day runs through the
world and dances in rhythmic measures.
It is the same life that is rocked in
the ocean-cradle of birth and death,
in ebb and in flow.

RABINDRANATH TAGORE

The house is quiet in the hours before dawn—as it's always been. Upstairs, at the end of the hall, Kiran still sleeps with her bedroom door open, a night-light glowing from her adjoining bath. I stand in the doorway and listen to the faint sound of her breathing, then head for the shower, a smile in my heart.

I turn on the spray, take a fresh towel from the folded stack in a wicker basket, and toss it into the dryer to toast. While I brush my teeth, steam fills the shower stall, fogs the glass door. Quickly, I undress, avoiding my reflection in the mirror, and step inside, cuddling the warm blanket of mist.

In minutes, my muscles relax, and I start to play my new daily game—climbing my fingers up the diagonal-laid tiles in front of me, counting off each diamond I pass, each milestone, reaching higher and higher elevations. I'm rock-climbing, I pretend, one precarious handhold after another. *How high will she go? Nobody knows.* Both arms overhead, victory is mine. I taste its sweetness, *amrit*—nectar of the gods—on my tongue. I savor my triumph. I'm an Olympic athlete who's beaten the odds, won a gold medal, not only for myself but for my countrywomen. The crowd goes wild. I take a bow and blow kisses to my fans.

How silly I've become! I laugh at myself. I don't care.

Didn't I serve my time? Earn the privileges that come with living to a ripe old age? Doesn't that include the right to be a little silly? Still, I am still *me,* and I can't help wondering: What would people think if they knew?

What will Kiran think when I tell her?

Now that she's home, it must be done. I can't avoid the subject any longer. She's bound to figure it out on her own—that would be the worst way to find out. I brace my heated forehead against the cool tiles. Close my eyes. *Haré Ram*...

Since my tropical Indian blood stubbornly refuses to thicken no matter how many winters I endure, I dress in layers. Bundled in fleece thermals and double socks straight from the warm dryer, I head downstairs to the northeast corner of the kitchen for my prayers. Northeast is the direction of Lord Shiva. From the north comes positive magnetic energy; from the east, positive solar energy.

Even if I *hadn't* started doing a daily morning *puja* this year, I would today, for Kiran.

My *pujas* aren't as elaborate as my mother's, but I find

serenity and comfort in many of the old rituals. Washing and drying the figurines of the gods. Using my ring finger to apply *gandha* (sandalwood paste) and *haldi-kumkum* (yellow turmeric and red vermilion powders) to their foreheads. Sprinkling rice and fresh flowers around them. Burning incense. Lighting a *diwa*—a small, *ghee*-fueled lamp. Offering *prasad*—sweets, nuts, fruit, or sweet milk—in a silver bowl to be blessed. Taking *prasad* as sacrament. Bringing my palms together in *namaskar*. Praying.

As a girl, I looked forward to my mother's *pujas*, not for any spiritual reasons, but because of my sweet tooth. If my two older brothers and I behaved, *Ai* let us have the leftover *prasad*. I always behaved; my brothers didn't. They forgot to remove their *chappals* before entering the *puja* room, or tipped over the figurines (claiming to lay them down for a nap), or dunked them upside-down underwater instead of using the silver *pali* to give them a bath. All of which meant: more *prasad* for me.

I also enjoyed gathering the offerings from our beautiful *baag*. *Bel* leaves for Lord Shiva. Twenty-one stems of *durva* for Shree Ganesh. *Tulsi* leaves for Lord Krishna. A red rose for Shree Lakshmi. And for all, whatever fragrant flowers were in season: marigolds, mums, tuberoses, jasmine, or white lilies.

If I close my eyes, I can still smell the perfume of *Ai*'s *puja* room, the heavenly mix of flowers, sandalwood paste, and incense. When performing *aarti*, *Ai* would chant a hymn while one of us circled the *diwa* clockwise before the gods to show respect and ask blessings, and another rang a small, handheld bell. We jockeyed for these positions, these privileges, the way Vivek and Kiran did over who rode in the passenger seat of the car. Then we did our *namaskars* and prayed.

I used to pray for *shakti* and *buddhi*—strength and wisdom—and that my parents would choose a good husband for me. Now, I pray for *shakti, buddhi,* and good health—for my loved ones and myself.

After my *puja,* I put the kettle on the stove and take out a cup and saucer. The good china. Purchased piece by painstaking piece back in the Boston Days—a dollar here, two dollars there, whatever I saved from my frugal management of the grocery money Yash gave me each week. When, at last, we had a formal dining room, a china cabinet, and those twelve precious place settings, I displayed each piece like artifacts in a museum: *Do Not Touch.* Yes, I was one of those women who hoards away my finery, taking it out only on Very Special Occasions. Not until this year did I realize *every day* is a Very Special Occasion.

Now that I know, I pour decaffeinated Darjeeling green tea into my Lenox teapot each morning. Inhaling the aroma of fresh ginger I add to the brew, I take my matching cup and saucer into the dining room, sit at the head of the table, and let the peace and quiet wash over me.

I savor this time, when the world is still, when I can hear every little sound—the hum of the refrigerator, the ticking of the wall clock, the settling of the house, the furnace igniting—but not the same way I did when three of the upstairs bedrooms were occupied, when my alone-time was scarce. I'm still deeply grateful for each morning God gifts me, but these days, I would gladly trade the stillness to hear the voices of my loved ones.

Last night on the phone, Yash asked, "Did you tell her?"

"Not yet." I paced the kitchen. "She's just come home. After so long . . . What's another day?"

He wanted to argue—I know he did—but it was late, and he was tired. I'm not surprised when the phone rings this morning. Anticipating our conversation, I tell Yash I'm coming over.

"What about Kiran?" he asks.

"Sleeping. I wrote a note."

At his apartment, he opens the door for me in his pajamas. When he kisses my cheek, I smell toothpaste and Listerine, the original medicinal kind. Brand loyal, he'd still use each and every product we grew up with, if he could.

Even without me, Yash keeps his bachelor pad meticulously neat. His shoes line the wall inside the coat closet. Not a spoon in the sink. If he isn't in it, the bed is always made. Crisp, starched shirts in plastic bags on wire hangers. Dirty clothes in the hamper. Toilet seat down.

An independent husband. Independent children. American ideals, not Indian. *Not mine.*

"Good morning," I chirp, breezing past him.

"Good morning." He stretches his arms over his bald head, eyeing the small cooler I'm carrying. His bare feet poke from the light blue pajama bottoms he's paired with a white, short-sleeved V-neck undershirt. Toenails trimmed.

"Breakfast," I answer his unasked question.

He helps me out of my coat. "Meena. You shouldn't have. The coffee shop around the corner—"

"Delivers. I know. But I woke up in a baking mood." I head for the kitchen, glancing over my shoulder. "*Sattvic* food."

He chuckles. "Of course." He's the one who encouraged

me toward ayurveda and yoga—complementary ancient Indian diet and lifestyle disciplines that detoxify and balance the body, mind, and spirit. I stand here today because of God's will, first and foremost, but also in large part because of this man before me, once a mere stranger whose astrological chart indicated my best match for a life partner.

How many times did I question the stars? Never in India. But in America, when I saw the attention men lavished on wives and girlfriends... I'm ashamed to say, too many to count. But no longer. Because now I know. I received a definitive answer this year.

In the kitchen, I make Yash's tea the way he likes, piping hot with lots of milk and sugar, and mix a blender of mango *lassi*—yogurt smoothie. The mangoes we get here aren't as fragrant or flavorful as those in India, especially luscious Alphonso mangoes that conjure such fond memories for me, but luckily, we have Alphonso canned pulp.

Yash and I sit together at the table. When he sips his *lassi,* he breaks into a wide grin. "Ahhh. Delicious. *Much* better than the coffee shop."

"Try a muffin."

He breaks off the muffin top, pops a piece into his mouth. "Ummmm. Tasty."

The way we were brought up, food was the main vehicle for displaying and withholding affection. In my parents' home, if *Ai* was upset with *Baba,* she refused to cook his favorite dishes. If *Baba* was upset with *Ai,* he refused to eat, or ate out, usually at a relative's home. Sandeep Chawla told me the first time Yash had one of Saroj's lunch *tiffins* back in the Boston Days, Yash remarked about her *aloo ghobi*—a spiced potatoes and cauliflower dish: *Very good, but I prefer my wife's.*

That was the moment I knew I loved my husband. It took considerably longer for me to know, *really know*, that my husband loved me.

Yash and I reach for the wooden napkin holder at the same time. He retreats, and I hand him a napkin.

"Thank you," he says.

"You're welcome."

How automatic we are with these expressions—*please, thank you, you're welcome*. How liberally we use them. How much we've grown to *like* them. The very expressions we poked fun at in the Boston Days, dismissed as gratuitous!

Over the rim of Yash's *lassi* glass, our gazes meet and hold.

"You know why I came over," I say. "I want you to make an effort with Kiran. I want our daughter in our lives. I want to see her more than once in five years. If that means meeting her more than halfway..."

Yash grunts and takes another bite of his muffin. "These American kids. They expect everything served to them on gold platters. They feel entitled. But where's *our* entitlement as parents?" He jabs a thumb at his chest. I brace for a tirade; he delivers as expected. "After all we do for our kids, all the sacrifices we make, what do we get in return? We indulge them, and they feel subjugated. They grow up and distance themselves from us. Having adult children in our lives is a privilege, not a right. What rights *do* parents have in this country? None. A better life, we thought we gave our kids by raising them here. Better in material things, yes. But *not* in respect. *Not* in family values." He thumps his palm atop the wooden table to punctuate his conclusion: "No respect for elders and family."

I fold my hands in my lap. This isn't a new topic. We've had this conversation for years. Though intervals between grow longer and viewpoints change with time and experience, it's our lot to compare and contrast, assess and reassess. We were born to one of the world's oldest civilizations—*five thousand* years old—and we emigrated to one of the youngest. Which values and customs are superior: those of our birthplace, or those of the land where we chose to settle? What to adopt? What to reject? What to preserve? What to discard?

The answers aren't as obvious as you may think. They're riddles. Brainteasers. Puzzles. You think this piece fits, but wait, you look again and realize you jammed it into place. A virtue in one land is a vice in another. In India, deference signifies respect, showing strength of character, not weakness. And the American notion that all men are created equal? Not in India. There, people openly acknowledge innate differences, a hierarchy of power and respect, and for the most part believe that like a card game, one plays the hand one's dealt. Rules of the game include: Seniors trump juniors. Males trump females. Priests trump nobles and warriors. Nobles and warriors trump merchants. Merchants trump laborers.

I used to shake my head at Uma. Uma and her compromises. Concessions that permitted her daughter to run wild. Now look whose daughter married a rock star wannabe, and whose daughter married a Bill Gates wannabe. Look who among our friends circle is closest to her daughter. Not me. Not even Saroj. It's Uma.

And it was Uma to whom I turned more than any other friend this past year. Uma who helped me the most.

Sometimes solutions are counterintuitive, I think, watching as Yash drains his *lassi*. The way you must turn your wheels in the direction you're skidding. The way you inject a virus into your body in order to build immunity. The way certain bacteria and toxins prove helpful because they attack more harmful cells. The way you must sometimes *let go* in order to *retrieve* something. *Or someone.*

"When will you come to the house?" I ask when Yash rises to clear the dishes.

"After you tell Kiran."

"By myself?" I shake my head. "I want you to be there."

"You'll want mother-daughter time."

"Later. After. I can't tell her by myself. I need—"

"Okay, okay," he says. "I'll be there."

"And you'll try your best to get along with Kiran, for me? Please, Yash. I miss her so much. I miss... having family... at home... all together."

He slants his gaze at me and scowls like a little boy. I picture him at age six wearing the same expression. "Only for you, Meenu," he says, making me wish—again—I didn't learn my lessons about love so late.

When Yash comes home, he tries to keep the mood light, easing into things with Kiran. She proceeds with the same caution. They are two porcupines in a fragile soap bubble, afraid to get too close. That evening at the dinner table, we three sit together for the first time in more than five years.

"Mom? Dad?" Kiran speaks first. "Here's a crazy idea... What would you think about me... potentially..."

When she doesn't finish, I glance up to see her pushing food around on her plate. From the corner of her eye, she watches her father, who's occupied with his eggplant *bhaji*. Deftly, he mixes milk, rice, and eggplant with his agile surgeon's fingertips.

Kiran's never been much for rice, preferring to eat *bhajis* and *daals* with *chappati*, pairing her bites just so. I prod her, "Potentially what?"

"Um, moving... to this area... when my contract's up?"

I suspect this isn't the question she originally intended, but I can't contain my joy. "We'd love it! Wouldn't we, Dad?"

Yash just took a bite. He stops chewing, looks at me, then Kiran. With a casual nod, he drops his gaze to his plate and resumes eating. "That would be nice," he says. "Better late than never. Meena, *dhai*, please."

I reach for the container of plain yogurt, spoon some onto his plate.

"So, while we're on the topic of better late than never..." Kiran says.

"Bas," Yash says. Enough.

I look at Kiran, waiting. Yash keeps eating.

She clears her throat. "What would you think about me, um, having a semi-arranged marriage?"

My mouth drops open. I snap it shut. Swallow.

"Ten years too late for that," Yash says.

With my foot, I nudge him under the table.

He grunts.

"Kiran? Did you mean...? Was that a joke?"

"No joke. I'm serious. Is it a possibility or not?"

"Not," Yash says.

I nudge him again, harder this time.

"What, Meena?" He makes a helpless gesture toward me. "She asked a question, I gave her an answer. Ten years ago, she had her pick of boys, all good boys. We always told her it would be better, easier for the families if she married a nice Indian boy. Someone like her—born here, with the same background and values. Look at Vivek and Anisha. Her brother listened to us, but did Kiran? No. She said all Indian boys felt like cousins to her. She said we were too conservative, *narrow-minded.* She said it was her life and her decision whom to wed.

"Fine, we certainly weren't going to force her. We aren't *that* old-fashioned. But did she choose wisely like Preity? Or Rani? No. And if we didn't approve, too bad. She didn't give a damn what we thought. *Now,* when she's messed up her life, when she's too old, when she's divorced . . . *Now* she comes to us. What can we do *now*? *Jyacha haat modla to tyachaach galyaat padla.*" A Marathi proverb, meaning: One who breaks his arm must carry it in a sling. He shakes his head. "She's leftovers. All she can get is leftovers, if that."

I feel sick. Want-to-keel-over-and-vomit sick.

Our daughter sets her jaw in a steely line, wads up her napkin, and tosses it onto her plate. "On that encouraging note . . ." She shoves back in her chair.

"Kiran, wait." I reach across the table. "Don't leave." When she bolts, the familiar, metallic taste of fear fills my mouth.

I remember five years ago when she stormed from the house after a fight with her father. After confiding in us: She'd caught her husband with another woman and filed for divorce.

"Did he ever raise a hand to you?" her father had asked. Learning no, he'd looked visibly relieved and advised working things out. But Kiran was adamant: Their trust was shattered, the marriage was over, she wanted out.

"Just like that?" he asked.

"Just like that," she said.

Yash's face twisted with disgust. "These American kids," he said. "No respect for family. You live in a disposable society. Bored with your clothes? Throw them out, get new ones. Your electronics and other luxury goods become outdated? Throw them out, get new ones. Dissatisfied with your marriage? Throw it out, get a new one. It's all the same to you, isn't it? You have so much, yet you're never satisfied. You obsess over what you *don't* have. You want it all. You believe it's your right. You think only of yourself, your own happiness, and nothing of duty. Duty to family is an oxymoron here. Family is optional. You're spoiled. Selfish. Self-gratifying."

And then there was Kiran. Kiran who never lowered her eyes or her neck. Kiran who stood with her arms crossed, jaw cocked, and fire blazing in her direct gaze. "Don't hold back, Pops. Go ahead, tell me how you really feel. Respect doesn't apply to subordinates, does it? And on the subject of double standards, God forbid if the tables were turned and *I* was the unfaithful one and *Anthony* wanted to divorce me. You'd say I deserved it, wouldn't you? *Wouldn't you?*"

I wanted to gag them both and send them to opposite corners to cool off, but before I could calm either of them down, Kiran packed her bags, slammed the door shut, and left without saying good-bye.

I will *not* let that happen again. *I will not.* I stand, my head swimming with the abrupt motion, ready to referee. "Please don't leave," I say again, glaring a warning at Yash, who keeps his mouth shut this time.

"I'm not leaving, Mom." Kiran gives a tight smile. "I'm just going upstairs. I seem to have lost my appetite."

I'm relieved, but numb, watching as she takes her half-eaten dinner to the counter. *R-r-rip.* She tears off a sheet of foil, covers the plate, and puts it in the refrigerator. Yash resumes eating. After Kiran goes, I sit.

"Meena, *dhai*, please."

I don't move.

"Meena? Please may I have more *dhai*?"

I stare straight ahead at Kiran's vacated spot. Yash sighs and reaches across the table; I move the container of yogurt out of his reach.

He slumps back in his chair. Sighs. "Okay, what's wrong?"

"What's wrong?" I echo. For an otherwise brilliant man, he astounds me with his blind spots in relationships. "*This* is how you try to get along with your daughter?"

He shrugs. "When there's a difficulty, she falls. When not, she goes on jumping," he says in Marathi, an expression meaning Kiran humbles herself only when she's faced with a problem she can't solve alone, otherwise she's independent.

"And every time she falls," I reply in Marathi, "you kick her."

"I don't—! I—!" he stammers in English, then appears to question himself.

"Yes, Yash," I say softly, also switching to English, "you do. You kick her when she's down."

He scowls. "What was I supposed to do? You tell me."

"You can't just say whatever you want, however you want."

"Why not? I'm her father. If I don't say these things to her, who will? She *asked* our opinion. Did I lie? Did I say a single thing that wasn't true? We have to be honest, don't we?"

"Kamaal aahé!" Unbelievable! "You keep doing what you've always done, and you're surprised when you get the same results you've always gotten."

We mix languages midsentence, sometimes midword, tapping all our available vocabulary in our attempt to *best* convey what we mean. It isn't always possible. My thinking is different from my children's because of culture, my husband's because of biology. What's obvious, simplistic, to me isn't necessarily to them. And vice versa.

"I don't know what you want from me," Yash says, frustrated, and it dawns on me he *really* doesn't know. He excels in complex, delicate surgery but flunks at taking a person's emotional pulse.

I used to get so fed up, having to explain myself over and over, trying to be understood. Often, I just gave up. What was the point? They obviously weren't going to understand *any* words in *any* language. I might as well have been talking to the walls. But this year, in therapy, I learned how to take something big and scary, something overwhelming, and break it down—one, two, three—into small, manageable chunks. Much easier to chew on. Digest. Let go. That's what I must do now, for my husband.

I take a breath, find my center, soften my voice. *"Aho . . ."* I respectfully ask him to listen and tick off specifics on my fingers. "One, I need you to *please* avoid criticizing Kiran—"

"But—"

"Even if you think it's constructive. It doesn't help her. It only pushes her further away. Two, if you feel the need to vent, to get something off your chest, then please vent to me, not at her. Three, if you want a better relationship with our grown-up, *American* daughter, you must learn to balance honesty with diplomacy. *Compromise.*"

"In other words, censor my speech."

"If that's how you define it, yes."

These are the words his supervisors used on his performance evaluations. Words that made sense of what previous supervisors had tried and failed to convey. Words that *finally* communicated their intended meaning.

Yash makes a face, as if sucking on a wedge of lemon. "I shouldn't have to censor myself with my children."

And I shouldn't have to verbalize *my feelings. My needs.* That's what I always thought, before therapy.

"Right or wrong, the fact remains, you *do* have to," I say. "Our ways don't always work, certain ones never will—not here, and not with those born and brought up here. Please, on this, with Kiran, will you try a new way, for me?"

"It's not so easy, Meena." He pinches the bridge of his nose, the way he used to when he removed his glasses—before contacts, before corrective vision surgery. "I'm an old dog. How can I learn new tricks?"

"You can if you try. Just *try*."

"Okay, *baba*. I'll try harder."

"Thank you."

"But not tonight. Tonight, I'll go back to the apartment—"

"No! Yash—"

"Yes, Meenu. I'm making things worse here. You know I am. You and Kiran need to spend time together, just the two of you."

He's right, but I'm nervous. I dread having to tell Kiran at all, more so by myself.

Yash lays his left hand on my arm. His touch is strong, capable, reassuring. "The worst is behind us. Remember that."

I nod, but in the distance, I hear the rumble of thunder. The monsoon approaches. One prays for the best, but one never knows for sure what *is* best. . . .

I remember how as a girl, I watched my mother attend to my father's every need, from serving his meals to helping him dress. *Subservient* we call such women today. *Chauvinistic* we call such men. Yet if you ask *Ai*, she'll tell you she wouldn't have it any other way. She *prefers* a division of male-female domains and responsibilities—complementary, rather than repetitive, often *competitive* roles. *Ai* derives immense pleasure and satisfaction from managing the household, being a dutiful wife. "He would be lost without me," she says with pride, and *Baba* wobbles his head in agreement.

To them, *Baba* isn't an oppressor but a provider; *Ai* isn't a caged bird but a revered partner. They believe interdependence makes for solid marriages. For them, *need* equals *love*. And for most of my adult life, I believed their equation, definition, was the only one, hence: *My family's independence means I'm unneeded, unloved.*

I was wrong. Love, like God, takes many forms.

No one can be certain if *this one* or *that one* is best. God alone determines; God gets the final word.

Meenal's Mango Lassi

SERVES 4

2 cups Alphonso mango pulp or fresh ripe mango, mashed

4 cups plain nonfat yogurt

1 cup water (adjust to desired liquidity)

1 cup ice cubes (adjust to desired liquidity)

4 fresh mint leaves (optional garnish)

1. In a blender, whirl mango, yogurt, and water until smooth.
2. Add ice cubes a few at a time. Whirl until smooth.
3. Pour into tall glasses with straws, optionally garnish with mint.
4. Serve immediately.

Saroj Chawla: Partition: A Division of Hearts

Today I say to Waris Shah:
Speak from your grave.
Today I beseech you to add a new page
to your Book of Love.
Once one daughter of Punjab wept,
and you penned verse upon verse;
Today thousands are weeping and calling you,
Waris Shah.
Arise, friend of the downtrodden,
Arise, and see your Punjab.
AMRITA PRITAM

Beta, last night I dreamed of Lahore again... Of running barefoot through the fields to the banks of the Ravi, of kites tangling high in the bluest of skies, the *kulfi-wallah* ringing his bicycle bell, and my best friend Zarkha and I abandoning the wedding ceremonies of our dolls for the old-fashioned, pistachio ice cream.

I dreamed I rode in a *tonga* along the Mall, past the old Mughal cannon Zamzama and the cricketers playing in Gol Bagh. When the *tonga-wallah* dropped me off at Kapoor

Road, I paid my fare with Cadbury chocolates and skipped home with the breeze rippling the white, embroidered *dupatta* covering my head.

A lock hung from our iron gate; I rang the bell and waited, but no one came. Cupping my hands around my mouth, I called to my mother, "*Biji!* Open the gate!" Hot, humid wind blew leaves of *peepal* and *shesham* trees and brought the perfume of *raat ki rani*, "queen of the night," to my nose. I leaned in, stuck my face between the rungs to smell the tiny white blooms, when I noticed a cobra sleeping underneath the bush and jumped back. "*Biji!* Open the gate!"

"Go away!" An irritable shout. Not *Biji*. No one I knew.

Squinting, I spotted an old, weather-beaten woman squatting on the veranda. "Who are you?" I demanded. "What are you doing there?"

"Who am *I*?" the crone asked with equal indignation. "Who are *you*?"

"I live here!"

At that, she threw back her head and cackled. Her lips, tongue, and few remaining teeth were stained bloodred from *betel*-nut juice. "*You* don't live here. *I* do. Now, scram! Before I call the police!"

Then the mustachioed police were there, dragging me away.

"But it's *my* house," I cried. "It's *my* house, not hers!"

Every few years, I have these kinds of dreams. These and worse. Since I had one just last month, I'm surprised another came so soon.

Sometimes you know what triggers a bad dream. Eating

too late. Cold medicine. A disturbing movie. Last month, I knew: It was Meenal.

She reminds me lately...of things I don't want to remember. And though I feel awful about it, I find myself avoiding my best friend. I drop off a care package with the *samosas* I promised Kiran and make excuses not to stay. "I'd love to, but my errand list's a mile long. You know the holidays. Crowds, crowds, crowds." I give Meenal a quick, one-armed hug, glad for the bag of *samosas* between us. "Engine's running. See you on New Year's if not sooner."

Halfway down the street, I pull over and flip open my cell phone. *Please answer. Please answer.* Damn, voicemail. I drop my head against the leather upholstery and wait for the beep to leave a message. "Hello, darling. Any chance you're free for lunch? I'm heading to Tyson's Galleria for some shopping. My cell's on. Love you. Bye."

Beta, have I told you about the walled city? Come here, sit with me a while, and I'll tell you about the place that haunts my dreams....

In Lahore, we lived outside the walled city in a two-story bungalow my father and his two brothers built. The old Lahore, where my parents were born and brought up, and where my *Nanaji* and *Naniji* lived, was a colorful, busy maze. Joint families occupied four-story row houses, or *makan*, crowded on narrow, crooked alleys called *gullis*. More and more, well-to-do and upwardly mobile families were breaking away from the cramped quarters, venturing to the open spaces and modern construction available outside the walled city. Our *mohalla*—neighborhood—was in one such new area: Krishanagar.

Kapoor Road was a wide, pretty, tree-lined lane with three bungalows on either side, four families total, each connected to the government. *Bauji,* my father, was a civil engineer, like his father. One of his brothers worked for the railways; the other taught at the Government College. They had two married sisters—one lived near Amritsar, the other in Delhi. *Dadaji* and *Dadiji*—my paternal grandparents—lived next door to us with my professor uncle, their eldest son.

Next to them lived a Muslim doctor from Ferozepur. He had two wives, a sign of prosperity. One was his first cousin, a custom common among Muslims, the other a blue-eyed widow from Kashmir, young enough to be his daughter. Surprisingly, the wives got along great.

Across the road lived my best friend Zarkha Ansari. We were born the same month, Zarkha on the sixth and me on the fifteenth, which made us both Number 6 in numerology. Our fathers, both London-returned engineers, played tennis and cards at the same club. And we both had older brothers who would have loved to bunk school to play cricket, *guli-danda,* football (soccer), *bantay* (marbles), *lattoo* (yo-yo), *kabbadi,* or their favorite winter sport: kite fighting.

Next to Zarkha lived the sons of a wealthy landowner. A retired senior government officer, he somehow accomplished the rare feat of infiltrating the exclusive Gymkhana Club. Membership couldn't be bought, at any price; entry was strictly by European pedigree. A sign outside read: "Dogs and Indians Not Allowed." No one knew for sure how he got in, but there was no end to the speculations. While living in the Cantt, as they called the Lahore Cantonment, he built two bungalows in Krishanagar in addition to his country estate, so that his grandchildren could attend St. Anthony's and Sacred Heart, two of Lahore's fine English-medium schools. We seldom saw a girl in their family wear the same *salwar-kameez* twice, never one made of homespun cloth, like most of mine and Zarkha's. "They're more English than the English," said *Bauji*.

In those early years of my life, every day brought a fun-filled adventure. I'll share one of my favorite memories with you. It happened when Zarkha and I were four.

You think a woman my age can't remember back that far? I remember *everything*. People, places, conversations... A good memory is both a gift and a curse.

Now, on to my story....

Kapoor Road had many kids, but most were either too young, or too old, or too male to play with Zarkha and me, and even so, we always preferred each other's company. One evening, after we tired of *kokla-chhapaki* (a game similar to duck-duck-goose), Zarkha and I were playing *kikli*—holding hands, leaning back, and spinning. Her brothers Tariq, Basit, and Usman were playing *guli-danda*, a ball-and-bat–type of street game where you whack a small stick with sharpened edges *(guli)* with a longer batting stick *(danda)*. *My* brothers would have been playing, too, but they were inside receiving lectures from *Biji* for neglecting their studies.

With his *danda*, Tariq struck a conical edge of the six-inch *guli*. When it flew up, he swung and sent the *guli* airborne over his brothers' heads. It was then that we noticed the stray dog.

"Hey!"

"Look there! Look there!"

"Where did he come from?"

When the *guli* landed, the dog picked it up. Tail wagging, he trotted to Tariq, deposited the *guli* at his feet, and nudged it forward a few times with his nose. He was a really cute dog. He looked like a cotton ball that had rolled around in the dirt.

Tariq laughed. "Looks like we have a new player."

"He smells mutton," Basit said. "*Ammiji*'s *biryani.*"

"Is that so, you hungry beggar?" Tariq hit the *guli,* and again the dog fetched it.

"I'd run all the way from Anarkali for *Ammiji*'s *biryani,*" Basit said.

"I'd run all the way from Rawalpindi," said Tariq.

"I'd run all the way from . . . from Kashmir," said Usman. He was the youngest of the brothers and didn't like to be left out of any one-upmanship.

Zarkha turned to me. "I'm hungry."

"Me, too," I said. We typically ate later than Zarkha's family.

She tugged my hand and led me behind her house. In those days, we had detached kitchens. "*Ammiji,* we're hungry," Zarkha said to her mother. "Can we eat *biryani?*"

Zarkha's mother wore a bunch of keys—*guchcha*—tied to the end of her *dupatta,* which she draped over her shoulder. Busy supervising the *naukarani* who was flipping *chappatis* on a hot *tawa,* she said, without looking at us, "Yes, go wash."

Half forgetting, half ignoring *Biji*'s rules about eating or drinking outside our house, I followed. We took turns washing at the hand pump and sat at the *chauki* on low, jute-woven stools. Only then did Zarkha's mother notice me. She looked surprised but greeted me warmly, as always.

"*Namaste,*" she said.

"*Namaste,*" I replied.

Good manners dictated the person who spoke first greeted the listener according to her religion, respecting each other's religions the golden rule of politeness. When I greeted Zarkha's mother first, I said, "*Salaam alaikum,*" and she replied, "*Walaikum as-salaam.*" Peace be with you.

Zarkha's mother smiled. "I think your mother's calling for you."

"I don't hear her," Zarkha said.

"Zarkha. It's time for Sonia to go home."

"But we're eating *biryani*... You said..."

Her eyes clouded. "Sonia can't eat with us. Her parents wouldn't like it. Isn't that right?"

How did she know Biji's rules? Mothers mysteriously knew everything!

I hung my head. "I have to go home. *Khuda hafiz,*" I said in parting. At the gate, when I peered back over my shoulder, Zarkha's mother's expression looked pained. At home, I asked *Biji*, "Why can't I eat or drink at Zarkha's house?"

She glanced up from her knitting. "Because you'll fall sick."

I couldn't very well tell her that Zarkha smuggled delicious *bakarkhani* from Gawalmandi to me all the time, and not once had I experienced ill effects from eating these layered, *chappati*-sized and -shaped crisps made by a Muslim baker.

"But Zarkha doesn't fall sick," I said. "Tariq doesn't fall sick. Basit—"

"Hindus and Muslims don't share food and drink. *Bas*." Period. End of discussion. That was the moment I realized although we had people over all the time—our family was social, friendly, and outgoing—our dinner guests were never Muslim.

In the days that followed, we adopted the dog. Or rather, the dog adopted us, spending his afternoons sleeping under what patches of shade he could find. We named him Moti—pearl.

"Is Moti a Hindu dog or a Muslim dog?" I asked Zarkha. "He eats your scraps and our scraps."

"He must be both," Zarkha said. "Some days, he's Hindu. Some days, he's Muslim."

Ah, yes. This made perfect sense. "Monday, he's a Hindu. Tuesday, a Muslim." I had learned the days of the week, and I counted each one on my fingers. "Wednesday, Hindu. Thursday, Muslim. Friday—"

"Friday must be Muslim."

"Okay." I started over. "Monday, Muslim. Tuesday . . ."

Zarkha joined in, and together we giggled and sang to the tune of a popular song.

It didn't take long before I reasoned if Moti could be both Hindu and Muslim, so could I. One Friday morning, I announced to *Biji* as she churned buttermilk, "Today I'm a Muslim. I can't eat here, only at Zarkha's." I hoped Zarkha's mother was making her *biryani* again. Maybe I should have waited to be sure.

Biji stopped churning. "Sonia, you can't be a Muslim. You were born a Hindu. You can only be a Hindu in this life."

"But Moti's both—"

"Moti's a dog. Moti doesn't have a religion. Only *people* have religions."

I frowned. This was all very confusing. *People* were very confusing.

In my next life, I wanted to be a bird. Or a cow. Or a cat. I didn't tell *Biji* this. Sweat beaded on her upper lip, and she looked pale. I thought maybe she was falling sick.

When I think back on those early years in Lahore and Kapoor Road, I rank them among the happiest, most carefree of my life. That's what makes me so sad.

Among the many things I left behind was a child's innocence.

At the Galleria, I stare at the display window of the Godiva boutique with yearning. *Don't do it. Don't do it. Be strong.* With a groan, I force my feet to move, drag myself away. Outside Nordstrom's, a Salvation Army Santa rings his bell for donations. I dig into my wallet and stuff a twenty into the cup.

"Thank you. God bless," he says.

"You, too. Merry Christmas."

Next on my list: *BUY PJs.* Every year for Christmas, I buy new nightclothes for the whole family. When Preity and Tarun were little, it was the one present we let them open the night before Christmas. They'd bathe before bed and wake up Christmas morning fresh and clean in their new jammies. I got the idea for this tradition from Uma back in the Boston Days.

A bunch of us were suffering another bout of homesickness reminiscing about the Hindu festivals we missed most.

Diwali, of course, our five-day Festival of Lights. Uma also missed Durga Puja. Meenal missed Ganpati. And I missed Lohri. We started swapping stories about our family traditions. Uma pointed out that going forward, we would create new favorite traditions, and we could certainly incorporate some of our old favorites. After all, the common themes of holidays are the triumph of the human spirit and giving thanks.

Leave it to Uma. She has a knack for turning lemons into lemonade. When she eloped with Patrick, she became the center of gossip in our Indian friends circle. People still blather over whether Uma's brave or brazen, but I have to tell you, I admire her. When we first met, I expected her to be a stuck-up smarty-pants Bong (Bengali) with her nose either in a book or up in the air, sniffing her disdain at the simpletons in her midst. Was I ever wrong! Instead, it felt as though Uma jimmied open a sticky window with a crowbar, airing out rooms that were stifling, choking with inbred fatalism. Sure, I coughed a while, but eventually, my lungs cleared.

Fifteen minutes on the phone with Uma can lift your spirits better than an hour of yoga and meditation. She's the most open-minded of my friends. Obviously. She defied convention and married a *firangi*—Westerner. Which doesn't mean I tell her everything. Even a loudmouth like me knows certain topics you just don't discuss, not even with the people closest to you.

Anyway, it's thanks to Uma that I meshed some well-loved traditions of Lohri with Halloween, Diwali with the 4th of July, and for Christmas, I recycled her family's Durga Puja tradition of getting new clothes.

As I cut through the lingerie department, a silk nightgown catches my eye. Red. Festive. Sexy. I find my size (hooray!) and remove the hanger from the rack.

A voice in my head says, "Old lady, have you no shame?"

"Shut up," I tell the voice. "I intend to enjoy this body as long as I've got it." As the Punjabi saying goes, *Wakt noon hath naen phar-da*. There is no hand to catch time.

Meenal may be ready to renounce worldly pleasures, but I'm not. And good sex, unlike good chocolate, has negative calories.

Do you know, *beta*, that everywhere I've lived, winter has been my favorite season? I love winter holidays. . . .

In Delhi, we had Lohri, the bonfire festival signifying the harvesting of winter crops, celebrating fertility and goodwill. While Indians all over celebrate winter solstice on January 14, the day the sun enters Capricorn according to Hindu astrology, different regions have different names and traditions for this day. For Punjabis, it's Lohri.

Some of our Lohri traditions are similar to fall harvest celebrations here. In the morning, kids go from door to door, caroling about a Punjabi Robin Hood and demanding *lohri*—loot—like trick-or-treating. When we received money or a sweet, we would sing, *"Ai ghar ameera da."* This house is full of the rich. If we didn't receive any *lohri*, we sang, *"Ai ghar bhukka."* This house is full of misers.

In the evening, we dressed in our best, warm clothes and gathered with our family and friends around festive bonfires. Lit sparklers and firecrackers. Tossed puffed rice, popcorn, sugarcane sticks, snacks, and sweets into the flames, singing, *"Aadar aye, dilather jaye!"* May honor come and poverty vanish. As the frigid air filled with the sweet-smoky aroma of burning sesame seeds and jaggery, we danced and sang the night away. I credit these jovial Lohri bonfires for helping me get over my phobia of fires, though I still have my moments. . . .

Beta, don't ask, I don't want to talk about it.

Have I told you about Basant in Lahore? The festival of kites and colors to exalt the onset of spring. We would say, *"Aaya basant, paala udant."* Warm weather comes, cold weather flies away. Kite flying was a cold-weather sport, mostly for boys. In winter, the boys of Kapoor Road came home from school and raced straight to rooftop terraces to send up their kites. Soon our *mohalla* echoed with cries of, *"Bo-kata! Bo-kata!"* The kite's been cut! You see, kite strings were coated in a paste of ultrafine powdered glass—harmless at rest, but with velocity, sharp enough to bloody fingers, much the same as a paper or cardboard cut—ouch! Fliers battled to cut each other's kite strings and chased booty that fell from the sky, finders keepers.

Once, Zarkha and I were playing *stapu*—hopscotch—in the courtyard behind my bungalow when a fancy, multi-cornered kite thunked down right in front of us. Our eyes went wide. This wasn't just any kite. It was a *patang,* the *maharaja* of kites. Far showier, pricier than the common *guddis* and *paris, patangs* were the most coveted booty of all.

Whoops of excitement sounded from the wooden parapet—from my brothers Sunil and Harinder and cousin Shankar, better known as Sunny, Dimples, and Chhotu.

While Dimples and Chhotu dashed for the stairs, Sunny, the eldest, rappelled down a banyan tree with the agility of a monkey! As *"Bo-kata!"* battle cries grew closer, Zarkha and I screamed and ran into the house because we knew any second, the courtyard would be swarming with boys. And it was! That is, until *Biji* came out and chased them all away because they were scaring the buffalos we kept for fresh milk.

Needless to say, Basant was a much-anticipated holiday, not just in our *mohalla*, but in every corner of Lahore. Before dawn, we awoke to the beating of drums, the *dhol-wallah* going down the road, signaling the arrival of Basant. Our gazes shot to the sky, filled with candlelit box kites. So beautiful, so peaceful that sight. As if stargazing, we watched the luminous lanterns twinkle, the only waking moments when not one of us talked.

By daybreak, we congregated on the rooftop terrace dressed in yellow, the first color to emerge after the biting cold winter with vibrant mustard flowers, *peeli chambeli*, scentless yellow jasmine, and Amaltas trees signaling new life. Soon, we could barely see the sky through all the kites! Every color, shape, size. Wind dancers and warriors. Dipping, swerving, tangling. Watching a kite ascend to the sky took my breath away. My heart soared higher and higher with the kite, climbing the stairway to heaven.

There wasn't an empty rooftop in all of Lahore. Regardless of age, gender, religion, caste, or social standing, all Lahoris participated in the major festivals of Basant, Holi, Diwali, Eid, and Christmas. Nowhere else did I witness such collective merrymaking and communal harmony.

Nowhere else and never again.

"Long years ago, we made a tryst with destiny, and now the time comes when we shall redeem our pledge..."

These are words, *beta,* every educated Indian knows. You'd already know them, if we'd raised you in India. Still, even if you are here, not there, you must know your heritage. It's *how* you got here.

On the eve of India's independence from the British Empire, as Lahore burned in communal riots, my family huddled around the radio, listening to Pandit Jawaharlal Nehru, India's first prime minister and father of later prime minister Indira Gandhi.

I remember *Dadaji,* usually aloof, removing his spectacles to dab tears as he grumbled over Panditji's decision to deliver his address in English, the foreign tongue of our now-former rulers, a language the vast majority of Indians didn't understand. The families of Kapoor Road, being Punjabi, shared a mother tongue. My generation also spoke English, or "*gulabi* English," as we called English sprinkled with Punjabi. While my father spoke English, my mother didn't; most of their generation and older spoke Punjabi exclusively.

"At the stroke of the midnight hour," Panditji's confident voice boomed, "when the world sleeps, India will awake to life and freedom. A moment comes which comes but rarely in history, when we step out from the old to the new; when an age ends; and when the soul of a nation, long suppressed, finds utterance..."

At six, I didn't understand the meaning of these words, or

the mixed emotions people had about them. Now I understand all too well.

"We end today a period of ill fortune, and India discovers herself again . . ."

Unfortunately, our period of ill fortune wasn't over yet.

In 1947, my world went crazy. Lahore—a modern, cultured, charming, progressive, and tolerant city—descended into chaos. Though Lahore was awarded to Pakistan, my family never intended to leave. And though we fled to escape the violence, we never dreamed it would be permanent, that the borders would be sealed, and we would be exiled forever. More than *Indians* or *Pakistanis*, we were Punjabis, *Lahoris*. For generations, the land of five rivers flowed through our veins, until the knife of Partition slit our wrists.

The Cost of Independence.

One night, my father came home pale and shaking. A train had arrived at Lahore Station. A ghost train. Every passenger dead. Slain. They were Muslim refugees migrating west. All men, not one young woman among the corpses. But bags and bags were found heaped full of bloody, severed breasts.

It was "retaliation" that led to more "retaliation," a vicious cycle of "you harm my people, I harm yours." People fighting terror with terror.

With the breakdown in administration and absence of adequate peacekeeping forces, savagery escalated on either side of our two new borders. Hindu, Muslim, and Sikh communities all had blood on their hands and loved ones to mourn. Riots and looting ran rampant. Homes were torched. Doused with gasoline, entire neighborhoods were reduced to cinders. From Amritsar to Lahore—both sides of the Wagah border—trains pulled into stations like crypts containing murdered and maimed refugees, Hindus and Sikhs migrating east, Muslims migrating west.

Men were often forced to drop their drawers to prove their religion. Hindu men aren't circumcised; Muslim men are. Women were kidnapped, stripped, robbed of jewelry, raped, and murdered. People jumped into wells to drown or otherwise committed suicide to avoid compulsory religious conversions and other fates deemed worse than death. Many women opted for "mercy killing" by a male relative in order to "protect their honor."

Hundreds of thousands were massacred, millions violated. Some abductees were rescued. Some remain missing. Some women, tragically, returned to their families only to be turned away, written off as unlucky, damaged goods, shameful.

To be fair, there are many accounts of communal compassion and heroism, people who risked everything to save their fellow human beings, regardless of religion or caste. Our *mohalla* in Krishanagar organized a twenty-four-hour watch, and people took turns keeping vigil. Our Muslim neighbors and friends helped us in every way possible—storing our belongings, sheltering us in their homes, aiding our escape. On the other side of the border, many Hindus and Sikhs similarly protected innocent Muslims.

But the volumes that showcase the underbelly of human nature are the ones that haunt me. The ones that taught me tolerance is too often superficial. In times of peace and prosperity, people from different communities can live and let live, but in times of fear and uncertainty, many—*far too many*—side with their own and turn against those who share their biology but not their ideology or heritage. Far too many fall in line behind leaders who rally: *You're either with us—"our kind"—or against us.* Or, *Death to a nation, or a people, not ours—not "our kind."*

I was only six, but I saw it. I lived through it. Others didn't.

Nanaji and *Naniji* refused to leave Lahore. "I was born here, and I will die here, if that is my karma," *Nanaji* said. And *Naniji* refused to leave *Nanaji.*

Relatives, friends, acquaintances pleaded with them to no avail. *Biji*'s eldest brother, after escorting family across the border, risked his life to return *twice* for his parents. The first time, they sent him away with a neighbor girl who later became his wife. On the second trip, he found them in the charred remains of their home in the walled city.

They rarely slept in the same bed, but they did on their last night. On *Nanaji*'s single divan, they died side by side.

In Delhi, we rebuilt our lives from scratch and assimilated into a new land, a new culture where we were not always welcome, where locals regarded our overflowing refugee community as loud and unrefined, our speech and mannerisms as accented and crude. But we were survivors; we proved that every day.

Biji had an intricately carved walnut jewelry box *Bauji* gifted her on a family holiday in Kashmir. She emptied it, selling her wedding jewelry to finance our new start. *Bauji* spent the next decade filling it back up again.

I remember watching *Gone With the Wind* with my girlfriends in college. How I related to Scarlett O'Hara! I loved the end when, after surviving the Civil War, she lifts a handful of the earth and vows never to go hungry again.

In time, we replanted ourselves in the soil of our new motherland. The mournful wails of chest-beating women in grief subsided, and laughter replaced the horror stories. Still, memories of 1947 hung over our Punju community, the silence between our gay notes.

More than half a century later, they still hang over me.

I close my eyes and see Lahore, Kapoor Road, our bungalow. Zarkha and me swinging from the iron gate, throwing sticks for Moti, playing *stapu* and *kikli,* arranging the marriages of our dolls, dressing in yellow for Basant, eating pistachio *kulfi,* sneaking *bakarkhani.*

I remember an old Punjabi saying: If only these walls of steel could be brought down forever, we could once again gaze upon each other.

Saroj's Famous Samosas

MAKES 16

PASTRY:

2 cups all-purpose flour, plus more for plate

½ teaspoon ajowan seeds,

½ teaspoon salt

⅓ cup vegetable shortening, chilled

⅓ cup butter, chilled

4–8 tablespoons very cold water

1. In a large mixing bowl, sift the flour, ajowan, and salt together. Cut in thin slices of shortening and butter. Using fingertips or pastry blender, rub mixture together until coarse and crumbly in texture.
2. Starting with 3 tablespoons, add water and work into mixture by hand or wooden spoon. Add more tablespoons as necessary until dough holds together, neither sticky nor dry. Knead on lightly floured surface 5–7 minutes or until smooth.
3. Wrap dough ball in plastic wrap and chill for 1 hour.

FILLING:

2 tablespoons canola oil

1 teaspoon cumin seeds

1 teaspoon fennel seeds

1 medium yellow onion, finely chopped

1 tablespoon fresh ginger root, peeled and minced

1–3 fresh green chili peppers, finely chopped (adjust to spicy preference)

4–5 medium potatoes, peeled, boiled, cooled, and cubed

¾ cup frozen green peas, thawed

1 tablespoon coriander powder

1 teaspoon cumin powder

1 teaspoon garam masala

½ teaspoon salt (adjust to preference)

½ teaspoon sugar (adjust to preference)

½ teaspoon turmeric powder

¼ cup water

¼ cup fresh coriander (cilantro), finely chopped

⅛ cup fresh mint, finely chopped

1 tablespoon anardana powder (dried pomegranate seeds) or amchur powder (dried mango) or lemon juice

1. In a wok or deep 12-inch skillet, heat 2 tablespoons oil over medium-high heat.
2. Add cumin seeds and fennel seeds. When they change color, about 30 seconds, reduce heat to medium.
3. Add onion, ginger, and chilies. Mix well. Sauté until onion is golden brown.
4. Add potatoes and peas. Mix well.
5. Add coriander powder, cumin powder, garam masala, salt, sugar, turmeric, and water. Mix well. Cover and reduce heat to medium-low. Simmer, stirring occasionally, until water is absorbed.
6. Remove from heat. Stir in fresh coriander, mint, and anardana (or substitution). Cover and let stand for 5 minutes. Uncover and let cool completely, about 20–30 minutes.

ASSEMBLING SAMOSAS:

1. On a lightly floured surface, knead the pastry dough 3–5 minutes. Divide dough into 8 equal portions. Work with 1 at a time.

2. Roll portion into 6-inch circle. Cut into 2 half-moons. Arrange with straight edges closest to you.
3. Spoon 2 tablespoons of filling onto the center.
4. Fold left and right corners over to form a cone.
5. Tuck the top flap inside, like an envelope. Samosa should resemble an inverted pyramid.
6. Seal flap carefully using a little water. (Note: Contents will leak into the oil if the flap isn't sealed completely.)
7. Place on floured plate to prevent sticking.
8. Repeat steps 2–7 for remaining dough.

COOKING SAMOSAS:

1 cup canola oil for deep-frying

1. Heat oil in a wok or deep 12-inch skillet over medium-high heat. Carefully lower 4 samosas into the oil. Turn frequently until light golden brown.
2. Remove with slotted spoon. Drain on paper towels. Serve with chutney.*

Mint-Cilantro Chutney

2 CUPS

2 cups fresh coriander (cilantro), chopped

1 cup fresh mint, chopped

½ cup yellow onion, finely chopped

2 cloves garlic, finely chopped

1 teaspoon fresh ginger root, peeled and finely chopped

1 fresh green chili pepper, finely chopped (adjust to preference)

1½ teaspoons sugar (adjust to taste)

¾ teaspoon salt (adjust to taste)

¼ cup lime juice

¼ cup water

1. In a blender or food processor, puree all ingredients until smooth. Pour into a bowl.
2. Serve immediately or cover and refrigerate until ready to serve.

Tamarind Chutney

1½ CUPS

⅓ cup tamarind

1 cup boiling water

1 teaspoon fresh ginger root, peeled and chopped

¾ cup jaggery or packed brown sugar

½ teaspoon cayenne pepper (adjust to preference)

½ teaspoon salt (adjust to preference)

2 tablespoons fresh coriander (cilantro), finely chopped

1. In a small glass bowl, soak tamarind in boiling water until soft, approximately 10–15 minutes. Mash through a wire strainer. Reserve pulp and juices. Discard solids.
2. In a blender or food processor, combine all ingredients except fresh coriander. Purée until smooth. Pour into bowl.
3. Stir in fresh coriander. Serve immediately or cover and refrigerate until ready to serve.*

* Saroj's Tips:

✔ Samosas are best fresh but can be preassembled and frozen, then fried straight from the freezer, no defrosting necessary.

✔ Chutney is best fresh, but can be refrigerated up to 2 days.

Uma Basu McGuiness: The Mother of a Hundred Daughters

How I cherished to be married to Krishna!
My husband turned out to be neither
Krishna, nor Vishnu, but the grandson of
Faringa, the buffoon weaver.

BENGALI PROVERB

Red is the color of love. Of passion. Of rage.

Red is the color of an Indian bride's *sari. Sindoor* in the part of her hair when married. Blood when she fails to conceive.

Red is the color I see when I think of my mother. Red, red, red...

Everyone believed *Ma* was mad, myself included. Even before The Unspeakable, signs that Something Was Not Right swirled like ever-present dust motes in the musty air of the Ballygunge house in South Calcutta where our large joint family resided.

Smaller signs we ignored, dismissed as we might a breeze that snuffs out the *prodeep*'s sacred flame and plunges a room into inauspicious darkness. But the bigger signs haunted our days and nights, as unshakable as horoscope predictions.

First we struggled to conceal, then to contain, and finally to survive, for no secret, not even the tiniest, remains secret for long in Calcutta's Bengali community. And no one, not even the wealthiest family, can escape destiny.

Next semester, my research sabbatical begins, and I embark on a voyage of discovery to fulfill a longtime goal, professional and personal: translating my mother's journals and poetry from Bengali to English. I want to preserve the enormous wealth of Bengali literature, to record new voices and recover lost ones, especially women's. I want Bengali writing accessible outside Bengal as it once was—Rabindranath Tagore won the Nobel Prize for literature after *Gitanjali* was translated into English by W. B. Yeats. I hope my experience proves enriching, cathartic. Right now, it's merely daunting.

My mother was highly creative. She painted, wrote poetry, narrated fabulous stories, danced, and sang with the voice of a goddess. As the daughter of a wealthy *zamindar*—landowner—it was out of the question for her to pursue any of these talents professionally, something respectable women didn't do. But she performed for her family and guests who came to dinner at the family home. After marriage, once settled in her *sasur-baari*—father-in-law's house—she encouraged (or should I say *coerced*?) all of us children to put on skits, sing, and dance to Tagore's plays and songs.

From family lore, we learned *Baba*, who also sang quite well, married *Ma* for her beautiful voice. After hearing her, he didn't want to marry anyone else. He pleaded with *Thakurda*—my paternal grandfather—to do whatever it took to convince *Ma*'s father to accept their proposal. *Ma* had numerous interested parties, and *Baba* was afraid, with such stiff competition, he would lose out to one of them. Later, *Thakurma*—my paternal grandmother—said *Ma* cast a spell on everyone when she sang at the bride-viewing. She didn't mean this nicely.

In *Ma*'s journals, she confessed though *Baba* wasn't her first choice, she didn't object to him when her father asked, so their match was fixed. Later, she lamented her lapse for not speaking up when she had the chance, for not voicing a single reservation, such as the smell of his hair oil, which grew to repulse her.

She wrote about her everyday life. Bargaining for *saris*. Lizards whose tails still wiggled after being severed from the rest of the body. Bolts on doors and bars on windows to "lock thieves out, and women in." Wanting to march in a rally and not being allowed. Accidentally burning the rice. Deliberately spoiling a favored dish. Modest praise and stern reprimands. Massaging babies with mustard oil. Power cuts at inopportune times. Loneliness in a crowded house. Fantasies about film stars and cricket players. Women's gossip, embellishments, deceptions. The escape of novels. Pleasure at possessing skills—reading, writing, singing—her mother-in-law didn't.

These things are not so difficult to translate. Others... I cannot imagine coming out of her mouth, not the *Ma* I knew.

I remember her voice was always sweet, whether singing or speaking. Even when she cried, it sounded like a bitter-sweet melody. *Ma* claimed this was because of the honey *Thakurma* gave her during the welcome ceremony when she and *Baba* first arrived home as newlyweds. *Thakurma* put a little honey on *Ma*'s tongue and dabbed a drop in each of her ears so that *Ma* should always speak sweetly and hear sweet things in her *sasur-baari*. "It worked," *Ma* told us, we who were too young to know any better.

The voice in *Ma*'s writing is her authentic one—the voice imprisoned in the body of a Bengali woman in the mid-twentieth century. The spirit I hope to set free.

My mother died far too young, when I was twelve. As to how... For that, I must back up a year to when I was eleven.

My parents had five daughters then. The firstborn was fair and ugly. The second was dark and lovely. I was in the middle, too tall, but otherwise unremarkable in all-important aesthetics. Finally after me, the goddess Parvati granted the most desirable female combination: two girls both fair and lovely. But by then it was too late.

Everyone knew three girls was triple unlucky, but *five* girls? *Five* dowries? And not a single penis to light the funeral pyre? That wasn't just unlucky. That was *cursed*.

In traditional Indian culture, daughters are a liability,

raised to be given away to another family. Sons are an asset, retained to support the family. And for Hindus, only sons can perform the parents' last rites. A common Indian blessing is: *May you be the mother of a hundred sons.*

"That poor man," people said about my father. "His wife can't bear sons." From shopkeepers to socialites, illiterate servants to *babus* in suits and boots, tongues wagged.

In the evenings, when we piled into *Baba*'s Ambassador and drove to Victoria Memorial for our family outings at the lush gardens, we felt the weight of people's gazes, heard whispers, sometimes snickers when *Baba* went across to the Maidan (think: New York's Central Park, with litter) to buy rolls, *jhaal muri*, or *phuchkas* from a vendor's stall. *Baba* was a well-known man. We were a well-known family.

When shopping on Chowringhee or Park Street or playing outside with siblings, cousins, or girlfriends from our *paara*—neighborhood—I overheard the speculations about my mother's condition.

"You can hear her wailing at night. You must have heard."

"I thought it was a stray cat or a baby crying."

"No, it's her. They say she's mad. They've locked her away."

"I heard she has a mysterious disease."

"A disease? Is it contagious?"

No one knew for sure. They only knew Something Was Not Right.

We knew it, too. For as long as I can remember, *Ma* suffered from an illness no doctor could diagnose, let alone cure, that periodically confined her to bed for days, weeks, and sometimes months. During this time, she struggled to eat or bathe, even with assistance.

Sometimes, *Thakurma* didn't so much mind having her daughter-in-law indisposed. With *Ma* out of the way, *Thakurma* could wait on *Baba,* her favorite son, as she'd done all his unmarried life, taking great pleasure in such simple expressions of affection as fanning him with a hand-fan while he ate.

But at other times, *Thakurma* grew skeptical and accused *Ma* of faking her ailment. "Why does she suddenly fall ill on gray, overcast days? After giving birth, why does it take her so long to recover? She's lazy. That's what she is." Or, "She's ashamed. She cannot face the humiliation of not bearing sons."

On occasion, even my father, who doted on his daughters, buckled under society's pressure and lashed out at my mother.

Thakurda intervened. He was the only one who could, who held the power. Though as a general rule, he steered clear of household squabbles, *Thakurda* had a soft spot for his *bouma*—daughter-in-law—who dutifully massaged his feet, plucked his gray hairs, and read aloud to him for hours if he so desired. "*Bouma* would never do this on purpose," *Thakurda* said in *Ma*'s defense. "It's not her nature."

Thakurma may not have agreed, for she had witnessed many of *Ma*'s erratic moodswings, but she held her tongue. *Thakurda* had spoken, and no one could contradict him, certainly not a self-respecting wife. To do so would be undignified. As for *Baba,* his duty as a good son meant he obeyed his parents.

"Shuncho?" Thakurma called to *Thakurda* one hot afternoon. (Neither she nor *Ma* addressed her husband by name, but by this expression that translates: *Are you listening to me?*) *Thakurma* handed *Thakurda* a tumbler of cold lime water and mused about my again-bedridden mother, "She must be cursed. There is no other explanation."

Thakurda didn't so much as glance up from the crossword puzzle in the *Statesman*, his daily newspaper, but over time, the notion of a curse seized *Thakurma*. One day, she whisked *Ma* away to consult a highly respected guru who confirmed her suspicions: Indeed, my mother had been cursed by the evil eye in a previous life. The blessing, "May you be the mother of a hundred sons" was inverted to: "May you be the mother of a hundred daughters."

To remove the curse, they had to perform various rituals. Among other things, my mother had to wear certain charms, fast, and make offerings at the Kalighat temple.

She followed the instructions to the letter, and with her next pregnancy, she grew so huge, everyone felt certain at long last, she carried the family heir. Suddenly, she was treated like a queen, instead of head servant. *Thakurma* pampered her and jumped to do her bidding. *Thakurma* felt vindicated her diagnosis of the problem had proven correct. The ring of keys she wore on her *palloo*—the long end of her *sari*—jingled as she walked with an extra bounce in every step, and she hummed as she rubbed *Ma*'s swollen feet with mustard oil.

As with all her previous deliveries, in *Ma*'s last trimester, she packed her suitcases and went to *Dadu* and *Dida*'s—my maternal grandparents'—house to have the baby.

I remember all of us standing on the veranda and running across the lawn to see her off. I remember *Ma* waving goodbye from *Baba*'s Ambassador. The *palloo* of her *taant*—Bengali *sari*—modestly covering her head. The *loha*—iron bangle—on her slim wrist. The newfound happiness on her round face. The hope in her eyes. The relief as she settled back, and the Ambassador drove off.

That was the last time I saw my mother.

After giving birth to twin girls, she selected one of her favorite *taants*, tied it to the ceiling fan, and hanged herself.

In grad school at Boston College, Colleen—then my best American friend, now my sister-in-law—asked if I blamed my parents, if I was angry with them. I told her no and no.

I lied.

I can't remember a time when I didn't struggle with anger. A constant battle. One I like to think I'm winning, but there's always the next round. Ask me then and my answer may change.

One's demons don't really go away. Have you noticed? They live, thrive in the shadows. Multiply if you let them, if you don't learn to diffuse their power, control them so they don't breed like the lower classes, don't overcome you, control you. Turn your heart to ice, or to fire. Destroy you. And others.

Patrick taught me this. He would know. He returned from Vietnam an expert on demons.

I tell myself *of course* I wish it could have been different with my parents. How could I not? But my parents were products of their times, their culture, as each of us is. I cannot blame them for what happened. That's what I tell myself. Most of the time, it works. Most of the time, but not always.

When intellect fails, Patrick takes me downstairs to our basement where the cinder-block walls contain a person's howls. He holds the punching bag, and I release my fury. Release the animal inside me, the animal a good Hindu wife—a *proper* woman—isn't supposed to have, let alone acknowledge. The animal whose existence I denied, until my husband called me on it.

"You aren't sucking it up," Patrick said. "You're sucking it in." He showed me the difference. Showed me what I could do, the ways of the warrior—the caste into which I was born—as he was shown by his fellow war veterans, his band of brothers and sisters.

In the basement, I hit and kick, scream and cry. I curse. If you saw me, you would think I had lost my mind, and you would be right. But I will let you in on a little secret, a paradox I believe my mother knew: Sometimes one must go insane, dance cheek-to-cheek with one's demons, in order to slay them, to *regain* one's sanity. This is the wisdom my husband gave me. Now, I'm giving it to you.

Uma's Shorshe Salmon Maachh [Grilled Salmon with Spicy Mustard Glaze]

SERVES 4

*3 tablespoons paanch phoron (Bengali five-spice—recipe follows)**

2 dried red chilies (adjust to taste)

¾ teaspoon salt (adjust to taste)

¼ cup water

4 salmon fillets (6-ounce pieces)

2 tablespoons mustard oil

banana leaves (optional)

1. In a blender or food processor, purée to a smooth paste paanch phoron, red chilies, salt, and water.
2. Brush both sides of fillets with oil, then rub both sides with the paste.
3. Place fillets in a glass bowl. Cover with plastic wrap and refrigerate for at least 1 hour, but no more than 24 hours.
4. Spray grill rack with nonstick cooking spray. Heat to high. Place fillets 5–6 inches from heat. Sear each side until lightly browned, about 1–2 minutes.
5. Remove from grill and wrap each fillet in a banana leaf (or aluminum foil). Secure leaf with string or toothpicks and return to grill, seam side up.
6. Grill each side 5–7 minutes, until fish flakes easily with a fork. (Caution: Don't overcook!)
7. Serve with rice.

Paanch Phoron

[Bengali Five-Spice]

MAKES 1/4 CUP

1 tablespoon cumin seeds

*1 tablespoon brown mustard seeds**

1 tablespoon fennel seeds

1 tablespoon fenugreek seeds

*1 tablespoon nigella seeds**

1. In a small, airtight plastic bag, combine all ingredients.
2. Seal and shake.
3. Use immediately or store in airtight container. Keeps up to 6 months at room temperature, 1 year refrigerated.

* Mom's Tips:

- ✔ Brown mustard seeds are sometimes called Chinese mustard.
- ✔ Caution: Nigella is erroneously called/confused with black cumin, royal cumin, onion seeds, or caraway.
- ✔ For store-bought paanch phoron, I like the "Maya" brand.

Meenal Deshpande: Monsoon Memories

Our bad experiences provide the contrast that enables us to recognize goodness. If you wrote a message with white chalk on a white board, no one would see it. Without the blackboard of bad, the good things in the world could not be magnified at all.

PARAMAHANSA YOGANANDA

Before Yash leaves to go back to the apartment, he says, "It's like waiting for the monsoon. Will it come today? Or tomorrow? Or the next day?"

He's right. The thought of breaking the news to Kiran *has* felt like waiting for the monsoon. Waiting and wondering. Will the rains cleanse and nourish life? Or will they overwhelm and destroy?

She's home now; it must be done.

Kiran brushes her teeth in front of the bathroom mirror. "Everyone wonders why I don't come home. *This* is why." She spits into the sink, rinses her mouth, and grabs a hand towel. "I don't need this grief."

I stand in the doorway, a folded newspaper in my hands. "No, you don't. I'm sorry."

She drags her hairbrush through her hair. "Why are you apologizing? You didn't do anything. You never do," she says, then winces, whether at her words or her tangles, I'm not sure.

I wait until she finishes, then pick up her hairbrush and pluck a few long strands of her hair with nostalgia. "I don't want to fight, Kiran."

"Neither do I."

"Life's too short."

"Yeah, it is."

I meet her gaze in the mirror. "What made you think of an arranged marriage?"

"Desperation," she says. "My biological clock's ticking. I'm ready to have a family, and there's no groom on the horizon. I don't know when, or even if..."

I nod and put down the hairbrush. "I want to show you something." I gesture for her to follow me and head for the door, but when I turn, she hasn't moved.

"Mom?" she asks, a waver in her voice. "Do *you* think I've messed up my life?" With her sweatpants and Redskins sweatshirt, hair in a ponytail, and fresh-scrubbed face, she could pass for a teenager. But she isn't, hasn't been for years.

You build your life around your children, then one day, they grow up on you. They don't need you anymore and make no bones about telling you so. That's life in America.

Now here she is, my grown-up and independent daughter, for the first time in God-only-knows-how-long, needing her parents. Needing *me*.

Making me want to move mountains for her.

"Complicated," I say. "Not messed up. Not at all. And your second-marriage prospects are challenging, not hopeless. *Definitely* not hopeless."

Kiran's smile is shaky—relief tinged with regret. "I never should have married Anthony. It was the biggest mistake of my life. I know it. You know it. Everyone knows it. You were right. I was wrong. Go ahead and say, 'I told you so.' "

I snap my tongue and suck a sharp breath between my teeth. "We didn't want to be right, Kiran. We just wanted the best for you. We still do. Forgive us if we . . . if we . . ." I struggle for the right words. "Forgive us for not being the parents you want us to be."

Her eyes water, but she blinks back her tears. Even as a girl, she hated to let anyone see her cry. *Let anyone see her vulnerability.*

"I know what Dad said was harsh, but please understand he didn't mean to hurt you. You know the way we were brought up, elders spoke their minds—it was a right of old age. We were used to this, so it didn't hurt us the way it hurts you."

"You'd think after forty-some years in this country, he'd—"

"That doesn't matter. If you move to another country where women don't have the rights you enjoy today, will you forget the freedoms of your upbringing? Elders command respect in India—unconditional respect. Outside his home, a man must play by the rules set by others, bend to their ways, but inside his home, *he* makes the rules, and others are expected to bend to *his* ways. In Dad's bones, he feels it's his right to speak his mind, however candid. The same way you will always feel entitled to certain 'inalienable rights' you've learned in this culture. Does that make sense?"

She nods. Grudgingly.

"I talked to Dad, and he promises to try harder to be more diplomatic."

"Right. I'll believe it when I see it."

"Fair enough," I say. "Come. Let's move our conversation out of the bathroom, huh?"

"I'm not up for another round with Dad—"

"Dad's gone back to the apartment. It's just you and me."

Her rigid posture softens, relaxes. "Good," she says and brushes past me, out the door.

"We'll need your laptop," I say, sitting on Kiran's bed. While she turns on her computer, I open the newspaper, *India Abroad,* to an ad I marked folding down the corner of the page. "Go here."

"What is this?"

"A new twist on the old ways. An Indian matrimonial website. You know, like computer dating."

"No way." She laughs in disbelief. "Arranged marriages have gone high-tech."

"Why not? The Internet has made the world a small village, and with all the computer engineers India produces, it was just a matter of time." I smile. "According to this ad, you can input specific requirements and search their database. Such as, U.S. citizens only."

"Interesting," Kiran says. "Very interesting."

"I think it's a good place to start. Get an idea of the fish in the sea. And you're good at corresponding in email. You may like this."

We do a trial search. She selects "looking for groom" and her acceptable age range. This yields fifty pages of profiles. Twenty profiles per page. Never married, divorced, and widowed. *One thousand available men.*

Kiran's head snaps back. "Whoa. That's a lot of fish." She leans in for a closer inspection. "Well, well, well... Looks like a decent 'recycled' market."

"Go ahead," I say. "Cast your line."

She selects a thirty-five-year-old divorced doctor in New York. "Education, occupation, income, religion, caste, birth place, values, languages, current residence, residency status, complexion, height, body type..." She reads his profile aloud, including the various attributes he seeks in his ideal partner.

"Thorough," she says.

"That's the idea. In arranged marriages, we lay all our cards on the table, so we can best gauge a potential couple's compatibility. We don't want to be surprised by some vital information *after* marriage."

"Vital info like, oh, *monogamy-challenged*, for example."

"You should discuss everything that's important to you openly and honestly."

She nods and turns back to the screen, reading a few more profiles, the difference of ten years' wisdom reflected in her thoughtful gaze. She's finished weeping over her *chaalu*, skirt-chasing Krishna; now she's ready for a stable, dependable Shiva.

I wish she didn't have to learn the hard, painful way that

sunshine burns if you get too much. I wish she'd heeded Yash's and my repeated warnings, our pleas, but some mistakes you must make for yourself if that's your karma.

"This isn't a bad idea, Kiran. Trying another route—a proven route for many. It may very well work for you, too. . . ."

The next afternoon, encouraged by our preliminary groom search, Kiran and I take a break. We play the soundtrack from *A Charlie Brown Christmas* and put up our tree. It's the eight-foot artificial one from the basement. I've never had the energy for a live tree, plus I feel sad when all those discarded trees line the curbs after the New Year.

"I can't believe you still have these," Kiran says as she opens a box of the kids' handmade ornaments.

"Oh, yes. I'll donate the other boxes to Goodwill when we sell the house, but not these." I hook the golden string of a ceramic candy cane engraved: TO MOM & DAD—LOVE, KIRAN—1979. "These are my favorites."

"Sell the house?" Kiran echoes.

My hand stills in midair. I could slap my forehead. "I didn't mean to blurt that out so insensitively."

"You're planning to sell the house *in the near future?*"

"Well, we've been thinking about it for a while. . . ."

"But why?" she demands. "I thought you loved this house. You and Dad designed it. It's your dream house."

"It is, but it's served its purpose. You kids are gone—"

"But I thought you'd retire here."

"It's too much space, Kiran. Too much work." *Too empty without you and Vivek.*

"Wow." She looks around, dazed. "I can't imagine other people living in our house."

"I know. Neither can I. But it's time to move on, to life's next phase."

She chews on her lower lip. I want to tell her to stop. *Ai* could always get me to stop whatever undesirable behavior by saying no one would want to marry a girl who did such things. That didn't work with Kiran. She'd tell me she didn't *want* to marry someone who wouldn't marry a girl for such petty reasons.

"So what exactly is the plan?" she asks.

"Exactly, we haven't decided. Probably, we'll list the house in summer."

"*This* summer?" At my nod, she frowns.

"After it sells, we'll buy a condo or a townhouse around here. And something else, somewhere warm. Florida. Arizona. Maybe India."

"Wow," she says again. "You're really considering being snowbirds in India?"

"I'm leaning in that direction." I've told her of my plans to winter in India this year. I leave soon after the New Year, and I'll be gone for three months. My parents, while in superb health for their ages, are both in their eighties, and they slow down more each year. This year, *Baba* rarely left the apartment building. "*Aji* and *Ajoba* are on bonus years," I say. "I want to spend as much time as I can with them. We'll see. Dad gets a vote, too."

When Yash's and my marriage was arranged, our agreement was: Stay in America for ten years, collect our money, and return to India. Then we had children. American kids in American schools with American friends. Excellent education.

So many cherished friends. How could we take them away from everything they knew and loved? We couldn't. So we stayed. For them. And as soon as they could, they left us. Still, here we remain....

Kiran and I lean back and admire our trimmed tree. We sit on the exquisite hand-loomed Kashmiri rug we carted from India (and unrolled for customs inspectors) the sole time Yash and I felt it was safe to take the kids to the stunning Kashmir Valley nestled in the Himalayas. (So devastating, that quagmire. So tragic the blood man spills in God's country.)

We are gazing up at our angel-topped tree without speaking when the soundtrack ends. I look at Kiran; she looks at me. I can't avoid the unavoidable any longer.

"Kiran, I have to tell you something." I turn toward her, tucking a leg underneath me. "I know this is a lot for you to swallow all at once—"

"There's more?"

"Yes—"

"Shit, now you're scaring me."

"No, don't be scared." I'm beyond telling her to clean up her language. "Everything's fine—"

"Have you and Dad split?"

"No! God, no."

"Just tell me, Mom."

"Stop interrupting, and I will."

She crosses her arms and presses her lips together. I comb my fingers through my hair, for a split second forgetting and expecting inches that aren't there anymore, haven't been for months. Both of our chests heave. I wish Yash was here.

I've rehearsed this a million times, what to say, how to

say it. Show-and-tell seems best. I tug the neckline of my sweater, reach down into my pima cotton bra. First one pocket, then the other. I remove both my prostheses, show them to my physician daughter.

Kiran stills. The deceptive, eerie calm before the storm. Her wide eyes, unblinking, fix on the objects in my hand. She knows what they are. Knows what they mean. Wishes she didn't. On her face, heavy storm clouds gather. The sky darkens, turns ominous.

She opens her mouth, but no sound emerges. She covers her mouth with her hand. She's in shock, as I was. Stunned. Numb. Frightened. Her gaze seeks, searches mine. A child afraid to look under the bed, fearing monsters. A doctor driven to look, preferring monsters she knows over those she doesn't.

Again, she opens her mouth, tries to speak. A single word. Barely audible. Except to a mother's ear, endowed by nature to hear the sound of her child, as dogs hear pitches humans cannot. In a noisy crowd. From a distance. Awake or asleep. Anytime, anywhere. Her voice is my beeper. My ears perk up, alert to my page: "*Mom.*"

"I was first diagnosed in February. Just one breast." My mouth feels like cotton. I want water, but I don't dare to stop now. "I . . . never expected it, didn't see it coming. You know we don't have a family history of cancer. I'd done my regular self-checks, and I didn't *feel* anything unusual. It was the mammogram that picked it up." I clasp my hands in *namaskar*. "Thank God I scheduled my annual on time this year.

"The doctors recommended a lumpectomy, chemotherapy, and radiation. After all that, the cancer showed up on my other breast. At that point, we went for bilateral mastectomies." I glance at my fake breasts. "I decided against reconstruction, for many reasons. Mostly, I didn't want to chance the cancer hiding behind an implant."

In Kiran's shallow breathing, I hear the ghostlike howl of the wind. "Are you . . . ?" Her voice wavers the way the ocean ripples. Tossed between the tides of daughter and doctor, she anchors one hand over her heart and draws a steadying breath. "What's the prognosis?"

"Excellent. Clear margins. Clear lymph nodes." This means no more chemo or radiation. The cancer didn't invade my blood or my bones.

She releases her breath with a *whoosh* and covers her eyes. "Oh, thank God. Thank God. Thank God."

"Yes. I'm very lucky. I've regained mobility, slowly but surely through yoga. My stamina still isn't what it used to be, but I'll get there."

When she lowers her hand, her lashes are wet, spiked. As she holds my gaze, lightning crackles between us. "When . . . was your surgery?"

My mouth goes dry. I swallow around my guilt. "October."

Ka-boom! Thunder rocks our world.

Fat teardrops spill from Kiran's eyes. She doesn't bother to wipe them. Twin streams flow down her cheeks and plunk into her lap. "Why, Mom? *Why* didn't you tell me? Why didn't *anyone* tell me?" The hurt in her voice and on her face is a dampness that creeps into my bones and makes me ache from the inside out. I didn't think I could bear her suffering on top of everything else I had to face. Now I know I can, and I must.

"Kiran . . ." I take her hands.

She sobs openly. "Does Vivek know yet?"

"Yes."

"When . . . ?"

I hesitate a second too long.

Her eyebrows dart up. She snatches back her hands, swipes her runny nose. "He's known! All this time! You told him and not me!"

"He came home for Thanksgiving—"

"Oh, *he* came home, and *I* didn't, so this is my punishment—"

"*Arré baba,* no. Nothing like that." I know her anger is inevitable, but let it stem from the truth, not misperceptions. I reach for her hands again, but she scrambles up, wobbling as she stands.

"I need a minute. I'll be back. I just . . . need . . . one minute." She runs from the room. Her footsteps sound up the stairs and overhead. I hear her on the phone, yelling at her brother, as she cannot yell at me.

So much fury. So much pain. So much love.

I close my eyes and drop back my head, face to the heavens. *Pausachi zad aali.*

The deluge has arrived.

The rainy season in Mumbai lasts from June to September. Everyone anticipates and prepares for the monsoon. Everywhere, vendors advertise umbrellas for sale. After months of muggy, suffocating heat, people look to the skies for relief.

But the skies often tease before they give up their goods. Dark clouds roll in, then keep right on rolling, not sparing a precious drop. Then come the sprinkles—gentle showers that sneak in and out on tiptoes. *Pausachi sar aali*, we say.

When I was a girl, my brothers Dilip and Girish—Dilu-*dada* and Giru-*dada*—often took me to the beach a few blocks from our home. We sipped coconut water from fresh-picked baby coconuts and munched *bhel puri* or *chev puri*, our favorite beach snacks. *Ai* strictly forbade us from eating street food from vendors of questionable hygiene during the rainy season when water gets dirty and must be strained and boiled, so on sticky June evenings, we gorged while we could. We'd sit on the sand, watch tides grow higher and dark clouds descend lower, listen to the sea and wind's roaring competition, and wager if the rains would come.

Finally, the inevitable happens, every year without fail: Heavy, swollen clouds burst open like water balloons smacking pavement. The rains pour. And pour. And pour. As the water bathes the hot ground, the air fills with the fragrant aroma of the earth. Baked-on, caked-on dirt and grime washes off trees and buildings, leaving them slick and clean. Exhilarated, people dance in the streets and on rooftop terraces. Children jump in puddles and come home wet and muddy. During high tide, the beach disappears, and waves slam into the ten-foot-high retaining wall, spilling over. Pigeons and sparrows take shelter in trees, under awnings, indoors if they can find a way inside.

Summer vacation from schools ends in May (mango season!), so when the monsoon arrives, the kids are back in school. I used to walk home from school with my girlfriends who lived on my street. During the rains, when water gushes like rivers over the grates of the gutters that line the streets, we loved to toss newspaper boats into the water, gleefully clapping and cheering and running after them as they floated downriver. Sometimes in the height of our excitement, we tossed in our little umbrellas, upside-down. *Ai* always scolded me when I returned home drenched, especially when I arrived without my umbrella. (Those currents moved fast!)

"The wind turned my umbrella inside out," I said. Or, "The wind snatched my umbrella."

My mother never bought it. "Meenal, *kaan pakad,*" *Ai* said. Grab your ear. I grew up to use this same Marathi expression with my kids when they got into trouble. Instead of the parent taking the kid by the ear, the kid's told to grab her own ear. "Do you want to fall sick?"

Every monsoon I caught a cold, but luckily, nothing worse. Illness is a downside of the rainy season, and the poor are the most susceptible.

To this day, whenever I get a cold, I recall the scents of lemongrass tea and Vicks Vapor Rub, *Ai*'s remedies. And whether it's my body, mind, or spirit that feels down, it's lemongrass tea I crave. Lemongrass tea to soothe the soul.

When my daughter comes downstairs, I'm in the kitchen—you guessed it—boiling water for tea. Not lemongrass, but *masala chai,* which Kiran prefers. In Mumbai, our family didn't take our tea with added spices, but I developed a liking for *masala chai* because of Saroj's North Indian influence.

"I want to see your medical records, please," Kiran says, and I know, as a mother who's observed her child since birth, that she's hiding behind an armor of professional detachment.

The same way she hid behind the chip on her shoulder as a teen. The same way she hid behind the folds of my *sari* as a toddler.

"Yes, of course. We have copies of everything upstairs. Can we have some tea first?"

She sits—more like *collapses*—on a barstool, her elbows propped on the granite island. If you didn't know Kiran *very* well, you might think she was aloof, like her father, out of touch with his feelings. She isn't.

It's not that Kiran doesn't feel; rather, she feels too much.

I pour her a mug. The steam of cardamom, cloves, ginger, cinnamon, and black pepper perfumes the air. "Cookies?"

"No, thanks."

"Pepperidge Farm. Mint Chocolate Milano and Gingerbread." Gingerbread is her favorite. I count to myself. *One. Two—*

"Okay, I'll get them."

As she goes to the snack cupboard, I remember when she and Vivek were little, I twisted rubber bands around the knobs to keep them out of the forbidden cupboards. Vivek understood *no* meant *no* much earlier than Kiran (I'm not convinced she accepts this, even now). Kiran endlessly questioned *why*. "Because I said so" was reason enough for Vivek. For me, it went without saying—I never dreamed of questioning *Ai* or *Baba*. Not Kiran. She viewed *rules* as *theories* she had to test out for herself.

"Little Monkey," I would say. "You're worse than Curious George." On occasion, I threatened to ship her off to the Man With the Yellow Hat if she didn't behave.

Was that really half my lifetime ago?

I stare at her back. I want to go to her, wrap my arms around her. I want to turn back the clock. I want my little girl again.

"Kiran, I'm sorry," I say. "I didn't mean to hurt you. Please forgive me." She glances over her shoulder, clearly surprised by my apology. "Come. Sit." I pat the barstool beside me.

She carries over a few pouches of cookies, scoots a plate between us, busies herself arranging white paper cookie cups.

"I didn't tell you for selfish reasons. I think I had the right to be self-absorbed this year—it's one of the perks of fighting for your life." I smile. "Getting out of chores is another."

She slants her gaze in the same way her father does and, without a word, decapitates a gingerbread man.

"Okay." I sigh. "No bad jokes. I do miss my breasts, I can't lie about that. I'm still adjusting to not having them. Two weeks after my surgery, a Victoria's Secret catalog came. For five minutes, I stood in the driveway in my bathrobe and cried like a baby. Then I came inside and cried some more."

Something flickers in Kiran's bloodshot eyes. She blinks it away and says, "Your life's more important than your breasts." Yash's exact words.

"I know. *Believe me,* I know. It's like this house." I gesture around us. "It served its purpose. So did my breasts. I nursed two babies. Still, I feel the loss of something that was part of me, something I loved for so long." I reach out, tuck Kiran's hair behind her ear—hair I used to braid into pigtails. I bring my hand to my lips and kiss my fingertips.

Kiran's lower lip quivers. She bites it. "Why didn't you tell me, Mom?"

I give a weak smile. "Because I wanted *one thing* in my life to stay normal. From everyone else, a simple 'How are you?' was a loaded question. Friends were so nicey-nicey. I tried to pick fights, so they'd be real. But they wouldn't. Whatever stupid thing I said, they let me. So many of my relationships changed in ways I never would have predicted. People close to me grew distant, people distant from me grew closer. Some relationships strengthened. Some weakened. Some just . . . I don't know. There were so many surprises, revelations. Your father, for example."

"What?" she says, apprehensive.

"Dad was incredible. I never thought . . ." I lift my hand, let it fall. "He held my hair out of my face as I vomited on the side of the highway. When my hair started falling out in clumps, he found me in tears in the bathroom. He handed me his electric razor and asked me to shave his head. You know what he said? 'We'll both be *tucklus*.' " Baldies. "After my surgery, he helped me dress. He was so gentle, with his touch, with his words. I didn't want him to see my body, but he sat beside me and said, 'We're growing old together, Meenu. We may lose our hair, our teeth, our memories, a few body parts here and there, but we'll never lose each other.' " I fold my hands over my heart. "After forty years together, you think you know everything about a person, and come to find out, there are still mysteries left."

Kiran hangs on my every word, without comment or question.

"And then there are my friends . . ." I take a Milano

cookie, break off a piece but don't eat it. "Uma Auntie stayed with me at the hospital when Dad couldn't, and Saroj Auntie stocked our freezer with dozens of single-serving dishes, so I never had to cook."

I don't tell her that since my surgery, something's changed with Saroj. It's subtle, but there. She still brings food, but there's a barrier between us, as if I'm contagious. I wonder if I'm imagining it. Maybe I'm overly sensitive. I don't know. I can't comprehend, let alone explain the change, why these days I feel like a leper around Saroj. (The problem with a threesome like Saroj, Uma, and me is that, as close as we are, like a game of musical chairs, someone inevitably feels squeezed out. Each of us takes a turn being the odd woman. Could be, it's my turn. Or Saroj's.)

"*You* were the only person who was *normal* with me, Kiran. Our phone calls were bright spots during some very dark times. Talking to you was my best therapy. I couldn't give that up. You took my mind off my illness. You kept me sane." Gently, I lay a hand on her tear-damp cheek. "I can't tell you how much you helped me, without knowing."

The barstool's wooden legs scrape the ceramic tile as Kiran vaults to her feet. She winds her arms around me and tucks her head on my shoulder. "I should've come home sooner." She sobs.

"You're here now." *And so am I.* "That's all that matters."

"I love you, Mom."

"I know." I kiss her head and rub her back. *"Maaji sonu ga ti."* My dearest one. "I love you, too."

Behind us, the curtain of rain clouds parts, and the sun peeks through the crack. In front of us, I see a magnificent rainbow. *My daughter is home at last. . . .*

FROM: "Meenal Deshpande" <dil_MD1@yahoo.com>

TO: Saroj Chawla; Uma Basu

SENT: December 14, 20XX 10:38 PM

SUBJECT: Update

Saroj & Uma,

Two important pieces of news to share . . .

First, I told Kiran. As expected, she was very upset, but things are better now. She's memorized my medical records, grilled my doctors (and Yash), and studied every book on breast cancer in print, it seems. Then, there is the Internet, too. How did we ever manage without the Internet??

This brings me to my second news. Kiran is ready for marriage again. This time, she's asked our help, so if you know of any suitable boys, please do let me know.

That's it for now. Look forward to seeing you on the 31st.

Meenal

FROM: "Uma Basu" <ubasu@gwu.edu>

TO: Meenal Deshpande; Saroj Chawla

SENT: December 15, 20XX 04:15 AM

SUBJECT: RE: Update

Dearest Meenal,

Terrific news! Heartfelt congratulations! I want to write more, but I'm on my way to the airport -- red-eye to San Francisco this AM. Please know you and Kiran are in my thoughts.

Affly,
Uma

FROM: "Saroj Chawla" <Saroj@ChawlaCatering.com>

TO: Meenal Deshpande; Uma Basu

SENT: December 15, 20XX 09:01 AM

SUBJECT: RE: Update

WOW!!! I did NOT expect the second news!!! WOW!!!

On the other, I'm glad it's done, and you can both move forward now. Secrets are never easy, but sometimes, they're necessary. Our girls may not understand this now, but one day, they will. When they've lived as long as we have! :-)

How I wish I could offer Tarun as a possible match for Kiran! Too bad: #1 -- he's too young for her, #2 -- he insists he's never getting married, a confirmed bachelor. Ha! In India I would have said, "Enough naatak. Time to settle down." & fixed his marriage. Here, my son threatens to sue me!

Chalo. My phone's already ringing this morning. Talk soon.

Saroj

Meenal's Masala Chai

SERVES 2–3

8 green cardamom pods

2 cups water

2 tablespoons loose black Assam or Darjeeling tea leaves

1 teaspoon fresh ginger root, peeled and grated

1 3-inch cinnamon stick

5 whole cloves

5 black peppercorns

1 cup milk

¼ cup sugar

1. Using a mortar and pestle, bruise cardamom pods.
2. In a saucepan over medium heat, combine all but milk and sugar. Bring to a boil.
3. Reduce heat to low and simmer 10 minutes.
4. Stir in milk and sugar. Simmer 5 minutes.
5. Strain *chai* and serve immediately.

PART THREE

Passing the Torch

Kiran Deshpande: Who's Your Goddess?

The possibility of stepping onto a higher plane is quite real for everyone. . . . It involves little more than changing our ideas about what is normal.

DEEPAK CHOPRA

The Big C has a way of altering the way you look at the world. Small stuff becomes big stuff, and big stuff becomes small. When I learned about my mother's breast cancer, I was angry, confused, and scared. Mostly, I was scared. A little girl terrified of losing her mommy.

Though Mom's prognosis is excellent and she tested negative for the breast cancer gene, a relief for both of us, my rotations in the E.R. taught me that you never know when the sands in the hourglass will run out. She may have another twenty-four years, or twenty-four months. Weeks or days. Hours or minutes. She may not die of cancer at all but something else, potentially unexpected.

All I know for sure is, I'm not ready. I'm *nowhere near*

ready to lose her. I might never be. Whenever the end comes, it'll be too soon.

I see the sands falling in the hourglass, future slipping into past like a thief in the night stealing the irreplaceable. I hear a watch ticking as if underneath my pillow, my sense of urgency, anxiety cranking up notch after notch. I've wasted enough time—a losing gamble on marriage, estrangement from my family. I can't afford to waste any more.

"How about this one?" I hold up a black lace camisole.

My mother's eyes go wide. She whispers, *"Parath thev. Parath thev."* Put it back.

We are in a classy intimates boutique in Georgetown that specializes in lingerie for women who've had mastectomies. I learned about it from a local Pink Ribbon support group's website.

Ignoring her embarrassment, I thrust the camisole toward her. "Feel it. It's pima cotton. Solid cloth on the inside, against your skin. Lace on the outside, so it doesn't touch you." Her skin itches, and she admitted feeling more comfortable without a bra but not wanting to go braless, or boobless. The saleslady, herself a breast cancer survivor, recommended these specially designed camis that have pockets for prostheses.

"It *is* soft," she says. "But the color . . . the style . . ."

"It's sexy." The mere word makes her flush and turn away. "Mom. *Really.*" I plant one hand on my hip Saroj Auntie–style. "You and I both know the stork didn't deliver Vivek and me. By my calculations, that's at least two occasions on which you and Dad—"

"Kiran!" She practically leaps into the air like a comic book superhero to cover my mouth with her hand. *"Chup bus!"* Be quiet. *"Tujya tondala kulup lawayla hava."* Your mouth should have a lock put on it.

If I had five bucks for every time she's said this to me, I could have paid off my student loans a long time ago.

"Just try it," I say. "Here, take the matching panties, too. *Chalaa, chalaa.*" I shoo her toward the dressing room. When she doesn't emerge for a while, I go after her. "Mom? Everything okay in there?"

"Yes."

"Did you try them?"

"Yes."

"And?"

She opens the door a crack, and I see her standing with one hand covering her mouth. Not in embarrassment, but in surprised pleasure. The camisole set is sexy but in a sweet, tasteful way. The color makes her skin look creamy and her complexion radiant. She looks beautiful—and she knows it.

"Those Victoria's Secret models don't have anything on you, Mom."

Her eyes fill with emotion. She lowers her hand and says, "Thank you."

"Stay put. I'll get some more," I say, closing the door.

Dad might get lucky, I think, but opt to keep that thought to myself.

Aside from physician-to-physician discussions regarding my mom, I've barely spoken to my dad. I figure the less said, the less chance of starting World War III.

After shopping, Mom and I lock the bags in the trunk of my car and decide to do lunch at Clyde's. We follow the hostess past tables with red-and-white checkered tablecloths, our heels knocking on the hardwood floors. She seats us by the windows where we can people-watch the passersby on M Street.

"What can I get you ladies to drink?" our waiter asks.

"Water for me, please," my mother says. "Wine for you, Kiran?"

I glance at her over my menu. She appears nonchalant, yet an age-old-programmed twinge of guilt prickles at me when I ask for a glass of Kendall Jackson Chardonnay.

The waiter cards me, and my mother laughs.

"He's just being kind, Mom."

"No, he's not. You still look like you're in college. My daughter's a doctor," she informs him with undisguised pride.

The waiter grins and returns my I.D. "Thank you, doctor."

"How embarrassing," I mumble as I replace the card in my wallet.

Outside, an Indian family strolls past the window, and I imagine our family must have looked the same. Yuppie immigrant mom and dad, their son and daughter sporting the latest trendy clothes and hairstyles, and the five-foot-tall grandmother, her silver hair in a bun, a big, round red *bindi* on her forehead, a coat over her *sari,* and tennis shoes on her feet.

Three generations: Indian → Immigrant → American.

"It feels like everyone knows," my mother whispers.

"Knows what?"

"What I'm wearing. Under here..."

"Oh..." I smile. "You mean that my mom's wearing black lace—"

"Kiran!" She bats my menu. "Stop!" But she's smiling, too, so I tease a little more.

"Didn't you see that *aji-bai* mouth *'arré wah, kitti chan'* just now?" Oh, wow. How nice.

She throws back her head and laughs deep from her throat. Music to my ears. *"Labaad mulgi,"* she says. Mischievous girl. *"Mummylah sataawayla majjah yeteh, nuh?"* It's fun to harass Mom, isn't it?

Whenever our parents speak to us in Marathi—commonplace from Mom, not as much from Dad—Vivek and I tend to reply in English, because we think in English: Input Marathi → Mental translation → Output English. The process can prove taxing.

Sometimes, we get translation overload and beseech Mom to please speak English. As teenagers, we also implored her for another reason: Marathi in public places caused embarrassment. She might not have given a rat's ass when strangers mistook her for a fuzzy foreigner, fresh off the boat, but Vivek and I sure did. It wasn't that we weren't proud of our heritage. We were. But we were *equally* proud of our nationality. That's what it *means* to be American. Like our friends, we were Americans of (insert your heritage here) descent, and we didn't like being mistaken for foreigners, or worse, *tourists* in our own country.

That was then; this is now. Today, it's enough that *I* know who I am. And as evidenced by my marriage and divorce, I'm not overly concerned with the (mis)perceptions of others, certainly not strangers.

I waggle my brows at my mother. *"Mummylah sata-awayla khup majjah yeté,"* I say. It's lots of fun to harass Mom.

I can tell my use of Marathi touches her.

Happiness and fear swirl in my heart. *Please, God. Don't take her away from me anytime soon.* Beneath the table, I clasp my hands, reminding myself I must stay positive.

When our lunch arrives, I bite into my jumbo lump crab cake sandwich and sigh with satisfaction. My mother steals one of my French fries.

"Excellent food. Excellent company," she says. "*Arré*, we forgot to toast."

I raise my wine, she her water. "To many more days like this for many more years to come," I say, and we clink glasses.

"Hey, Mom." I carry my laptop into the kitchen. "You have to hear some of these." My mother caps her pen, lays it on the opened page of her recipe notebook, and swivels her barstool toward me. I read a profile from the matrimonial website, " 'WANTED: A GOOD-HEARTED WOMAN to cook, clean, wash, sew, milk cows and goats, and do all household and farm chores.' " My mother looks as mortified as I felt when I read those words. "Then he adds, 'Just kidding!' "

She laughs and drops her forehead onto her palm.

"Had you going, didn't he?" At her nod, I say, "Me, too!"

"Is he a doctor?"

"Architect. Commercial. Builds hospitals. Have to admit, I'm intrigued. I love his sense of humor. Cute, too." I bring up his photo. "Not that looks are everything, but there *is* that little technicality about how babies are made. . . ."

Mom ducks her head and lowers her eyelashes, but I glimpse an upturned corner of her mouth. That's Indian modesty/prudery, and it cracks me up.

Not all the aunties, but many, including my prim and proper mother, act as if they found their children in the cabbage patch. They're of the old school that believes respectable women have sex for procreation, not recreation. Missionary position only. Oral sex? *Chi-chi-chi!* (Dirty-dirty-dirty!) Forget about it!

This from the culture that produced the bible of sexuality, *The Kama-Sutra* (*Art of Lovemaking*), and erotic temple sculptures and cave drawings over one thousand years ago. Go figure.

Mom clears her throat. "So, do any doctors intrigue you?"

"Some, but I'm not sure what I think about doctor couples. I see advantages and disadvantages."

"Never say never."

"I'm not. Okay, here's another one. He does his spiel about himself and what he's looking for, then at the end, he writes, 'Serious inquiries only. I'm NOT looking to be just friends. I have enough friends. If one of them becomes an enemy, I'll let you know there's an opening.' "

"*Kamaal aahé.*" She laughs and shakes her head. "Doctor?"

"Engineer." Before she can ask, I say, "No." I turn the screen toward her, so she can see the photo. She flinches and waves her hand for me to take back the laptop.

I read several more, and we share smiles and grimaces. Together, we compose my profile. After lengthy discussions mingled with healthy debates over profiles that pique my interest, we compile a list of first choices and initiate contact, both of us giddy as schoolgirls.

I nibble on my index finger. "What if everyone says *no*?" Each has the option of accepting or declining contact with me.

"We'll curse their lineage."

"Mom!"

"Kidding!" She nudges my shoulder.

That evening, I check to see if anyone responded, telling myself it's probably too early, but just in case... "Oh! Oh! Look!" Chills race up and down my arms, and I tap the screen. "Someone accepted!"

My mother comes running. "Who is it?" She peers over my shoulder as I break into a huge grin.

"The architect," we say in unison.

"*Chalaa*, Kiran-*bai*." She pats my hand. "You better get ready to milk your cows and goats." *Bai* means lady; it's also the polite way to address one's maid.

"Eight maids-a-milking..." I hum. "I don't believe I'm saying this, but... this is exciting."

"It is! I never dreamed I would arrange *your* marriage."

"Semi-arrange."

"Semi-arrange." She smiles. "It's really just matchmaking. Parents help make the introductions. What you decide to do after that is up to you."

It doesn't sound at all strange when she puts it like that. The irony is, I heard these exact words growing up but couldn't get past the "ick" factor. I'm ashamed to admit that, more than once, I stuck my index finger in my mouth and made gagging noises when my parents suggested pairing me with a "nice Indian boy." In my paltry defense, the Indian immigrant community was *much* smaller back then. All the nice Indian boys I knew felt like cousins to me. We called each other's parents *auntie* and *uncle*, after all. And last I checked, "our people" didn't do that—no cousin intermarriage. Obviously, it wasn't the right time.

Over the next days, I'm floored at the number of contacts that pour in from the matrimonial website. People I contacted. People who contact me. To keep everyone straight, my mother and I make handy-dandy folders, separating each profile into YES, NO, MAYBE. People think I get my anal-retentiveness from my father, when really, it's Mom. Obsessive-compulsiveness I get from Dad.

"Thank you for sharing this with me," my mom says. "It's nice to be a part of it."

"An integral part," I say. "Thank *you*, *Mummyji*." I show off my (very limited) Hindi. The suffix *-ji* denotes respect. "Couldn't do it without you."

I think of all the times my mother has said, "Kiran, learn at least the *basics* of Indian cooking. It's a mother's duty to teach her daughter."

A mother's duty to pass along her wisdom before she dies.

This is the reason she's writing, recording her recipes, I realize. But recipes aren't all that my mother has to impart. It hits me, the sheer magnitude of how much I don't know, how much I still have to learn, how much I can *only* learn from her and no one else. All the stories I haven't heard. The family history. The life lessons.

Deliberately, I lend a hand in the kitchen, try to take an interest, or at least "fake it until I feel it" for her benefit.

This morning, we're making *kheer*, a holiday dessert. To many, *kheer* is a kind of rice pudding, but in my family it's a porridge of vermicelli—chockful of pistachios and golden raisins, and laced with fragrant cardamom and saffron threads.

I'm assigned to spice preparation, the old-fashioned way, which Mom maintains is the best way to achieve optimal flavor. With a brass mortar and pestle, I bruise sage-colored cardamom pods, extract their sticky black seeds, and crush them into a fine powder. (Note to self: Grinding spices by hand is a good way to take out pent-up aggression.)

"Mom?" I ask. "How many marriage proposals did you have? Do you remember?"

Stirring a big pot of milk on the stove, she smiles. "I remember. I had six offers before your father."

"And the others, the rejects? What made them unacceptable?"

"Unsuitable," she corrects. "Oh, different things."

And here they are. *Meenal's Top Five Reasons to Ding an "Unsuitable" Groom Candidate:*

1. His family
2. Differing goals
3. Differing values
4. Socioeconomic concerns
5. Horoscopes

According to Mom, the groom's family was a big, big deal. Living as a joint family *really* meant marrying the boy's whole family, not just him. "You can imagine the atmosphere of grown women living together. At best, it's a sorority.

At worst, a women's correctional center. In all cases, the mother-in-law reigns supreme. I remember there was this one boy we all liked, but his mother..." She shudders. "She was a scary character. She asked me to wash my face, so she could see my 'natural look.' What she really wanted was to inspect the natural shade of my skin, to make sure I wasn't wearing a skin-lightening powder. After they left, *Aji* vetoed them."

"What made Dad stand out from the others?"

"Everything. Our horoscopes matched perfectly—a match made in heaven, according to the stars. Our goals, values, everything matched. His mother was sweet and gentle. Not the domineering type every girl fears will make life miserable for her daughters-in-law. Still, *Ajoba* had some reservations," she says about my grandfather. "Dad's family wasn't well-off financially. His father's death left him with many responsibilities. And, if we married, he would take me far away. In America, there would be no servants. A wife was expected to do all the domestic labor. I wouldn't be able to see or talk to my family more than once a year. All these things worried *Ajoba*, but when Dad came to the house, he so impressed everyone.... He turned all the minuses into pluses!

"His family was humble but cultured. His profession and the lure of an American green card made him a catch. Though America was far from my family, it was also far from his. I could run my own household. I wouldn't have servants, but I would have modern conveniences. Refrigerator, dishwasher, washing machine, dryer, vacuum cleaner. It sounded very exciting, like a movie. *Ajoba* saw Dad as a practical boy with great potential. *Aji* noted Dad was tall, fair, and handsome. That didn't hurt."

I laugh. "I'll bet." I recall many a time when my gray-haired granny swooned over the popular Hindi film hero Amitabh Bachchan, and she likened my father's appearance to the star's.

I learn my parents "interviewed" each other before they agreed to marry. They also had a chance to talk alone. The adults told them to go out onto the balcony. That way, they could keep an eye on them—in those days, girls of marriageable age from good families were always chaperoned to protect their reputations, their honor. They couldn't risk anyone questioning the girl's virtue. That would ruin the family's name and the girl's chances for a good match, as no decent family wanted an "impure" wife for their son. Of course, such impurities didn't tarnish the halos of angel sons one bit.

Bam-bam-bam! I clobber spices with my mallet, er, pestle.

Mom tells me she and Dad were both very nervous and trying hard not to show it. They knew that was the only conversation they'd have before they had to make up their minds, make their decisions. Dad was only in town a few weeks—Harvard's winter break—and he planned to return to Boston a married man, not uncommon, even for today's modern arranged marriages. Mind-boggling, I think, what little interaction the couples have before arranged marriages... and the enormous success rates. Obviously, there's something to it.

Outside, the clouds move in, a thick wall blocking the sun, and the kitchen darkens. We flick on the lights, recessed bulbs over the range and stained-glass lamps that hang over the center island, creating a cozy glow. In the cocoon of the kitchen with my mom, I have the same snuggly feeling as curling into bed with a good book on a rainy day... only better.

I ask her, "Did you discuss any deal-breakers beforehand? Things you wouldn't tolerate in a marriage?"

No shocker: Dad said that while he respected modern career women, he didn't want to marry one. He wanted a wife who would be content as a homemaker, so if Mom was even remotely thinking of working outside the home one day, she should do them both a favor and marry someone else.

Shocker: Mom said that if her husband hit her, even once, she'd leave. No apologies. No second chances. She would pack up her bags and children and go back to her parents—she'd live with society shunning her before she died in an abusive home.

Hearing this, my mouth gapes. "That was *bold*."

She grimaces. "It was, wasn't it? I might not have thought to say it, or had the courage, but my friend Usha was killed in a dowry death."

"Dowry? But I thought... Am I off in my time line? Didn't they make dowry illegal before then?"

"It was illegal, the same way speeding's illegal. It still happens. Often."

With Usha, her in-laws kept demanding money and gifts from her family, and sons from her. She wasn't conceiving, and her monster-in-law was in the habit of regularly caning her, so it wasn't any stretch of the imagination when Usha "accidentally" died from burns in a kitchen fire.

"You always read about dowry deaths in *The Times of India*," Mom says, "but that was the first time it happened to someone I knew, from a supposedly good family."

"How awful," I say.

She nods. "From start to finish. Usha tried to go back to

her parents many times, but they wouldn't have her. They said her place was with her husband, and she must have brought the punishment on herself. If not in the present, then in a past lifetime—bad *karma*. They were very orthodox. They believed once parents gave a girl away in marriage, she wasn't their daughter anymore. They had no rights or responsibilities."

"So they just washed their hands of her?"

"Sadly, yes."

I close my eyes. "Man."

"Now, *Aji* and *Ajoba* were traditional about most things, as you know, but this was an issue where they were *very* progressive. They sat me down and told me in no uncertain terms that a wife's duty does *not* include abuse. It was one thing to be willing to die for your husband, and another to die at his hand. If I ever found myself in that situation, I was to come home immediately," she pronounces the word *im-ME-jet-ly*, "or I should send word to them, and *Ajoba* and my brothers would come and get me, with the police if necessary. I'd always be welcome in their home."

"Good for them! And good for you, too, for putting it out there with Dad. I had no idea—"

"Not just Dad. I told every boy who came to see me."

I'm floored—*beyond* floored—by her revelations. There have been times when I've thought my mother was a doormat, when she put up with things I never would, deferred to my father as lord and master even when she knew he was wrong. But, like me, my parents were molded by the culture in which *they* were raised. They had their own benchmarks, values, challenges to the status quo. For her time and place, her generation of Indian women, my mom *did* stand up for herself, assert herself in ways many others wouldn't have, even today, even in *this* country.

I look at her anew and say, "That couldn't have been easy, sticking your neck out like that."

"It was a calculated risk," she says, explaining she didn't want to be branded unmarriageable.

A girl who came across too headstrong, too liberated from tradition, could be perceived as a threat to family harmony, especially in a joint family with its existing hierarchy. But Mom wanted her marriage to have the best possible foundation, best chances of success, so it was critical both sides, girl's and boy's, understood what they were signing up for, made sure they were compatible.

"Here, you talk about *love*. There, it's *compatibility*. Love's fickle. Compatibility endures, sustains marriages," she says. "Here, marriage is about the two people on the wedding cake. Couples don't need permission slips from their parents. Families have a lower priority than the couple. But in India, marriage is the joining of two families, a strategic alliance. The couple's a lower priority than the family as a whole, and permission slips are essential. Understand, Kiran, it was only because my parents dared to stick their necks out that I could. You think of parents as a net that traps you. For Dad and me, parents were our safety nets. We wouldn't have dared walk the tightrope of life without their support."

I squirm in discomfort. *Guilty as charged.*

Midway through the *kheer*, Mom asks me to take over for her. She raps the wooden spoon against the rim of the milk pot, then hands it to me with instructions to stir every few minutes and make sure I scrape the bottom and sides. We trade places, and she flops onto my vacated barstool.

Concerned, I ask, "You okay?"

She nods. "It's just frustrating not to have the stamina."

"Patience, Mom. You're doing great. I mean it. But you can't overdo. Listen to your body. If you need to rest, rest. You want to go lie down for a while? I can finish the *kheer*."

She laughs. "You and what personal chef?"

"Very funny."

She writes the recipe as we go, refusing my suggestion to dictate directions I can jot on scrap paper, then follow while she naps. "My body's tired, but my mind isn't," she says. "I need you to talk to me. Wear out my brain like you usually do."

"Hey!" I lift my chin. "I resemble that remark!"

She smiles and gives me instructions for the vermicelli. Since I can't cook and talk at the same time, I focus on the *kheer* until I get to a place where all I have to do is stir and scrape the pot again. "Mom?" I ask once I'm on cruise control. "Can I ask you a personal question . . . ?" I hasten to add, "You don't have to answer, but it would help me if you did."

She tilts her head, both curious and apprehensive. "What?"

"Did Dad ever . . . fool around on you?"

Right away, she drops her gaze somewhere around her ankles. Her lips tighten. But then, she takes a deep breath and looks up, meeting my gaze unflinching. "Honestly?" she asks. At my nod, she says, "I don't know. There were a few times when I suspected there might have been someone. He's had plenty of opportunities, but I've never found proof. If there *was* any hanky-panky, I've never caught him."

"Did you ever ask?"

She laughs. "All the time."

I blink. I'd expected her to say no. "What did he say?"

"What do you think?"

"*No*. Of course. Okay, dumb question." I laugh at myself. "But what would you have done if you *had* found proof, if you'd caught him?" I lean one hip against the counter, stirring and scraping, the aroma of saffron and cardamom wafting in the air.

"We wouldn't have divorced, if that's what you're asking."

I nod. This doesn't surprise me. Traditional Hindus—in addition to believing the man can do no wrong and should never be questioned—don't believe in divorce. You can't trade in your "partner for life" (marriage being a sacred, heavenly ordained, *permanent* union) for a new, better model. You must accept what you can't change, and you can't change what's been predetermined. That's fatalism.

"You know my *Ajoba* had a mistress," my mother says.

No, I didn't know this about my great-grandfather, a High Court judge! The name of the floozy, er, mistress was Gajra-*bai*. *Gajra* means "garland of flowers." Everyone, even his wife, knew about her. There wasn't a need for secrecy because society accepted it. It was common practice to have "a big house and a little house." A wife and kids in a big house, a mistress in a little house. A respectable, presentable wife for public show, prestige, procreation, and child rearing. A mistress for private pleasure. Unwinding after a hard day.

"In India, we don't expect any one person to fulfill all

our needs the way you do here," Mom says. "We aren't as disappointed when they don't because our expectations are different. I don't know if you remember that perfume commercial—you might have been too little—about a woman who could bring home the bacon, fry it up in a pan, and never let her husband forget he's a man?" She makes a sound of disgust. "That's a lot of pressure, isn't it? Earn a paycheck, cook, and perform in the bedroom. If you ask me, that's why you have such high divorce rates. I don't know that it's realistic to expect so much from a spouse. You set each other up to fail."

I never thought of it that way. *Did I set Anthony up to fail?*

"You know, in some societies, it was, and still is, a sign of prestige for a man to have a mistress or a second wife. Not every man's capable of keeping more than one woman happy. Most have their hands full with just one."

Ah. *The Joy of Sex in Patriarchal Societies.* There's a best-seller for you.

I whack the wooden spoon against the pot—*boom-boom-boom!*—arguing that it's a double standard. Countering that wasn't always the case, Mom cites the example of ancient India when women sometimes had more than one husband.

"In the *Mahabharata,*" she says, referring to the *Great Tale of India,* the longest poem in world literature and a cornerstone of Hindu culture, "Draupadi has five husbands. She's the wife of the Pandava brothers, who are sons of the deceased King Pandu. She's considered a role model for wives and cooks in parts of India, like Bengal. At the Rays', you might hear Subhro Uncle call Chitra Auntie 'Draupadi.' That's a high compliment to a woman who's a good cook."

Some compliment. I'd take it as an insult. And how much

do you want to bet there was a shortage of women, thus polyandry? It was more about satisfying *his* needs *(quelle surprise)* than *her* needs, I'm sure.

A *man* wants a madonna and a whore, and society shrugs its shoulders. *What can you do? Men will be men. A man has his needs. It's his nature.* So, *he* gets two houses. *He* gets a harem. But a woman who wants a faithful Ram and a passionate Krishna? Oh, no. *That's* unrealistic. She has to adjust her expectations. Or wear a scarlet letter.

"Let me get this straight..." I deposit the spoon on a ceramic dish shaped like a celery stalk. "Our heroine got to cook and clean and service—er, perform conjugal duties—for multiple men. And here I thought Cinderella had it bad. But little girls in parts of India want to grow up to be *just like that*? Yeesh." I wrinkle my nose. "I'd say they need better role models. Like Kali. Now *there's* a role model, if you ask me." The goddess Kali, destroyer of evil, reminds me of Buffy the Vampire Slayer. "She kicks ass and takes names."

My mom laughs. "Obviously, there's more than one way of looking at such things."

"Spin, Mom. It's all about the spin."

"Exactly my point. Society's interpretations, our *taboos* change, but actual human behavior has been the same since the dawn of time. Consider this.... President Clinton was tarred and feathered, and people marveled his wife didn't divorce him. But Kennedy and Nehru? They got off scot-free. Whether it's front-page news or strictly hush-hush, humans have always behaved this way. Monogamy's held up and publicly touted as a moral value, but that doesn't change the fact humans as a species... Well, some of us can accept one mate for life, some can't. Men and women. Even in societies where they stone adulterers. Preach all you want. Punish all you want. It's still going to happen."

I cross my arms, lean against the counter. "Reality or not, I can't accept adultery. I *won't*. Please don't tell me you're advocating—"

"No, no. I'm not—"

"Just because something's *always been* a certain way doesn't make it right."

"True. I guess what I'm *trying* to say is...I want you to be able to look at certain situations...without ego. Anthony's womanizing—it wasn't about you, Kiran. It doesn't matter how wonderful the pistachio ice cream is if you want all thirty-one flavors. If that's right or wrong depends. On many factors. It's taken me a while, but I've finally realized there are no hard and fast rules, no absolutes in life. Think about it. We say *thou shalt not kill*, that we have a culture of life. In the next breath, we send our young men and women off to wars that claim innocent lives, and we support the death penalty. Is this consistent moral reasoning? Is *consistency* necessarily *right*?"

I frown. "I'm not sure."

"Me neither," she says, "which is a different answer than I would have given you a year ago. A brush with death changes the way you look at things. It's made me more philosophical. Less judgmental." She makes an analogy about sunlight hitting a cut crystal, the multitude of prisms. "That's how I see things now."

"I noticed that this year. When we talked. On the phone."

"Now you know why." She rises from the barstool, inspects my pot, and reaches for the wooden spoon. I take it from her and try to nudge her away, but she remains at my elbow, looking over my shoulder. "I'm learning, *understanding* that what's right for one person, in one situation, may or may not be right for another person, or another situation. There are things that seemed so important to me in my twenties, thirties, forties, fifties. Now I look back and see so many of those things don't matter at all in the long run. It was my ego that got in my way. Egos cloud our vision. We need to pierce the veil in order to see clearly. Cancer did that for me.

"When I'm vomiting on the side of the road, when my hair's falling out in clumps, when I fear losing my life, and I *do* lose my breasts, it doesn't matter if my husband had other women. What matters is that he stands by me through thick and thin, that he supports me in every way, that we take care of each other and grow old together. To me, that's the ultimate test of fidelity, the ultimate expression of love. Everything else..." She lifts one shoulder. "It pales in comparison."

I swallow and meet her eyes.

"But that's me," she says. "You are you. And each of us has our own *dharma*." She takes one of my hands, turns it over, and traces the lines on my palm with the soft pad of her index finger.

I stare at her aged hand, at the life flowing in her blue veins. Life that created mine.

...it was because my parents *dared to stick their necks out that I could.*

"You *will* have problems in your next marriage, Kiran. *Every* marriage has its problems. But good marriages are the ones where both parties are committed to *working through* problems, riding it out even when the road gets bumpy. Remember, life is a journey. We're here on earth to learn and grow, to fulfill a purpose, a mission. And marriage... Marriage is a vehicle of evolution." With those words, she pats my palm and closes my hand.

The warm, comforting scent of *kheer* wafts around us. I stir pistachios and raisins into the pot, and Mom gets spoons from the drawer, so we can taste test. I blow on my spoonful, cooling it, then sample a bite—ambrosia on my tongue.

"Ummmm. Good."

"Does it need anything?"

"Not to me. You try."

She takes a bite and appears to mull it over. "Another cup of sugar—?"

"No!"

She laughs. "I'm kidding. It's perfect."

Most Indian *mithai*—sweets—are so sweet they induce a sugar headache in all but the native Indian-born. Even with my wicked sweet tooth, I need the usual dose of sugar scaled way, way back.

"Congratulations, Kiran. You just made *kheer*. Now, tell me. Was it really so difficult?" There's something about her tone. It is...? Could it be...? *Smugness?*

Suspicious, I slant my gaze at her. "Were you really so tired?"

She smiles—more like *preens*—and rubs her hand over my back. "Better late than never, *nuh*?"

"You're bad, Mom."

"I am, aren't I?" She beams, not the least repentant.

FROM: "Vivek Deshpande" <Vivek_Deshpande@mckinsey.com>

TO: Kiran Deshpande, MD

SENT: December 27, 20XX 8:35 PM

SUBJECT: Doghouse

K,

Speaking to me yet?

V

This message may contain confidential and/or privileged information. If you are not the addressee or authorized to receive this for the addressee, you must not use, copy, disclose or take any action based on this message or any information herein. If you have received this message in error, please advise the sender immediately by reply e-mail and delete this message. Thank you for your cooperation.

FROM: "Kiran Deshpande"
<Kiran.Deshpande@yahoo.com>

TO: Vivek Deshpande

SENT: December 27, 20XX 10:11 PM

SUBJECT: RE: Doghouse

V,

Yeah, I'm speaking to you. But only in short sentences. ::wry grin:: I don't like it, but I get it. I understand why you didn't tell me. I just hope you don't have to do it again.

As you can guess, this was some wake-up call. Things are better between Mom and me. (Same old, same old with Dad . . . Some things never change.) I went through her medical records, talked to her doctors, confirmed prognosis is excellent. All the same, do keep her in your prayers.

In other news, I may have a shocker -- of the GOOD sort -- to report soon. Stay tuned . . .

K

Kiran's Kheer

[Dessert Porridge]

SERVES 8

8 green cardamom pods

8 cups whole milk

¼ cup unsalted butter, divided

1 cup uncooked vermicelli, broken into 1-inch pieces (substitute: angel hair pasta)

1 cup sweetened condensed milk

½ teaspoon saffron threads

¼ cup unsalted pistachios, coarsely chopped

¼ cup golden raisins

1. Remove cardamom seeds from pods. Using a mortar and pestle, crush seeds and set aside for later. Discard pods.
2. In a large Dutch oven over medium heat, bring milk to a boil, stirring constantly to prevent burning.
3. Reduce heat to medium. Stirring occasionally and scraping bottom and sides of pot, cook until reduced in half, about 40–45 minutes.
4. In a wok or deep 12-inch skillet, melt 2 tablespoons of butter over medium heat. Add vermicelli and stir-fry until golden brown, about 1–3 minutes. Transfer to Dutch oven with slotted spoon to drain butter. Stir.
5. Stir in condensed milk, cardamom, and saffron. Cook until thickened, stirring occasionally, about 8–10 minutes.
6. Melt remaining butter in wok or skillet over medium heat. Add pistachios and raisins. Stir-fry until raisins plump, about 2–3 minutes. Stir into Dutch oven.
7. Serve warm or chilled.

Saroj Chawla: Pyar Hota Hai [Love Happens]

The stomach is full,
but the heart still wants.
SANSKRIT PROVERB

Every New Year's Eve, Sandeep and I try to outdo the last, to best ourselves. I can't begin to tell you how proud we feel when our friends circle jokes that rather than "keeping up with the Joneses," it should be "keeping up with the Chawlas."

The days before our New Year's Eve bash, our house resembles a bride's house before her big wedding day, bursting at the seams with overnight guests, excitement, and nervous energy. Everyone pitches in, performs whatever assigned tasks. The women prepare mass quantities of food in assembly lines, gabbing and gossiping and having a grand time. Since we remodeled the kitchen and doubled the former space with a spectacular, state-of-the-art addition, catering runs smoother than ever.

"Close your eyes," Sandeep says. "I have a surprise for you."

"What is it? Tell me."

"Hold out your hand."

Jewelry. It must be jewelry. He knows I've had my eye on this exquisite pair of diamond earrings at Tiffany's, but I'm not about to pay such outrageous prices when I can have any design created—or replicated—in India, much cheaper. Ooooh. If he's bought me those earrings, I don't know whether I'll jump up and down with excitement or launch into a tirade. Probably both.

"Are your eyes closed?"

"Yes!"

"Good. Keep them closed." He takes my hand and leads me through the house.

"Where are we going?"

"No peeking. Are you peeking?"

"No!"

When I hear the door to the basement open, I drag my feet. "Deepu," I say. "Are you going to bury me in the basement?"

"Of course not," he says. "After all we shelled out to have it finished? I can't ruin the dance floor."

"Ha, ha."

Deepu is my nickname for Sandeep, but not for the obvious reason. As newlyweds, we lived as a joint family. My orthodox mother-in-law, who ran a tight ship, didn't approve of me being so bold and disrespectful as to address my husband by his first name. Traditionally, a wife referred to her husband as the-name-of-their-eldest-child's father ("Preity's father"), *my husband*, or *he*. Caught between tradition and modern times, neither his first name nor his lack-of-name felt right, so Sandeep said to come up with a nickname of my choosing. One night in bed, I was fantasizing about my last, burning crush before marriage. His name was Deepak Sharma, and he wanted to marry me, but it wasn't possible—his family wouldn't allow marriage out of caste. By accident, I blurted *his* nickname.

"Deepu." Sandeep laughed. "Is that my new nickname?"

Oops! And that is how the two great loves of my life came to share the same nickname. How convenient!

Sandeep guides me down the stairs, one at a time. "Okay, open your eyes. Ta-da!"

At the new state-of-the-art entertainment center, I squeal and cover my mouth. "Deepu! A wide-screen *plasma* television?"

"With surround sound." He grins.

"I love it, but can we afford so much right now?" With our latest round of remodeling and Tarun at Georgetown Law School—

"No payments for a year," Sandeep says. "And . . . check this out." He opens a cabinet stocked with DVDs. "Hollywood meets Bollywood."

I squeal again and give him a giant hug. "We'll host the best parties!"

"Don't we always?"

"Yes, and we must uphold our reputation, after all." I plant a noisy kiss on his cheek. "Thank you, Deepu. I love you."

There's a Hindi expression pertaining to arranged marriages: *Pyar hota hai*. Love happens. That's how it was with Sandeep and me. We barely knew each other when we married.

We met one time only—at the bride-viewing, as we called the question-and-answer session over tea and snacks I served—before his father offered a proposal to mine. My father accepted *with my consent*, which was progressive for the times. "I won't have you blame me if you're unhappy," *Bauji* said. "The final decision is yours."

After marriage, Sandeep and I actively worked on bonding. We courted. We weren't yet in love with each other, but we were in love with the *idea* of being in love, and we worked toward it. As we spent time together and learned more about each other, we grew on each other, grew to care. The best thing we did for our relationship was to leave India. In those early days abroad, we may as well have been shipwrecked on a deserted island. It was during this time, when we only had each other, that my husband of six months and I fell in love.

At Chawla Catering, I employ mostly recent Indian immigrant women. They work for different reasons: finances, boredom, love of cooking, or the kinship of women like themselves. Where else can they make Indian cultural references and jokes? Or say, "So many flavors of yogurt!" or "SNOW!" or "*Huggies* diapers? *Chi, chi, chi!*" and expect everyone to understand? Same when they lament over their children "losing their Indian-ness."

I remember well my own experiences, Sandeep's and my fears of cultural dilution, our struggles to preserve our identities, values, heritage, and traditions in the American melting pot. I sympathize and share what wisdom I have accumulated in my years.

In case you haven't already figured it out, I'm not your

"typical Indian woman." Preity laughs whenever she hears this because most of her aunties here, the ones of my generation who emigrated around my time, will tell you this exact same thing. We may not mean it in the same way, but to Preity, a claim of being atypical *is* typical. I believe only a native can fully grasp what *is* and *is not* typical, in any culture.

One of the biggest factors that sets me apart from other immigrants is the fact I didn't have the same qualms (at least not to the same degree) about "uprooting" from India that most immigrants do. My family had already been separated from our homeland, yanked from our native soil, weeds in a Mughal garden.

Though I grew up to love India, I was always aware my roots lay across a border I couldn't cross, in a country no longer mine. I wore my displacement like my starched school uniform, perfectly comfortable in the cardboard-stiff fabric because I knew nothing else. My parents had a harder time.

Like many immigrants, they never felt they belonged, in any country. They suffered chronic homesickness, longing for a home that didn't exist anymore. It was wrenching to be so close, yet so far from their ancestral land, the place where they had left shattered pieces of their hearts, never to be retrieved. When the first of our relatives settled abroad, my father said with a touch of envy, "It's better to be separated by God's oceans than man's borders."

The second time I left the world I knew behind, I took two big suitcases. It wasn't enough, but it was two suitcases more than I was able to take when we left Lahore, and I felt lucky.

When Sandeep and I arrived in the States in the mid-

1960s, there weren't so many people from India living here. We couldn't have created a Little India like those you see now, say, in New Jersey, if we'd wanted to: There simply weren't enough of us. If we said we were Indian, people asked, "Which tribe?" Honorary Indian, Patrick McGuiness often clarified, "Dots, not feathers."

Though it was harder for us in many ways back then, in some ways, I think it was actually easier.

For example, today, it's easy for Indian subcultures to stick together, birds of a feather: Bengalis with Bengalis, Maharashtrians with Maharashtrians, Punjabis with Punjabis, etc. Major cities have organizations, community centers, activities dedicated to specific subcultures. Not so then. In those days, we had "slim pickin's," as the kids say. The dearth of Punjabis *forced* us to mix, not be so cliquey. We didn't have any choice! Starved for company, we found ourselves socializing with Punjus, other Indians, Americans, and immigrants from other countries whom we otherwise would not have. And lo and behold, a most peculiar thing happened.... *Everyone—we and they—benefited.*

Did we lose some of our Indian-ness? Yes. But we learned the difference between cultural pride and elitism. We lost our superiority complexes *and* our inferiority complexes. We gained awareness and appreciation of other cultures, and others—non-Punjabis and non-Indians—gained awareness and appreciation of *ours*. (Meenal, Uma, and I couldn't be more different. In India, we *never* would have been friends, our husbands *never* would have mixed, yet for almost half a century, ours are the friendships that have thrived the longest, ripened the sweetest, and borne the most fruit.)

It feels good to share my stories with these women, to let them know others have walked in these same steps—and succeeded. I hope to console, and to inspire.

Some women have the support of their husbands; others don't. This, too, is a marked improvement since my time when, by and large, women from good families didn't work. For wages, that was. Volunteering was acceptable, provided family obligations were met. Oh, the fights Sandeep and I had!

"It looks bad," he would say. "As if I can't support my family on my own."

"You have a Ph.D. from M.I.T. You're an engineer at a top company," I'd reply. "Everyone knows you can support us. But think, what if something happened to you? An illness, or an accident? We have children now in addition to our family in India who depend on us. It isn't a bad thing to have backup. Hope for the best, prepare for the worst."

Then I would bring up my own education—education *Biji* and *Bauji* didn't want me to pursue too rigorously for fear it would scare off potential grooms. "Men don't like women who are too clever," *Biji* advised, "or too aggressive." But I refused to hide my intellect from my husband, especially in this New Land that redefined self-respect, where fewer men ruled over their families as dictators in a totalitarian regime and more women had voices and choices. Where a woman who suffers in silence, sacrifices, and devotes herself to a man who lacks consideration for her needs *isn't* a heroine. And the threat of a woman, when wronged, isn't suicide but homicide.

"I have a brain and a B.Com.," I would say. A bachelor's degree in commerce. "I want to use them."

"And *I* want a traditional wife," Sandeep would bemoan. "A woman who puts her duties as a wife and mother first."

Of course, family has always come *first*. He meant a woman who lived *only* to serve, expecting no reciprocation. A woman with no identity beyond dutiful wife and mother. Ideally, the Indian version of a Stepford Wife: fair but not white, lovely, homey, chaste, modest, fertile, nurturing, soft-spoken, loyal, obedient . . . and a good cook!

A woman like Meenal.

Back in the Boston Days, Sandeep would have traded me for Meenal in a heartbeat. He flirted openly, shamelessly with her, as he does with most pretty women—he *is* a charmer by nature. But when it came to graceful, first-class Meenal, I suspected underneath his lighthearted banter, he really did "covet thy neighbor's wife." Lucky for me, I knew my pious best friend didn't return his interest—and lucky for Sandeep, so did her husband.

What I also knew, though I'd never tell a soul, is that Sandeep's all show. He is, in fact, a lackluster lover. A few thrusts, and the party's over. He doesn't see any problem—*he's* satisfied, so mission accomplished, right?—and I can't bear to crush his ego. He fancies himself Don Juan de Punjab; I find our sex as exciting as inserting and removing a tampon. Nor can I tutor him in the countless *other* ways a man pleases a woman, for how would a proper, respectable woman possess knowledge about such things?

Every now and then, Sandeep raised the subject, "Maybe we should go back to India."

India, where his mother, sisters, and aunts pampered him, and he was never expected to wash his own dishes, take out the trash, clean toilets, change diapers, or baby-sit his children. India, where his independent-minded wife could spend her life serving endless cups of tea under the critical eye of her mother-in-law and rehash ad nauseam such scintillating topics as:

1. Good help being hard to find;
2. Society's moral decay—due to corrupting Western influences;
3. Duties of a good Hindu wife—being barefoot and pregnant-with-sons in the kitchen, obeying her husband and in-laws, fasting and praying for the health and long life of her husband.

"Okay, I'll pack our bags," I said, knowing we'd never go. We both knew Sandeep couldn't earn in India the income America provided. Our families on both sides of the globe were better off if we remained here.

I don't know if he came around or simply resigned himself to my working. Likely, it was the prestige I accelerated for us. In a good year, I earn almost twice his engineering salary, and in a calculated ego-stroke early on, I hand the bulk of it over to him to manage however he wants. Because of my contributions to the family income, of all our Indian friends, we always have the biggest house, best toys, fanciest clothes, and splashiest parties.

"What man doesn't welcome the coming of Lakshmi incarnate into his home?" Sandeep boasts, likening me to the goddess of wealth. Wise man. He's learned the secret of a happy life—a happy wife. When a husband treats his wife as the goddess she is, riches naturally follow.

Preity, Eric, and the kids arrive the day after Christmas, filling the house with laughter and joy. Sandeep and I relish our roles as *Nanaji* and *Naniji*, playing with our grandchildren. Though we wish they lived closer to us, I know Preity wouldn't like me breathing down her neck more than I already do! Can I help it? It's my duty as her mother to instruct her, correct her. If I don't, who will?

For dinner, I serve up requested favorites: *murgh makhani*—butter chicken—tender chunks of chicken breast in a tomato-cream sauce. *Chhole*, a kind of chickpea chili Preity calls "Punjabi comfort food," delicious year-round, but especially satisfying on cold winter nights like tonight. And *sarson da saag* on *makki di roti*, another winter favorite of Sandeep's and mine since childhood. *Sarson da saag* is tender mustard greens, spinach, and spices that I cook either very slowly over very low heat or in a pressure cooker. We eat it with *makki di roti*, a soft, golden griddle bread made with cornmeal and wheat flour. Sometimes, I'll add grated radish or fresh *kasuri methi* (fenugreek) or cilantro to the dough for a little variety, but even plain *makki di roti*, piping hot off the griddle with a pat of butter, tastes out of this world.

After dinner, I unbutton my pants when no one's looking, sticking out my tongue and biting it in embarrassment. If I don't watch it, I'll outgrow my new nightgown before I get a chance to wear it!

After Lina and Jack are tucked in bed, Preity and I put up our feet and unwind in the family room while the boys watch

TV downstairs. The angle and light combination makes me notice her face is fuller, her cheekbones less prominent.

"Have you gained weight?" I ask. "You look like you have."

She shrugs. "Don't know, don't care. I stopped weighing myself."

"*Eh!* Don't say that! You don't want to be one of those women who lets herself go after marriage. I know winters are tough in your frozen tundra. That's why God made treadmills. Preity? Are you listening? What did I just say?"

She parrots back all my words. "Duly noted."

"Good, and while we're on the subject of harsh winters.... Your skin's showing some wear and tear. Do you use a night cream? Make sure you invest in the best moisturizers, *beta*. Otherwise, you'll be looking at premature wrinkles."

"We wouldn't want that."

"No, who would? Add moisturizer to your resolutions, hmm?" At her pointed stare, I say, "What? Why are you looking at me like that?"

She gives a tight smile. "Oh, no reason."

The next night, we find ourselves in the same spot after putting the kids to bed.

"Say, Mom? Do you, by chance, remember the boy I met in Goa?"

I blink. Where did *that* come from? Keeping a straight face, I murmur, "Vaguely," though I remember perfectly.

As if a mother forgets her daughter nearly giving her a heart attack.

From upstairs, she retrieves a white plastic bag. Her show-and-tell: an illustrated children's book her *Mussalman* boyfriend made her. "I wonder what ever happened to him...

We never did say good-bye. . . ." She doesn't mask an undercurrent of accusation: *You saw to that.*

Hai Rabba, why this bad trip down Memory Lane?

"I'm thinking about looking him up," she says.

Okay, trip's over. "Preity, enough nonsense. You aren't eighteen anymore. You have a wonderful life. Great marriage, children, career. What more could you want?" I hold open the plastic bag, direct her to pack up her little storybook and forget about it. "Now, on to more pleasant subjects." I straighten my clothing, fluff my hair, smile. "Kiran looks fantastic. Did I tell you she works out regularly? Yoga, weights, cardio. Of course, being a doctor, she's health conscious. Isn't it great she's home?"

"Yeah. Great."

"Is that all the enthusiasm you can muster for one of your best friends?"

"Uh, Kiran and I were never best friends."

"Sure you were. You were inseparable."

"No, that would be you and Meenal Auntie and Uma Auntie. Kiran tolerated me, at best. In case you didn't notice, she didn't like me."

I frown. I don't know what's gotten into my angel daughter tonight. "Of course she liked you. Everyone likes you. What's not to like?"

Preity looks away. "You know, just because you choose not to talk about something doesn't make it go away."

"I don't know what you're talking about."

Her eyes pin me. "Arsallan. I'm talking about *Arsallan.*"

"Beta." I smile, shifting uncomfortably. Is it hot in here? "Don't be difficult, please."

"You're the one being difficult—"

"Preity!" Blood rushes to my cheeks. "Since when do you talk to your mother like this?"

"I'm sorry. It's just..." She holds out a hand in appeal, then drops it on the storybook with a thump. "You always change the subject when it gets awkward for you. You shut *me* down when *you've* had enough. I wish... You're my mother, my *one and only* mother. I want to be able to talk to you, *really* talk. Not just about my figure and complexion—"

"You're upset about what I said last night."

"Honestly, I don't care. That's my point. There are so many other, more important things in life. Why exclude those—"

"Fine-fine-fine. You're making my head hurt." I rub my throbbing temples. "You want to talk. Go ahead. Talk. But first, get me some aspirin." I drop my head back against the cushions, already regretting this.

My daughter thinks I'm prejudiced. *Prejudiced!* What an oversimplification!

Hindu–Muslim conflicts date back centuries, to the time Muslim invaders conquered Indian kingdoms—looting, raping, killing; desecrating and destroying Hindu temples, erecting mosques on the foundations, sometimes using the same stones.

"You know how a volcano can lie dormant for years, then erupt with little notice?" I say, trying to explain a complex subject in terms she'll understand. "That's how it is with Hindu–Muslim communal relations. The threat of violence is always there, lava bubbling beneath the surface. Partition taught me there are lines that separate certain communities. Lines that cannot be crossed."

Preity shakes her head. "We cry the same tears, bleed the same blood—"

"I didn't make the rules," I say. "They are what they are."

"If everyone in this country believed that, women wouldn't have the right to vote, and we'd still have racial segregation. If everyone in India believed it, only descendants of Brahmin priests would be educated. And just the men, at that."

She's comparing apples and onions. I tell her so, but I'm wasting my breath.

"God gave us brains, Mom. If rules are unjust, we should change them. Didn't Akbar the Great abolish unfair taxes on non-Muslims?" she says about the sixteenth-century Mughal emperor's revocation of nonbeliever *jizya* and pilgrimage taxes. "Wasn't his favorite wife—the mother of his successor—a Hindu? While Christian Inquisitions and witch hunts were terrorizing Europe, an Islamic emperor in India was making policies to respect and protect *all* religions and treat believers of *all* faiths equally."

"Akbar was an exception. Have you heard of Aurangzeb? In comparison to *him,* Saddam Hussein and Osama bin Laden are pussycats."

"I knew you'd say that."

I can't help but smile at her example from Indian history. "You finally got around to reading the books Dad and I got you."

"Those, and a lot more. I just needed time."

Sandeep and I tried our best to plug holes in our children's school curriculums, but it proved an uphill struggle to squeeze in *our* lessons with *their* lessons. We couldn't deny their need to master the civilization and cultures they encountered firsthand every time they left the house. Immediacy took priority. It makes me so proud to know they *did* expand their scope as we hoped, in their own time, and in their own way. Though at the moment, it appears a mixed blessing. . . .

"My studies confirm what I know to be true," Preity says. "Discrimination's always wrong. Violence in the name of God is always wrong. And when mankind takes a wrong turn and strays from these fundamental truths, we need to correct our course." She rattles off more examples: caste discrimination, female education and inheritance rights, child marriage, dowry, bride burning, widow remarriage, and *sati*—the now outlawed practice of a widow self-immolating on her husband's funeral pyre, a supposed act of piety. "From east to west, ancient to present, people from all different backgrounds have crossed those lines, those *artificial barriers,* and unified in common fights for humanity. *That* is what I've learned."

Wah-wah. What a performance. Give the girl a round of applause. She, not Tarun, should have been the lawyer in the family. She never could back down from a perceived injustice. When she was five, she saw a mother spanking her child in the supermarket. All the way home, she pleaded for me to call the police, arguing about the rights of the child. It's not fair, she cried until she went hoarse. If I *didn't* shut her down, she'd carry on indefinitely from her soap box. Wind her up, watch her go. . . .

"Getting back to Arsallan," she says.

"Hai Rabba." I press the heel of my hand to my forehead.

"I'm going to ask around."

"Hai Rabba!" I feel pain in my chest.

"I'll start with Riya-*didi*, see if anyone—"

"HAI RABBA!" I'm breathing heavy now, sweat on my brow, armpits damp. "You'll do NO SUCH THING. What would people think? My married daughter chasing after a married man. A *Mussalman*. Can you just imagine the talk?"

"I'm not chasing him. And who cares about gossip-mongers—"

"*I* care. *Your father* cares. *You* should care. You have a family reputation to protect, too. If your husband finds out—"

"I told Eric."

I wince and cover my eyes. Did I drop her on her head when she was little? Did she crack her coconut open? Did her common sense leak out with the milk? "*Never* talk to your husband about other men," I say what should be obvious to a woman with a fully functioning brain. "Husbands get jealous, too."

Preity just bats a hand, dismissive. "Jealous of what? I have nothing to hide. Eric and I don't have secrets."

"*Humph*. Keep this up, and you will."

I don't understand this younger generation. A wife talks to her husband as if he's her girlfriend. Spouses expect to be best friends. It's unnatural!

I get up and sit beside my daughter, grip her shoulders, and say firmly, "Listen to me. I'm your mother. I brought you into this world. I know you better than anyone, better than you know yourself, and *I* know what's best for you. Hindu–Muslim relations aside, reputations aside, do *not* jeopardize your marriage. You have a *lot* to lose, and I don't want to see you, or anyone else, get hurt. There are people who can handle affairs. *You* aren't one of them. You're Sita, not Radha."

In the Hindu epics, both Sita and Radha have great loves. Sita's is a conjugal relationship with her husband Ram, while Radha's is an adulterous relationship with Krishna. The epics romanticize both couples, but in reality . . . Show me a society that openly accepts the Krishnas and Radhas of the world.

"Affair?" Preity sputters. "Who said *anything* about an affair? I'm in love with my husband. I'd never cheat on him. And Arsallan is hardly Ravan." Ravan, villain of the Ram-Sita-Ravan triangle, tricks Sita into leaving her safety zone, then kidnaps her and tries to woo her into falling in love with him. "Trust me, Mom. He wasn't *at all* the presumptuous, lecherous type you warned me about. The kind who compartmentalizes women as madonnas or whores, pure or impure. Who can't conceive of drinking, dating, bikini-wearing females being *good girls* with our own standards and rules of etiquette. Please. I wouldn't give a guy like that the time of day." She huffs, lifting her chin. "Arsallan was one of the enlightened. Romantic *and* respectful. A perfect gentleman. And a devoted family man—you'd agree if you'd seen him. He was so good with his nieces and nephews. I'm sure he's a wonderful husband and father."

I sigh. For all Preity's reading, my whimsical daughter lives in an idealistic world of right and wrong, good and bad, innocent until proven guilty—I can just hear her arguing that poor Ravan was misunderstood—and God bless her naiveté, I want her to stay in that nice, safe world. But it's my job, my duty as her mother to warn her about the big, bad realities in life.

"I'm sure he takes excellent care of his family," I say. "Family's very important in Indian culture. A family man will never leave his wife, break up the family unit, but Preity..." How do I phrase this? "That doesn't mean he doesn't run around with other women, discreetly, on the side. Trust *me*. The sweet, innocent girl he knew has grown into a mature, desirable woman. He'd take one look at you, assume you're a loose American, and want an affair."

"Oh, brother." Preity rolls her eyes. "The Hindi-Bindi Club's been watching too many Bollywood flicks."

She doesn't understand, but what more can I possibly say?

I have always tried to be open, frank with Preity, as the women in my family were when I was growing up. But there were limits to mother–daughter candor then, and there still are, as far as I'm concerned, lines that can't be crossed, circumstances in which a mother shouldn't talk to her daughter as a friend, a peer. A daughter can have any number of friends, but as Preity pointed out, she has one and only one (birth) mother. A mother can't forget she serves a different, *higher* purpose than a mere friend. Maybe it's the way I was brought up, but that's how I see it. I wasn't raised to be a best friend to my daughter; I was raised to present her a role model.

I straighten my spine and speak with calm and conviction. "Don't play with fire, Preity. Past is past. You both doused your old flames and moved on. For heaven's sake, *let this go*."

That night in bed, I say to my husband, "Your daughter is the most stubborn, willful—"

"Yes, I know," Sandeep says. "She takes after her mother."

"You have no idea." I turn out the bedside lamp, punch my pillows a few times, and flop onto my side. Behind me, Sandeep chuckles. He's only amused because he doesn't know what I know. If he did, he'd take out a contract.

He hooks an arm around my waist, hauls me against him, kisses my shoulder. "We can't protect her from the world."

"It's our duty to try," I say, though at the moment, the world at large doesn't concern me, just one Arsallan Khan.

In my red silk nightgown, I stretch my arms to my sides, turning in a circle.

"Beautiful," he says. "As always."

Is there a woman in all the world who is immune to this compliment, especially from the lips of a man she loves? If there is, I haven't met her.

An hour later, I slip out of bed, retrieve the nightgown from the floor, and tiptoe toward the bathroom to dress.

"Sonu..." An arm reaches out.

Sonu is an endearment, like sweetie. It's also a nickname for Sonia, my name before marriage. In traditional Hindu custom, the groom gives the bride an entirely new married name: first, middle, and last. His first name becomes her middle name, and the middle name of their future children, male and female. My father was Gurpreet Malhotra. At birth, I was: Sonia Gurpreet Malhotra. After marriage: Saroj Sandeep Chawla.

"Sonu," he whines again. "Don't leave. Come back."

"Sorry, Deepu, I have to go."

"Not yet," he protests, throwing back the covers from my side of the bed and patting my vacated spot.

"I can't. You know we have a houseful of guests. . . ."

A groan. A whimper. A sigh.

Pitiful. I laugh as I dress. "Men are such big babies."

"Only with the women they love. Can I help it if I love you? If I can't get enough of you? If no amount of time is ever—"

"And I love you, darling, so I will make it up to you."

"Soon?"

"Soon."

"Promise?"

"Promise."

"Okay." He climbs out of bed, gathers me close, and frames my face between his hands. His kisses are soft, sweet, coaxing, each brush of his lips punctuated with "I love you."

I melt. I let him take off my clothes and lead me back to bed. Every time we're together, every time we touch, I'm awed. Humbled. "All this time," I whispered, spent, after our first time. "I didn't know what I was missing."

"I did," Deepak said.

That's right, *Deepak*. As in, Deepak Sharma, my first love. He is the one in my arms. Ten years ago, our lives intersected again. We meet at a condo at the Rotunda, an upscale complex near Tyson's Galleria. The owner, a bachelor friend of Deepak's, travels extensively. In Hindi, we have a saying: *Teri bhi chup; meri bhi chup.* You be quiet; I'll be quiet.

Affairs destroy many marriages; others, they save. Deepak will never leave his wife, and I'll never leave my husband; nor will we leave each other. Because of our affair, our marriages work. Endure. Flourish. I don't fault my husband for what he can't provide. I'm perfectly happy, content with what he can. No bitterness or resentment. Only appreciation and affection.

I love two men. Differently but equally. It's a fate I wouldn't choose for my daughter. A fate I pray doesn't await her. I can't help but worry. What if Arsallan is her Deepak?

The consequences for Preity would be disastrous. Rock the foundations of everything she believes in. Shatter her self-image. Her marriage wouldn't survive. I don't know that *she* would. Unlike me, the guilt would kill her.

Sometimes, in Preity, I see the girl I was, the woman I might have been, believing in a world without boundaries and barriers, believing in one planet, one people.

If only I could believe again. . . .

FROM: "Saroj Chawla" <Saroj@ChawlaCatering.com>
TO: Meenal Deshpande; Uma Basu
SENT: December 28, 20XX 09:15 AM
SUBJECT: Favor

Meenal & Uma,

I have a favor to ask. I would like to find my childhood friend. We were separated after Partition. Do you or your husbands know any Pakistanis in the area? As a starting point, I would like to talk to any local Lahoris (who would be willing to talk to me).

Saroj

FROM: "Meenal Deshpande" <dil_MD1@yahoo.com>

TO: Saroj Chawla; Uma Basu

SENT: December 28, 20XX 10:22 AM

SUBJECT: RE: Favor

Yash knows some Pakistani doctors. He will inquire. It's not such a big world these days. You will find your friend.

Meenal

P.S. Kiran thanks you again for the samosas!

FROM: "Uma Basu" <ubasu@gwu.edu>

TO: Meenal Deshpande; Saroj Chawla

SENT: December 28, 20XX 11:01 AM

SUBJECT: RE: Favor

Dearest Saroj,

The "Pakistani Student Associations" will surely have Lahoris. If you're able, do an Internet search to find out which of the local universities have PSA websites and email the presidents. If you'd like, I can do this for you tomorrow.

Warmest wishes,

Uma

FROM: "Saroj Chawla" <Saroj@ChawlaCatering.com>
TO: Meenal Deshpande; Uma Basu
SENT: December 28, 20XX 01:45 PM
SUBJECT: RE: Favor

Thank you both so much!!!

In other news, Preity wants to learn to read/write Punjabi so she can read Punjabi children's books to Lina, Jack, & Eric (!). She says their Punjabi should be at least as good as Patrick Uncle's Bengali! :) I'm so tickled... There's SO MUCH wonderful Punju lit/poetry I would LOVE Preity to experience, but I will wait until the right time to bring that up. It's always better if these things are HER idea. ;)

Saroj

FROM: "Meenal Deshpande" <dil_MD1@yahoo.com>
TO: Saroj Chawla; Uma Basu
SENT: December 28, 20XX 08:57 PM
SUBJECT: RE: Favor

Saroj, good for Preity! How wonderful that SHE initiated this! It's such a delicate balance between exposing the American-born generation(s) to Indian culture vs. forcing it on them. We want them to appreciate, not resent; to feel enriched, not alienated by their heritage.

Preity's thirst for knowledge is commendable and, I must admit, enviable. I'm lucky Vivek and Kiran still understand Marathi. When they speak it, it's a rare treat. They still sound 4 yrs old, the age when they started school and their Marathi skills froze in time. :) It's very cute to hear baby talk from the mouths of my physician daughter and management consultant son. :)

I make a conscious effort to speak to them in Marathi, so they won't forget what little they know. If I don't, who will?

I'm happy to bring back Punjabi books from India. Bulleh Shah's poetry? Anyone else? I'd love to read some Sufi poetry myself. The world could use some Sufi saints' wisdom these days. As Uma says: "Where have all the Sufis gone?"

Uma, are you still in San Francisco?

Meenal

Saroj's Sarson da Saag

[Spinach and Mustard Greens]

SERVES 4

1 bunch/bag spinach

1 bunch mustard greens

1 teaspoon salt

2 tablespoons canola oil, divided

2 cloves garlic, minced

1-inch piece of fresh ginger root, peeled and minced

2 green chili peppers, minced

½ teaspoon amchur (mango powder) or lemon juice

*1 pinch asafetida (hing)**

1 cup water

1 small yellow onion, diced

garam masala

1 tablespoon cornmeal

1. In a colander, wash spinach and mustard greens under cold water. Repeat with cold salt water. Drain and chop finely.
2. In a pressure cooker, heat 1 tablespoon oil. Add spinach and mustard greens. Stirring constantly, mix in garlic, ginger, chili peppers, amchur, and asafetida.
3. Pressure cook for 5–10 minutes. Mash with water.
4. In a wok or large skillet, heat remaining 1 tablespoon oil over medium-high heat. Add onion. Stir-fry until light brown.
5. Stir in spinach and mustard greens. Reduce heat to medium. Sauté 2 minutes.
6. Stir in garam masala. Sauté 1 minute.
7. Stir in cornmeal. Cover and simmer until done, about 2–5 minutes.
8. Eat with *makki di roti* or corn bread and fresh butter.

* *Mom's Tips:*

✔ Asafetida will stink up your spice cabinet. Refrigerate in an airtight plastic bag.

Uma Basu McGuinness: Your Fate or Mine?

There are two ways of passing from this world—one in light and one in darkness. When one passes in light, he does not come back; but when one passes in darkness, he returns.

BHAGAVAD GITA

The day before we leave for San Francisco, my husband stacks hundreds of gift bags and boxes for our haul to Walter Reed Army Medical Center. "You and the elves have been busy, Mrs. Claus," he says, kissing me under the mistletoe.

Our library resembles Santa's workshop not only during the holidays but all year long. Just as my mother and her friends packed medicines every week for Mother Teresa's lepers, so my friends and I work on our humanitarian projects. Every week, we put together care packages for the world's children in need and our soldiers in harm's way, two causes near and dear to my heart.

It was during the Vietnam War that Patrick and I fell in

love, through letters. Before he left for his tour of duty, I was still getting used to the social mixing of men and women in America. I was shy and reserved around him, as I was with most men. I didn't speak unless spoken to, I never said their names, and I averted my gaze, looking down when they were present.

Our letters changed everything.

In the Bengali community, we have something called *adda*—friendly, casual conversation about every topic under the sun. For my college girlfriends and me, *addas* went beyond social gossip and family politics to include world events, economics, philosophy, psychology, sociology, science, religion, sports, weather, history, the arts. You name it. We hung out at the Coffee House of Calcutta, pontificated about life, and solved the world's problems over cups of Assam and Darjeeling tea and snacks like *chanachur*, *kachuri*, *muri*, *nimki*, and *shingara*. How I missed the camaraderie and intellectual stimulation, the mind-dump of *addas*. How grateful I was when Patrick's and my pen-friendship filled that void.

Have you noticed how the written word can be deeper, more intimate, more honest than verbal, face-to-face conversation? Maybe it's because you sit alone and have time to reflect and revise and get the words right. The written word can take you beyond the superficial, beyond the façades, and allow glimpses into people's inner worlds.

With time, familiarity, and trust, social barriers fell away. Patrick and I found ourselves opening up, rambling on, giving and taking comfort. We didn't wait to receive each other's letters before responding. We just wrote and kept writing regularly, so a steady stream of mail came and went.

Those were dark days for both my homelands. When

I wasn't worrying about Vietnam, I worried about India, and vice versa. The Indian subcontinent experienced much tragedy in the 1960s. China invaded an unprepared India in 1962. India and Pakistan went to war for the second time in 1965 over Kashmir. The 1970 cyclone—imagine a nightlong tsunami—killed millions in East Bengal, which was then East Pakistan. The Pakistani civil war soon followed, claiming even more lives in already devastated East Bengal. With India's assistance, East Pakistan seceded from West Pakistan and won independence as Bangladesh in 1971.

As desperate as I was to talk about these events—of major consequence in India, but minor in America—Patrick needed to talk about Vietnam to someone who wasn't directly involved. He was more open with me than his family because he didn't want to worry them more than they already were. Since the day he left, his mother went to church twice a day and kept a candle burning for him. Any mention of him brought tears to her eyes.

There are three wars, Patrick wrote in one letter. *The political war, the war on the ground, and the war inside every human being.* When he confided in me, sharing his fears and the abject horrors of witnessing the cruelties man can inflict on man, I wrote to him about Lord Krishna's counsel to Arjuna on the battlefield in the *Gita*. The *Bhagavad Gita*—Song of the Lord—is the gem of Hindu spiritual wisdom, an ancient Sanskrit epic poem comparable to Homer's *Iliad,* with the interaction of gods and mortals in which Arjuna, an esteemed warrior like Achilles, questions the virtue of war.

In our letters, we ruminated over the existence of God, the failures of man, the meaning of life and death, the codes by which we lived, and the unique role each of us is destined to fulfill. I confided to him my family's deep, dark secrets, my unfavorable birth chart, my father's dwindling wealth with so many daughters and nieces to marry off, all of whom, for one reason or another, necessitated a sizeable dowry in order to secure a good match.

In my case, even a hefty dowry wouldn't have guaranteed any takers. In Vedic astrological terms, I am what we call a "strong *manglik*." Sparing you the scientific techno-babble, suffice it to say: It's very bad for one's marriage prospects. One look at my birth chart—and they usually consult birth charts—and it was difficult to find an Indian family who would consider me as a prospective bride for their son, as *mangliks* are believed to jeopardize the health of their spouses. Even bring an early death.

My great-aunt, widowed at fourteen, was a *manglik*. Three months after marriage, her husband was hit by a double-decker bus. He died instantly at the age of twenty-one. As custom dictated, she never again wore jewelry, or a tip (*bindi*) on her forehead, or *sindoor* in the part of her hair—all symbols of a married woman. Nor did she remarry, as widow remarriage was—still is, but to a much lesser extent—considered shameful in traditional Hindu culture.

One may argue correlation doesn't mean causality in such cases of *manglik* widows. But not many parents are willing to stake their son's life on it.

This was the underlying reason why *Thakurda*—my paternal grandfather—encouraged my education, first at the elite Loreto House, where the nuns stoked the embers of my English proficiency, then at Presidency College, where I earned a bachelor's degree in English literature, and most controversially, abroad for further studies.

"No," *Baba* said, and ripped my admission letter from Boston College in half, twice. As far as he was concerned, that was the end of it. The full scholarship and generous-by-Indian-standards teaching stipend didn't sway his opinion. At the time, most upper-middle-class girls attended college only for time-pass before marriage and/or to enhance their appeal on the bridal market. Increasingly, good families were seeking college-educated brides for their sons, though as wives, most were prohibited from earning wages.

But the combination of unlucky factors led everyone in my family, including me, to suspect that my fate was sealed as a spinster, a social pariah. Knowing this likelihood, *Thakurda* couldn't deny my fervent wish for higher studies abroad and a career as a professor upon my return when chances were I might not have a husband and children. "One who doesn't go forth and explore all the earth is a well frog," *Thakurda* said, a Sanskrit proverb. "My granddaughter may end up a spinster, but she will *not* be a well frog." With that, *Baba*'s lower court ruling was overturned by the supreme court of *Thakurda*.

When I told all this to Patrick, he said no, my destiny was *not* that of a well frog. Nor a spinster. Because if he made it out of that hellhole alive, he wanted to marry me, and together, we would explore all of the earth.

Gulp.

With each letter I received, I sobbed with relief that he was alive, and I felt my heart being torn because I didn't know what I would do if he didn't make it. Or what I'd do if he did.

"Cross that bridge when you come to it," advised Colleen, his sister and my American best friend.

When the time finally came, when at long last Patrick

came home, I flew right over that bridge and into his awaiting arms.

"You're the reason I'm alive," he said, on one knee on his parents' porch, with his family peeking out the windows. "You kept me going. You gave me hope. You saved my life. I came back for you, Uma. If that isn't fate, I don't know what is. Marry me. Please. Be my wife."

I couldn't say no. After all we'd been through together... I didn't *want* to say no.

There's a Bengali expression: *Tumi bina ke achhe amar?* Who is there for me without you?

"I have to see your horoscope," I said.

Patrick agreed, not so much because *he* believed, but out of respect for *my* beliefs—one of the many, many reasons I love and admire this man—and we covertly arranged for his chart, which is prepared by taking the date, time, and place of birth and mapping the planets' positions.

When we met with the astrologer in New York City, my heart hitched into my throat.

You remember what I told you about me being a *manglik*? Well, there is a catch. If one spouse is a *manglik*, it's bad news. However, it's neutralized if *both* spouses are *mangliks*. According to every astrologer my family consulted, their best chance at marrying me off was to hope for another *manglik*.

Patrick, as it turns out, is a *manglik*, too.

"If that isn't fate," I said, "I don't know what is."

In San Francisco, my husband and I sit across from our daughter and son-in-law in the living room of their posh two-bedroom condo. A wilting sunflower, Rani sags against Bryan, drooping her head on his shoulder. "Do we have to go to the Chawlas' New Year's Eve party?" she asks, causing Patrick and myself to exchange glances.

"Well, that answers that question," Patrick says. "Yes, you *can* still land a plane on Boo's lower lip." Boo, short for Boo-Boo, is our nickname for Rani. From the time she was an infant, her pout wrapped us around her little finger. Patrick called it her "boo-boo face."

Bryan glances down at her. "What's wrong, hon? You love New Year's at the Chawlas'."

Rani shrugs. "I just thought maybe we could do something different this year."

"Like what?" I ask.

"Stay home. Order takeout. Rent movies. You know, Q.T. with the fami-ly."

"Umm-hmm . . ." I stare at her, waiting.

"I'm socialized out," she says, "after the exhibit and all."

"Umm-hmm . . ."

She plucks imaginary lint from Bryan's sweater. "The last thing I need is two dozen aunties pestering me about children."

Aha. The truth comes out. I can't suppress a tiny chuckle.

Rani frowns. "You could *pretend* to be sympathetic, Mom."

"Sorry, *shonu*, but you think your aunties' pestering is bad here. You have no idea how bad it would be in India, where it's inconceivable a couple would *choose* not to have children."

"I know. I know," she says. "But I'm tired of having to explain and defend my reproductive choices. It's not just the aunties. Everyone asks these days. You start pushing thirty, and perfect strangers feel it's their right to inquire. And to offer unsolicited advice."

"It's your call," I say. "If you don't want to go to the party, you don't have to."

"Thank—"

"But Dad and I are going."

"Oh. Well. Of course..."

"The food alone," I say. "No way can we miss out on that."

Over her head, Bryan winks. "You realize denying me Saroj Auntie's buffet is cruel and unusual punishment, don't you?"

I love my son-in-law. Patrick and I couldn't have chosen a better husband for Rani if we handpicked him and arranged their marriage ourselves.

"Hey, Bryan can go with Mom, and I'll stay home with Boo," Patrick says.

I shake my head. "I don't think so."

"Yeah, nice try, Dad, but *you're* going," Rani says. "*And* you're going to dance with Mom."

He makes a face. "You want to talk cruel and unusual..." Patrick doesn't have many shortcomings; this is one of them. He hates to dance—a staple of Chawla parties, along with excellent cuisine. He and Meenal typically sit on the sidelines and watch. "I'm not going if you're not going." Patrick laces his fingers behind his neck, his elbows wide, and stares up at the ceiling.

Rani laughs and rolls her eyes. "What is this, a pouting contest?"

Patrick sticks out his lower lip in imitation; Bryan and I follow suit.

Rani gasps in mock outrage. "Gang up on me, why don't you? Okay, fine. I move, we *all* go to the party. Happy now?" At our resounding noises and gestures of affirmation, she pretends to scribble on her palm, then holds it out. "The secretary notes three *yes* votes from the colluding trio. One abstention. The motion passes. Chawlas', here we come."

The following afternoon, we go to the art gallery where Rani's work hangs on exhibit. Patrick and I wanted so badly to attend the opening, but now we get our own V.I.P. private tour. And what a tour it is.

"Boo, this is incredible." Patrick's deep voice vibrates with a father's pride.

I, too, feel my heart swell. "You have a gift, sweetie. Saraswati definitely blessed you." I refer to the goddess of knowledge and the fine arts, gesturing around us in awe. "*This* from the girl who was scolded for drawing on the walls at home and constantly doodling during class." Rani's teachers thought she wasn't paying attention, but every time they called on her, she shocked them by answering the question correctly. I smile, half musing to myself, "Isn't it funny to look back and see how the signs of our personalities are there, right from the start? With Rani, the writing was literally *all over* the walls."

"You really like it?" Rani asks, and it pleases me that our opinion still means something to her, that she still asks for it. Even if she ignores our advice as often as she follows it.

"We really do," I say, and Patrick nods.

She crooks a lopsided grin and inspects her fingernails—short and ragged with chipped polish. "Well, it's not rocket science."

That draws chuckles all around.

"You would know," Bryan says, draping an arm around her.

Yes, she would. In case no one told you: Our celebrated artist holds an advanced degree in aerospace engineering, not art. In fact, Rani has little formal art education. Before pursuing her lifelong passion full time, she worked for NASA. A rocket scientist turned artist. Or, as she puts it, an artist masquerading as a rocket scientist.

I must admit I wasn't thrilled with the idea of her quitting her day job, abandoning a well-paid, respected career. I didn't understand why she couldn't continue to do her hobby on the side. But this was an issue where my vote didn't count, especially with Bryan's steadfast support and encouragement.

Patrick was Switzerland—neutral. She can always go back, he said.

I thought for sure she would. Especially when the bottom fell out of Bryan's company in the Silicon Valley dot-com bust. And now I find myself wondering again...

Last night we stayed up late chatting, just the two of us. Rani told me she's burned out. *Burnt to a crisp,* to be precise. Understandable, I said. She worked so hard that her creative well's run dry. Even as these words left my lips, alarm bells sounded. *Is it more than creative burnout?*

"Have you seen the doctor?" I asked. "Checked your meds?"

"Yes," Rani said. "No changes yet, but we'll follow up in another month. We agreed it's situational this time."

This time, as opposed to two previous times when she slipped into clinical depression—the first in high school, the second in college—due to chemical imbalances in her brain. The hereditary disease she inherited from me.

I always told her: *Look for the signs. Pay attention. No one will think less of you. This isn't India.*

"Good girl." I gave her hand a squeeze. "I'm so glad you went. You did the right thing."

"On that score. The jury's still out on this artist gig."

"Meaning?"

She shrugged. "Maybe you were right. I shouldn't have put all my eggs in one basket."

"Why do you say that?" *What's changed?*

She confessed that when her hobby became her career, it put a lot of pressure on her creativity she didn't have before. Art became more perspiration, less inspiration. And all this recent attention had been a mixed bag. Flattering and validating, yes. At the same time stifling.

"I feel people looking over my shoulder now, heaping more pressure, more expectations on top of my own," she said. "It's not just *me* and *my art* anymore. Right now, it's just me. No art." She slouched in a corner of the couch, hugging a cushion to her chest. "I can't believe I'm saying this, but I actually miss rocket science. A job where I could Just Do It. Instant gratification. Clock in. Do my work. Pass GO. Collect two hundred dollars."

I let her talk. I just listened.

"There's no certainty in art," she said. "You can spend your whole life working and reworking something, and never get it right, never pass GO, never collect two hundred. There's no surefire methodology you can follow. No process works every time. Success is *never* guaranteed. Even if you taste it once, that's no assurance for the future. Every day, every moment, you're back to square one."

Then she said it. The surrender I'd awaited.

"I don't think I'm cut out for being a full-time artist," she said. "My self-esteem can't handle the uncertainty, the constant failures. I think maybe I should go back to rocket science. It was a lot easier."

I should have been overjoyed. I wasn't.

I felt a strange apprehension, like indigestion churning in my stomach. Now I know why. Looking around the gallery, I see so clearly into my daughter's heart, her soul. The same way I did when I read my mother's journals, the poetry she scribbled and hid away from critical, judging eyes.

There's a reason God gives us the gifts we have, obstacles that test us and force us to grow; our strengths, weaknesses, opportunities, threats. For the first time, I can see enough dots to connect them. I realize I don't want Rani to go back.

I want her to go forward.

I often wonder what unknown fallacies today's societies accept as truth, what cultural norms our future generations will dispel as backward rubbish. Today I understand the science of sex determination and postpartum depression. It infuriates me that society automatically blamed the woman for not conceiving sons, when the man's sperm carries the Y chromosome. And for clinical depressions, as with most baffling illnesses before scientists discover a cure, it's heartbreaking to think: *One little pill might have saved Ma*. That is, if they could have gotten past the social stigmas of "mental illness" and "pill-popping" Western medicine.

I'm thankful to live in a different time and place now, thankful I married a man like Patrick. Though it cost me my father, I believe things happen as they are meant to happen. Everything happens for a reason. Patrick was meant to be my husband, and Rani my daughter.

I remember feeling so helpless watching *Ma* suffer, being powerless to do anything to help. Today I realize: I couldn't help my mother, but I *can* help my daughter.

Another chance for me.

And for her.

When we get home to our townhouse in Old Town Alexandria, Rani goes straight up to bed. Her room is exactly the way she left it. Aside from occasional dusting, vacuuming, and airing out, we don't touch it.

On the wall opposite the bed, she painted movie-screen-sized brown eyes, lush eyelashes, upper lids lined with black kohl, and a ruby *bindi* set between arched brows. Depending on the angle (and my mood), the eyes appear happy or melancholy, hopeful or despondent, seductive or innocent. But always, the eyes watch me. Wherever I am in the bedroom. Wherever I move. It creeps me out at times. I don't know how Rani—or Bryan!—can sleep, or do anything else, with those eyes watching.

"I feel like such a loser," Rani says, pulling the covers up to her chin.

I sit beside her on her bed, my back to the Enigmatic Eyes. "You're *not* a loser. You're drained. That's all."

"Uh-huh. I couldn't hack it as a full-time artist." She forms an *L* with her thumb and index finger and drops her hand over her forehead. "Loser."

"Stop that." I tug her wrist. "You're way too hard on yourself. Do you remember all the times I told you depression isn't some indulgence of the weak? A chemical imbalance is a chemical imbalance? That big, clever brain of yours needed to get recalibrated, and it *would*? The same concepts apply here. Your battery's dead. Out of juice. It happens. You need to recharge, and you *will*."

"I don't know . . ."

"Okay, tell me something. A genie pops out of a bottle and grants you one wish for the career of your choice. The opinions of others, talent, money—none of that matters. There are no obstacles. Success is guaranteed. Now, what career would you choose?"

"An artist," she says without hesitation.

"There's your answer—"

"In an ideal world."

"So art isn't the easy road you thought it would be. So what? If it's the road you want, make it work. Fight for it. Easier said than done, I know. But I also know you can do it. You can, Rani. I have faith in you. Have faith in yourself."

My daughter looks at me as if I've grown two heads. "I don't believe you're saying this. *You*."

"I had an epiphany at the gallery."

Hope and fear war in Rani's eyes. "Mom . . . ?" she says in a small voice. "*You* tell *me* something. What if it doesn't work? What if I try and try, and the magic's gone forever and never comes back? If I'm a washed-up artist, a *has-been*? Will you still love me?"

I don't reassure her those things aren't going to happen. That's not what she needs to hear. I smooth her hair from her forehead. "Yes, my Boo-Boo. I will love you, no matter what."

"Even if I don't go back to rocket science?"

"Even if you don't go back to rocket science."

"If I don't have kids and just stay home and eat bonbons all day?"

I smile. "If that's what you want to do with your life."

She smiles, too. A crooked grin that makes my heart turn over. "Thanks, Mom. You're the best."

"No, just Top Ten," I tease. We hug. "Come down," I say. "Grab a bite. I've made your favorite *shorshe salmon maachh*." Salmon in mustard sauce.

"Thanks, but I'm not hungry yet."

"Not even for *chingri maachher malai* curry?" Prawns in coconut curry, another of her favorites.

"Not yet, thanks."

This is her standard answer, and it worries me. "Rani, I understand that you don't have much of an appetite, but you're losing too much weight."

"Not this again."

"Yes, this again. You know the drill. You have to eat. Put something in your stomach. Not a nine-course meal but at least a little. Even if you aren't hungry."

"Later, please."

"How about a walk, then? It's a gorgeous day. Sunny and—"

"Mom." She groans—long and loud—and rolls away from me. "I'm tired."

"You can nap *later*. Come on, let's get up. You've slept enough. It's almost noon now." I pat her bottom. "Let's get some fresh air."

"Let's not and say we did."

"Rani." I use my sternest voice. "Do you want me to get your husband and father up here?"

"Moth-er! That is *so* not fair, calling in reinforcements. You play dirty."

I'll play any way I have to for you.

"Up. Up." I tug the covers off her, step back, and cross my arms. Good thing Bryan and Patrick aren't here. Her kicked-puppy whimper could bring the strongest man to his knees. But a mother endures what she has to for the sake of her children.

Rani gets up like an arthritic old lady. When I hug her, she sags against me. "Did I mention how much depression sucks?" she says into my shoulder.

"I know, sweetie, but we'll get through it. Together as a family. I promise you it *will* get better. Just don't give up." I pull back, raise Rani's chin with my curved index finger, and hold her gaze. "Don't *ever* give up."

"I won't," she says, her eyes solemn. "I'll never do that to you again."

Oh, my sweet, intuitive girl. I hug her again, tightly. She, too, knows the reassurance *I* need to hear.

My daughter has my mother's eyes. Undoubtedly you'll think I'm crazy when I tell you it's more than mere resemblance I see. But then, that's what everyone thought about *Ma*.

It is said the eyes are windows to the soul, and from the moment I first held Rani, I glimpsed in the depths of her gray newborn eyes my mother's soul.

I might have dismissed it, if that's all there was to it. But that was only the beginning....

From birth, Rani's had an almost phobic aversion to anything around her neck, fear of strangulation. I've never told her how exactly *Ma* died, only that her death resulted from complications after childbirth.

As a teen, in addition to doodling, Rani jotted conflicted, suicidal verses in the margins of her school notebooks. One may find her scribbling reminiscent of Sylvia Plath—many phrases are verbatim from *Ma*'s tablets, written in Bengali script that Rani cannot read.

When Patrick and I awoke one Saturday to find our rebellious fifteen-year-old lying beside a pool of her vomit from swallowing a bottle of sleeping pills, I surrendered, opening my mind to *all* possibilities. Reincarnation. Clinical depression. Therapy. With my daughter's life at stake, I no longer had the luxury to be a skeptic, to cling to false pride.

Though we don't speak of this incident outside our family—it's no one's business but ours—inside our family, everything changed from that point on.

In family counseling, we learned that I was a significant contributing factor to Rani's suicide attempt. Until then, I'd always reprimanded her for answering back. I come from a land where dissent means disrespect; therefore in the name of Respect to Elders, I conditioned my daughter to bite back any words that questioned my authority. I forced her into submission, the mold of a good Indian daughter and my duty as a good Indian mother, I believed. But the words I prohibited? They didn't vanish into thin air; they accumulated, as voices trapped inside her head, screaming ever louder for release. Like *Ma*.

The guilt of what I caused, however unintentional, almost did *me* in. Our tiny family could easily have fallen apart that year. Instead, we pulled together. Forgave each other. Took pains to try to understand others' viewpoints. We learned to communicate as a family. How to talk, how to listen, how to dissent, and how to accept dissent. *I* learned to guide Rani without gagging or straitjacketing her.

Meenal and Saroj were none too pleased with the drastic change in my child-rearing practices, and they weren't alone. Disapproval came at me from both sides: Indian friends questioned my Western attitudes, and American friends questioned my Eastern beliefs. But none of them ever walked in my mismatched shoes—one *chappal* paired with one sneaker—and I refused to succumb to peer pressure. Society's ignorance, closed-mindedness, killed *Ma*. I wouldn't let that happen again, to Rani.

From the outside looking in, one might say—and many did—that I let my daughter go wild. Call it whatever you want, but from where I stand, I let my daughter express herself. As long as she wasn't hurting anyone, or herself, I refused to trap her in her own skin. Never again did I want her to feel she had to escape the prison of her body and her only way out was to take her life. Never again would *I* be a contributing factor with my actions or inactions.

I believe Rani is *Ma*'s reincarnation. I believe she is destined to face in this lifetime the same tests she failed in the last. I believe that's true of us all. Our eternal souls are reborn in different mortal bodies until we get it right.

Scoff if you must, but history has proven time and again that one person's religion is another's superstition, and one person's superstition is another's science. What's truth and what's *maya*—illusion? Time will tell.

FROM: "Uma Basu" <ubasu@gwu.edu>

TO: Meenal Deshpande; Saroj Chawla

SENT: December 29, 20XX 09:52 AM

SUBJECT: Here I am . . .

Dearest Meenal and Saroj,

My apologies for not writing sooner. We had a great time in SF. Home now. Rani and Bryan are with us. Bryan must return to work after the New Year. I'm trying to convince Rani to stay through January since I'm on sabbatical next semester. Rani could use a sabbatical, too, and my project -- translating her grandmother's writings -- might benefit her.

It's so wonderful to have the kids home. I know we say this all the time, but it bears repeating: They grow up too fast! Wasn't it just yesterday we were their age???

Warmest wishes,
Uma

FROM: "Meenal Deshpande" <dil_MD1@yahoo.com>

TO: Uma Basu; Saroj Chawla

SENT: December 29, 20XX 12:19 PM

SUBJECT: RE: Here I am. . .

Uma, YES!!!!! It is SO wonderful to have the kids home!!! :) Fingers crossed Rani will stay on thru January. Give her our love, and if you need any arm-twisting, just holler.

Meenal

FROM: "Saroj Chawla"
<Saroj@ChawlaCatering.com>

TO: Uma Basu; Meenal Deshpande

SENT: December 29, 20XX 1:30 PM

SUBJECT: RE: Here I am. . .

Yes, they do grow up way too fast, yet in some ways, they remain children even as adults. Is it only because we're their mothers that we see this???

Lately I'm afraid that in trying to protect my children from the ugliness I've seen in this world, I sheltered them too much. :(We came to this country to give our children better lives and opportunities than WE had in India, but there were trade-offs. . .

Despite my angel daughter's vastly superior intelligence, her privileged education, and the enviable social charms that she gets from her mother (hahaha!), the little Disney Princess I brought up in this Land of Milk & Money is out of touch with reality sometimes. Certain "facts of life" elude her grasp. Nothing I say makes any difference. Sigh.

OK, different subject . . . Uma, what goodies shall I send for Rani? Kiran wanted samosas. How about Rani? Does she still like chickpeas? Preity's come up with another crazy culinary fusion, Chhole Caesar Salad (!). Rani might like it. Grated paneer in place of parm, too. Want to try it?

Chalo, back to work . . .

Saroj

FROM: "Uma Basu" <ubasu@gwu.edu>
TO: Saroj Chawla; Meenal Deshpande
SENT: December 29, 20XX 04:43 PM
SUBJECT: RE: Here I am . . .

Dearest Saroj,

I've been mulling over your email all afternoon. I understand all too well the frustration of trying to communicate a message that isn't getting through. I also understand the helplessness of being unable to lock your precious princess up in her Ivory Tower and wear the key on your palloo like we could in India <g>, so she doesn't learn the hard way what a LONG drop down it is.

I tell myself that I can't prevent Rani from getting hurt, but I can prepare her as best I can, and I can be there for her when it happens, as it inevitably will. I can be a safe place for her, always. Even if it's just having a ready hug and a kiss and a shoulder to cry on. That's what I did when she was 3, and I'm still doing it at 30.

All that said, I respectfully submit the following for your consideration:

1) "The Facts of Life" constitute material, physical reality;
2) Perhaps Preity's world view is the TRUTH, and yours is the ILLUSION.

Just something to ponder. And if you aren't hurling rotten tomatoes at me, Rani says she'd LOVE to try Preity's Chhole Caesar Salad!

Yours affectionately,
Uma

FROM: "Meenal Deshpande" <dil_MD1@yahoo.com>

TO: Uma Basu; Saroj Chawla

SENT: December 29, 20XX 06:05 PM

SUBJECT: RE: Here I am . . .

Uma, before this year, I would have been first in line to throw rotten tomatoes. Today, you've managed to take my breath away. My dearest Bengali friend, you embody Gopal Krishna Gokhale's: "What Bengal thinks today, the rest of India thinks tomorrow." :)

For obvious reasons, I've thought a lot about "material, physical reality vs. ultimate reality" this year. The body and mind are conditioned/ contained by our physical reality (ILLUSION). The spirit is boundless, aware of all possibilities, the ultimate reality (TRUTH). Thus the saying, "From the mouths of babes . . ." Babies come to us unconditioned spirits. We condition them to our reality, but who is wiser to the TRUTH?

I'll stop now, before Saroj thinks we're ganging up on her. :)

Saroj, I've been trying to call you. Preity said you're running errands. Either your cell phone is off, or you aren't taking my calls. Hmmm . . . which is it?

Meenal

FROM: "Saroj Chawla" <Saroj@ChawlaCatering.com>
TO: Uma Basu; Meenal Deshpande
SENT: December 29, 20XX 7:11 PM
SUBJECT: RE: Here I am...

Uma, aren't you the clever one? You KNEW I would throw rotten tomatoes if I HAD any, but since Chawla Catering uses only the freshest ingredients, you're safe!! Hahaha!!

Meenal, sooo sorry I missed your call. I was at the supermarket and forgot to switch on my cell. Will try you later, traitor. ;)

What's one to do when her two best friends abandon her in samsara while they proceed to vanaprastha??

Saroj

FROM: "Uma Basu" <ubasu@gwu.edu>
TO: Meenal Deshpande; Saroj Chawla
SENT: December 29, 20XX 08:59 PM
SUBJECT: RE: Here I am...

Dearest Meenal, you've leapfrogged this Bengali. I hope you know what an inspiration you have been, and continue to be, to us all.

Dearest Saroj, you live it up, that's what you do! And no one does it better than you -- you, too, are an inspiration to all -- so take a well-deserved bow!

Looking forward to celebrating another Happy New Year with you, my cherished friends,

Uma

Uma's Ghee Bhat

[Rice Pilaf with Clarified Butter]

SERVES 4–6

1½ cups basmati rice

2 tablespoons ghee or unsalted butter or canola oil

2 bay leaves

8 whole green cardamom pods

1 3-inch cinnamon stick

3 whole cloves

¼ cup unsalted raw cashews

¼ cup golden raisins

¾ teaspoon salt (adjust to taste)

½ teaspoon sugar (adjust to taste)

2¼ cups water

1. In a colander in the sink, rinse rice under tepid water until water runs clear.
2. Transfer rice to a bowl. Fill with cold water, submerging rice by 3 inches. Soak 30 minutes. Drain.
3. In a wok or deep 12-inch skillet, heat ghee over medium-low heat.
4. Add bay leaves, cardamom pods, cinnamon, and cloves. Sauté for 1 minute.
5. Add cashews and raisins. Sauté for a few seconds.
6. Stir in salt, sugar, and rice. Sauté until rice begins to brown, about 3 minutes.
7. Add water. Increase heat to high and bring to boil. Cover and reduce heat to low. Simmer until water is absorbed and rice is tender, about 15–20 minutes.
8. Sprinkle rice with warm melted ghee. Fluff grains with a fork, removing cloves and cardamom pods. Serve hot.

Ghee [Clarified Butter]

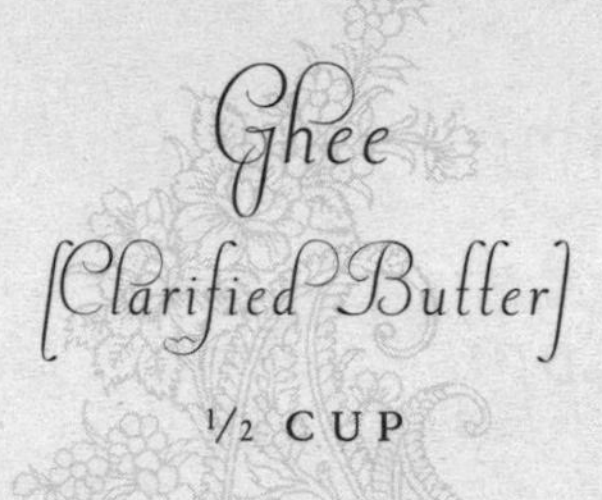

½ CUP

2 sticks unsalted butter

1. Cut butter into 1-inch slices.
2. In a heavy saucepan over medium heat, bring to a boil.
3. When foam covers butter, reduce heat to lowest possible setting.
4. Simmer, stirring occasionally, until butter separates into milky-white solids and fat, about 8 minutes.
5. Stir constantly until butter turns golden/translucent and sediment at bottom turns golden brown, about 3 minutes. When bubbling stops, remove from heat.
6. Line a colander with 4 layers of dampened cheesecloth. Place over a glass jar. Pour butter into cheesecloth, straining ghee from sediment. Discard sediment.
7. Repeat straining process until all sediment is extracted and discarded.
8. Store in glass jar or bottle with a shaker top.

Ghee keeps at room temperature for 2 months.

Kiran Deshpande: Happy New Year

Yesterday is but a dream
And tomorrow is only a vision;
But today well lived makes
Every yesterday a dream of happiness
And every tomorrow a vision of hope.
Look well, therefore, to this day!

KALIDASA

At the Chawlas' New Year's Eve party, Sandeep Uncle meets and greets arriving guests at the door. Assorted kids shuttle coats upstairs. As my father helps my mother out of her coat, Preity appears at the top of the wide curving staircase.

"Meenal Auntie!" She picks up the hem of her full-length black velvet skirt and glides down to the foyer like royalty, jewels dripping from her earlobes, neck, and wrist, her arms extended to receive my mother. "You look beautiful! What a lovely *sari*!" gushes the Queen of Suck-Up.

My mother smiles, brown eyes sparkling under the crystal chandelier. "Do you like it?"

"I love it! Lavender is your color. Classy, like you."

Barf tray. Stat.

Mom's face goes all soft and mushy. "Still as sweet as ever, aren't you?" She cups Preity's cheeks with both hands, makes a kissing sound.

Chubby cheeks, I notice. Underneath her long flowing tunic and skirt, Little Miss Perfect's becoming Little Miss Butterball. There *is* some justice in this world.

Preity drones on about the damn *sari*—you know, on the off chance her nose isn't brown enough. "I've never seen this kind of print..."

"It's a Rajasthani design called *bhandhani,* meaning tie-dye. I'm told it's made a recent comeback in popularity, all the rage these days."

"Oooh, Meenal Auntie." She winks. "You fashion diva, you."

Mom laughs. "Right, that's me. Fashion-Diva Auntie."

Are we done yet?

I'm aware such immaturity on my part is highly unbecoming, especially for a woman of my age and (supposed) accomplishments, but there you have it. Preity Chawla Lindstrom brings out the worst in me. Always has. Always will.

My father and Sandeep Uncle have been chatting until now. Sandeep Uncle clears his throat and says, "Preity, aren't you forgetting someone?" He gives my father a He-Man clap on the back.

Preity flashes her orthodontically impeccable Miss World smile, her arms outstretched. "I can never forget you, Yash Uncle."

I'm next in her reception line. Still hugging my father, she meets my eyes, smiles, raises a hand in greeting. I do the same, forcing my smile to stay in place. Our turn comes. With the parental units watching us expectantly, we shuffle toward each other, exchange perfunctory stiff hugs and stiffer small talk.

"So good to see you," she says.

"You, too. Is Rani here yet?"

"Downstairs. You have to see the new dance floor."

"That's right. I heard."

"Tarun and his roommate are deejays for the night."

With the lull in arriving guests, Sandeep Uncle asks Preity to take over meet-and-greet duty and turns to my parents. "Come, we'll leave the girls to catch up."

Thanks, Sandeep Uncle. I owe you one.

"What are you drinking tonight?" he asks. "Meenal, I have San Pellegrino just for you." He wedges between my parents and drapes a casual arm around my mother.

She turns as if to say something to me or Preity, breaking the contact. She opens her mouth, pauses, gestures *never mind*, and smiles sweetly. Turning back, she tucks her hand into the crook of my dad's arm and glides into step with him.

"Smooth," Preity says with admiration.

I nod. "Very smooth."

"Meenal Auntie hasn't lost her touch."

"Neither has Sandeep Uncle."

Everyone knows that Sandeep Uncle's an incorrigible flirt. He's the ham of the Indian friends circle. My mother, however, is the Guru of Covert Evasion.

"Remember that plaque in Uma Auntie's kitchen?" Preity says. "From Patrick Uncle's sister? *'Irish Diplomacy: The ability to tell a man to go to hell in such a way that he looks forward to making the trip.'* Meenal Auntie must've been Irish in a former life."

Isn't it interesting to see how others view your parents?

Not often the way you do. I wonder, if my parents saw me in my element—my world, not theirs—would they, too, notice the difference in the way others view me? My father, especially. . . .

A (balding) Nordic God materializes at Preity's side. He sports a red-and-black sweater and black slacks and appears as though he's stepped out of the pages of a J.Crew catalog. "Hi, you must be Kiran." He puts one arm around Preity. With the other, he offers a hand to me.

"And you must be Ken—er, *Eric*. I knew that, sorry." I thump the side of my head before shaking his hand. "Too many names on the brain at these parties."

"Yeah, no kidding. Preity tells me when in doubt, just say Uncle and Auntie." He smiles. Nice smile. Confident handshake. Strong without breaking my hand. "Nice to finally meet you."

"Same here." *Thank you for not saying you've heard a lot about me.*

"Mommy! Mommy!" A little boy runs up and wraps himself around Preity's legs. He wears spiffy black-and-cream cotton *kurta-pajamas* embroidered with red, green, and gold threads. Jumping, he says, "I want jingle bells, too!"

"You can't," says a little girl in a watermelon-pink-and-green-apple *ghagara-choli*. "You're a *boy*." She wears a dozen glass bangles and silver anklets with bells. Her French braid bounces as she hops, jostling her arms and tinkling with every move.

"Lina, be nice to your brother. Don't worry, bud. We'll figure something out. I'll bet *Nanaji* can rig his wind chimes for you. Eric, will you get Dad for me, please? I think he's downstairs. Tell him Jack and I require his services A.S.A.P."

"You bet." Eric takes off.

Lina's brows perk up with interest as she looks after her father. "Wind chimes?"

"It's for boys," Jack says. "Not girls."

"Nuh-uh."

"Yeah-huh."

"Mommy." Both turn to Preity for backup.

"Enough," Preity says. "Lina, you already jingle. Jack, you're *going* to jingle. Now, if you two can't be nice to each other, I'm going to take away *all* the jingles from both of you. Understand?" They nod, eyes wide. "No more whining?" More nodding. "Okay, how about you show some manners, then? Say hello to Kiran Auntie."

My hand flutters to my throat. "*Kiran Auntie*... Wow..."

Preity laughs. "First time you're hearing that?" At my nod, she says, "You get used to it. But, yeah, I remember the first time I heard *Preity Auntie*. Right up there with being called *ma'am* for the first time. Makes you want to reach for your walking stick and Centrum Silver, doesn't it?"

"*Auntie*'s not so bad. *Ma'am* definitely gave me the heebie-jeebies." I shudder and rub my arms. "But *auntie* has a ring to it. Kiran Auntie..." I test it out. Let it roll off my tongue. "Kiran Auntie..."

"Kiran Auntie!" Lina says.

"Kiran Auntie!" Jack joins in.

My heart turns over. Squeezes painfully. Her children are precious; her husband still looks at her like she's a svelte sex kitten when she's obviously battling the bulge (and losing). I may have to kill her. I'm a doctor; I know of many ways. Fast and painless. Long and agonizing. Untraceable...

Sandeep Uncle comes around the corner, dangling wind

chimes, and the kids squeal and take off with grandpa, leaving Preity and me staring at each other again.

That's two I owe you, Sandeep Uncle.

"Kiran, I . . ." From Preity's tone alone, I don't like where this is going. "I just heard about Meenal Auntie. I'm so sorry. I had no idea. I didn't know what to say when I saw her, thought I'd better ask you before I stuck my foot in my mouth. Should I say something to her or avoid the topic?"

"Avoid it tonight," I say. "But give her a call before you leave. She'd like that."

Preity nods. "I would have called you. If I'd known."

"That's probably why no one told you, either."

"Kiran, I . . ." She frowns and takes a breath.

Please, no. Whatever it is, just keep it to yourself.

"I know we never really got along," she says, "but I'm hoping we can move past that. You know, *we're* aunties now."

Read: We shouldn't still behave as children.

"If there's anything I can do . . . Anything at all . . ." Preity reaches out, squeezes my arm.

Cooties! I want to shriek and run from the room.

"I'm here," she says. "I want you to know that."

Can I just say sympathy from a rival, even a childhood rival, is the pits? It is. The absolute pits. And it sucks that much worse when it's genuine, from the heart. As with Preity. The bitch. Why can't she lower herself, stoop to my level? Is it too much to ask for her to be catty like other estrogen-charged females? How the hell am I supposed to fight with someone who won't fight me back? What kind of lame-ass rivalry is that? Does she care nothing for tradition?

"Thanks," I mumble.

"Oh, there's Tarun!" Preity flags down her brother. "T, look who's here!"

"Hey! Kiran!"

"Hey yourself, Little T!"

"Not so little anymore." He scoops me off the ground, my legs dangling. "Six foot."

"Doesn't matter," I say. "You'll always be little in my book."

He laughs. "Like Little John. He wasn't little, either."

"Exactly."

"T, are you headed down? Will you show Kiran the new digs?" Preity preempts my own request. "And see if you can find Rani. Go on, I'll catch up. I'm going to see if Mom needs any help. . . ."

Grateful for the opportunity to exit stage left, I toss a glance over my shoulder. "See you . . ." *Wouldn't want to be you,* I think, wrapping my immaturity around me, a ratty, moth-eaten security blanket. But of course that's a lie—that I wouldn't want to be Preity—always has been, always will be.

The Chawlas finished their huge walk-out basement this year and relocated the traditional dance floor downstairs. Out the sliding glass door, a heated tent covers the brick patio and Saroj Auntie's lavish buffet. Tarun and roommate Jeb, a law school buddy, are in charge of tunes. In addition to *bhangra*—hip Indian dance music, kinda like Indian disco—they lined up music videos to show on the (new) projection and wide-screen televisions. Little T tells me they made a mix of MTV, VH-1, and *filmi* videos (song-and-dance numbers from Bollywood musicals). Add to this, flashing colored and strobe lights. All that's missing is a disco ball.

When she spots me, Rani screams. Runs over. Throws her arms around my neck. Kisses me soundly on the cheek. On her breath, I smell a hint of peppermint.

"Schnapps?" I ask.

"Yep," she says. "Preity spiked a thermos of hot chocolate. Want some?"

"Not yet, thanks."

"I was freezing when I got here. Now I'm broiling. But enough about me. What's this I hear about an arranged second marriage?"

I laugh. "*Semi*-arranged, and why am I not surprised you already heard?"

"Word travels fast on the Hindi-Bindi Express."

"Does it ever!"

"So tell, tell." Rani wiggles her fingers. "Give up the goods. Inquiring minds want to know and all. Details, woman."

I grasp her fingers. "Later, later."

"Fine. Make me wait. But it's gonna cost you. Come on, let's dance." She tugs my hand.

"Oh, no." I snatch back my hand. "Nonono. Where's your darling husband?"

"Upstairs, losing his darling shirt at *teen pathi*." (The Indian equivalent of poker.) She takes aim for my hand again, but I'm faster.

"Rani, you know I don't—"

"You're going to tonight. I won't take no for an answer. We already have your mom and my dad holding up the wall. That wall doesn't need any more help, believe me."

Sure enough, my mom and Patrick Uncle have assumed their customary positions, standing against the wall and chatting. Rani takes me by the arm and drags me onto the dance floor, shaking her hips and pointing her index fingers in the air (I wasn't kidding about the disco reference) to the beat of some incomprehensible Hindi song.

Rani's always had amazing rhythm. And I've always had an amazing lack thereof.

You won't see dancing at our house. My parents are sedate people; Deshpande parties are sedate affairs. But Saroj Auntie and Sandeep Uncle are as over-the-top as my parents are sticks-in-the-mud. Auntie and Uncle embody *masti*, as they call it. A zest for life.

"Rani, I can't dance like this."

"You can, and you will."

"It's not in my genetic code."

"You do *not* want to get into nature versus nurture with me. You will not win. Now, watch. I had private lessons with Saroj Auntie earlier." She demonstrates dance steps. "Imagine you're picking up fairy dust and tossing it. Pick it up. Toss it." She gestures with a dainty flourish of her hands. "Pick up. Toss. See. Easy. You try."

"Maybe after a drink, or three—"

"Would you stop with the analysis-paralysis and just do it with me? Come on. Gather, sprinkle. Gather, sprinkle. Wheee! Isn't it a trip?"

I flip her the bird as I try not to trip over my own feet.

Right foot crosses left. Stomp. Pretend to pick up fairy dust on left.

Uncross. Stomp. Pretend to sprinkle fairy dust high into the air to your right.

"There you go ... That's it ... Accentuate your fingers ... Good ... Now, to the beat ..."

Beat-beat. Beat-beat. Pick-up. Toss-out.

I smile through my teeth. "I hate you, you know."

"I know." She puckers her lips, blows me a kiss.

Rani McGuiness Tomashot was the girl who could sell, or at least rent, a native New Yorker the Brooklyn Bridge.

And I don't remember the last time I had such a blast.

Uma Auntie comes up to us. "Hello, girls. Having fun, I see. Glad you came, hmmm?" she asks Rani in a rhetorical tone.

"Yes, Mother. You were right."

Uma Auntie shrugs and teases, "It happens."

"Yeah, waaay too often, if you ask me."

With a wink, Uma Auntie dances away, rejoining some aunties.

"I've been a party pooper lately," Rani says in explanation. "Lucky you, I snapped out of it tonight."

"Lucky me."

When we take a break to chug some water, our hearts pumping, brows sweating, I ask Rani, "Who are they?" *They* being the fun, fashionable, outgoing newbies cutting it up on the dance floor. Though they appear to be in Rani's and my age group, I'm certain I haven't seen them before. I would remember.... The chicks are decked out in modern, ultra-hip *salwar-kameezes*, *ghagara-cholis*, and *saris* and shake their booties as if styling the latest club-wear! "I've always thought of *saris* as graceful, elegant ..."

"Matronly?" Rani offers.

"Yes! *Sexy* isn't a word that's ever come to *my* mind before because, you know ..."

She nods. "You associate *saris* with aunties and grandmas."

"Right! But these *bindi*-babes... The way they move..."

Rani smiles. "They make *saris* look downright hot!"

"Exactly!" I say in amazement. *"Who knew?"*

We laugh.

"Now, before you try this at home," Rani says, "be warned they've had a *lot* more practice than we have. They're the *New* Hindi-Bindi Club. Hindi-Bindi, Next Generation? Hindi-Bindi Babes? Hmmm, I wonder what *their* kids will nickname them...."

"Oh! I thought—" Realization dawns. They're the *recent* Indian immigrants. "So *theeeese* are our infamous counterparts. The good Indian girls we 'would have been,' 'should have been,' 'ought to be,' take your pick." The only people on the planet with whom my parents compared me even more than Perfect Preity. *If we'd stayed in India... If you'd been brought up in India*... I narrow my gaze, study the *bindi*-babes closer. *"Our nemeses."*

"You got it." Rani leans against me, shoulder to shoulder, folding her arms in contemplation. "Here we have live, in-the-flesh specimens of that rare, endangered species. She represents the impossible. Sets standards you can never live up to. Why? Because you've been corrupted by the West. Americanized. That's right... she is... none other than... *the Good Indian Girl*." Rani arches an eyebrow. "Now observe, if you will, doctor. Tell me, do you see what I see?"

I squint. "I'm not sure. What?"

"Aha! It's a trick question. She-*ji* isn't, in fact, all that different from you-*ji* or me *ji*. Just more discreet."

"And a better dancer."

"Much." Rani nods. "Than you, you meant, right?"

I shove her with my shoulder. She shoves me back. We laugh. "You're still a goofball," I say as we head for the buffet, having worked up ravenous appetites.

"Takes one to know one," Rani says, not missing a beat.

"God, I missed you."

"Don't sound so surprised." She hands me a plate—rather, pokes it into my ribs. "I've been known to have that effect on people. It's rare, but it happens."

"And you have supporting documentation of this?"

"I do. Would you like to see it?"

"Sappy love letters from Bryan? No, thanks. I'll pass."

"Suit yourself."

Glancing across the room, my gaze collides with Preity's. We share that awkward moment of indecision when you don't know whether to maintain or break eye contact.

I hold her gaze. She looks away. For some reason, I keep looking, and in the space of a blink, she looks back. Her eyes register surprise—she didn't expect me to maintain the contact. When she smiles, hesitantly, I see myself reflected in her eyes as the jerk I am. Have been. Will be . . . ?

To be or not to be a jerk? That is the question.

"She's scared of you," Rani says.

"And I'm scared of *you*."

"You should be."

"Well, as long as we're all clear on the pecking order . . ." I wave Preity over.

She's in the middle of a circle of conversation, but she nods, signaling she'll join us when she can.

"You might like her better now that you're *all grown up*." Rani cracks herself up; I shake my head. "Seriously, can you believe you're *really* a doctor? Preity's *really* a corporate-suit-slash-budding-exec? I'm *really* a rocket scientist?"

"No. No. And hell, no."

"Did you meet Lina and Jack?"

"I did."

"Damn cute, huh?"

I nod. "In a big way. Speaking of which..." I tilt my head. "How about you and Bryan? Any plans—?"

"Aaaaah!" She wheezes. "*Et tu*, Bruté?"

I wince. "Oops. Sorry. Sore subject?"

"Very."

"Alrighty then..." I slink farther down the buffet line. "Butting out now..."

Rani sighs. "We can talk about it later."

"That's okay. We don't have to—"

"Actually, I could use a good rant. And you still owe me details. Preity *and* me." She smiles and wiggles her eyebrows. "Unless you want to take another twirl around the dance floor.... Saroj Auntie taught me another—"

"Uh, Rani?"

"Yes, Kiran?"

"Shut up and eat your *chhole*."

Her smile widens.

"Kiran, *pillu*?" My mom lays a hand on my shoulder. "I'm not going to last until midnight. Dad's taking me home. You have two offers. Saroj Auntie invited you to spend the night. Patrick Uncle offered to give you a ride home when they leave."

"I should go with you and Dad."

"No, no. Don't be silly. It's New Year's Eve. You stay. Have fun."

"But I'd rather be with you, Mom."

Her eyes soften. "Thank you, *pillu,* that's very sweet of you, but you won't be *with me* at home. I'll be fast asleep in bed."

And I'll be left with Dad. Alone.

"Okay, I'll stay. But not overnight. I'll bum a ride."

"Good girl."

I hug her before she goes. "Happy New Year, Mom. I love you."

"I love you, too, *Mummychi pillu.*" She kisses me on the cheek, smoothes my hair from my face, smiles. "Toast the New Year for me. It's going to be a good one. The best ever."

I nod, swallowing around the tightness in my throat. My mom hasn't called me *pillu* since I was in elementary school. I don't even know the exact definition. To me, the endearment means the equivalent of *little one*. That's how it makes me feel. Like my mother's little one again. In a good way.

A *very* good way.

Soon after midnight, Rani, Preity, and I slip away from the still-hopping party and hole up in the seclusion of the Florida room. Under the bright flashlight of the moon reflecting off the snow, we pass around a bag of marshmallows and a thermos of spiked hot chocolate, filling our Styrofoam cups and laughing at ourselves for still feeling like we're "getting away with something," even at our age.

"Just a heads-up," Rani says after I bring them up to speed on my semi-arranged marriage plans. "Beware of men who talk the talk but don't walk the walk."

Preity nods. "Don't assume because arranged marriage is a legit, respectable part of Indian culture, everyone's on the up-and-up. Ask my mom about her widow friend who was swept off her feet by this dashing smooth-talker. Turned out, he was just after her money. He had another wife back in the old country. He figured a lonely widow would be easy prey. Every culture has its snakes—venomous con artists and your garden-variety losers-who-can't-get-a-date—who pretend to be something they're not."

"Exactly," Rani says. "I have a friend. Beautiful, smart, the whole nine yards. Her career took off—I-banking, you know how that is—and with mergers and acquisitions up the ying-yang, she didn't have time to play the dating game. She checked out a popular matrimonial site and hooked up with a supposed 'doctor.' Everything was going great guns until her parents ran a routine background check. Turned out the guy didn't just stretch the truth, he was a *complete* fraud. Made up his *entire* identity."

"Wow," I say. "He was either really twisted, really lonely, or both."

"Moral of the story?" Rani says. "Verify all claims before you get in too deep with anyone."

"Good advice. Thank—"

Rani holds up a hand. "I'm not done, babe. Hang on to the thanks."

"But wait, there's more!" Preity teases.

"Now, allow me to preface this next bit by saying I'm *not*

making any generalizations here," Rani says. "I've just heard enough stories that I feel I have a fiduciary duty to give you advanced warning on something you *might* encounter."

I nod. "Forewarned is forearmed."

"Right. So. You may, just *may* encounter Indian immigrant men who come on way too strong, then end up being clueless when it comes to performance."

"And by 'performance,' we *are* talking—"

"In bed," Preity says before Rani can. "I've heard that, too."

"Why is that, do you think?" I ask.

"Inexperience," Preity says.

"But Bollywood, the *Kama-Sutra*—"

"There's *knowledge*, and there's *experience*," Rani says. "You go to med school—knowledge—then do your rotations and residency—experience. They might watch, and they might read, but they lack *hands-on* experience in the steps of our Western Mating Dance. The nuances of flirtation, seduction, kissing, lovemaking. Remember, dating's a fairly recent, cosmopolitan phenomenon in India, exclusive to younger generations. P.D.A.'s still taboo," she says regarding Public Displays of Affection. "Even the stuff we consider chaste, like pecks on the lips and holding hands."

"I have a theory," Preity says. "I don't have firsthand experience, mind you. All the Indian men I've encountered have been perfect gentlemen, but I do know others who've reported differently. I think this is because, by Eastern standards, Westerners can be perceived as loose."

"Can be?" I smile. "Preity, you should be a diplomat."

"She'd make a great diplomat," Rani says.

"Thank you," Preity says. "But we digress. My theory is

that some Indians, particularly in the age groups ahead of us, believe an unmarried woman who has physical relations with the opposite sex is automatically . . . How shall I put this . . . ?"

"A slut?" Rani says.

"Um, maybe not an out-and-out slut. But definitely *of ill repute*."

I nod. "You're either a good girl or a bad girl. There's nothing in between. They have no real concept or understanding of the infinite spectrum between those two poles."

"Exactly," Preity says. "Girls only come in two flavors. Naughty and nice. If you put out, you're bad. If not, you're good. And in a two-toned world, when they equate a woman who drinks, dances, and/or dates with being easy, indiscriminate, they may come on too strong because they can't differentiate what's considered healthy, respectful sensuality in our society and what's offensive vulgarity. That's my take on it, anyway."

"Interesting," I say. "Very interesting."

"Still." Rani raises a finger. "Let's not lose sight of the common denominator here."

"Which is . . . ?" I ask.

With a fairy-dust-dispensing flourish of her hands, she says, "Men are like puppies. Most can be trained to correct undesired behavior, so if you find one that goes straight for your crotch or piddles on your shoes when he gets excited but otherwise shows good character, there may still be hope."

We laugh.

Preity raises her hand.

"What, are we in school, now?" I say. "Yes, you there. Little girl in the front row."

"I've been trying to wrap my brain around something,

and well, I could use your insight. You're both strong, independent women. Nonconformists. Free-thinkers. Would you agree?"

Rani and I look at each other, shrug, nod.

"Both of you also have a long history of, um, challenging your parents. Defying, if you will."

Rani exaggerates a yawn. "Any year now..."

I smile sweetly. "Spare us the formality and get to the point, would ya?"

"What I want to know is, did guilt ever enter the picture with either of you when you disobeyed your parents?"

"No," I say.

"Yes," Rani says at the same time. "Why? What's up *chez* Chawlas?"

Preity shakes her head. "I don't want to get into details, but suffice it to say, it's one of those trapped-between-a-rock-and-a-hard-place times, and I don't know what to do. I mean, I know what I should do, what I want to do, but man..." She holds her head in her hands. "It's the guilt. The guilt! How do you deal with the *guilt* of blatant defiance?"

I understand her reticence to disclose specifics. That's a limitation of family friendships, a reason Preity, Rani, and I could never be confidantes, why when we played Truth or Dare, Rani and I opted for dare, and Preity opted out. Opening up, exposing yourself, makes you vulnerable to a breach. There's always the risk one of us may, over the course of a lifetime, divulge what we know to another (a family member is the usual fear), who may, in turn, divulge to another, and so on. Better to err on the side of silence. Keep to yourself any sensitive info you wouldn't want getting around the friends circle—and coming back to bite you in the ass.

"Now there's your first problem," Rani says. "Do you have to be *blatant* in your defiance? Can't you be subtle? Or even sneaky?"

"Sneaky doesn't work for me. I'm not the sneaky type."

She got that right. The word *guileless* comes to mind.

"Okay, scratch sneaky. What about subtle?" Rani asks.

"How subtly can a person fart?"

I laugh, despite myself.

"Right. Scratch subtle."

"Which takes us back to the guilt factor," Preity says. "How do you deal with it?"

"Ancient Catholic secret," I whisper. "Confession."

"No," Rani says. "My father doesn't believe in confession, says you don't need a middleman with God. Likewise, I prefer to go directly to the source. If the problem's between my parents and me, then I'll talk it out with them. Shout it out. Pout. Cry. Apologize. Whatever it takes. For as long as it takes."

"What if you reach an impasse?" Preity says. "And there's no getting around it? Or have you always resolved—?"

"No, we've deadlocked lots of times. When I lived under their roof, they automatically won any stalemate. Since I've been on my own, we agree to disagree, shelve the subject, and move on," Rani says, matter-of-fact.

I look at Preity; she looks at me. Together we bust out laughing.

"Oh, man. That's a good one. A classic." I wipe tears from my eyes. *"Agree to disagree."*

"Shelve the subject and move on," Preity says. "Tell me another one."

Rani's gaze shifts between us. "O-kay, and that's funny because . . . ?"

"Because," I say, "it might work if your parents are Uma Auntie and Patrick Uncle, but it won't fly with mine."

"Amen, sister." Preity nods, solidarity from an uncommon source.

Rani just shrugs.

"So again, getting back to guilt," I say, curious myself now. "Let's say you agree to disagree and shelve the subject, but you still feel guilty? What then?"

"Yeah, does that ever happen?" Preity asks.

"It happens."

"And?"

"Well, my friends," Rani says, "I hate to break it to you, but sometimes, there's no magic cure-all. You have to learn to live with the pain. Think of it as the cost of doing business. The cost of being human."

"In other words," Preity says, "you're fucked." I expect her to say *pardon my French*, like she used to, but she doesn't.

"Pretty much," Rani says. "Sorry, Preity."

"Yeah, well, I suspected as much," Preity says. "I just wanted confirmation from someone who's been there, felt that." She draws her knees to her chest, tucking the hem of her long skirt under her feet.

Rani raises a hand. "Been there. Felt that. Got the T-shirt. Welcome to the club."

"Is there a secret handshake?" Preity tries to laugh it off, but she's just covering, I can tell.

"You, uh, want to talk about it, Preity?" I say. "I mean, your guilt, not the disagreement, if that's possible." I don't want her to think I'm trying to get the dirt or anything. I've just heard enough to recognize she's having a Victoria's Secret Dressing Room Moment of her own.

Preity shrugs. "I guess the thing of it is . . . I love my parents. I respect them, admire them. I can't easily dismiss their opinions. Not when they only want the best for me, when they love me more than life. I'm sure that sounds corny to you." She flicks her gaze at me. "But it's the truth. And when they love me that much, when they've struggled and sacrificed so much to provide for Tarun and me, to give us the Good Life, how can I let them down? I feel like a bad daughter, thumbing my nose at them. That's the rub. It kills me to hurt people I love, and I know my parents interpret my disobedience as: 'I don't love you. I don't respect you.' That's complete and utter bullshit, but it's their perception, their reality. My words won't change it. Actions speak louder and all that." She drops her chin onto her knees and hugs her legs. "Go ahead, Kiran." She gives a short laugh of self-deprecation. "Serenade me with 'Goody Two-Shoes.' You know you want to."

Actually, I don't.

There are times in your life when a lightbulb clicks on. When you see for the first time something that was there all along, only you were sitting in the dark. Blind. Ignorant. Worst of all: blind to your ignorance.

"You're a good daughter, Preity," I say. Okay, *mutter*. From the side of my mouth.

"What was that?" Rani cups a hand behind her ear. "I didn't quite catch that. Could you say it a little louder, please?"

I narrow my gaze at her. Brat, she heard me perfectly.

So did Preity, who laughs. "That's okay. She doesn't have to. . . ."

Actually, I do. And if you're wondering: No, crow does not, in fact, taste like chicken.

"You're a good daughter, Preity," I say again, louder, minus the 'tude, a simple statement of fact. "You're conscientious and caring, and you have a lifelong track record of love and respect for your parents. Everyone knows that. Including your parents. So you aren't the Perfect Indian Daughter. Rest assured, you're nauseatingly close."

Preity chuckles. "Thanks, Kiran."

I don't tell her this is the real reason I could never stand her. Because she had what I lacked, and I was jealous, resentful that it came so easily to her.

She still has what I lack, and I'm still jealous, but not resentful. I don't hate her anymore; I might even (gasp) like her.

She deserves to know. I *should* tell her. But let's get real. You can only eat so much crow in one sitting. For now, it's enough that *I* know.

"Don't mention it," I say. Then add, "*Ever.* Or I swear I'll deny everything."

"Um, hi. Hello. Yoo-hoo. Over here?" Rani points to herself. "Witness."

"Who may have to go into the Protection Program," Preity says, while I leisurely scratch my chin with my middle finger.

"Ah, just like old times," Rani says.

"No," Preity says. "New and improved."

"A toast . . ." I raise my hot chocolate. "May each of us realize her goals in the New Year."

Saroj's Chhole
[Chickpea Chili]

SERVES 4–6

3 teaspoons cumin seeds, divided, 2, 1

2 teaspoons anardana seeds (dried pomegranate) or amchur powder (dried mango) or lemon juice

2 tablespoons canola oil

1 2-inch cinnamon stick

3 green cardamom pods, bruised

3 whole cloves

4 black peppercorns

1 cup onion, finely chopped

1 tablespoon fresh ginger root, peeled and finely grated

2 fresh green chili peppers, finely chopped

1½ cups tomatoes, finely chopped

½ teaspoon cayenne powder

1 teaspoon coriander powder

½ teaspoon turmeric powder

2 (15-ounce cans) chickpeas, rinsed and drained

1 cup water

1 teaspoon salt

2 teaspoons tomato paste

1 teaspoon garam masala

¼ cup fresh coriander (cilantro), chopped

1 lemon, cut into wedges

1. In a small skillet over medium heat, dry roast 2 teaspoons each of cumin seeds and anardana seeds (if using), stirring constantly until lightly browned, about 2–3 minutes. Allow to cool, then ground into powder using a mortar and pestle. Set aside.
2. In a 2-quart saucepan, heat oil over medium heat. When hot, add remaining cumin seeds. Stir-fry until seeds begin to splutter.

3. Add cinnamon, cardamom, cloves, and peppercorns. Sauté 2 minutes.
4. Add onion, ginger, and chilies. Sauté until onion turns light brown.
5. Add tomatoes, cayenne, coriander powder, turmeric, and the ground, toasted cumin and anardana (or amchur if using, but *not* lemon juice). Sauté until tomatoes melt and the sauce thickens.
6. Stir in chickpeas, water, and salt. Increase heat to medium-high. Bring to a boil.
7. Reduce heat to low and cover. Simmer gently, stirring occasionally, until sauce thickens, about 15–20 minutes.
8. Remove from heat. Remove and discard cardamom pods, cinnamon stick, cloves, and peppercorns.
9. Stir in lemon juice if using. Stir in tomato paste and garam masala.
10. Garnish with fresh coriander. Serve with lemon wedges.

PART FOUR

No Place Like Home[s]

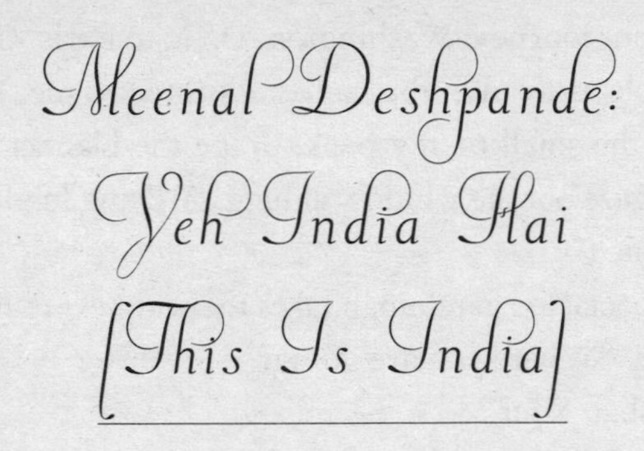

Meenal Deshpande: Yeh India Hai [This Is India]

One's mother and one's motherland are superior to heaven itself.

SANSKRIT PROVERB

My Indian bones can't stand another cold winter. This year, I'm wintering in India. I'll spend time with my family *and* stay warm.

There's something about strangers on a plane, I reflect as I board my flight, observe the others settling in. For better or worse, they're often compelled to share their life stories. When you're trapped on an international flight, you're at God's mercy in more ways than one. Ordinarily I like to chat with strangers. I never know what I'll get, like the toy surprise at the bottom of the box. But, on an international flight, whatever you get, you're stuck with for six hours or more, so I proceed with the utmost caution. And carry sound-cutting headphones.

I slide into my seat for the first, seven-hour leg of my

twenty-hour journey: Washington, D.C., to Paris. Getting as comfortable as I can in the inches allocated to me, I adjust a pillow in the small of my back, drape the blanket over my legs, and gaze out the window at luggage being loaded onto a conveyer belt.

A bespectacled gentleman takes the seat next to me, nods, and smiles. "Where you are going?"

"Mumbai. You?"

"Gujarat."

"Going home?" I ask.

"*Gi.* You, too?" At my nod, he asks, "How long you were here, in America?"

"Forty years."

"*Achah,* you are *living* in America. You are N.R.I." Non-Resident Indian.

"Yes," I say. "I have family here and there."

"Very good, very good." He smiles and wobbles his head. "Which you're liking better, India or America?" Everyone wants to know this. They might as well ask whom I like better, Vivek or Kiran.

"I like them both," I say. "They're both my homes."

It's not enough.

"But you must be preferring some things about India, some things about America."

"Yes."

"What things?"

And so it goes.

Things I prefer in India... Real men ask for directions. Spirituality. Hospitality. Community. Respect for elders. Cultural diversity. Multiple languages. Traditions and celebrations. Family values. Family values. Family values.

Things I prefer in America... Cleanliness. Relatively low corruption. Safety. Education. Efficiency. Use of *please* and *thank you.* Orderly lines (queues) and the concept of "first-come-first-served." Infrastructure. Conveniences. Work ethic. Respect for manual laborers and subordinates. Acceptance of outsiders. Cultural diversity. Accurate, detailed maps.

FROM: "Meenal Deshpande" <dil_MD1@yahoo.com>

TO: Undisclosed recipients

SENT: January 5, 20XX 06:45 AM

SUBJECT: Paris

Family & Friends,

Bonjour from Paris! I'm writing this from a "cyber-café" at the Orly airport. I've always been curious about these places where you can pay to use a computer, like a copier in a photocopy shop. But you know how it can be with trying new things, especially all by myself... Scary! But this time, I said to myself: no excuses, Meenal, be adventurous!

And here I am. :)

I purchased 1 hr of computer access time because I wasn't sure how long it would take me to figure this out. As it turns out, it's easier than I thought! You just enter a temporary code, almost like the way you do at the car wash, and then it's the same as using your computer at home!

50 min left. Oh well. What to do? Next time I'll buy 15 min instead of 1 hr. :)

Now I'm going to walk around a while and stretch my legs before my next plane leaves. I will call/email when I reach Mumbai.

Love,
Meenal

On the plane to Mumbai, I take my seat and watch passengers board. Most are Indians, and I hear many regional languages. My heart goes out to a young mother traveling alone with two small, fussing children. They sit in the bulkhead row of the center section. Poor things. I remember when that was me with Vivek and Kiran. Between the singing, whining, and crying, I thought the other passengers would throw us out the emergency exit door if they could.

The young mother keeps glancing around, her face anxious. A flight attendant stops to say she's located the baby's bassinet, and she'll bring it when we're in the air. "Let me know if you need anything," she says. "We know how hard it can be traveling with small children, and we want to do everything we can to make your journey comfortable." She stays and chats a bit, inquiring about them, and the mother smiles and relaxes.

"Ma'am?" The rumble of a deep voice startles me. I was so impressed with the flight attendant's warmth, I didn't notice the young man standing in the aisle next to my row. Tall and blond, he has a receding hairline, a heart-shaped forehead, and a pink baby face. "I'll be sitting next to you," he says in a slight drawl and asks if he can fetch me another pillow or blanket or anything from the overhead compartment while he's up.

"No, thank you." I smile. "I'm fine."

He ducks his head and folds his frame into the aisle seat beside me, tucking in his booted feet and long legs.

"You fit," I say.

"Barely." He grins. "Where you coming from?"

"Washington, D.C. You?"

"Austin, Texas."

I nod. "My son's in Houston."

"Yeah? How's he like it?"

"Better than Dallas. Not as much as Austin."

He chuckles. "Same here."

Here we go again . . .

As the plane accelerates, I peer out the window. I love takeoffs. Speeding faster and faster. Climbing into the sky. The aerial view of the world. The geometric shapes of the land. With international flights, I'm continually awed when these big, lumbering birds take flight. A tiny part of me always thinks, no way can this huge lug make it off the ground, but it always does, taking to the skies like a magic school bus.

Once we level out, I turn my head to my neighbor, thinking: *Let's get niceties over and go to sleep, shall we?*

"Are you traveling to Mumbai on business?" I ask.

"Actually, I'm living in India right now with a host family. I was just home for Christmas. Now I'm headed back to Pune."

"Oh. I'm going there next week. Our family divides their time between Mumbai and Pune."

"That's pretty common, it seems," he says. "Like New York. Lots of people live in the city and have retreats on Long Island or upstate."

"Good analogy." I learn he did his undergraduate studies in the Big Apple and tell him Kiran went to Columbia Medical School. "What are you doing in Pune?"

"Learning Marathi," he says, making me do a double take.

I laugh, amazed and delighted. "This is a new one..."

"Yeah." He rubs the back of his neck. "I get that a lot."

"I'll bet. So why in the world are you learning Marathi? Trying to impress an Indian girlfriend?"

"No..." He grins, the pink of his cheeks deepening. "I'm a music professor at U.T.-Austin, and I'm studying Indian classical music. I want to learn Marathi to understand the music better. I'm studying and teaching at Symbiosis University. Been there almost two years. I finish in May."

"Mug thumala chan Marathi boltha yet ashnar?" I say. Then you must be speaking very good Marathi.

"Aho, me sagla Marathi bolu shakto." Yes, ma'am, I can say anything in Marathi.

My jaw drops. I can't believe it. I just can't believe it. This blond-haired, blue-eyed, pink-cheeked cowboy from Austin, Texas, speaks beautiful, grammatically flawless Marathi like a native!

Our conversation proceeds exclusively in Marathi.

"Which do you prefer, Mumbai or Pune?" he asks.

"I like them both, for different reasons. I love the sound of the ocean, but it's cooler and drier in the mountains, which I prefer. Communities mix more in Mumbai, but Pune's catching up. Pune's quieter. Less polluted."

"Compared to Mumbai, yes, but Pune's local people say it's more congested than it used to be. Urban sprawl is everywhere. Bangalore and Mysore have much less pollution than Pune. And a lot more greenery."

"At my age, you'd think not a lot surprises me, but this... this..." I laugh and shake my head. "A year and a half, and you're speaking better Marathi than my children!"

He laughs, too. "A year and a half *at the college level.* In their defense."

"Amazing. We should have sent them for a year abroad. I never even thought of it."

"Maybe the grandchildren."

"Maybe." I smile. "My name's Meenal." I offer my hand.

He takes it. "John Cooper. Pleasure to meet you, ma'am."

Texas John proves an excellent travel companion, providing the optimal balance of quiet and conversation. At Vivek's age, he's sadly already a widower, having lost his beloved Madelline, a concert pianist, to ovarian cancer three years ago. I don't mention my own ordeal. I'm fed up with this damned disease defining my life, my identity. I just want to be Meenal—not Meenal the Breast Cancer Survivor—and for my three months in India, I plan to be.

Before his wife passed away, she made a list of things she wanted him to do for her. A long, handwritten list. He carries a copy with him, and I'm honored and touched he lets me read it.

Maddie's List for John, she wrote at the top in block print, with a heart on each side. On five pages, she listed numerous tasks, which would surely take a lifetime to complete, but he's made a good dent, as evidenced by checkmarks. He smiles when I point out *learn to play the sitar, hike the Himalayas,* and *see the Taj Mahal.*

Delicately, I ask if he knows the history behind the Taj, checking to make sure he knows the white marble architectural wonder is a mausoleum built for a deceased empress, not a palace, as many mistakenly think.

He knows. That's one of the reasons Maddie chose it—the symbolism—and why he's delayed going. "It's gonna be tough." He thumps his fist over his broad chest, the way one does to settle a cough. "Hits close to home."

Bichara mulga. Poor guy.

I pat his arm. "You go when the time is right. You'll know." I tap my own chest, the part that's real, that still feels, between the prostheses. "In here."

Later, after we eat and sleep, watch a movie, sleep some more, when the projection screen displays our plane's location two hours away from the Indian border, John tells me that he enjoys hearing the story of the Taj told by different people, picks up something new each time.

"Would you like me . . . ?"

"If you wouldn't mind."

I smile. "Not at all. Moms love to tell stories, right?" I take a sip from my water bottle, rest my head back, and begin the tale of Mughal Emperor Shah Jahan and the love of his life, his favorite wife whom he gave the name Mumtaz Mahal—meaning in her native Persian "beloved ornament of the palace"—who died at the age of thirty-eight while giving birth to their fourteenth child.

When the time comes to fill in our immigration and customs forms, John and I exchange contact information. We deplane in Mumbai in the early hours of morning. The warm, muggy airport feels good after the bone-chilling air-conditioning. We march through two immigration lines like a procession of ants, Indian citizens in one line, visitors in another. I've always been a little annoyed to be viewed as a foreigner in my birth country. I'm so glad dual citizenship's finally an option.

At the counter, I fork over my American passport with its Indian visa stamp. A few basic questions and I'm on my way to the luggage carousel. What a zoo. I maneuver my luggage cart through the bodies and spot one of my suitcases already pulled from the conveyor belt. As I raise the handle to tow it, John approaches.

"I got it," he says. Hefting the sixty-pound bag onto the cart, he teases, "You remembered to pack the kitchen sink."

I laugh. "Hey, I'm ten pounds underweight this time!"

Funny how the things I carry to and from India have changed over the years. In the Boston Days, I packed food, toys, makeup, sneakers, and linens (clothes, bed sheets, tablecloths) to take to India. And Indian snacks, sweets, spices, sandals, clothes, and jewelry to bring back to the States. Today, we get so many things here and there. One hardly has to go without. The need to transport precious goods isn't anywhere near as dire anymore.

This trip, I stuffed my suitcases with things like pretzels, baking mixes, flavored gelatin and pudding, mayonnaise, shelf-stable cheese spreads, powdered salad dressing, instant soups, and pasta sauces.

I stand with the cart while John fetches the remaining bags. Uniformed boys scramble around me. "Madam, do you have anything to declare? I can take you to the Red Zone quickly. Only five hundred bucks."

Only! The most you'd tip in India is one hundred rupees—and this in a five-star hotel.

"No, thank you," I say.

"You have electronics?"

"No, I don't." I eye the Green Zone. Long, long lines.

"Madam, I'll take you out in five minutes from Red Zone," the coolie insists. "You don't have to worry."

"No, thank you."

"Madam—"

I hold up a palm in front of me like a stop sign, cutting off his sales pitch.

John appears at my elbow. "Madam doesn't need your help," he says in Marathi.

At the coolie's startled expression, I can't help smiling. A Marathi-speaking cowboy is good entertainment.

I point to John's lone suitcase and carry-on duffle bag. "That's all you have?" At his nod, I say, "Light traveler."

The cumbersome luggage and security screening process is something like the checkout of a self-serve supermarket with *very heavy* groceries. First, you unload your seventy-pound suitcases from the luggage carousel and load them onto a cart. Then, you push your cart to a security screening line, where you unload luggage from the cart and load it onto a conveyor belt to be X-rayed. Finally, you load it back onto the cart.

John pushes the cart to our final security checkpoint. A guard checks our passports and paperwork. Then we're out the automatic glass doors that take us into the warm blanket of a tropical winter night.

I heave a sigh. "Free at last."

"You can say that again."

A crowd waits behind an iron railing, on the lookout for arriving family and friends. I spot Dilu-*dada* and Giru-*dada* waving and grinning like little boys. Little boys with *ajoba* faces.

"That's me," I say.

Up front, a shuttle service representative holds a sign reading *Mr. Cooper*. "And this is me," John says.

I hug my brothers and introduce my new friend, whom they promptly invite over, offering tea, food, a bed for the night. That's Indian hospitality for you.

John thanks them, requests a rain check, and invites us to a concert in Pune where he is playing sitar. We promise to try to make it. Dilu-*dada* and I escort him to his shuttle van. We make sure he's all set before we take our leave and join Giru-*dada* and Ramesh, our driver of five years, who've loaded my bags into the trunk of our silver Hyundai Accent.

Ramesh grins from ear to ear, as overjoyed to see me as my brothers. "*Namaste,* madam. How was your trip? Was everything okay?"

I smile at the trio. "It sure is nice to be back in India."

When I was a girl, joint families usually lived in a single house or flat. Now, joint families often occupy multiple flats in a single building, appealing because nuclear families have a bit more personal space and autonomy, but the extended family's still together.

As the eldest son, Yash provided for his side of the family two adjacent flats in Mumbai. On my side, *Baba* and *Ai* had a big windfall when they sold our family bungalow that enabled them to purchase two sets of two adjacent flats—four flats in total—in Mumbai and Pune.

Dilu-*dada* and Giru-*dada* told me that a renowned builder has broken ground on a multistory complex a few blocks from ours in Pune. The flats have gone fast; only a few remain. I'm anxious to visit the sales office, check out the designs and floor plans. I'd love if Yash and I could have a flat nearby, especially new construction.

India is a great place to be old. Society heaps respect upon your feet like marigold petals. Your son (at least one), his wife and children live with you. They'd never dream of putting you in a nursing home. They don't consider elderly parents a burden. Nor guests, even when they stay for weeks, sometimes months. Western concepts of privacy are alien; an Indian is rarely alone, rarely wants to be, rarely likes it.

In India, I am never lonely.

---

9 January

Dear Kiran,

Greetings from Mom in Mumbai! How are you? How is the groom search progressing? I'm anxious to hear the latest! ☺

You must be surprised to receive a handwritten letter. Aji and I were talking over tea and Shrewsbury biscuits from Kayani Bakery, and she said what a pity it is that with new technology, we've lost the art and beauty of writing letters by hand... email can't replace the personal touch of seeing and feeling what you're right now holding in your hands. Our handwriting lives and breathes.

I realized she's right. I remember when I first came to Boston... with my two suitcases of saris and silverware. ☺ How eagerly I awaited the mailman each day, always hoping he would bring me a blue aerogramme from home. Here, everyone similarly anticipated aerogrammes from Boston. In fact, Aji saved them! Yours and Vivek's, too! I want to read every one, but I'm not ready yet. Just the sight of the handwriting on the envelopes makes me teary, so I fully expect a sobfest.

I remember that in the beginning, we wrote frequently... every sparrow and crow's story, as Aji says. (Remember this expression for "every little detail"? Sounds much better in Marathi ☺). Then fewer details, less often over time.

Now, Aji tells me she loves hearing my voice on the phone, but she misses my letters. "No one wants to write letters to an old lady anymore," she says. And you think YOUR mom is good at guilt trips! Ha ha.

I promised Aji I will return to writing genuine letters, with stamps. Then I thought it might be nice to write to my daughter, too. You don't have to write me back this way. Your time is more limited than mine. But you may enjoy receiving a letter in the mail every now and then, instead of the usual junk... bills and catalogs. ☺ Anyway, let me try it out, and we'll see how it goes.

All is well here. Neelima-mami and I are having a great time sari and jewelry shopping for Sneha's wedding. No new saris for me... I already have enough for several lifetimes. You know I'm not like Saroj Auntie who must always have AT LEAST a dozen of the latest styles, but I sure did feel like her when I met with the tailor to have a dozen new sari blouses stitched! ☺ (Higher necklines, you know why.)

Sneha's trousseau is impressive! So many saris, collected since the day she was born, most of which she'll never wear (she dresses exclusively in Western-style), but each so lovely. Her bridal sari is absolutely breathtaking, silk Banarasi, the kind every little Indian girl and her mother dream of. The bride's sari is traditionally a gift from her mama, but Dilu-mama said rather than Hema-mami selecting and him getting credit, Sneha should choose whatever shalu she wanted. Of course, Dilu-mama still got credit, because he paid! But everyone was happy... that's what matters!

It's so hard to believe I'm not feeling my usual jealousy, not even a tiny bit. I learned so many things this year I keep wishing I could have learned sooner. If I knew then what I know now, I wouldn't have wasted so much energy on petty jealousy. Take it from me, preoccupation with what others have that you don't blinds you to what you DO have. And jealousy, like all insidious negativity, is every bit as toxic as cancer. Sometimes, I think that's what caused my cancer. And getting rid of it cured me.

Lately, I've been dreaming about your wedding. Not just daydreams, but at night, too. Mostly they're good dreams, but sometimes, I dream I've forgotten something critical... like my CLOTHES!! Typical Mother-of-the-Bride anxieties. ☺

Kiran, you've given me a ray of hope I never expected, so please, even if you already know you're dead-set against having an Indian wedding, don't tell me just yet. Let me dream for a while longer...

There is something I never told you. It's difficult for me to think about, let alone write... I, too, collected saris for your wedding trousseau every time we visited India, until Dad and I decided to settle permanently in the U.S. So there were not too many. I say "were," because I gave them all away when you married Anthony. I can't tell you how sad, angry, and ashamed that makes me feel (about myself).

I'm sorry, Kiran. We can't change the past, but we can change the future, with each day we have, and each lesson we learn.

Take good care. I love you very much, pillu.

Love,
Mom

P.S. I want to hear "every sparrow and crow's story" on your groom search!! ☺

---

18 January

Dear Kiran,

How are you? I'm still wearing a smile from our phone conversation yesterday. It was wonderful to share the latest twists and turns of your roller coaster! As I told you, ups and downs are to be expected. I'm proud of how you're handling them. I'm VERY proud of you for getting on, and staying on, this crazy ride! ☺

Selfishly speaking, it's been such a joy for Mom to hold her baby's hand again, even if my baby's a big girl and doesn't need Mom's hand-holding. More so, actually. Somehow, it means that much more to me because it's your CHOICE. You don't NEED me... but you WANT me. (Another of God's late revelations!!)

While I was disappointed to hear Mr. Pediatrician declined our contact, it's his loss. Forget him. Same with the others. Don't try to second-guess their reasons. Move on. Dwelling on the negative gets us nowhere. Focus on the positive. You have plenty of it!

I was glad to hear you and Mr. Architect clicked in email. I can't wait to hear how it goes on your first "phone date"! ☺ (Do NOT use that term with Aji or Ajoba! Or any Indians of my generation and up! Phone INTERVIEW. You're INTERVIEWING each other. ☺)

Saroj Auntie phoned this morning. She's been busy! ☺ She has an ever-growing list of "leads" she's going to email to me. I'll forward the list to you when I get it, and we can discuss. Saroj Auntie volunteered to prescreen/make introductions, but don't feel pressured. These are only options, not obligations.

It's funny... The more I write, the more I want to write. I can go a long time without talking to someone, but once I do, I'm itching to talk again soon afterward. It's like breaking a fast. Once you eat, you hunger for more. Is that how you felt (feel?) about cigarettes?

Yes, I know. Are you surprised? You weren't as good of a storyteller as you thought. But then, your mother comes from a land of storytellers. ☺

I knew you smoked, not just your friends whom you blamed for your smelly clothes and hair when I noticed. I might not have caught you red-handed, or found hard evidence (though I looked), but moms know these things. You'll find that out for yourself when you have children. (If they're anything like you, I'm in for quite a show as the Aji who gets to sit back and watch! ☺)

Now, while we're on the topic of smoking... Yes, here comes Mom's lecture, and you'd better read every word—there WILL be a quiz!

As a doctor, you know the dangers, the health risks of this filthy habit. Specifically, the correlation between smoking and cancer. But for some reason I've never understood, you doctors can be the worst offenders! So I urge you: Please do NOT gamble with stakes this high. We now have a documented case of breast cancer in our family. Take it from me, the temporary pleasure you might get from a cigarette isn't worth permanently cutting off your breasts, or cutting short your life.

Okay, end of lecture. For now. I reserve the right to resume at will. ☺

It rained in the mountains yesterday, starting late in the afternoon and pouring all through the night. The soothing patter of raindrops lulled me into the most heavenly sleep, but I awoke to a miserable cold dampness and had a terrible time getting out of bed. We turned on the single space heater in the living room, which toasted us up nicely, but I'm going out this afternoon to buy one for every room. If I tell Ajoba, he will protest that it's wasteful to have so many when they're hardly ever used, so I'm following Aji's example of saying nothing and quietly doing what I want. Ha, ha.

That reminds me... You might get a kick out of this...

I had an incident with Aji this morning. You know I've always worn saris in India. This trip, I've taken to wearing salwar-kameezes—better camouflage for my chest. Aji noticed this change but accepted it easily enough (so far). It's not that drastic, still within reason. Today, however, it's cold, and thinking only of warmth and comfort, I dressed in jeans and sweatshirt. Aji was horrified! "What's this??? You can't go out dressed like that! Go change your clothes right away!" ☺

Women my age don't wear jeans. It would be like wearing a miniskirt. People would snicker, "Look, the old bat's dressed like a college girl, doesn't feel any shame!"

Funnier than Aji's reaction, though, was MINE... Before, I would have been thoroughly embarrassed at my lapse in judgment and dashed off to change without hesitation. Today, I thought: So what? Frankly, I don't give a damn. I'm too old, and I've been through too much this year to care about people's judgments. Let them laugh at me. My physical comfort's more important than their stupid opinions. Then, ZAP!!! In that instant, something hit me like a lightning bolt! I thought: My God, I'm Kiran, and Aji's me!!! ☺ It was a FREAKY FRIDAY moment!!! ☺ Of course, I returned to my own body shortly thereafter and changed clothes. It doesn't matter to me, but it does to Aji, and she matters to me, so that's that.

Okay, enough for today. Take good care. I love you, baby.

Love,
Mom

---

22 January

Dear Kiran,

We've just returned from seeing Texas John in concert—what a treat! By the time this reaches you, I will have told you the entire contents on the phone, I'm sure.

We had John over for dinner a few nights ago. Aji and Ajoba were very impressed when he knew to touch their feet in respect, but when he started speaking Marathi, they nearly dropped their false teeth!! It was priceless!! ☺

At dinner, John fit right in. Since he's been living with an Indian family for the past year, he's learned Indian manners and mannerisms. He ate everything with his hand—even Neelima mami's varan bhat, which he said was the best he's tasted! No surprise, everyone loved him. Even Ajoba, who rarely goes out anymore, insisted on attending John's concert.

John made such a point of warning us it was strictly amateur night and not to expect Ravi Shankar. We went into the concert hall with our bar lowered so far, it was lying on the ground. And then... after all that... I should have guessed it... Texas John, our kurta-pajamas-wearing cowboy, played the sitar so beautifully, I could have wept. Afterward, Ajoba flicked his wrist and joked, "Now, I've seen everything. God can take me." ☺

I've saved the best for last...

Aji took John's arm in that way of hers, the one that signals she's about to sweet-talk someone out of something. "John? Do you know any nice Indian-American boys, bachelor friends looking to settle down, who would be interested in meeting Meenal's daughter, Kiran?"

NOT ONLY did Aji take it upon herself to ask this, she scolded ME for not thinking of it/doing it first!!

But wait, it gets better...

I had talked to John about you, but nothing about semi-arranging your second marriage. After I filled in the blanks, he told me to wait there, don't move, he'd be back in a minute. He returned with Maddie's List. Remember I told you about the list John's wife made before she passed away? On it, he pointed to: "Find a wife for N.T."

As it turns out, N.T. is Nikhil Tipnis, one of John's best friends from high school. Quick summary: born in North

Carolina, brought up in Texas, divorced 4 years back (from his high school sweetheart), 2 years older than you, lives in Austin, works for Dell Computer. I'll tell you more details when we talk, but he sounds terrific, and Texas John volunteered to introduce you in email!! I gave John your email address, so expect to hear from him shortly.

I'm crossing my fingers. Aji will be doing puja. And now that I've gotten all this excitement out on paper, I hope I can fall asleep. My coach turned into a pumpkin hours ago... ☺

Lots of love,
Mom

Neelima Mami's Moong Daal

[Mung Bean Stew]

SERVES 4

1 cup dried split moong daal, without skin (mung beans)

7 cups water, divided 3, 4

1 teaspoon salt

2 tablespoons canola oil

½ teaspoon black mustard seeds

6–8 curry leaves (kadhi patta)

*3 dried red chilies**

2 pinches asafetida (hing)

1 teaspoon brown sugar

1 teaspoon coriander powder

1 teaspoon cumin powder

⅛ teaspoon turmeric powder

1 cup tomato, chopped

¾ cup fresh coriander (cilantro), chopped and divided, ½, ¼

1 tablespoon ghee or unsalted butter

1. Sift through mung beans, removing and discarding debris. Rinse and submerge in 3 cups water for 15 minutes. Drain. Rinse again.
2. In a 2-quart saucepan over high heat, combine 4 cups of water, mung beans, and salt. Mix well. Bring to a boil. Reduce heat to medium. Simmer to a stew, about 15–20 minutes, skimming and discarding surface foam. Remove from heat, mash with wooden spoon or potato masher, and set aside.
3. In a small skillet, heat oil over medium-high heat. Add mustard seeds. When seeds begin to sputter, reduce heat to medium. Stir in curry leaves, red chilies, and asafetida.

Stir-fry until asafetida changes color, about 30 seconds. Pour over mung beans. Mix well.

4. Stir in brown sugar, coriander powder, cumin, and turmeric.
5. Return saucepan to stove over medium-high heat. Stir in ½ cup fresh coriander and tomato. Bring to a boil. Reduce heat to medium. Cook to desired consistency, stirring in some water if needed.
6. Remove from heat. Stir in ghee. Garnish with remaining fresh coriander. Serve hot with rice.

* *Neelima's Tips:*

✔ Do *not* eat the red chilies!

Saroj Chawla: Lahore, Meri Jaan

One who hasn't seen Lahore hasn't been born.

PUNJABI PROVERB

FROM: "Meenal Deshpande" <dil_MD1@yahoo.com>

TO: Saroj Chawla

SENT: January 15, 20XX 07:02 PM

SUBJECT: What's wrong?

Dear Saroj,

Have I done or said something to upset you? If I have, I'm sorry. But I can't fix it if I don't know what I did wrong.

Please don't brush me off and say it's nothing. We've been friends too long and know each other much too well for that.

Please talk to me. Whatever it is, let's work it out, okay?

Love,
Meenal

FROM: "Saroj Chawla" <Saroj@ChawlaCatering.com>
TO: Meenal Deshpande
SENT: January 16, 20XX 05:55 PM
SUBJECT: RE: What's wrong?

It's not you, it's me. When's a good time to phone you there?

Saroj

Hypothetically speaking, if I was to visit Lahore, who would accompany me? I'm afraid to travel in an Islamic country without a male escort, preferably four, but I wouldn't want to put my "infidel" husband at risk in potentially hostile territory. I would also worry about the possible ramifications of Sandeep's passport carrying the stamp of an Islamic country.

Since 9/11, it can be challenging enough to be a brown man, more so when traveling by air. I fear giving authorities (more) reason to question my husband, subject him to increased scrutiny.

It doesn't matter if you're Hindu, Sikh, Christian, Jewish, Parsi, Jain, or Buddhist. It doesn't matter if you're a doctor or an engineer or any other educated professional. If you're a man with brown skin and/or a name that appears Muslim, even to the ignorant eye, you risk fitting the profile of a terrorist.

These are my thoughts as I push my grocery cart through the supermarket. I buy smoked Gouda, Brie, grapes, strawberries, kiwi, crackers, and fresh bread. I'm in and out in ten minutes. We've shopped in this store for twenty-five years. I know the location of every item, could find my entire grocery list in the dark. When Sandeep used to run the occasional errand for me on weekends, he, like many men on weekends, didn't bother to shave. Not anymore.

After 9/11, we had armed guards in our supermarket. At first, Sandeep didn't understand why the guards were giving him dirty looks and trailing him. Then, he caught on. He calmly went about his business, and no one approached him. Still, it rattled him, and he resolved to appear clean-shaven in public. And poor Yash Deshpande, who has dedicated his life to saving others, told us how he inspired fear and suspicion in parking lots and elevators.

This is what non-Muslims experience. It makes me wonder about innocent Muslims.

Sandeep says India saw worse in 1984 when Prime Minister Indira Gandhi's assassination by her Sikh bodyguards sparked rampages of violence against random bearded and turbaned men. The bloodbath of thousands drove many men—against religious custom—to shave their faces and cut their hair.

If this is supposed to make me feel better, it doesn't.

In the elevator at the Rotunda, I set down my grocery bag, press the button for my floor, and watch the numbers light up.

1984. I find myself thinking about *1984,* not the year but the novel by George Orwell that I read in a neighborhood ladies' book group. Big Brother Is Watching You. America's Patriot Act reminds me of *1984.* As much as terrorists frighten me, so does an act that allows authorities to detain "suspected terrorists" indefinitely, deprived of due process. No formal charges. No lawyer. No phone call. No "innocent until proven guilty."

Am I not a patriot because I don't support this?

Some people believe a patriot puts the nation's safety before an individual's rights. Some people believe national security justifies whatever margin of error (some mistakes, whether or not you own up to them, are inevitable). But be honest. That's as long as we're talking about *other people,* right? Them. Not us.

What if it's *you*? Or *your husband*? Or *your son*?

What if there's some terrible mix-up? If you're in the wrong place at the wrong time? If there's one rotten apple in the bunch of officials, and that lone apple's assigned to *you*? What if somehow, some way, *you* or *your loved ones* get screwed?

Do you know the American expression "S.O.L."? In case you don't, I will tell you. It means: Shit Out of Luck.

These are my fears. Will they keep me from going to Lahore? I don't know. But if perchance I go, I won't allow my family to accompany me.

Through Yash Deshpande's contacts in the medical community, I hook up with a young Punjabi Lahori couple named Farani. The husband Yousef is a surgeon. The wife Saira is a hematologist.

I want to invite them to dinner, but I'm torn between my desire to meet Lahoris and my wariness of associating with them. I know my American history. I know about the infamous McCarthy trials where people were arrested, scapegoated, their lives ruined because of suspicion of communist relations. In the 1950s, it was the Red Scare. Today, it's the Green Scare. (Green is the color of Islam.)

It is said history repeats, and I witnessed the ruin of a civilization so advanced no one expected its annihilation. Not even Mohammad Ali Jinnah, founding father of Pakistan. In his inaugural speech as Pakistan's first governor-general, Jinnah said, "You will find that in the course of time, Hindus would cease to be Hindus and Muslims would cease to be Muslims, not in the religious sense because that is the personal faith of each individual, but in the political sense as citizens of the state."

So much for that prediction.

Once you've seen a sophisticated civilization crumble, you know no nation is invincible from self-destruction. Just as her people have the power to make a nation great, they also have the power to destroy all that is great. Where nation-building takes generations, evisceration requires only a minuscule fraction of this time. After the holocaust of Partition, I recall everyone saying in shell shock, it happened so fast....

The other day, I saw a bumper sticker that read: "I pray to God to protect me from His followers." With this prayer, I bite the bullet and invite the Faranis—Yousef, Saira, and their five-year-old son Aamir—to dinner at our house.

When I hear their car pull into the driveway, I lift a slat in the blinds with the tip of my fingernail. Squinting through the crack, I watch them get out. Aamir has sneakers like Jack's with lights that flash with each step. Yousef is clean-shaven. Saira wears a *salwar-kameez* but doesn't cover her head. Like Kiran, they look too young to be doctors.

The doorbell rings. I don't wait for Sandeep but dash for the door, getting there before him. I stop with my hand on the knob, try to catch my breath. Can't. My heartbeat drums in my ears. *Boom-boom. Boom-boom. Boom-boom.*

My husband bellows my name from upstairs. (We have the fanciest intercom system, but does anyone ever use it? No.) "Did I hear the doorbell?"

"Yes! They're here!"

"What?"

"Come down!" I turn the knob, swing open the door. *"As sal—"* The words *as salaam alaikum* dry on my lips.

There they stand. Papa Bear. Mama Bear. And Baby Bear. With three pairs of hands clasped in *namaskar*.

They beat me to it.

"*Namaste*, Auntie-*ji*," they say. Even Baby Bear in his squeaky, innocent-little-boy voice.

I, too, put my hands together at my heart. *"Namaste."*

Before I register what he's doing, Yousef bends and touches one hand to my feet then his heart, a sign of respect to elders.

A wave of emotion rises inside me. My throat closes, and my eyes sting. As I touch his head, blessing him, the wave crashes. A sob rips free of my chest, and I burst into noisy tears like a maudlin Bollywood heroine.

Sandeep rushes to my rescue with a joke about emotional Punjabis, the true test of a Punjabi, making everyone laugh, including me. We speak in Punjabi. Such an intimate language, our mother tongue, spoken only by our community. Before long, we're swapping life stories. Pakistani-born Yousef and Saira inherited their stories of Partition. . . .

Their families, not related, emigrated from the Indian side. Before Partition, Yousef's family owned mango orchards. They were wealthy, but Partition sliced through class hierarchies, leveling the field. Whatever you had, whether a mud hut or a mansion, you lost it, abandoning anything you couldn't carry. Like everyone else in the overflowing refugee camps, they crossed the border into Pakistan with next to nothing, struggled to reestablish themselves in a new land, a society that wasn't always welcoming of *muhajirs,* refugees. Locals threatened them into selling the parcel of land allotted to them by the Pakistani government in compensation for their relinquished mango groves. They missed the people, the places, the way of life they left behind. Bit by bit, things improved; still, it often feels like "two steps forward, one step back" with the country's problems.

It's been my experience that in social settings, Americans generally avoid talking about religion and politics, and

Indians talk of little else. Conversely, Indians avoid public sex-talk, and Americans talk of little else! I find the Faranis are like us in this regard, too.

"We are an Islamic nation," Yousef says, "but there's great debate amongst our people as to *what is* and *what is not* Islamic."

"There's great debate in America," Sandeep points out, "as to *what is* and *what is not* constitutional."

Yousef and Saira grew up loving Pakistan but wishing they could see India ("We've always wanted to see the Taj Mahal..."), the way I grew up loving India but wishing I could see Lahore ("Are the Shalimar Gardens still as beautiful as I remember?").

Neither of our families went back after they left. Besides emotional issues, visas between India and Pakistan are difficult to procure in good times, impossible in bad. Likewise, cross-border travel.

"Ironically, now that we're U.S. citizens, we can easily visit our ancestral lands," Saira says.

It's not right, we agree. Peace-loving, nonviolent citizens of India and Pakistan should have access to their shared culture, heritage, and loved ones across the border.

But how to tell a peace-loving, nonviolent person from one who is not?

That is the problem.

"My *nanaji* says it's a conspiracy," Yousef says, "by power-hungry leaders who use fear tactics, propaganda, and the almighty 'patriotic card' to serve their own interests, feed their greedy addictions. It's to their advantage to keep ordinary Pakistanis and Indians apart, to fuel mistrust and hatred, because if we got together, one-on-one, we'd catch on to their scam, see the truth behind their lies—that the average person is not so threatening, not the enemy, that we are most capable of loving thy neighbor. Then what would happen to their power base? Poof. Gone. This is my *nanaji*'s theory."

"Are they power-hungry or passion-starved?" I ask. "Don't we Punjabis know best the human need for passion? Like air, it cannot be denied. A person must feel passion for some*thing*, if not some*one*, in order to live. A goal. A cause. Conveniently, 'serving God' and 'serving country' carry universal honor. Even more, '*defending* God' and '*defending* country.' Tap into those, and voilà, you transform into a Pied Piper. Play those magical tunes on your flute, and watch how the hypnotized masses follow anywhere you lead."

"Religion is the opiate of the masses," Yousef quotes Karl Marx.

"Exactly," I say. "So in these impoverished, repressed societies, some leader comes along and offers passion-starved people a reason to live, a reason to die. Reason to get fired up, to partake in an orgy of righteousness. A gift of passion, wrapped up in the validation of serving God and country, tied with a pretty bow of honor."

"Not only in impoverished, repressed societies," Sandeep says. "Manipulating people's passions is universal."

"But Auntie-*ji*'s right," Saira says, "in that it all gets back to the human need for passion. In the absence of healthy choices, humans will choose unhealthy ones."

"What is violence," I say, "but the dark side of passion?"

When I go to check on dinner, Saira rises and follows me. We take our conversation into the kitchen.

"Is it foolish to hope for a mutually acceptable solution

for India and Pakistan?" I ask. "Does such a thing even exist?"

"It might," Saira says, "if the *desi* diaspora joined hands. We have the numbers, the power, to affect change. And outside the wire, we women can leverage our strengths more effectively. We are the nurturers, the experts at human relationships and community-building. We are the ones who break up children's fights and teach them to play nicely, to respect one another. We, mothers and daughters, can be the greatest of healers. . . ."

Here is another idealist, I think. But unlike my daughter, Saira knows what she's talking about. She's lived it, not just read about it in books, or watched it on CNN's *Headline News*. From her experience alone, I cannot discount her as a Pollyanna.

"If anyone can reach out across divides and rebuild burned bridges, women can," Saira says. "But first, we have to stop undermining each other. We're quick to blame men for all our troubles, overlooking our own culpability. We, too, must observe human rights, starting in our own homes, our own families, in how we treat each other, and our daughters versus our sons. That's not to say men don't need more accountability. They do. A *lot* more. In fact, if it was up to me, if I had to pick one gender to quarantine in *purdah* for the greater good, it would be the male, not the female. It's males who have a harder time curbing base urges with the opposite sex, provoked or not. Therefore, to *best* reduce moral corruption and promote social harmony, we should put the males on short leashes, restrict *their* movements, *hai na*?"

"Ha! Saira for President!" I tie my apron around my waist. "What a platform. Can you imagine? Move over,

Benazir Bhutto." A controversial political figure, twice democratically elected Benazir Bhutto was Pakistan's first and only—to date—female prime minister. When she took office in 1988, at thirty-five years old, she was the youngest person and first woman to head an Islamic government in modern times.

Saira goes on, "I remember once, I told my mother it wasn't Eve's fault Adam lacked self-control and succumbed to temptation. Was God's solution to veil all the apples, to camouflage their appeal? No. If God intended to *remove* temptation, to prevent Adam from *seeing* things he might desire, why not poke out Adam's eyes, blindfold, or otherwise take away Adam's sight? Instead, a loving God, just and merciful, banished Adam from Paradise to a world of temptations, so Adam could learn to act properly *in the face of* temptations. That would include infinite apple orchards with buck-naked Eves in plain sight, *hai na*?"

I laugh. "Oh, *beta*. You must have given your poor mother many gray hairs."

"Oh, no." Saira grins and tucks her hair behind her ear. "*Ammiji* was quite proud. She is ten times the feminist I am. Some of my friends here are surprised when I say that. They think 'Muslim feminist' is an oxymoron, but it's not at all. My mother raised all of us—three sons and two daughters—to read the holy Koran ourselves, so we understood the rights of gender equality, among other things, in Islam. She's always insisted if more people could actually *read* for themselves the teachings in the Koran, they wouldn't be so easily misled by interpretations, distortions, and misrepresentations of others."

"She sounds like a very wise woman."

"She's a Sufi."

"Ah." I nod. "That says it all."

Sufis are mystics. Often controversial, often corrupted by man, Sufism is rejected by some as a legitimate form of Islam. Others maintain it's Islam's purest essence. Sufis believe God exists in all, and all exist in God.

"You've read Sufi literature?" Saira asks.

"Of course." Whatever you think about Sufism, no one can deny it has inspired a treasure chest of literature and music. Sufis believe human love—including consensual physical love—awakens the heart to spiritual love, bringing one closer to God. I've never known anyone whose heart couldn't be stirred by the beauty of Sufi poetry, including me. "I adored Waris Shah and Bulleh Shah."

"The classics."

"And you?"

"I favor the modern poets."

"Does anyone still write in Punjabi these days?" I ask.

"Punjabi and Urdu both," Saira says. "Soon they'll be writing in English."

"God, I hope not." I grimace. "Even the very best English translations are watered-down versions of the original language."

"I know it. Punjabi has wings to soar to places English can't even imagine with its lead feet shackled to the ground."

We laugh.

It's been so long since I had a spirited discussion about Punjabi poetry and literature. I didn't realize how much I'd missed it. I find myself wishing I could talk to Preity like this. And wishing Saira could join our book group—she would make a wonderful addition.

When it's time to eat, I take out the good silver plates,

bowls, and cups. "I hope this is okay," I say, unveiling my *murgh Mughalai* (Mughalai chicken). Growing up, we had this dish on special occasions, as chicken was the most expensive meat. I like to make mine with lots of toasted almond slivers and plump golden raisins. "I was too intimidated to attempt *biryani* with such connoisseurs."

"Nonsense, Auntie-*ji*," Saira says. "Everyone knows Punjabi mothers make the best *biryani*. But *murgh Mughalai* is a favorite, and it's been ages since we've had it. What a treat!"

"Will Aamir eat what we're eating?" I ask. "Otherwise, I can toss a cheeseburger on the grill if he'd prefer."

"Shhhh, Auntie-*ji*." Saira places a finger over her lips. "As long as he doesn't hear B-U-R-G-E-R, he'll eat whatever we eat without complaint."

I chuckle. "Just like my grandchildren."

"Your family eats beef?" she asks.

"Here, yes. In India, no."

Dinner's a hit, and I bask in everyone's lavish compliments, though I pretend to be modest, not easy, ha ha. I'm pleased to see little Aamir eat with gusto, trying each dish. How lucky he isn't a fussy one! Preity and Tarun were the worst. Here I slaved to prepare meals fit for kings and queens, and my kids whined for macaroni and cheese.... Not even homemade with real cheese, but the kind that comes in a cheap cardboard box with a packet of bright yellow *powder*!

"We're going to Lahore for Basant," Yousef says, accepting my offer of second helpings. "Aamir starts first grade in fall, so we won't be able to go at this time of year anymore."

Sandeep nods. "We had the same problem with our kids. We didn't want to pull them out of school in winter, but we didn't want to go to India in summer during the monsoon, either."

"It's a dilemma," Yousef says.

"We just hope Aamir's old enough to remember this trip," Saira says. "We want him to have memories of Basant."

I smile. "I do..."

Yousef and Saira exchange glances. "Uncle-*ji*, Auntie-*ji*?" Yousef asks. "Would you like to come with us?"

He can't mean...

"Where?" I ask cautiously.

"To Lahore. For Basant."

My heart skips a beat. Starts thudding triple-time.

"Our family's in Defence," Yousef says, "but we have plenty of friends in Krishanagar."

Saira nods. "They can help find your old *mohalla*. Someone there must know someone who knows someone who can tell you about your friend."

It's obvious they discussed this subject before now.

I look at Sandeep. He nods, but still, I hesitate. It's what I want, but I'm afraid. It's so much, so fast. I didn't expect this. I'd hoped to spend a nice, cordial evening with the Faranis. I hoped to like them. But never did I think I would—that I *could*!—like them this much. Never did I expect such rapport. *Never* did I expect Mussalmans—*Pakistanis*—to feel like family. But that's exactly how Yousef, Saira, and Aamir feel. Like long-lost family.

"Have you ever had problems?" I ask. "With Immigration..."

"No," Saira says.

"Never," Yousef says at the same time.

"Just think about it, won't you, Auntie-*ji*?" Saira smiles.

"If not this time, then another," Yousef says. "Though we won't be able to make it for Basant again for a long time."

Lahore for Basant . . .

Lahore for BASANT . . .

LAHORE!

"Our families, especially our remaining grandparents, would love to meet you," Saira says, and I must press my lips together to stop their quivering.

My emotions, long suppressed, ooze like pus from an infected wound.

There is a Hindi word, *jaan*. It means life force. When a person dies, we say his *jaan* has left his body. We may call our loved one *meri jaan*. Many times, when I heard refugees weep for Lahore, they said, *Lahore, meri jaan*.

"They're getting old, and it would be good . . ." She doesn't have to finish. I know what she means.

Partition survivors are dying off. Soon, we'll be extinct. The time for closure is now. Now or never.

There are Indians who would call Sandeep and me traitors. There are Pakistanis who would call the Faranis the same. Yet other calls are echoing ever louder in my conscience. Calls of children who don't see boundaries until adults teach them, and still, they resist.

When we take a wrong turn, we need to correct our course.

If anyone can rebuild burned bridges, women can.

Is it possible? In this age of *Kali Yuga*, when the world's religions are increasingly blind beliefs, ripe for man's misuse as instruments of dominance, persecution, and division... Do I dare to hope?

FROM: "Saroj Chawla" <Saroj@ChawlaCatering.com>
TO: Meenal Deshpande
SENT: January 18, 20XX 10:55 PM
SUBJECT: RE: What's wrong?

Meenal,

It was SO good to hear your voice, and clear the air! Thank you for forgiving me. I don't deserve such a good friend as you. I swear it was never YOU, it was bad memories I couldn't deal with. Partition happened so long ago, when I was so young, I thought I was over it. Now I realize if I'm to have any chance of getting over it, I need to break my silence.

OK, enough on that subject. I'm sending your list of potential boys for Kiran in next email. Talk soon.

Saroj

Saroj's Murgh Mughalai

[Chicken with Almonds and Raisins]

SERVES 6

½ cup blanched slivered almonds, divided

4 cloves fresh garlic, peeled

1-inch piece of fresh ginger root, peeled

2 cups yellow onion, chopped

2 tablespoons canola oil

3 bay leaves

4 whole green cardamom pods

1 2-inch cinnamon stick

4 whole cloves

1 teaspoon cumin seeds

3 pounds boneless, skinless chicken breasts, cubed

1 cup milk, divided into thirds

¼ cup water

½ teaspoon cayenne powder (adjust to spicy-hot preference)

1 teaspoon coriander powder

1 teaspoon salt (adjust to preference)

½ cup golden raisins

½ cup fresh coriander (cilantro), chopped and divided

½ teaspoon garam masala

1. Preheat oven to 300 degrees. Spray a disposable aluminum pie dish with nonstick cooking spray. Add almonds. Roast until they turn light brown, shaking and stirring often, about 15–20 minutes. Set aside.
2. In a blender or food processor, purée to a smooth paste: garlic, ginger, and onion. Set aside.
3. In a wok or deep 12-inch skillet, heat oil over medium heat. When it's hot, add the whole spices: bay leaves, cardamom pods, cinnamon, cloves, and cumin.

Stir-fry until cumin seeds turn golden brown, about 10–15 seconds.

4. Add chicken. Sear all sides to lock in the juices, about 3–5 minutes. Using a slotted spoon, transfer chicken to a plate. Set aside.
5. In the same skillet, add the paste. Stir-fry until liquid evaporates.
6. Stir in ⅓ cup milk. Reduce heat to medium-low, cover, and simmer until milk evaporates, about 3–5 minutes, stirring occasionally. Repeat twice until reduced to thick sauce.
7. Stir in chicken, cayenne, coriander powder, salt, and water. Increase heat to medium-high, bring to a gentle boil, then reduce heat to medium-low, cover, and simmer 15–20 minutes, stirring every 5 minutes.
8. Stir in raisins. Cover and simmer 5 minutes. Remove from heat.
9. Remove and discard bay leaves, cardamom pods, cinnamon stick, and cloves. Stir in ¼ cup almonds, ¼ cup fresh coriander, and garam masala.
10. Transfer to serving bowl or platter. Garnish with remaining almonds and fresh coriander. Eat with rice or roti.

Uma Basu McGuiness: Refilling the Well

With problems, you have food for creation.
You have your material.
SATYAJIT RAY

Day after day, I wear my holy amulets, consume herbal roots, perform occult rituals. I battle sweaty, smelly crowds, endless queues to offer prayers at Kalighat. Inside, the temple crackles with a potent energy. Sizzles between secret lovers who have come to elope, circumventing their families. People from near and far offer their fondest possessions as honorable sacrifices. Marigolds, tuberoses, hibiscus blooms. Rupee notes and coins. Slain goats. Long snips of tresses, women's prized beauty. But where, then, are the heaps of castrated penises? I hear Kali-Ma laughing.

The first time I read these words scribbled in one of *Ma*'s tablets, I was a student at Presidency College. I was shocked! Refined Indian women don't use crude language. They don't make overt dirty jokes. Such behavior, as innumerable others, falls strictly within the men's domain.

If I hadn't come to America, if I hadn't married Patrick, if we didn't have Rani, I would have omitted these passages from my English translations. And in so doing, I would have committed a grave injustice, not only to my mother, but to our posterity who deserve nothing less than the complete, uncensored truth.

"They won't give me the tablets," says my sister Anandita (ON-un-DEE-tha) over her mobile from Kolkata.

Our connection is so clear, I feel I'm on the adjacent balcony. I hear the blaring of horns, barks of pariah dogs, whistles of night watchmen.

"Not even copies?" I ask.

"Not even copies," she says, frustration evident in her voice. "I tried reason. I tried sweets. I tried guilt. I tried everything. Still, they refuse."

I, too, have tried to persuade three of my six sisters—the stubborn ones—to part with their prized volumes of *Ma*'s writing, so I can translate and include them in my anthology. Tried and failed.

Some of her writing—a smattering of poetry, a short story here and there—*Ma* shared with others during her lifetime. But most of her words, written as well as spoken, she guarded. Her inner world was too private. Radical. *Damning*.

After filling tablet after tablet with neat Bengali script, she mailed them to her mother, requesting her to lock them up in her metal cupboard. Before *Dida*—our maternal grandmother—died, she divvied and distributed them among my sisters and me. With precious few mementoes of our mother, we hoarded each and every one. Even a hairpin was an heirloom. So you can imagine how we felt hearing *Ma*'s voice, recorded in her writing, speaking to us.

"Bharati claims hers are lost."

I roll my eyes. "She's lying."

"I know, but what to do?"

Cut up their ATM cards, Patrick says, meaning *stop sending them money,* but that's too American, too cold for me. In India, family—even extended family—takes care of family. Though we don't subsidize others as we do Anandita, we do what we can to help with health care, education, weddings. It's not a choice for me, but a duty.

"What to do, *Sejdi*?" my sister asks again, this time not rhetorically, but expecting an answer. Instructions from me. Next Steps.

In our family, I'm called *Sejdi,* which means third-oldest sister. Anandita is one of the twins. I call her *Choto didi,* youngest sister. The other twin, Oindrilla, lives in Australia.

"I don't know," I say. "Short of stealing them—?"

"Impossible. Even spices are under lock and key."

We laugh. Tinny, nervous laughs of desperation.

Though Anandita and Oindrilla are twelve years my junior, my bond with them is tighter than with my other sisters. From their rocky beginnings, I felt protective of the twins. Of all my sisters, they—the ones who never had the chance to know *Ma*—are closest to my heart.

When our father arranged Oindrilla's marriage to a Bengali economist who chanced to move abroad, to *Baba*'s dismay and my relief, I prayed for the same for Anandita. In Kolkata, the twins lived under a cloud of culpability for their role in *Ma*'s death. I wanted to get them away from that. But for Anandita, it wasn't to be. No family could get past her epilepsy. They viewed her as damaged goods. Unacceptable.

Thankfully, *Baba* allowed her to attend Santiniketan, "abode of peace," the college founded by Tagore, our Bengali Renaissance Man. This brought her great happiness and a lifelong network of friends. But he wouldn't permit her further studies after she completed her B.A., certainly not abroad, not after my example.

Despite repeated offers to bring her to the States, to have her stay with Patrick and me, Anandita refused to abandon *Baba,* as the rest of us did when we married and joined our husband's families. Though *Baba* showed little similar consideration for her, she continually fretted over his well-being.

"Who'll look after him in his old age?" Anandita said time and again. "He has no son."

Nephews could light a funeral pyre, but could they care for him the way his own children would? We had witnessed that, when push came to shove in our large joint family with its constant power struggles, a nephew's loyalty laid with his own parents.

So it was that Anandita alone stayed by *Baba*'s side to the end, after which she had no desire to leave Kolkata. There she remains today, in Ballygunge, living with her black cat named Hulo in a luxury two-bedroom flat we purchased for her after *Baba* passed away.

"Sejdi?" Anandita says. "Why don't you come here? They won't refuse you in person."

I squeeze my eyes shut, grip the phone tighter, my palms growing slippery.

"*Baba*'s gone," she says, reading my mind. "Gone-gone.

Body and spirit. He isn't lurking in the *neem* trees, poised to drop on you if you walk under them." Only with me does she feel free enough to aim her slingshot at superstitions. With others, she guards her inner world, as did *Ma*.

Ma's deep, dark secret? Encrypted in innocuous poetry, but laid bare in journal entries: her unconventional, independent, clever mind. People could control *Ma*'s actions, imprison her body, but never her thoughts.

Now that I think about it, Anandita's deep, dark secret is similar. She's an atheist.

She won't admit to it. Not even to me. Doesn't live in a world where one safely can. To varying degrees, most of today's world—East, West, and Middle; First, Second, and Third Worlds—still largely fears and shuns, if not punishes, nonbelievers, equating *godless* with *immoral*. Self-preservation spurs Anandita through the motions of socially accepted piety, not belief in a higher power.

How do I know? The same way I know about Saroj's extramarital affair, Meenal's crush on my husband, and a whole host of other secrets no one suspects. I pay attention. Not only to what's said, but what isn't. Not just actions, but inactions.

Take Anandita's tireless humanitarian work, as an example. That's real. It's her passion, her raison d'être. But observe her body language, listen to her response when people tell her, as they often do, that she's doing God's work or earning her wings in heaven. She bristles. Averts her gaze. Turns away. If she replies, she says things like: "I'm doing *man's* work." Or: "It's not for my *karma* that I do what I do." She may quote the *Gita:* "Let right deeds be your motive, not the fruit which comes from them." Such qualifiers, disclaimers, hardly register on a radar screen; but over time, tiny blips add up.

"*Sejdi*, are you still there?" Anandita's voice comes over the line. In the background, a dog howls.

"I'm here," I say. "And I must stay here. You know that."

Because she was there, Anandita's the only living person, besides me, who knows what *Baba* said to me before he died, words I could never repeat verbatim, even to my husband, *especially* to him, because what hurts me hurts Patrick. With the last of his weak breaths, my father used all his remaining strength to cane these words on my soul: *Never step foot on Bengali soil again.*

"This is your bloody soil," Anandita says, and my vision blurs. "Your birthright."

I cover my eyes. "*Choto didi*, please. I can't."

"You mean you *won't*."

"Yes. That's right. I won't."

It's my choice to honor *Baba*'s deathbed request. This is the sacrifice, penance by which I hope to wipe my karmic slate clean with my father. Patrick understands this. When he and I were in Kolkata, I caught the tail end of a conversation he was having with my sisters.

"So the Christian notion of Hell exists here on earth for those paying off bad *karma*?" he asked.

"Yes," Moitreyee said.

"He is getting it," Tapasi said.

"Fascinating, isn't it?" Anandita murmured from the corner divan where she absently stroked Hulo, a cat who thinks she's a dog. "The gospels to which humans, in all cultures, cling to ease the pain of living and dying?"

Anandita knows my beliefs, even if she doesn't accept

them. And, as evidenced in the letter I receive weeks after our phone conversation, she's clever enough to speak to them.

My dearest Sejdi,

After great thought, prayer, meditation, consultation with gurus, and pilgrimage to Kalighat, I have reached the following conclusions: You have stayed away long enough in deference to Baba's wishes. Come back, and we shall do all the necessary spiritual cleansing. As you know, these important rituals are best performed in India, and there's no holy place better than our Ganges.

I eagerly await the news of your imminent arrival.

Yours affectionately,
Choto didi

P.S. Your presence in Kolkata is the only hope of compiling a comprehensive anthology.

"I'll go if you go," Saroj says, offering her hand to me in pact. "We'll do it together, at the same time."

She understands as no one else can: When you are thrown out of a place, it's not easy to return, under any circumstances, no matter how much you may want to.

I take her hand. "You go to Lahore. I'll go to Kolkata."

"Deal."

We shake, two live wires of nervous energy coiling together.

FROM: "Rani Tomashot"
<RaniTomashot@hotmail.com>
TO: Uma Basu
SENT: January 14, 20XX 02:15 AM
SUBJECT: Life

Hi, Mom!

Can't sleep. Decided to get up and write you. How are you and Dad doing? Do you miss me terribly? Everything here's fine. I finally unpacked my suitcases. That's gotta be a new record for me. Just don't ask if I've done laundry. :P

In the Good-News department: My chronic fatigue has lifted. I'm not feeling the terrible lows anymore. In not-so-good-news: My passion's definitely missing. My highs are gone. I'm listless. And yes, I'm wishing I listened to you and stayed there another month. Is the latest "being right" streak giving you a swelled head??? <g>

I feel like I'm wasting so much time, on this extended vacation from my life. I know Bryan's going through the same thing. In our own ways, we're both floating . . . drifting . . . aimlessly. Don't get me wrong, floating's a helluva lot better than drowning -- NO danger of that, believe me. It's just that I want to SWIM again. I want purpose. I want passion. I miss it!

And now that I've written all this, I want to go to sleep . . . Zzzzz . . . :-)

Thanks for listening, Mom.

XOXOXO,

Boo

FROM: "Uma Basu" <ubasu@gwu.edu>

TO: Rani Tomashot

SENT: January 14, 20XX 08:33 AM

SUBJECT: RE: Life

Dearest Boo-Boo,

We miss you more than stars in the heavens, raindrops in the monsoons, sands on every beach, and colors in all the world. Raised to the power of infinity -- that's how much we love you.

Let's talk later tonight, okay? I have a proposition that may spur you in the right direction.

In the meantime, remember we talked about your creative well being dry and how you cannot continuously take from that place without occasionally replenishing it? Boo-Boo, you refill the well by living in the world, =experiencing= life. Stopping to smell the roses is NOT wasting time.

Love,
Mom & Dad

FROM: "Rani Tomashot" <RaniTomashot@hotmail.com>
TO: Uma Basu
SENT: January 14, 20XX 03:01 PM
SUBJECT: RE: Life

What about stopping to SMOKE the roses? <g>

Seriously, thanks for the pep talk. Nothing on tap here tonight, so call anytime.

XOXOXO,
Boo

Kolkata is a city of juxtaposed contradictions. Splendor and squalor. Fragrance and stench. Intellect and ignorance. Humanity and apathy. Culture and uncouthness. Arrogance and humility. Cutting-edge technology and Stone Age backwardness. Generosity and avarice. Joy and despair.

Once the capital of British India, this wonderful, horrible

city represents (to me) a microcosm of the world. The full range of the human experience. If ever there was a place to inspire an artist, Kolkata is it.

Just what Rani needs.

I always wanted to show Rani the city, country of my birth. *Really* show her, not the emotionally wrenching IN/OUT we did when *Baba* died, but full-blown adventures on par with our travels in Europe, Australia, New Zealand, Thailand, Bali, and Singapore, like my Indian friends in America who traveled to India with their children.

"India is as much a part of Rani's heritage as Italy and Ireland," I said to Patrick after we returned from two glorious weeks at a rented ten-bedroom villa in Tuscany with my in-laws (before Patrick's parents passed away, we were fortunate enough to go on two McGuiness family vacations to Ireland and Italy). "She has every right to experience the land, to know the people, the culture."

"She does," Patrick said. "So do you." That's my husband, always hearing unspoken words, even more perceptive at reading people than I am. "We could go to other parts of the country."

I thought of the spectacular palaces of the Hindu maharajas. The cave paintings and sculptures, wrinkles in time to ancient civilizations. The Himalayas. Hill stations. Beaches and bazaars. Tea plantations. Temples, mosques, churches, and monasteries.

I thought of all these places and so many more I longed to see with Patrick and Rani, but how could I bypass the one city that dwelled in my heart, my memories? How could I go to India and *not* to Kolkata? I couldn't. For me, India began and ended in Kolkata.

"Do you want to go to Kolkata with me?" I tentatively ask Rani and hold my breath, waiting for her answer. Waiting to see if the coin I tossed into the air lands head or tail up. If she says no, I won't try to change her mind, I decided. I'll take it as a sign. A sign of what exactly I'm not sure. Something bad.

She says yes; I book our tickets.

It's been a long time since Rani and I bunked together. Since Anandita snores, Rani and I will share the guest-room's king-sized bed. As Patrick hauls our two largest suitcases upstairs from the basement to Rani's bedroom for me to begin packing, we reminisce about our Boo's old bedtime rituals.

Until Rani was twelve, either Patrick or I had to lie with her in her narrow twin bed until she fell asleep. If we didn't, she would have dark circles under her eyes the next morning from staying up late, unable to sleep. So one of us kept her company for an hour each night, and Rani would ask a myriad of questions, as if downloading her brain to free up necessary space for sleep. Afterward, Patrick and I would share highlights of that night's Boo-Boo Hour, as we called it, marveling over the little wonder we created.

Did the dinosaurs go to heaven? Are people safe—does God brainwash the dinosaurs not to hurt us? If God made everything, who made God? Did Jesus really say no one goes to heaven except through Him, or did somebody mess up/make up His message? When Ganesh was little, did people make fun of his elephant head, or did elephants make fun of his human body like Dumbo's big ears? Did people who aren't/weren't nice to the Untouchables (Dalits) come back as poop-eating flies in their next lives? (This after watching Bimal Roy's touching masterpiece *Sujata* about an orphan untouchable girl raised by a high-caste family.)

I wonder what questions await me in Kolkata. . . .

"Report back," Patrick says.

I promise I will. "I'm going to miss you terribly." Since marriage, we've never been separated more than a week at a time.

"Me, too, hon, but this is important. You need this trip."

"I wish you were going."

"We'll talk every day."

"I know," I say. "But I don't like being away from you . . ."

He chuckles and kisses my brow. "I'd be in trouble if you did."

Rani and I fly out of Dulles. Connect at Heathrow. Arrive at Dum Dum—Lollypop Airport, Rani called it on our last trip—around one in the morning on a Saturday night. This trip, she keeps reminding me the airport was renamed, but it's hopeless. It will always be Dum Dum to me.

Five of my sisters meet us. Anandita, Shukla, Moitreyee, Tapasi, and Bharati—everyone but Oindrilla. They have their husbands, drivers, various children, and grandchildren in tow. All of my *taant*-clad sisters are sobbing—the same picture as when I left—and soon, I am, too.

"So skinny, this one," says Tapasi as she hugs Rani, who shoots a look at me.

"*Sejdi,* you are not feeding her?" says Shukla.

I smile at Rani, a mother's patented I-told-you-so smile. Nothing like a trip to India to put my hovering in perspective.

"Does she speak Bengali?" asks a wide-eyed little girl in Bengali.

To whom does this girl belong? I don't know.

"She understands better than she speaks Bengali," Rani replies in tongue, eliciting cries of *Oh! Wah! Her accent!*

Quickly overwhelmed by the commotion, Rani's eyes glaze over. I'll need to whisk my baby out of the limelight soon.

Moitreyee cups Rani's cheek. "Sho shweet..."

Bharati: "You must be feeling hungry, *nuh*?"

Shukla: "Poor *shonu*, such a long trip."

Tapasi: "We've brought snacks for you."

Anandita: "Everything homemade and bottled water only. No stomach upsets on this trip."

Last trip, Rani suffered a terrible bout of diarrhea. She never divulged the culprit, but I suspected it was street food or drink I'd expressly forbidden her, and she chose to learn her lesson the hard way. The sole Western toilet in our old family home happened to go out of order at the same time. I don't know which was worse, Rani's physical or emotional misery, constantly having to crouch over Straddle-n-Squats, as Patrick calls Indian toilets—oblong-shaped, recessed, ceramic floor basins—*S&S* for short. Both sufficiently traumatized her. Especially when the toilet paper ran out.

Sensing Rani has exceeded maximum capacity, I link my arm with hers and say to our throng of relatives, "We'll ride with *Choto didi*."

Anandita averts her gaze in modesty, but I know my blatant favoritism, especially in front of the others, thrills her. It thrills me, too, to flaunt that the pup everyone else treats as the runt of the litter is my most cherished.

As our motorcade drives to Ballygunge, I'm glad we arrived at night. Nighttime is the best time to view Kolkata, her grime cloaked in darkness, her lights sparkling like jewels. Rani rides shotgun next to the driver to have a better view, while Anandita and I sit in back, holding hands and gabbing 90 M.P.H. Rani laughs at us because we talk on the phone all the time and still never run out of things to say.

"You know Mrs. Chaudhury on the tenth floor?" Anandita says. "The one whose cousin-sister slipped on the wet granite and broke her hip two weeks back? Her doctor's niece's friend's brother, Dr. Ghosh, teaches at Presidency College . . . chemistry, I think. Anyway, his colleague's neighbors, good people, I hear, they live half-year here, half-year in America with their kids."

I nod, certain she's leading up to something. She always is. Even if she takes a circuitous route, the scenic road, to her destination.

"Well, they know a boy there . . . thirty-nine, American-born, good family, surgeon, divorced long time back, no kids. He's interested in Meenal's daughter, the divorced family doctor."

"Sounds interesting. What's the family's name?"

"Hmmm . . . DasGupta or SenGupta, were they?" She frowns, trying to recall.

"Not plain Gupta?" I tease.

"No, no. They're Bengali," Anandita says. "*That* much I remember. Oh! Before I forget again, I must share Rohit's good news!" She tells of a favorite nephew's engagement with a South Indian girl he met in college. "Today's boys and girls go to coed colleges and mix with people from all over. It's good. Opens their eyes."

"Very good," I say. "We need more world citizens."

Though everyone doesn't share this viewpoint, I, of course, am ecstatic that caste and culture prejudices and exclusivity continue to erode daily, and intercaste, intercultural, and love marriages are on the rise.

"That surgeon?" I ask. "Do you remember his good name?"

She bites her tongue in chagrin. "I wrote everything down when Mrs. Chaudhury rang me up. I'll give you my notes at home."

"Great. I'll find a cyber café where I can email Meenal."

Rani glances over her shoulder. "Better get on the stick, huh, Mom? Saroj Auntie's scoped *how* many prospects now? Team Basu's lagging."

I laugh. "Is that a fair comparison? Saroj Auntie's far more networked than I am."

"Sorry, we don't grade on a curve here. Results, results. It's all about results."

I shake my head. "Silly girl."

"Silly girl-*ji*," she emphasizes the Hindi suffix of respect, a family joke, Patrick's "Hinglish" spin on the American jest. "That's *Mister* Lazy Bum to you" becomes "That's Lazy Bum-*ji* to you." That's my husband, who by his own admission, knows just enough to cause an international incident in any given country.

As Rani chats with Anandita, I look out the window at all that is familiar and all that is new, foreign to me. I've had butterflies in my stomach for so long, I don't remember how it feels not to have them. I remind myself to keep my eye on the goal: *Ma*'s tablets.

I glance at a Maruti subcompact that zips by, startled by

the sight of a little boy in the driver's seat. It takes me a second to reorient: *That's the passenger seat!* In India, as in England, they drive on the left side of the road, the driver's seat on the right, passenger seat on the left.

The city of Kolkata never sleeps, not even the children. From the sound of it, you'd think all accelerators and brakes came attached to horns. Trucks even have signs: *Please Honk*. No designated lanes, unmarked and undivided roads the norm, drivers blast each other with friendly honks, warning honks, and angry honks often accompanied with curses. In organized chaos, an array of vehicles vie for the city's scarcest resource: space.

Matchbox-sized subcompacts. Yellow Ambassador taxis and their miniature versions—three-wheeled, diesel-belching auto-rickshaws. Buses with arms dangling out the glassless windows. Scooters, often with a *sari*-clad woman nonchalantly sidesaddle behind a man, a baby in her arms, perhaps one more kid squeezed in there, not a helmet in sight.... I shudder to think of them taking a corner too fast.

Approaching a traffic light, dense exhaust forces us to raise the windows. Not a moment too soon. The light turns red; street urchins attack the trapped vehicles like ants to picnic baskets. They dart from one to the next, tap on windows, peddle their wares, clean windshields without asking, and hold out grubby hands for money, inspiring more irritation than pity.

On one side of us idles a sleek new high-end Mercedes. On the other side, a woman in a ratty *sari* squats on the pavement, cooking over an open flame. An old man holds his index finger against one nostril and empties the contents of the other onto the street. This oft-seen behavior, along with public urination, which I'm sure is coming up in our city tour, is *not* indicative of Indian culture but, rather, a lack thereof. You won't see a cultured Indian blow his nose onto the sidewalk. Sorry to say, however, you may see one—deserving of a good smack on his bum with a *chappal,* or *lathi,* if I had my way—watering the plants, or a wall.

Ahead, billboards advertise the latest new Bollywood films, television serials, Nokia mobiles, Amul Butter, luxury apartment buildings, Marlboro cigarettes, Lay's Potato Chips, Amulya Rich Marie Biscuits, Close Up toothpaste.

At the corner dumpster, a trio of cows gathers, swishing their tails like southern belles with fans gossiping about the stupid people going by. Their blasé expressions as they chomp away remind me of the *Far Side* comics.

The light turns green. Our car lurches forward, careens through the obstacle course. At the next red light, we find the same show, next act, different players. A dirt-caked young girl knocks on my window, a half-naked baby boy on her hip. I ignore her, but she persists. I look at her. Make eye contact. Force myself not to look away, despite my discomfort.

Who are you? What is your story? Do you think I'm cold-blooded, stingy for not giving you money? I want to take you home, clean you up, fill your belly with nourishment, send you to school. It pains me that I can't give you money—I'm not immune to your suffering—but to do so would cause more harm than good. Incite a riot. Encourage more begging. I'm sorry, little one. I can't help you here and now, but I'll donate to a charity that works to empower you, not shackle you tighter in your chains of poverty.

"Don't look," Anandita says. "You're encouraging her."

At the iron gates of the multistory apartment building, the driver honks, rousing the dozing night watchman from his catnap in a chair beside the guard shack. Recognizing the Honda City, the watchman opens the gate. We pull in, park in a designated spot, climb out, stretch. Automatically, I reach into the flower bed, touch the soil in reverence. Bengali soil. Forbidden soil.

My soil.

"We're in India, Mom," Rani says with incredulity. "We're really in India."

The wind kicks up. Leaves whisper in the giant *neem* trees, *shhhhh,* as if telling secrets. The hot air breathes in my ears. Grazes my face, neck, shoulders. Like a warm hand skimmed over my bare skin. The tickle of fingertips. I shiver in the heat. Chilled. Sweating. Fine hairs on my nape, arms, stand on end.

"Yes, we are," I say, a hitch in my voice.

Too late to turn back now.

I rub the earth between my fingers. Touch my forehead and my heart. Kiss my fingers. Turn to Rani. "Welcome to Kolkata."

Welcome back.

FROM: "Uma Basu" <ubasu@gwu.edu>

TO: Meenal Deshpande

SENT: February 10, 20XX 09:20 AM

SUBJECT: Nice Indian Boy

Dearest Meenal,

I'm delighted to report that I have a groom candidate to submit for your consideration! Shall

I give you details in e-mail, or on the phone? I would love to chat if you have time.

Rani and I arrived safely in Kolkata. Her jet lag isn't too bad. Mine's worse. Old age . . . grumble, grumble.

Interestingly, Rani's asthma has returned. She jokes that she's allergic to Kolkata since we were here when her childhood attacks started. The doctor's seen her, and she's now well-armed with inhaler/nose spray/meds.

While I have nothing against Western medicine, when necessary, being back in the East, I find myself thinking like an Indian again. East and West are like our right and left hands, don't you think? I'm wondering if air quality's the only factor at work here, and if it wouldn't be prudent to consider others . . .

Affly,
Uma

Anandita's Alu-Phulkopir Dalna
[Potato-Cauliflower Curry]

SERVES 6

2-inch piece of fresh ginger root, peeled

2 teaspoons coriander powder

1 teaspoon cumin powder

1¼ cups water, divided

3 tablespoons mustard oil, divided, or canola oil

4 cups cauliflower florets, leaves removed

2 cups quartered potatoes, skins removed

1 tablespoon ghee or unsalted butter, plus more for serving

⅛ teaspoon cumin seeds

2 bay leaves

1 2-inch cinnamon stick

2 green cardamom pods, bruised

2 whole cloves

½ teaspoon cayenne powder

½ teaspoon turmeric powder

salt (to taste)

sugar (to taste)

1. In a blender or food processor, combine ginger root, coriander powder, cumin powder, and 2 tablespoons water. Purée to a smooth paste. Set aside.
2. In a wok or deep 12-inch skillet, heat 2 tablespoons oil over medium-high heat.
3. Add cauliflower. Stir-fry until florets begin to brown. Remove with a slotted spoon. Set aside on plates covered with paper towels to drain.
4. In the same skillet, heat another 1 tablespoon oil. Add potatoes. Stir-fry until golden brown. Remove with slotted spoon. Set aside on plates covered with paper towels to drain.

5. In the same skillet, heat ghee on medium heat. Add cumin seeds, bay leaves, cinnamon, cardamom, and cloves. Stir-fry 2–3 minutes. If necessary, add 1 tablespoon water to keep from scorching.
6. Stir in cayenne, turmeric, and coriander paste. Sauté 3–5 minutes.
7. Add cauliflower, potato, and 1 cup water. Mix well.
8. Increase heat to medium-high. Bring to a boil.
9. Reduce heat to medium. Cover and simmer, stirring occasionally—gently, so that the potatoes and cauliflower florets remain intact—until vegetables soften, leaving a little gravy.
10. Remove from heat. Remove and discard bay leaves, cinnamon, cardamom, and cloves.
11. Drizzle with ghee, salt, and sugar to taste. Eat with luchis or ghee bhat.

PART FIVE

East Meets West

Meenal Deshpande: A Suitable Boy

As the rivers flowing east and west
Merge in the sea and become one with it,
Forgetting they were ever separate rivers,
So do all creatures lose their separateness
When they merge at last into pure Being.

THE UPANISHADS

"Mom, I have a problem," Kiran says, calling from Georgia. "Are you alone?"

"One minute," I say. I just finished yoga—I can now raise my arms over my head, palms together, for sun salutes!—and was about to join *Ai* and *Baba* downstairs for a little stroll in the *baag* when my cell phone burst into song. With all these mobiles ringing all the time, you need a unique ring tone to know which one is yours. I chose a tune from *Star Wars,* not the main one, that's too popular, but another.

I duck into an empty bedroom and close the door. "Okay. What's wrong, *pillu*?"

"Well, to start, it didn't work out with Nikhil Tipnis."

I shut my eyes. Lean my back against the door. Swallow my disappointment. The latest of many. After so many promising starts, we've hit one dead end after another. Either Kiran doesn't like the boy enough to proceed, or he doesn't like her enough, or both. Her father said, "She's too fussy. A spoiled American with so many options she can't make up her mind. A closet full of clothes and nothing to wear. But can we, her parents, choose for her, put an end to this nonsense? No. I tell you, we should have moved back to India, married her off when we had the chance."

God, give me the strength to keep this family together. I can't do it alone.

I sit on the side of the king-sized bed, ease my spine one vertebra at a time until I'm lying on my back, my legs hooked over the edge of the bed, my bare feet on the cool white ceramic tile. The ceiling fan, on the lowest mouse-power setting, stirs the dry air ever so softly. Later, it will die for three hours, our daily scheduled power cut—load-sharing to supply the rural areas with free electricity.

"What happened?" I ask my daughter. *Why didn't this one work?*

"We didn't click," she says. "At all. I'm sorry, Mom—"

"Me, too. But are you sure, Kiran? Maybe you should give it more time before you write him off? It's only been, what . . . ? A month?"

"Five weeks."

"Five weeks, then, since John introduced you. . . . Is that enough—?"

"Yes."

"You could grow on each other."

"We did. I mean, not—" Kiran exhales into the receiver. "Nik and I would only grow on each other's nerves, Mom."

I cluck my tongue, unable to hide my disappointment. "He was my favorite. He sounded *so* good, so perfect for you—"

"On paper, yes. But only on paper. He's a great guy, no doubt about it, but for someone else, not for me. He felt the same about me. Believe me, we tried. We really did. We knew how thrilled the families would be, how thrilled *we'd* be, if it worked. We gave it our best shot, but we just couldn't connect. There was no mental spark."

"Nothing?"

"Nothing. When you connect with someone, you know it. And when you don't, you know that, too. Nik and I ran out of things to say after ten minutes. It was a constant struggle to come up with conversation topics that interested both of us. If we bore each other already, where would we go from here?"

"But what about your shared heritage? That's a connection."

"It's not enough. There has to be more. Shared heritage can be a good start. I see how it gives people a shortcut to narrow the field, find some common ground, but it still boils down to personality types and how they mesh. Goals. Values. Interests. Priorities. Like you said, compatibility."

"Okay, Kiran." What can I do? "If you're *that* sure..."

"I'm *that* sure."

"And it was mutual?"

"Very."

"Then that's that." Another one bites the dust. I lay the back of my hand over my forehead. "I'll break the news to John. He just phoned. He's on his way over—"

"He knows. Actually, that's the problem, Mom. See, um... John and I were emailing, and... Are you sitting down? You might want to sit—"

"I don't like the sound of this."

"Please sit—"

"I'm lying flat on my back. Do you want me to get up?"

"No. That's good. Stay like that."

I wait. Silence. "Kiran, tell me what happened and tell me quickly. He'll be here any second." *What kind of mess do I have to clean up?* "You didn't get in an argument, did you? Over this Nik business? Is John upset?"

"No... He... I..."

The doorbell rings. "He's here."

"I love him."

"We all do—"

She groans. "Let me talk, Mom. I'm trying to tell you I'm *in love* with him."

"Oh, God." I bolt upright. My head swims. "John? We're talking about *John* here? Texas John?"

"Yes, Mom. And he's in love with me, too."

"Oh, God." I fall back down. "But...? How...? What...?" I can't form a coherent thought, let alone put words together. "Maddie," I manage to say. "What about *Madelline*?"

"It's been three years. He went to the Taj. He said his good-byes. It was beautiful... difficult, but cathartic. He'll love her forever, but she's moved on, and he's ready now, too. To live. The rest of *his* life. With me."

"Oh, God." I draw my knees to my chest. Stare at a crack in the ceiling. *"How did this happen?"* I ask the universe more than Kiran, but she's the one who answers me.

"It snuck up on us," she says. "Neither of us expected it. We were trading emails just as friends, nothing more. Then, we started talking on the phone. Again, just friends. No agenda. But the more we talked, the more we found we liked each other. And the more we got to know each other, the more compatible we realized we are."

"You and *John*...?" My voice sounds hollow to my own ears, as if someone else is speaking, not me.

"Like I said, when you connect with someone, you know it," Kiran says, "and John and I connect on multiple levels. We've emailed or talked every day for five weeks. No matter how long, or how often, we never get bored with each other. Even when we talk about really boring things. How do I explain it? We don't constantly have to be 'on' to enjoy each other. There isn't any pressure to put our best foot forward. Our attachment feels... well, normal. Natural. I've never felt so in synch with another person. Even when we argue. And you know me, so that's saying *a lot*." She laughs.

I open my mouth, but no words come out.

Kiran continues, "Before, I always thought love was enough. I thought it was everything, the be-all, end-all of a successful marriage. Now I get what you mean about compatibility. Anthony and I may have loved each other, but we didn't share the same values. John and I do. He's The One, Mom. The one I've been waiting for. The one I want to marry. He's going to ask your permission today—"

"Today?" My heart lodges in my throat. "It's only been *five weeks*!"

"And how long did you and Dad know each other before you agreed to marry?"

"You can't compare yourself to your father and me—"

"Why not? *You* always have."

"Don't get fresh with me, young lady. You're talking to your mother, not your girlfriend."

"I'm sorry. I—"

"You haven't even seen each other."

"We've exchanged photos. Lots of—"

"You haven't met *in person*, Kiran."

"But *you* have. *You* made the introductions."

I cover my eyes. *Yash is going to kill me.*

"Do you think physical attraction's going to be an issue, for either of us?" Kiran asks.

No. I bite my lip. *That's not the point....*

When I don't reply, she says, "Neither do we. Don't you see, Mom? It's just like a traditional arranged marriage..."

Not *just*.

Nausea churns my stomach. I feel seasick, not unlike how I felt during chemo. I hug my knees with one arm. Roll onto my side. "Your father isn't going to see it that way," I whisper.

The unspoken shrieks across the miles. *John isn't Indian.*

"That's what I'm afraid of," Kiran says in a shaky voice. "I don't want to go down the same road with you and Dad again. It was too hard, for all of us. I don't know what to do, Mom."

You and me both, pillu.

I take John by the arm and lead him out the door, making excuses to my confused parents. I hail an auto-rickshaw, hop inside, not bothering to barter on the fare into town.

"Kiran told you," John says as we rumble down the street.

"Yes, she did."

"You're in shock."

"Yes, I am."

"You want to put me in cement *chappals*."

"I'm thinking about it."

The driver flies over a speed bump, jarring our spines. John reprimands him in Marathi before I can, then continues speaking in Marathi to me, but I shake my head.

"Not today, John," I say. "Today, we speak in English."

"Yes, ma'am," he says.

We go to Saffron restaurant in Chandani Chauk. I wait until we order, then grill John.

"You don't know what we've been through with Kiran."

"I have an idea."

"I don't mean to sound rude, John, but you and I need to have a frank discussion here."

"I understand, ma'am."

Everything I tell him about Anthony he's already heard from Kiran. I don't enjoy enumerating her faults, but full disclosure is compulsory. "My daughter is very stubborn," I say. "And sarcastic. She argues for the sake of arguing. She can be difficult at times, and she'll try your patience regularly."

"Umm-hmm." He grins. "Never a dull moment."

Never a moment's peace, I was thinking. "Often, she gets an idea in her head and won't let it go. She can be like a dog with a bone."

John nods. "Been there, experienced that."

He isn't surprised by anything I tell him. I don't get it. "Answer me this, John," I say. "*Why* do you want to marry Kiran?"

"She makes me laugh. She's tough, but not as tough as

she wants people to think. A paper tiger. She's sensitive, though she tries hard to hide it. She's smart and makes *no* attempt to hide that. She's passionate. Focused. Loyal. Maternal. You want me to go on?"

"Yes. Please."

"We both fell in love with pianists..."

As I listen to him, I see that for every negative quality, he has a positive interpretation. He assures me he's committed to working through the challenges they are certain to have. He had a *very* successful marriage, and he knows how to have them.

"John, you know more about Indian culture than Kiran does. I'm not discounting that. But it's one thing to live with an Indian family as a paying guest and another to marry into one. You have no idea what you're getting into, what marrying into another culture entails."

"That's not true—with all due respect, ma'am." John takes out his wallet. "We have an expression in Texas. *This ain't my first rodeo.*" He hands me a photograph of a pretty Asian girl sitting at a grand piano, her slender ankles crossed, a single long-stemmed red rose in her delicate hands. "That's my Maddie," he says. "Madelline Chang Cooper. Her parents emigrated from Korea. Maddie was first-generation American, too."

I cover my open mouth. I don't know whether to laugh or cry. "John, you never fail to surprise me...."

His ears turn pink. "Thank you, ma'am. I think." He rubs the back of his neck.

"It's definitely a compliment." I hand back Maddie's photo. "May I speak with the Changs about you?"

"Yes, ma'am."

"And your parents? Have you told them your intentions?"

"Yes, ma'am."

"What do they think?"

"They're nervous but keeping open minds. They're anxious to meet Kiran. Mostly, they're happy I'm happy again. They watched me bury Maddie. They know..." His voice thickens, and he clears his throat. "They know me."

If we were in the States, I would reach across the table and pat his hand. But here, it's not proper to touch in public, so I smile my empathy and hope he understands.

"As you know, Indians commonly consult astrologers," I say. "Would you mind if we arranged for your chart?"

"No, ma'am." He provides all the necessary details.

I close my eyes. Draw a long, slow breath through my nose. Fill my lungs. Release at the same pace. Open my eyes. "I'll talk to Kiran's father."

Through the blue windowpanes of his eyes, I see his relief. "Thank you, ma'am. I swear, you won't regret—"

"Don't thank me yet," I say. "This isn't going to be easy. For me, or for you."

Texas John just grins and says, "Nothing worth having ever is."

"*What?*" Yash barks into the phone. "No Indian boy is good enough for this *maharani*?"

"It's not that," I say, but I'm not even going to *attempt* to have this discussion over the phone. Yash will not listen. This is where Kiran gets her stubbornness. Her father. He and Kiran lock horns precisely because in this one aspect, they're exactly alike. Neither will back down; each needs to have the last word.

"You tell me she's grown in the past five years," Yash says. "What grown-drone is this? *Kamaal aahé*."

"Come to India, Yash," I say in as soothing a tone as I can. "Meet John for yourself."

"Why should I come there? He should come here. And why should I waste my time meeting someone even Kiran hasn't met? How do we know they'll still want to marry after they see each other? They might take one look and say no way. God, I tell you, Meenal, this daughter of yours is going to give me a heart attack!" I know what's coming next; I mouth it along with my husband: "And send me to an early death, just like my father!"

He said this in his twenties; he says it in his sixties. Watch now, he'll outlive Kiran and Vivek.

I hold the mobile away from my ear. I'm lying on my back across the bed again, my newly adopted position for long and/or stressful phone calls. I learned many tricks this year to cope with toxins, including negativity. Negativity never goes away; you must learn how to handle it. Right now, I must disengage.

I raise my feet straight up in the air, flex and point my toes, stretch my calves, admire my pedicure.

I usually favor pinks, but I found red to my liking today. A fire engine red, that's what I chose from the sweet girl who comes to our flats each week to indulge the women of the house (only the women) with home massages, manicures, and pedicures. All for a minuscule fraction of what I would pay in the States but *don't*. There, I consider it a frivolous, overpriced expense; here such a small, easily affordable amount I can rationalize as doing my part to support gainful employment.

My feet have aged, I notice. Thickened toenails, cracked heels no amount of oils and lotions will repair. Oh, well... I've become an old lady. Who shall wear red toenail polish.

Periodically, when I hear an opening, I replace the mobile over my ear and say, "Yash, I would like you to come to India."

Two seconds, and he starts again. "What is this nonsense, Meenal? Have they brainwashed you?"

I put the mobile down. On the mattress. Next to my pillow. Maybe next week, I'll try a purple. There was this one shade, a pale lilac that caught my eye. Hmmmm... I lower my feet. Raise my hands. Splay my fingers.

Baba shuffles into the bedroom dressed in his usual evening loungewear of comfy white cotton *kurta-pajamas.* He pushes the black frame of his thick-lensed glasses higher on the bridge of his nose, hitches his chin at me, turns up one hand in question. *Getting anywhere?*

I shake my head.

He thrusts out his hand and gestures for the mobile. *"Eh, Yashwant! Me Baba bolthath! Huh, thik aahé! Huh. Huh."* He talks for five minutes, ends the call, drops the mobile on the bed. "Meenu," he says, all seriousness, "more than this, pink was much prettier. This red..." He wrinkles his nose, waves a palm in distaste. "This is not you. Too *ghatty*. Your husband's coming next week. Wear pink, huh?" He squeezes my big toe and shuffles from the room.

When I informed my parents of Kiran and John's intentions, *Ai* gasped and blamed herself. Why did she interfere? Did she make some mistake in her *puja*, accidentally switching John and Nikhil?

I reminded *Ai* that Kiran's fate is what it is. What is meant to be *will* be. We are all players in destiny's plans, vehicles through which God operates.

As fate would have it, after Yash arrives, it's *Baba* who makes the strongest case for John during the family gathering.

"The boy *is* Indian," *Baba* says, "in the most important way. *His heart* is Indian."

All around, heads wobble. I see in Yash's eyes, in the way only a wife can, that he is moved by the overwhelming endorsement of my family, but he remains quiet, stoic. That night in bed, he holds me close, burrowing his face against my neck. He's scared. He has every reason to be. Cancer taught me that true courage isn't the absence of fear but perseverance in the face of fear.

"God, Meenu. *Why* another American music-*wallah*?"

"Because, like John, she's attracted to the exotic. *He* is exotic to *her*."

"Didn't she learn from her mistakes?"

"Yes, she did." I stroke the back of his head, still bald because he can't tolerate stubble and lacks the patience to let it grow out. "The question is, *did we*?"

Yash raises his head. Frowns at me. "What does that mean?"

I trace his brow, ironing out the wrinkles with my fingers. "Ask yourself, as I did, when you're sick and dying, what's more important, your self-righteousness or your daughter's love? And when your soul leaves this body, departs this life, which would you rather take with you? We can't have everything, so we have to decide. What is it we value the most?"

These are the tough questions Uma put to me in the hospital, when I flatly refused counseling, and now I put them to Yash.

"Kiran isn't a child anymore," I say. "For better or worse, her personality has been formed. We can influence her decisions, but we can't impose our will on her. She doesn't need us, or our approval, but she still wants both. For how long, I don't know."

"In other words," Yash says, "if we want our grown daughter in our lives, it has to be on her terms."

"No, in other words, *there are no terms.*"

Yash shakes his head. "You lost me, Meenu."

Before cancer, I would have given up at this point. Given in to thoughts like: *How can he* not *understand what I'm saying? Haven't I said it enough times, spelled it out in the clearest possible terms? If I bash my head against this wall anymore, I'll knock myself unconscious.* The temptation to quit is still there, but I can't succumb. This is too important. Yes, it's true everything can't be conveyed, contained, in words. But if it's important enough, we have to keep trying—using new ways, *and* the old—to stretch our boundaries, increase our awareness.

I used to think saying the same old words, over and over, was wasting my breath. But what, then, is chanting? Doesn't repetition of a mantra heighten consciousness? Revisiting the old, familiar, over time reveals new meaning. Truth comes not at once but in layers. Life isn't a straight line but a circle. And this year, I feel myself coming full circle....

I breathe deeply, find my center, and try again, beginning with familiar building blocks, "Is there only one way to have a relationship with God? Only one way to worship? Only one path to *moksha*? No. We don't believe in any 'my way or the highway' terms with God, do we?"

So far, Yash is with me. "And God is love of the highest. The purest. The truest. God is the ultimate truth. It follows, then, that there are no 'my way or the highway' terms with true love. If you truly love someone, it's immaterial who's right or wrong, who wins or loses. There are no sides. We are all One."

Yash groans. "Meenu..." I've heard my husband's sounds enough to know what they mean. This kind of groan is physical pain. I'm hurting his head. A plea to let up.

I gentle my voice and forge ahead, building on familiar but less abstract concepts this time. "With every new discovery, the world feels like a smaller place, doesn't it? Remember when we watched Neil Armstrong walk on the moon? You were so excited, you phoned your mother, even though we couldn't afford it, and the first thing your mother said when you told her was, *'Kai, Ai la bandal noko maaru, Yash.'* She was convinced you were pulling her leg. Today, the rickshaw-*wallah* has a mobile. A village with no plumbing has a cyber-café. The world isn't shrinking, our awareness of all the possibilities is growing, right?"

A noncommittal grunt.

I'll take it. At least he's listening. I continue, "Well, in today's world, we are seeing, *discovering* how a child born to Indian parents can become American, and a child born to American parents can become Indian."

Silence. A sigh. "Meenu, you do craft beautiful prose—of that, there's no doubt—but it doesn't matter how mumbo-jumbo or one-two-three you say it, I see it how I see it, I'm sorry. *East is East, and West is West*... Please don't be angry. I just..."

"I know." I take his hand in mine. He isn't ready. Not yet, and perhaps not ever, in this life. We all have our own spiritual path. Though our eventual destination—the ultimate reality—is the same, everyone's at a different place, proceeding at a different pace. Before cancer, had Uma spoken these same words, they would have gone in one ear and out the other for me, *and* I would have judged her pretentious. It took cancer to heighten my awareness, my consciousness of *all* possibilities.

The infinite. Eternal. Dimensionless. *God.*

Cancer created a *new* material reality for me and brought me closer to the ultimate truth, to God. I saw the light—as a ray hitting cut crystal. The prisms are many; the light is one. I laughed in amazement, laughed at *myself*. There it was, right in front of me all along, plain as daylight, but I couldn't see it. And just as suddenly, yet again, I'm struck by a blinding flash of the obvious.

When you can't see the question, how can you see the answer?

Tenderly, I lay my hand on Yash's cheek. "It comes down to this," I say. "Can you forgive Kiran for not being the daughter you want, and accept the daughter you have?"

Yash rolls onto his back and flings an arm over his eyes. "I don't know, Meenu," he whispers, anguish clogging his voice. "I just don't know...."

Green Beans Bhaji

SERVES 4

3 tablespoons canola oil

2 pinches asafetida (hing)

1 medium onion, finely chopped

4 cups string beans, chopped into ¼-inch pieces

⅛ teaspoon turmeric powder

1 teaspoon coriander powder

1 teaspoon cumin powder

½ teaspoon cayenne powder

½ cup water, divided

1 teaspoon salt

½ teaspoon brown sugar

1. In a wok or deep 12-inch skillet, heat oil over medium heat.
2. Stir in asafetida. After the asafetida changes color, about 30 seconds, add onion. Sauté until golden brown.
3. Stir in beans. Sauté 2–3 minutes.
4. Stir in turmeric, coriander, cumin, and cayenne. Reduce heat to medium-low. Cover and simmer for 3–4 minutes, stirring occasionally.
5. Stir in ¼ cup water. Cover and simmer until water is absorbed.
6. Stir in remaining ¼ cup water. Cover and simmer until beans change color.
7. Stir in salt and brown sugar. Reduce heat to low. Cover and simmer until water is absorbed.
8. Remove from heat. Serve warm.

Chappati

MAKES 6

2 cups whole wheat flour, plus 2–3 tablespoons (for dusting)

½ teaspoon salt

2 tablespoons canola oil

1 cup water

ghee or butter to taste

1. In a large mixing bowl, sift together 2 cups flour and salt.
2. Using your hand to knead, stir in oil and water, ¼ cup at a time, until dough forms into a ball.
3. Transfer dough to a clean, unfloured work surface. Knead until smooth, about 5–10 minutes. Dough should be soft and pliable, neither too wet nor too dry. Add a little water or a little flour if necessary.
4. Cover with clean kitchen towel. Allow to sit for 30 minutes.
5. Dust a clean work surface with flour.
6. Tear off wedges of dough, making 6 equal portions between the size of a plum and an apricot.
7. Roll portion between your palms into a ball, then press your palms together to flatten somewhat. Set on work surface.
8. With a rolling pin, flatten portion into a 6-inch circle of uniform thickness. Dust work surface as necessary to keep dough from sticking.
9. Repeat for all 6 portions.
10. Heat a large nonstick skillet over medium-high heat. Test heat with a few drops of water. Water should sizzle.

11. Carefully place one chappati onto the skillet. Cook until chappati lightens somewhat and bubbles puff beneath the surface, about 30–60 seconds.
12. Using a spatula, flip chappati and cook other side about 30–40 seconds.
13. Make one last flip, if necessary, to cook any remaining raw dough, then remove to a plate.*
14. Spread a little ghee or butter over the surface. Should melt upon contact.
15. Repeat for remaining chappatis.
16. Stack on top of each other, so top of one chappati butters bottom of next.

Tips:

✔ Be careful not to overcook. Some brown spots are okay, but chappatis should remain soft, not cardboard stiff or crisp.

✔ If chappatis are cooking too quickly, or scorching too much, decrease heat.

✔ Chappatis are best served hot, right off the skillet, but can also be enjoyed warm or at room temperature.

Rani McGuiness Tomashot: Reincarnation

A diamond was lying in the street
covered with dirt.
Many fools passed by.
Someone who knew diamonds picked it up.
KABIR

Have you ever had one of those How-the-Hell-Did-I-End-Up-Here moments? And when you look back, you see that it started innocuously enough, as most life-altering courses tend to, one baby step after another? That's what happened to Bryan and me this year.

It all began when I agreed to accompany my mother on her research trip to Kolkata. . . .

There I was, playing tourist, and doing a bang-up job, if I do say so myself. No jet lag. No diarrhea. No communication problems. What more could a Third-World tourist want? Then, a weird thing happened. My asthma—wait, more precisely, *all the symptoms of my childhood asthma*—came back.

That's not the weird part. I'm getting there. Hold your horses. First, the symptoms. Basic stuff. Should be all-too-familiar to my fellow asthma sufferers: I woke up gasping in the dead of night. Couldn't breathe. Felt like someone was sitting on my chest and strangling me.

I woke my mom, who woke Anandita-*mashi*, who woke her doctor, who came right over. The doctor happens to live in the building, but house calls aren't uncommon, I'm told. Afterward, I was loaded up with the usual paraphernalia, including my old best friend I'd hoped never to lay eyes on again: the dreaded inhaler. So there I was, rapidly sucking my inhaler bone-dry, like in the not-so-good old days, when my mother decided she wanted a second opinion and carted my wheezing butt to another doctor.

This doctor, a stooped old woman with a reedy silver braid hanging down to her butt who appeared to be about a hundred, give or take ten years, didn't instruct me to say "ah," didn't look in my mouth or my ears, didn't instruct me to take a deep breath or listen to my lungs with a stethoscope. She didn't even feel the glands at the sides of my throat. She just sat me down in front of her on a low string-bed and put her wrinkly hand on my head—her fleshy heel against my forehead, bony fingers on my crown.

"This is not asthma," she said.

"Allergies?" Mom asked.

"No."

"I had a feeling..." Mom said.

"What?" I asked.

Neither of them replied. The doc instructed me to lie down, close my eyes, relax. She whispered something to Mom in Bengali, something I couldn't hear and had the distinct impression, from her tone, she didn't *want* me to hear.

I cracked open my eyelids just enough to peep through

my lashes and saw the Ancient One gesture for Mom to follow her. Slipping from the room through a curtained doorway, my mother looked back over her shoulder at me. Quickly, I shut my eyes. Minutes later, she retrieved me, and we left. Outside on the footpath, she asked if I wanted to go to a nearby café. I was pooped, but it sounded like she wanted to go, so I said sure.

Navigating through the traffic—animal, vegetable, *and* mineral—I surmised she wasn't planning to clue me in on the Ancient One's diagnosis until we sat down, but I was curious.

"If it isn't asthma or allergies, what is it?" I asked.

"You're adjusting," she replied. "To being here. Some people are more susceptible than others to . . . the elements."

B.F.D., I thought. "So, where's the big deal in that? Why'd you have to leave the room?"

Her gaze shot to mine, then darted away. She stopped, squinted into the distance, appeared to look down the road. "We . . . uh . . . were settling the bill."

Oh. That made sense. "So, did you haggle with her?"

"No—"

"*What?* Mom! The one time you *should* have, you didn't—!"

"No *need,* I was going to say, silly goose. She works pro bono."

"Well, seeing as she doesn't actually *do* anything. Nothing for nothing. Hey, what a bargain!"

Mom gave a short laugh. "I'd gladly pay *any* amount for her services."

"What services—?" A rickshaw whipped around the corner where we were standing, waiting to cross. In the nick of time, Mom yanked me out of the way before the wheel ran over my foot, then made me hold her hand like a five-year-old.

She tugged me out to the middle of the road, stopped in the midst of traffic, put her hand out in front of a slow-moving taxi and halted the driver, so we could cross in front of him—in the fine art of Kolkata Jaywalking, my mother is a master.

"What services?" I asked again.

"Spiritual healing. Watch out!"

I sidestepped a big ol' cow patty. "Eeewwwww."

"Someone will be along to collect that shortly."

A word to the wise: If you can't walk, chew gum, and carry on multiple threads of conversation at the same time, you won't last long in Kolkata.

Focusing on my feet, I said, "I guess anyone can put up a sign and call themselves a healer these days."

She laughed. "You think your mother can't sniff a phony? You can take the girl out of Bengal, but you can't take Bengal out of the girl. That healer was one of the best. You were asleep for half an hour."

That brought my chin up. "I was not!" When she made a snoring sound, I bumped my shoulder against hers. "Moth-er! Come on! I *don't* snore. And I closed my eyes for a minute. Two, tops."

"*Thirty*-two, Boo, I kid you not. I clocked you. I sat there and watched the entire time."

My gaze searched hers. She *was* serious. "No shit . . ."

The chic café looked just like a bookstore-café back home: hardwood floors, comfy furniture, air-conditioning. Sparkling clean and inviting, it was understandably packed. Mom went and struck up a conversation with a group of college students—just small talk, she said!—and another friendly group, behind them, overheard and invited us to join them as they were leaving soon.

I had to use the facilities, but I wasn't dying, so I held it. On that count, our last trip to Kolkata scarred me for life. My cousins, expecting me to be a stereotypical stuck-up American, thought it would be funny to play a practical joke on me—via my stuck-up, foreigner bowels. That was before they got to know me, and boy, did they feel rotten. (Hey, I may be stuck-up, but I'm also smart, cute, and funny!) Not as rotten as *I* felt, however, having already consumed the street food that worked faster than Ex-Lax. And did I mention they'd deliberately "accidentally" clogged the only Western toilet in the house beforehand? That would be the flip side of "brilliant." *Diabolical.*

T.P. wasn't in abundance, even in the big cities, back then. Paper, a costly commodity in India, is associated with books and newspapers, highly respected mediums of knowledge and wisdom—not something on which you wipe excrement. Though readily available today, T.P. still doesn't substitute for the traditional hygiene practice of washing thoroughly with water, but adds an optional, luxury "dry cycle" after the "rinse cycle."

Mom said unless we were in a five-star hotel, we couldn't assume the public restrooms had T.P. Western toilets might be plentiful, but T.P. isn't. Ditto paper towels.

"You packing?" Dad had asked before we left the house for the airport. "Make sure." Not guns, but packs of tissues and antibacterial wipes, he meant. And yes, I was—*at all times.*

At the café, Mom joined the intellectuals intellectualizing, but my brain was too tired to keep up with that many people, all talking at the same time, over each other. I was glad when they left, and Mom and I could do our own thing.

Over tea and snacks, she explained that the body's seven major energy centers—*chakras,* Sanskrit for *wheel*—aligned along the spinal chord can get blocked. Blockage causes imbalance, as each *chakra* correlates with specific physical, mental, emotional attributes. Apparently, my throat *chakra,* which is associated with creativity and expression, was clogged.

A healer's hands are highly attuned to energy fields, like how blind people can sense walls, doors, and other objects in close proximity without actually coming into contact with them. *Aura* is the term coined by the ancients, still widely used today in reference to these electromagnetic/quantum fields. "Think of the negative and positive poles of a magnet, of the earth," Mom said. By moving her ultrasensitive hands over my energy pathways, the Ancient One removed the negative energy, the cause of blockages, and infused positive energy that heals, rinsing my *chakras* and aura squeaky clean. After this energy "tune-up and oil change," I passed my emissions test.

Now, while much of this makes sense to my scientific brain, not all of it does. But I listened over two cups of Darjeeling tea—after which I *did* use the facilities, without incident, I'm happy to report—and I gave my mother an indulgent smile because I love the woman to pieces, and whether or not she's a fruitcake is irrelevant, though I seriously doubted I'd find any asthmatic relief while we remained in that polluted city.

Oddly enough, Mom smiled back at *me* in the exact same way.

When we got back to the flat, I was one tuckered puppy. I went to take a nap and ended up sleeping through the night, not uncommon with jet lag. The next morning, I was lying in bed, still groggy, watching dust motes dance in the sunlight when something felt "off."

I thought to myself: *Self, what's wrong with this picture?* Suddenly, I realized: *I'm not choked up. I'm not hacking. I'm breathing just fine.*

All my asthma symptoms vanished overnight, never to return. Cue the *Twilight Zone* music. Was it all in my head, psychosomatic? Is there a scientific basis to spiritual energy yet to be fully understood, explained? Beats me. But from then on, I started seeing things in a new light. Possibilities where none before existed....

Hip deep in boxes, I'm in the throes of packing up Bryan's and my recently sold Pacific Heights condo when the phone rings. I hop toward a clearing, aim for the cradle where the portable rests. Make that, *used to* rest.

Uh-oh...

Another ring. I scan the room. Clutter and more clutter. In what heap did I bury the flippin' phone? Color me clueless.

Oh, man, tell me I didn't pack it...

I eye the caller I.D. display. LINDSTROM, ERIC. Preity! And I know exactly why she's calling. "Hang on! I'm coming!" Following the rings, I unearth the phone and answer a second before voicemail kicks in. "Preity!" I say without preamble. "Can you believe it?"

"No! Can you?"

"No!"

"You sound out of breath. Am I catching you at a bad time?"

"No, I could use a break." I plop down onto the floor, back against the wall, feet on a box, ankles crossed, and wipe my brow with the sleeve of my T-shirt.

"I got your number from my mom, who of course got it from *your* mom. I had to call you. Who else would understand this? *Really* understand? I mean, it's Kiran. *Our* Kiran!"

"I know! I've been dying to call *you*!" Though I can count on one hand the number of times Preity and I have talked on the phone—all of them when we were kids—I, too, have had a burning urge to pick up the phone. "I've been going on and on to Bryan, the neighbors, the cats—"

"They don't get it," Preity says.

"They *can't* get it," I say.

"And we can't explain it to them!"

"Exactly!"

Neither of us has talked to Kiran yet. I left voicemail. Preity emailed. No replies yet. Preity doubts she's getting one, but I predict she will.

"So what have *you* heard?" she asks.

"You first. Saroj Auntie always has her ear to the ground."

"Yeah, but Uma Auntie's been instrumental. She totally has Meenal Auntie's ear."

"Meenal Auntie isn't the problem," I say.

"It's Yash Uncle."

"Yep."

"Is Patrick Uncle going to talk to him?" Preity asks.

"Nope, won't get involved. How about Sandeep Uncle?"

"Same."

"Humph. Typical," I say. "When you actually *want* a guy to interfere, he won't."

Preity laughs. "Isn't *that* the truth?"

We compare notes....

"Well, according to *The Basu Gazette*," I report, "Kiran says she won't get married without Yash Uncle's blessing. Sounds like *she's* come around."

"Depends. Is she making a promise or a threat? *The Chawla Times* wasn't clear on that. I mean, what's the alternative, if Yash Uncle doesn't give his blessing? Will she end the romance and walk away? Or will she play house without getting married?"

"That's the million-dollar question," I say.

"Okay, let's cut to the chase," Preity says. "I'm totally floored Kiran wants to marry a guy she's never met. Or touched. Or *you know*..." She drops her voice. "*No* sample of the goods?"

"I'm sure they've had phone sex. Or cybersex. Probably both."

"You think? Kiran doesn't strike me as the kinky type."

"Sweetheart, think romance, not porn. Erotic, not vulgar." I give her various examples. "See the difference? The spoken word can be very seductive. So can the written word."

"Umm-hmm. Just so you know, my office, where I'm sitting, is an open cubicle. And all those words? They happen to work for me, so show a little mercy and *quit it.*"

I make noisy kisses into the phone. "Hey, think about it. Isn't it kind of romantic, getting to know each other from the inside out, instead of the outside in? Exploring each other's hearts and minds before bodies?"

"Hmmm . . . Now that you say that . . . That *is* how it *should* be," Preity says. "Society's too damn fixated on appearances."

"Survival of the prettiest."

We break for half an hour. I finish packing my books from the library bookcases, leaving Bryan's for him to sort through. Preity calls back from the privacy of a conference room, and we resume our conversation. . . .

She predicts if Kiran's *really* serious about wanting to marry this Texas John—that's what our moms call him—and he's *really* serious about marrying her, it'll happen. Yash Uncle will realize the train's leaving the station with or without him. Either he gets on board, or waves good-bye from the platform. This time forever.

I'm not so sure. Kiran and Meenal Auntie have worked really hard at their relationship, getting it back on track after a near-fatal derailment. Kiran's realized the perils of solo travel, and Meenal Auntie and Yash Uncle are a joint ticket. "Plus, after all poor Meenal Auntie's been through with her cancer, Kiran won't do anything to unduly upset her."

"Neither will Yash Uncle," Preity says. "He worships the ground she walks on. Did you see how he kept checking in with her at the New Year's party?"

"That was sweet," I agree.

"So, if Kiran defers to her mom this time, and Yash Uncle defers to his wife this time, then..."

"The buck stops at Meenal Auntie."

We spend the next hour speculating and gossiping. What's going to happen when Kiran and John see each other in person? When and where will they meet? How can they stand to wait? If it works out, where would their wedding take place? Indian or American style? Hindu, Christian, or secular? How would they raise their children?

"Eeek! Listen to us," Preity says. "We sound like *them*!"

I gasp. "Not *them*! Say it isn't so! Horror of horrors! Have we become our mothers?"

"They warned us it would happen one day."

"I never believed them. Did you?"

"Heck, no. Old wives' tale," Preity says. "Nothing more."

"Yeah," I say. "Urban myth."

Preity clears her throat. "I won't tell if you don't tell."

"Tell what? Who is this? Do I know you?"

"Sorry. Wrong number. Hanging up now..."

On an evening stroll along the Maidan, Mom and *Mashi* eating *misti dohi*—jaggery-sweetened yogurt—from disposable terra-cotta bowls, while I had to pass on this and all other oh-so-tempting snacks from street vendors, my mother commented, "It's terrific to see all the progress, the Indian economy taking off in leaps and bounds."

"For the middle-class only, *Sejdi*—"

"Mostly, yes, but not exclusively. Remember when we were young? Servants wore torn clothes, no shoes. They barely had enough food to fill their bellies. What leftovers we gave them each day, they took home, so their children wouldn't go hungry. Fast forward to the present, look at Mrs. Chaudhury's *ayah*—"

"*Ayah*'s educated."

Mom acceded this point and switched her case study to the maid who worked part-time for *Mashi*, full-time for Mrs. Ray on the second floor. The maid wore decent *saris* and *chappals*. Her children were clothed, fed, sheltered, schooled—even her girl who was fourteen, which *never* happened in the old days. There was every chance they wouldn't grow up to be servants like their parents. Regardless, they had more choice in the matter, better opportunities than previous generations. True, the maid earned a pittance, but she and her chauffeur husband together made enough to support family here and in their native Bihari village. Mr. and Mrs. Ray paid their big-ticket expenses like medical bills, tuition, wedding expenses. It *was* progress.

Anandita-*mashi* argued the progress was disproportionate and made her case for a more equitable distribution of wealth, more benefits trickling down to those with the greatest need.

The two of them started debating, hot and heavy, I jumped into the fray, and the three of us had a rip-roaring, Bengali-style *adda*. We agreed on the "end" goal, disagreed on the "means" to achieve it. I wore the capitalist hat, Mom the socialist, *Mashi* the Marxist/communist.

After stimulating my cranium, I felt winded, yet energized. Invigorated, clearheaded, revitalized. Exactly the way I felt after a good run.

My runner's high was back!

My mother had piles of papers, stacked and spread, all over our room. She was trying to get a bird's-eye, big-picture visual of the body of my grandmother's work, to see how best to organize it. Randomly, I picked up one of the tablets, flipped through some pages, and shrugged. "It's all Bengali to me," I joked, unable to read the Bengali script.

Mom patted a spot next to her on the bed. "Come. I'll translate for you. She opens with a quote from Tagore." Mom read first in Bengali, then provided the English translation:

Let me not look for allies in life's battlefield,
But to my own strength.
Let me not crave in anxious fear to be saved,
But for the patience to win my freedom.

I listened, fascinated, exploring the hidden terrain of my grandmother's heart. Like me, she suffered clinical depression. Unlike me, they didn't know what it was back then and labeled her a madwoman, among other asinine things. Because she died when Mom and her sisters were little, she was always something of an enigma, which made the heirlooms she passed down even more precious, nothing more precious than *her words*.

Until then, everything I knew about my grandmother I'd been told secondhand. That was the first time I heard straight from the source. And wow, the power of that voice! I could hear her speak, her voice resonating deep inside me. Her handwriting seemed to pulse with life, breathing for her long after she'd stopped breathing for herself. Her handwriting often changed, sometimes on the same page, her pen strokes fanciful, crisp and clean, cramped, shaky. She crossed out words, sometimes whole lines of prose. Thinking of all my botched attempts and false starts this year, I understood. I could visualize myself in her place. Correcting. Tweaking. Ripping entire pages out of the tablets. Tearing them up. Starting over.

She wrote for herself, diarylike, about her life. An intimate view of a private world inside her head that no one knew, and no one cared to know. Recurring themes: unrequited love, unfulfilled desire, competition, failure, death.

There's such passion in her voice. Such intensity in her emotions, high and low. Vivid word pictures transported me to another world. I was right there, in her skin, breathing her breath. I saw what she saw. Smelled it. Heard it. Felt it. Tasted it. Mundane details, like the tiny brushstrokes of Impressionist painting, added up to a haunting portrait of a woman I never met.

A familiar stranger...

Just like that, my nose started to tingle. Then the backs of my arms and thighs. I knew that tingling. Slowly, I pulled myself upright as if chasing a sneeze. *Ahhh...? Ahhh...?* Oh, come on... *Ahhh-choo!* "Hey, Mom? Wouldn't it be cool if your anthology had Bengali script on the left page, and the English, or Hindi, or whatever other language translation on the right? You keep talking about the importance of preserving regional languages, making them accessible outside the region. Why not make a bilingual, or trilingual, anthology? And... Ooooh... How about illustrations? Wouldn't that be fun?"

Once I started talking, I couldn't stop. The ideas came. They came and came and came.

When I got back to San Francisco, I could tell something was up with Bryan, so I wasn't surprised when he said, "Rani, we need to talk."

Patience does not rank high on my list of virtues. "What's wrong? Who died? Is there someone else? Who is it? I'll kill her. Or him. You aren't . . . ? *Are you?*"

"No one died. There's no one else. And no, I'm not." He wiped a hand over his brow. "Whew! Thanks for putting things into perspective. Suddenly, investing in a computer animation start-up and relocating to Bangalore for a few years isn't the *most* life-altering thing that could happen to us."

"What???"

As he filled me in on a proposal that had fallen into his lap just that week, I drank in a sight I hadn't seen in a long time: the big, dorky grin I fell in love with. His *masti*!

In a nutshell: Bangalore is India's Silicon Valley and hometown of Bryan's college buddy and fellow computer genius, Rajesh. The start-up, Rajesh's brainchild, was seeking venture capital to create high-tech animated films. Think: *Shrek*, *Toy Story*, and *Monsters, Inc*. Except: *Indian* stories for *Indian* markets. Dubbed in English, Hindi, and the regional Indian languages. New markets. New opportunities. New jobs here, there, anywhere Rajesh finds the talent.

"Would you have any interest—?"

"Is the Pope Catholic?" I pounced on him like a puppy,

knocking him over and showering his face with kisses. "Yes! Yes, yes, yes, yes, yes..."

He laughed. "Wow, absence really does make the heart grow fonder.... Feel free to go to Kolkata with your mother *anytime*."

We stayed up until dawn talking and laughing and dreaming....

Before, I never understood how my mother found the courage to leave the world she knew behind. Now I get it. Very simply, she had a dream she couldn't realize at home, so she went where it took her, to the Land of Opportunity.

As the world's economies grow, so do Lands of Opportunity, benefiting *all* the world's people.

FROM: "Rani Tomashot" <RaniTomashot@hotmail.com>
TO: Kiran Deshpande; Preity Lindstrom
SENT: September 5, 20XX 02:20 AM
SUBJECT: Scriptwriters R Us

Hello, chickies! Salutations from Bangalore! How's life there? Soggy here, but drying out. Pics attached. As you can see, our apartment rocks! The whole building/city does! Just the nicest, coolest people. And having a domestic staff (that looooves us firangis!) doesn't suck. We expected to be more homesick, but we actually see/call/email family and friends MORE now that we're farther away. No one visits the other side of the world for a weekend, ya know. They camp out for weeks/months! Thank God I have domestic help . . . the "hostess with the most-est" I am NOT! And: Good Darn Thing we're moving BACK in 2 yrs cuz I'm seeing waaaay too much mother-in-law!! <ggg> You'd think the monsoon would keep/scare her away, but nooooo!!

Now, since I'm not only after Preity's "Multitasking Goddess" crown, BUT counting down the days to ***A Certain Someone's*** wedding, AND practicing scriptwriting for "Raj-Rani Animated Pictures" (!!!), check out a warm-up exercise I wrote today . . . Kiran, love, did I forget anything from our conversation? <wg>

XOXOXO,
Rani

RANI: (smug but in a cute, endearing way) You're talking to the new part-owner of a computer animation start-up!

KIRAN: (gasps) I don't believe it! How *perfect*!

RANI: Scary-perfect. I almost fell to my knees and kissed the ground. It's stuff like this . . . invitations that fall into your lap . . . synchronicity . . . that prevents me from being a card-carrying atheist, keeping me solidly in Camp Agnostic.

KIRAN: I'm so happy for you!

RANI: Thanks, babe. I'm pretty stoked for you and me both. So, hey, can I ask you a personal question?

KIRAN: How personal?

RANI: Have you and John had phone sex?

KIRAN: No comment.

RANI: Cybersex?

KIRAN: No comment.

RANI: (laughing) I knew it . . .

Anandita's Shukto

[Bitter & Sweet Mixed Veggies]

SERVES 6–8

VEGETABLES:

1 medium eggplant

1 cup chopped bitter gourd or 1 cup chopped kale or Swiss chard or collard greens

1 plantain or green banana, peeled and sliced

1 cup sliced radish

2 medium tomatoes, diced

1 cup sweet potato, peeled

1 medium potato, peeled

1 cup baby lima beans

1 cup sliced carrots, peeled

1 cup cauliflower

2 tender drumstick bean pods, or 8 asparagus spears*

SPICES:

2 tablespoons poppy seeds, divided

1½ tablespoons mustard seeds, divided

2-inch piece of fresh ginger root, peeled and chopped

¼ cup canola oil, divided

¾ teaspoon paanch phoron (Bengali five-spice)

2 bay leaves

1 cup coconut milk

1 teaspoon ghee or butter

salt (to taste)

sugar (to taste)

1. In a small bowl of warm water, soak mustard seeds and poppy seeds. Set aside.
2. Wash all veggies thoroughly.
3. For drumstick bean pods or asparagus: Using a vegetable peeler, scrape off tough outer skin. Cut tender stalks into 2-inch pieces.

4. For eggplant: Quarter lengthwise, then crosswise into ½-inch-thick slices.
5. For bitter gourd: Halve lengthwise. Remove and discard seeds. Chop halves crosswise into very fine, ⅛-inch slices.
6. For potatoes: Halve lengthwise, then cut crosswise into ¼-inch-thick slices.
7. Chop remaining veggies into bite-sized cubes.
8. In a blender or food processor, combine the soaked mustard and poppy seeds with ginger root. Purée to a smooth paste. Set aside.
9. Eggplant: In a large wok, heat 1 tablespoon oil over medium-high heat. Add eggplant. Stir-fry for 2–3 minutes. Remove with a slotted spoon. Set aside.
10. Bitter gourd: Heat another 1 tablespoon oil. Add bitter gourd. Reduce heat to medium. Sauté 3–4 minutes. Remove with a slotted spoon. Set aside.
11. Heat remaining 2 tablespoons oil over medium-high heat. Add bay leaves and paanch phoron. When spices begin to sputter, add remaining raw vegetables. Stir-fry 5–7 minutes.
12. Reduce heat to medium. Stir in ginger paste. Sauté for 2 minutes, stirring constantly.
13. Add cooked eggplant and bitter gourd, coconut milk, salt, and sugar. Cover until almost cooked, about 3–5 minutes, stirring occasionally.
14. Lower heat and remove cover. Allow gravy to thicken, then remove from heat.
15. Stir in ghee. Eat with rice.

* Anandita's Notes:

- ✔ Eat only the inside of drumstick bean pods, the fleshy innermost pulp and seeds. Slice open lengthwise and extract edible parts with spoon or thumbnail, if eating with your hand.
- ✔ There are absolutely no onion, garlic, or chilies in shukto. Remember the inept "Rani" who is mocked in the Bengali nursery rhyme: "Chhie chhie Rani randhtey shekheni, mashima key boley jholey mashla debo ki? Shuktani tey jhaal diyechhey, amboleytey ghee." *(Shame on Rani who doesn't know how to cook curry and puts chilies in* shukto *and* ghee *in chutney!)*

Preity Chawla Lindstrom: Soulprints

Even the man who is happy glimpses
something, or a hair of sound touches him,
and his heart overflows with a longing he
does not recognize. Then it must be that he
is remembering, in a place out of reach,
shapes he has loved in a life before this, the
print of them still there in him, waiting.

KALIDASA

FROM: "Preity Sharma Lindstrom" <ToyGirl@comcast.net>
TO: <TriDelta_BetaSigma_Smarties@yahoogroups.com>
DATE: October 23, 20XX 7:29 AM
SUBJECT: [TDBSS] Trivia question

Hello, Sorority Sister Types! I have a question for the 30-somethings on this list: At 35, how well would you remember a two-week romance from when you were 20? Vaguely? Pretty well? Quite well?

Preity

FROM: "Kathryn Serafin" <k.serafin@hotmail.com>

TO: <TriDelta_BetaSigma_Smarties@yahoogroups.com>

DATE: October 23, 20XX 7:33 AM

SUBJECT: RE: [TDBSS] Trivia question

Was it all physical or were there deeper emotions involved?

Kate <--former vixen

FROM: "Preity Sharma Lindstrom" <ToyGirl@comcast.net>

TO: <TriDelta_BetaSigma_Smarties@yahoogroups.com>

DATE: October 23, 20XX 7:36 AM

SUBJECT: RE: [TDBSS] Trivia question

Very emotional -- at the time, you THOUGHT you were falling in love. Physically restrained -- first base only. :-) Then an abrupt and possibly unexplained end that may or may not have hurt/pissed you off.

Preity

FROM: "Helen Twomey" <HBTwomey@earthlink.net>

TO: <TriDelta_BetaSigma_Smarties@
yahoogroups.com>

DATE: October 23, 20XX 7:41 AM

SUBJECT: RE: [TDBSS] Trivia question

I'd remember every wonderful intimate detail and have sugarcoated the more awkward ones. Painful ones would still be there, but not as searing as when they occurred. Call them manageable. But the good memories would still make me smile real big. :D

Helen

FROM: "Nancy Bogatka"
<appleforteacher@hotmail.com>

TO: <TriDelta_BetaSigma_Smarties@
yahoogroups.com>

DATE: October 23, 20XX 7:48 AM

SUBJECT: RE: [TDBSS] Trivia question

Oh, yeah. That hurt/pissed off part would sear it into my memory. Like Helen said, the sweet parts would be sweeter, polished with the ideal sheen. The end would seal it.

My two cents, er bucks (CA cost-of-living adjustment <g>),

Miss Nancy

FROM: "Preity Sharma Lindstrom"
<ToyGirl@comcast.net>

TO: <TriDelta_BetaSigma_Smarties@
yahoogroups.com>

DATE: October 23, 20XX 7:56 AM

SUBJECT: RE: [TDBSS] Trivia question

And if this long-lost (maybe) love you thought was gone forever popped back into your life? Say, maybe sent a brief message of hello. Would you be curious? Or would you be more crawl-back-under-that-rock-and-leave-me-alone?

Preity

FROM: "Valentina Swiridow"
<gypsy_007@yahoo.com>

TO: <TriDelta_BetaSigma_Smarties@
yahoogroups.com>

DATE: October 23, 20XX 8:14 AM

SUBJECT: RE: [TDBSS] Trivia question

Good God! Six posts before 8 AM! Y'all are wild women this morning! ;)

> And if this long-lost (maybe) love (that you
> thought was gone forever) popped back into your
> life.

I would have a panic attack. Really. I would have a physical reaction -- tightness in my chest, maybe the shakes, I would not be smiling, I would be excited but also sort of scared. I would call my close girlfriends, email my sorority sisters <g>, guess and second-guess and triple-guess whether or not to answer (and how long I should delay my response to not seem too eager). I would be VERY curious.

Tina Bambina

FROM: "Leydiana Martinez" <Leydi.Martinez@pobox.com>
TO: <TriDelta_BetaSigma_Smarties@yahoogroups.com>
DATE: October 23, 20XX 8:15 AM
SUBJECT: RE: [TDBSS] Trivia question

I would assume if he were to contact me, he would have grown up a bit. I sure have. I'd have to be pretty immature at 35 to still be pissed off.

Leydi

FROM: "Inglath Johnson" <Inglath@JohnsonHorseShelter.com>
TO: <TriDelta_BetaSigma_Smarties@yahoogroups.com>
DATE: October 23, 20XX 8:27 AM
SUBJECT: RE: [TDBSS] Trivia question

Depends on what's transpired in the meantime, personal growth-wise. It could be mild curiosity.

With maturity, contact could be made with a "bygones are bygones" mindset. If there hasn't been a lot of personal growth, or ill will is still harbored, then it might could fall into the "piss off, I don't have time for you" arena.

Inglath

FROM: "Lisa B. Ruddy" <GracesMommy@hotmail.com>
TO: <TriDelta_BetaSigma_Smarties@yahoogroups.com>
DATE: October 23, 20XX 8:33 AM
SUBJECT: RE: [TDBSS] Trivia question

Okay, spill it, Preity. What's this all about? :-)

FROM: "Carmella Grimaldi" <thegrimaldifamily@erols.com>
TO: <TriDelta_BetaSigma_Smarties@yahoogroups.com>
DATE: October 23, 20XX 9:01 AM
SUBJECT: RE: [TDBSS] Trivia question

spill what???? i thought this was a trivia question???? carm

FROM: "Heather V. Taylor"
<HeatherV@3TaylorLegal.com>

TO: "Preity Sharma Lindstrom"
<ToyGirl@comcast.net>

DATE: October 23, 20XX 9:05 AM

SUBJECT: FOR YOUR EYES ONLY!

Sending this off-list, private to you...

Oh. My. God.

I just turned on the computer, and I'm skimming all these posts, and it HITS me...

This is about that Indian guy from first year! The one you met over winter break! And oh, coincidentally, SOMEONE is going to India for a wedding next month! ARE YOU GOING TO CONTACT HIM?!

Just so you know, I have goose bumps as I type this!!!!!!!!!!!

Heather <--first-year roommate who remembers ALL

I wasn't going to go to Kiran's wedding. I hadn't planned on it, even after she returned my email, and we exchanged a few more. I didn't go to her first wedding; she didn't go to mine.

Then she phoned, and we both felt the winds of change that had blown through our adult lives. Afterward, I knew I couldn't miss this, even if it meant leaving my husband and kids for the first time and traveling alone to the Other Side of the World.

"I've always been jealous of you," Kiran said to me on the phone. "That's why I was such a little shit."

"First of all," I said, "you were a *big* shit. And second, jealous of *me*? Why on earth would *you* be jealous of *me*?"

"Because you're perfect, Preity."

I about laughed my ass off. "No one's perfect. Least of all people who appear to be."

"Yeah, that's what you hear all the time, but—"

"Did you know I was bulimic?" I couldn't believe I said it, to *Kiran* of all people, but once it was out, I felt like a ton of bricks lifted from the top of my head. (Picture a female Indian laborer here.)

"*No,* I did *not*—! Geez, no one tells me *anything* about *anyone's* medical condition. And why would they? I'm only a *doctor*."

"No one knew. Except my dentist."

A pause, and then, "No one . . . ?"

"Not even my parents. They still don't."

"When was this? How long—? Are you still—?"

"I'm fine now. It went on for about five years, on and off, starting in college when the ole metabolism took a nosedive, and a lifetime of '*khaa, beta, khaa*' caught up with me."

At our house, "eat, dear, eat" was my mother's *mantra*. She practically ran after Tarun and me with food in her outstretched hand. It was never, "Are you hungry?" but "Have some" of this and "Have some more" of that. We could say *no, thank you* all we wanted; still she heaped another helping on our plates, striving to ensure our stomachs never rumbled and we never experienced a single hunger pang. Mom said she knew she and Dad "had arrived" (meaning attained success) when they could afford ($$, not lbs.) to eat ice cream, a luxury in India, until they puked. Needless to say, ice cream was a staple of our diet.

My little brother, being "Joe Athlete," can still get away with pigging out, no worries of packing on the pudge, but my *Get Out of Jail Free* card expired in college. "Welcome to my world," my best friend Veronica said when I stepped onto the scale and shrieked in horror. (Picture Munch's *The Scream.*) I thought my jeans had shrunk in the wash, but no, it was me who had expanded. And only through the midsection. My figure resembled a toothpick spearing an olive! "No more gorging on ice cream in the dining hall," Veronica said. "Desserts go straight to the hips." But try as I might, I couldn't control myself with ice cream. Even today, I lack portion-control with certain foods and must avoid them entirely, like an alcoholic must abstain from alcohol.

"I rotted my teeth with all the stomach acid," I told Kiran. "And still, I couldn't tell my parents. Can't you just imagine? I'd never hear the end of it. 'All these starving people in the world, and here, this spoiled rotten girl not only has the luxury of eating like a queen, afterward, she sticks her finger down her throat and *intentionally* throws up. She's puking enough food to feed a village! We should send her to India. Let her volunteer in the Peace Corps. That will teach her.' So, since I couldn't tell the folks my shameful secret, I couldn't afford to pay for the kind of dental work I *really* needed until after grad school."

"Oh, Preity..."

"Hey, on the upside, no college loans. But yes, downside, I'll be making payments on the Mercedes in my mouth for several more years."

"And I was *just* noticing your lovely smile at New Year's..." Kiran said. "I'm so sorry."

"Don't be," I said. "It's over and done. All's well that ends well."

And that's what brought me to the Other Side of the World....

In Mumbai, I feel like a woman waking from a coma, then more like a ghost. A dead wife looking down from heaven, able to see, but not touch her loved ones.

Life in India went on without me. My memories, flash-frozen in time, thaw and feel fresh. Raw. This is how my parents feel, I realize. Why my mother never wants to come here, and my father never wants to leave.

I learn Riya-*didi* never delivered the letter to Arsallan. I locate him—he's a pediatrician, how wonderfully fitting for him. I wait outside his office, just wanting a glimpse of him before I decide how and when I'll approach. But when he steps out, when I see him, I'm bowled over by a barrage of emotions.

He looks the same. Aside from his hair, now threaded with copper and silver. Otherwise, *the same.*

It doesn't feel like sixteen years have passed. It hardly feels like sixteen minutes. *Didn't we just walk on the beach? Didn't you just kiss me under the stars?*

Don't I want to go to the bookmark we placed at the end of our chapter, to resume our story?

I'm stunned to realize my mother was right.

My feelings *are* too strong. The risks *are* too great.

How can we just have coffee, or lunch, or dinner? It won't be enough.

Tears spring to my eyes. I whirl in the opposite direction, walk for blocks in a stupor before hailing a cab. At the hotel, I have myself a good, cleansing cry, then pick myself up, brush myself off, and go downstairs to the lobby. I ask the concierge to recommend a Goan restaurant. Once there, I order *bebinca* and start to write.

It takes several drafts to get the words right. When I'm satisfied, I print a final copy and phone Rani in Pune. "Hi, I need a huge favor, no questions asked. Would you be willing—?"

"Just name it."

This time, I watch from a distance, observe the delivery, make sure it reaches Arsallan's hands, wait until he opens my envelope...

Once upon a time long, long ago, in a land far, far away, there was a young princess who met a young prince from another kingdom. For some unknown reason, the princess and prince were instantly familiar to each other, drawn together, as if their hearts recognized one another from another time, another place.

The princess loved the prince before she had any concrete concept of love. She had no need to label her feelings, knew that whatever she felt, the prince felt. A mirror reflection. That's how it is when two souls connect. No insecurities, no second-guessing. You just know...

Their romance was sweet and innocent and pure. But before their love could take root, or take flight, the princess died a sudden, mysterious death. She journeyed to her next life, not realizing that her soul, like all souls, carried the memories, the lessons of her past, including the prince's love. You see, once you are touched by true love, it remains part of you, even if you don't consciously know it.

Among other things, the former princess' experience of the Real Thing set the bar for every subsequent suitor. She knew to wait, not to settle. And sure enough, when the love of her new life came along, she recognized him as the one fate intended for her. Together, they built an enchanted life. It wasn't always easy. Life challenged them plenty, but they held fast to their commitment to each other, trusted and supported each other, and overcame every obstacle, learning and growing stronger together.

Then one night, out of nowhere, the past whispered in her ear. She remembered. Memories of her past life, her past love came to her, as messages in bottles, thrown out to sea, finally washing ashore, reaching their intended destination. Amid happy memories, she recalled a terrible injustice that occurred before she died. A mistake she was never able to put right because the prince never received the last, parting letter she wrote to him. It broke her heart to realize she'd unwittingly broken his.

The former princess couldn't bear this. She had to find the prince—an old man now—wherever he was. Even if she had to turn the world upside-down and shake it. He had to know the truth; she had to set the record straight: She loved him. Now. Then. Always. Forever.

When she found his dimension, many changes had taken place in her absence. At evidence of the prince's wonderful life and achievements, her heart filled with joy. At the same time, a bittersweet realization came to her: Though she could see the prince's dimension, she couldn't touch it. Even with a pure heart, she couldn't reenter, not without grave peril, for the words she wanted most to gift him were forbidden to them now, fraught with danger. Contained in their sweet nectar was a poison capable of killing the others to whom they'd pledged their love.

With utmost care, she composed another letter and watched from a distance as the courier hand-delivered it to the prince. Then she turned and walked away without looking back, secure in the knowledge the prince would understand the message contained therein:

"We were together before; we shall be together again. We need never say good-bye; with soul mates, it's until next time..."

Bebinca

[Layered, Upside-Down Coconut Custard Cake]

SERVES 6–8

2 cups coconut milk

2 cups dark brown sugar

1 cup rice flour

½ teaspoon salt

¼ teaspoon ground cardamom

¼ teaspoon ground nutmeg

10 egg yolks, lightly beaten

¾ cup melted ghee or unsalted butter, divided

3 tablespoons toasted almond slices

1. Preheat oven to 350 degrees.
2. In a small saucepan over very low heat, combine coconut milk and brown sugar, stirring frequently until sugar dissolves. Remove from heat. Allow to cool to room temperature.
3. In a mixing bowl, sift together flour, salt, cardamom, and nutmeg.
4. Stir in coconut milk mixture to dry ingredients, then add the egg yolks. Mix until smooth—neither too dry, nor too runny. (Add a little water if too dry, or a little flour if too thin.)
5. Grease a deep, 7-inch round aluminum pan with 2 tablespoons ghee.
6. Pour 1 cup of batter into pregreased pan. Set on middle rack of oven. Bake until top turns golden. Remove from oven. Pour 1 tablespoon ghee over top layer. Bake until

top turns golden brown. Remove from oven. Using spatula, remove "pancake" and stack on plate.

7. Repeat step #6 until batter is finished. Stack all pancakes in pan and bake 15 minutes.
8. Cool to room temperature. Turn pan upside down onto plate. Gently extract bebinca, so the shape stays intact.
9. Garnish with toasted almond slices. Serve at room temperature.

Kiran Deshpande: Shaadi

Be not parted—growing old,
taking thought, thriving together,
moving under a common yoke.
Come speaking sweetly to one another;
I'll make you have one aim
and be of one mind.

ATHARVA VEDA

Kiran & John

TOGETHER WITH THEIR PARENTS

YASHWANT AND MEENAL DESHPANDE
WILLIAM AND LAURA LEIGH COOPER

INVITE YOU
TO SHARE IN THE JOY OF THEIR MARRIAGE
IN PUNE, INDIA
ON NOVEMBER 24, 20XX

At the altar, John and I stand facing each other, but we don't see each other.

The countdown to the zero hour, the *muhurta*, has begun...

"Kuryat sada mangalam...shubha mangala savdhan..." wedding guests recite ancient, sacred verses in Sanskrit, reading from their programs, which provide the English translations as well: *May this marriage bring happiness...the auspicious time for the marriage is coming...*

Per tradition, I stand on the west side of the *mandap*, an outdoor gazebo, facing east. John stands on the east, facing west. Both of us in clear view of the officiating priest and guests—north and south respectively—we're hidden from each other. Between us hangs the *antarpat*, a white curtain with a *kumkum*-drawn auspicious swastika—right-facing, rotated forty-five degrees, a dot in each quadrant—a sacred symbol of good luck in Hinduism dating back to the fifteenth century B.C.E.

The *antarpat* symbolizes our separate identities, poised on the threshold, about to come together in holy matrimony. At the precise time of our *muhurta*, not a minute before or after, the *antarpat* will be removed—from the north. Amid much fanfare, John and I will gaze upon each other, garland each other with fresh flowers, and be pronounced husband and wife. Until then, the priest continuously chants the *mangalashtaka*, eight *shlokas* of prayers and blessings, and guests shower *akshata*—uncooked, unbroken grains of vermilion-dusted rice—while they recite, excitement mounting, *"Kuryat sada mangalam...shubha mangala savdhan..."*

From where they sit, it's excitement. From where I stand,

it's anxiety. Waiting to see and be seen by my groom, I'm a nervous wreck! I expected it to be nail-biting to stand up in front of everyone, the center of attention, but I didn't realize quite how unnerving it feels knowing everyone *else* is seeing what I can't, *the whole picture*, while John and I are limited to half, a partitioned pair of goldfish in a fishbowl.

What's the other goldfish doing over there? I want to see his face. His eyes. *Some* gauge of what he's thinking. Is he thinking what I am? That he's either crazy in love with me, or just plain crazy, or else he wouldn't be here! Can he feel my presence? Can I send a telepathic message? *E.T. phone home!*

Holding the garland I'll give him, I think of the brides and grooms who came before, over *thousands* of years, who stood as we are. At their *mandaps*. Separated by their *antarpats*. Awaiting their *muhurtas*. In the olden days, brides and grooms had little to no prior contact. Imagine what *they* must have felt in these agonizing moments.... *Uh, then again, Kiran: Let's not go there right now.*

I'm fasting this morning, as is John. That's all we need after everything everyone's been through getting to this point, for me to start hyperventilating and pass out at the altar.

"Kuryat sada mangalam... shubha mangala savdhan..."

My father finally gave his blessing. I wasn't expecting a Hallmark card, but I'd be lying if I said I wasn't disappointed. The unvarnished version is, Dad felt outnumbered, beleaguered by the army of open-minded people that surrounded him. He didn't have the energy left to fight anymore, so he surrendered. His "blessing" went, and I quote: *"Do what you want. It's your life."*

Makes you all warm and tingly, doesn't it?

My mother said, "Give him time. No one changes overnight."

I kept thinking of Uma Auntie, who would have loved even that much from her father. I tried to focus on what I *did* have, to be grateful, and see the glass as half full. But as wedding plans kicked into high gear, and Dad went through the motions on autopilot, doing what was expected of him—his duty, as written in some instruction manual titled *Responsibilities of the Father of the Bride*—I couldn't help but feel pinpricks of sorrow, never far beneath the surface of any joy. I wished he and I could see eye to eye, that he could share my happiness. But we never had, and it was unlikely he ever would.

The first time John and I met in person, my nerves were so frazzled, I had to take a valium beforehand. "What if he doesn't like what he sees?" I said to my mother. "What if I don't? What if he smells funny? What if . . . ? What if . . . ?"

She sat me down, took my hands, and looked me in the eye. In a voice as serene as a yoga instructor, she said, "Trust me. Do you think I *ever* would have let things go this far if I had *any* doubts?"

It was late summer, and John and I had continued to "date" long-distance. That was my father's mandate, his prerequisite for any chance at his blessing.

"If you haven't changed your minds by then, we'll see. . . ."

"Fair enough," John said.

We were going to meet in Paris, just the two of us, in May. We planned our itinerary and everything. Then, right before we booked it, we both—independently—reached the same conclusion: We'd come this far, let's keep doing this Indian-style, the old-fashioned way, by the book. For the novelty, if nothing else.

And so, in August, John and his family flew from Austin to D.C. to meet my family and me. Traditionally this was called a "bride-viewing." Mom seated his family in the living room; Dad escorted and presented me.

When I came in, John was the first to stand. He shot up from the couch, clutching a huge bouquet of roses, lilies, and freesia. He wore a navy sports jacket with gold buttons over a white shirt that showed off his golden tan. The instant I saw him, the moment our eyes met, my heart turned to mush. All those clichés—weak in the knees, short of breath, you name it—I felt every one. And from the besotted look on John's face, I knew he felt the same.

It was so cute—his mother nudged his arm with her elbow a few times, and when he didn't respond, she whispered, "Flowers, Johnny. Give her the flowers."

We hugged, but with everyone watching, nowhere near as long as we wanted. Separation was pure agony. Minutes crawled by as I poured tea, served snacks, did the customary chitchat. It was disconcerting to hear John, his voice so familiar I'd recognize it anywhere, coming from this handsome stranger's mouth. To be sure, it was great packaging, but unfamiliar. I kept stealing glances at him—I wanted to stare outright—trying to reconcile the known and the unknown.

Finally—*finally!*—our parents left us alone. We lunged

for each other. Smushed together. Clung. Breathless. I pressed my cheek to his chest, my ear over his racing heart. He threaded his fingers into my hair, cradling my head, cradling *me* against him.

"You're so tall," I whispered.

Him, "You're so beautiful."

"You smell good."

"You *feel* great."

"I can't believe you're real."

A chuckle. "You're shaking."

"I'm nervous."

He leaned down, whispered near my ear, "Don't be nervous . . . I love you, Kiran."

My eyes stung. My fingers bunched his shirt. I looked up, into his eyes, blue irises swallowed by desire-enlarged pupils. "That's what I was waiting to hear. I love you, too. So much."

He kissed me then. A soul kiss. A you-were-meant-for-me-and-I-was-meant-for-you kiss. Pure magic.

We both agreed: It was worth the wait.

Trying to incorporate two faiths to show respect for both families, their traditions and beliefs, is no easy feat.

I asked Rani, "How did you and Bryan do it?"

"A secular ceremony at the university chapel," Rani said.

"Okay, you're no help to me."

"Sorry. Ask Preity."

I did. I called. We bonded. It was weird. Imagine if Batman and the Joker struck up an alliance—there's something hinky about that, isn't there?

Preity and Eric had two ceremonies, two weeks apart. A Lutheran ceremony at his family's church in Minnesota, and a Hindu ceremony at a mansion in Middleburg—Northern Virginia horse country. Eric rode in on a white mare!

I should have gone, I was kicking myself.

John and I were leaning toward one combined-faith ceremony until I talked to Preity. "I have one word for you," she said. *"Wardrobe."*

An excellent point, which steered John and me toward the idea of two separate wedding ceremonies in one whirlwind day.

I found myself phoning, none other than, Preity—again—for a gut-check. Was it too much? Was it feasible to pull off? We brainstormed, and at the end of the conversation when everything met with her enthusiastic approval, I was not only excited but relieved. I thanked her profusely for letting me bend her ear, for being my sounding board.

No one else in my life could have related to the thousandth decimal point the way Preity could. I didn't have to explain myself to her. She could explain me to me! And she did! She knew exactly what I was trying to accomplish with the nuptials and what I was up against, because she'd lived it.

As children, we didn't have anything in common beyond our parents being born in the same country. Now, like our parents, Preity and I, too, had shared life experiences.

Holy samosas, Batman.

For my first wedding, I did all the planning, and I did it all *my* way. This time, I deferred to my mother. "Whatever you want," I said, handing over John's and my proxies. "Just tell us when and where to show up, and what we're supposed to do."

Mom and the aunties got right on it. She must have thought, *If only you'd done this sooner, my* pillu, *life could have been so much less complicated.* Not that *this* way was any cakewalk, mind you.

Since Indian wedding rituals and traditions differ according to subculture, each auntie had her own must-haves. I happened to be interviewing with family practices in the D.C. area, so I was in town for the Hindi-Bindi Club's first brainstorming session, lucky me, and watched with amusement as Mom presided, something akin to herding hamsters.

"Any minute now, *someone*'s going to suggest conch shells," one auntie said.

"Am I that predictable?" said Uma Auntie.

"You're that *Bengali,*" said Saroj Auntie.

Uma Auntie was pushing for the blowing of conch shells. Minor, compared to Saroj Auntie, who was lobbying hard for two prewedding bashes and for the groom to ride to the wedding ceremony on a white horse, accompanied by a marching band. All this before anyone had even *broached* the subject of food!

Across the room, Mom's and my gazes met. *Arré deva!*

"Maharashtrian weddings are *simple* affairs," Mom said, ever so diplomatically to the aunties. "It's more about *sanskar* than *naatik.*"

Here, I leaned over and consulted the nearest auntie for English subtitles. *Sanskar* means "rite of passage." *Naatik* is "theatrics."

"So let the wedding ceremony be boring—I mean, simple," Saroj Auntie said.

"You meant boring," Mom said. She turned to Uma Auntie, tattling like a schoolgirl, "She meant boring."

"Come now, Meenu," Saroj Auntie said in her conciliatory voice. "What's a little *masala* between friends?"

"And don't Punjus have enough to spare?" said Uma Auntie with a wink.

"I just think if you're going to do it, do it up," Saroj Auntie said. "Let the wedding ceremonies be traditional, but before and after? Why ho-hum if you don't have to? When will you and your guests all be together again? This is once-in-a-lifetime only. Everyone should have fun, fun, fun, *hai na?*"

Mom appeared to reconsider. "Maybe a little *chutpata* . . ." She asked me, "Would you like a *sangeet* the night before the wedding? And a *mehendi* party before your *chuda*?"

I leaned back, held up my palms. "Whatever you want, Mom."

At this, the aunties crooned over what a good daughter I am. (Ha! Selective amnesia, anyone?)

Sangeet means "singing session." It's a song-and-dance bash.

Chuda, the Maharashtrian version of a bridal shower, is a bangle party. The bangle-*wallah* brings his wares to the home, and the bride and her girlfriends play games and select their bangles. The bride's bangles are green glass—the auspicious color of new life—which the mother of the bride ceremonially presents at the *chuda*.

Mehendi is henna. With a cone akin to that used for icing decoration on a cake, a skilled artist paints intricate designs on the palms and feet of a bride, a gesture of wishing the bride luck. *Mehendi* takes several hours to dry and stains the skin for up to two months—at first, a deep red that fades to terra-cotta tones, then gradually disappears, like a temporary tattoo. A *mehendi* shindig, like the *chuda*, is a women's party. Attendees often have their palms decorated, too, for kicks—though nowhere near as elaborately as the bride's.

I didn't tell the aunties this, but the day before, when my fiancé (I've loved saying that... but will love *husband* far more!) and I were discussing wardrobe requirements for our impending East-West fashion show, John said he was *most* looking forward to me modeling one outfit in particular.... He couldn't wait to see me dressed in just "*mehendi* and moonlight" on our wedding night.

Did I mention I'm in love with him? I am. Big time.

Mom said, "Yes, on *mehendi*. Maybe, on a *sangeet*, but *if* we do it, no weepy farewell songs." She directed her gaze at Saroj Auntie, who inched up a lone index finger, wordlessly inquiring *just one*? "Not even one. And no *baarat*." She nixed the horse and marching band.

Saroj Auntie's mouth dropped open. "But John's a *cowboy*. Don't you see the parallel—?"

"I see that our cowboy is six foot three. If the 'horse' winds up being a weak, malnourished Arabian pony, we'll be in trouble."

Uma Auntie added, "And if he needs a tetanus shot the next day for sitting on a saddle with a rusty, protruding nail?"

"*Yeh India hai,*" Mom said, a reminder that we'd be in India, not the States. "And don't forget our most critical constraint. For a *Maharashtrian* wedding, the *muhurta* will be in the morning." This is the most auspicious hour to conduct the hour-and-a-half wedding ceremony as calculated by the *pandit* (priest), factoring the time of year and the *patrikas*—horoscopes—of the bride and groom.

From the "O" of Saroj Auntie's mouth, she *had* forgotten. She settled right down. "Like I was saying, the groom should arrive in a nice, quiet stretch limo . . ."

Everyone laughed, and the afternoon passed that way.

Mom compiled the suggestions, culled them into a select list of those she liked best, and instructed John and me to order à la carte off the menu.

"Are you sure there aren't some Muslim and Jewish traditions they'd like to incorporate?" I overheard Dad say to Mom. "Parsi? Buddhist? Jain? Wiccan?" My father has the best sense of humor when he doesn't intend to be funny.

Oh, well. You can't have everything. That's what they tell me. Over and over. Like a mantra.

"*Kuryat sada mangalam . . . shubha mangala savdhan . . .*"

My mother can't hear any of this. Until the *muhurta*, she's staying in the dressing room—with her ears plugged, she told us.

Traditionally, the bride's mother wasn't present because hearing these *shlokas* was too emotional for her. Today, it's simply considered bad luck.

Before the ceremony started, Mom did a reading. My dressing room was upstairs, John's downstairs. I peeked from the balcony. John did the same directly below me, out of my sight.

Mom gave an overview of the process—also in the program—and explained, for the benefit of those who didn't know, why she was "bunking" the ceremony, reappearing only after garlands were exchanged. "So no one can think I don't love my daughter." She wagged her index finger. "Or my future son-in-law. I love both very much. That's why I'm leaving at the end of this reading."

"Kuryat sada mangalam . . . shubha mangala savdhan . . ."

My parents bought a brand-new, three-bedroom, three-bath, two-balcony flat on the outskirts of Pune, in the foothills. Hoping to nudge Dad into retirement, Mom declared she would winter in India with or without him. Vivek and I placed bets on how quickly Dad would cave; he can't function without Mom.

The new digs served as our *lagna-ghar,* wedding house; John's family made their camp his former host family's home. Vivek, his wife, Anisha, and I arrived ten days before the wedding. We were surprised at how Scottsdale, Arizona–like these new developments felt. Our parents had a First-World oasis in the Third World. Mountain view. Gated community. Ritzy brick driveway. Plush lawns. Immaculate gardens. Swimming pool. Gym. Mom and Dad weren't roughing it here—this place was posh!

After an exhausting day of power shopping, I wished I could take my feet off and carry them home. I showered, changed into my jammies, and tumbled onto my parents' bed beside my mother.

"Uh-oh . . . She's making another list . . ."

She knew I was kidding. No way could I have pulled off this highly complicated, long-distance wedding without her stupendous organizational skills. The previous month, she'd sent me the mock-up of the wedding program she made for the three days of festivities. An individual pamphlet for each day. Blurbs on Hindu rituals—definitions, translations, history, anecdotes, jokes. (Inspired, John's mom did the same for the Christian ones.) I was so moved, so deeply touched by the massive time, effort, *love* she'd poured into everything. I broke down in tears, phoning her right away. "You really do love me . . ." I said, and she said, "Of course I do, *pillu*," as if there had never been any question.

The latest of her infamous lists read: *Things I Want to Do Before I Die*. "Don't tell me it's morbid," she said. "We all need goals."

I skimmed the page. "Impressive. But where's 'Have sex in a public place'?" I tapped the page with my fingernail. "That needs to be on here."

She sighed, the long-suffering-mother kind, and shook her head. All the encouragement I needed.

"You know, your building elevators are pretty cozy. That could work—"

"Kiran."

"What? Oh. Sorry. They call it a *lift*. British English takes some getting used to, doesn't it? Here, give me the pen. I'll add it for you." I reached for her pen.

She switched it to her other hand. *"Pooré."* Enough. As in, cut the crap.

"My mouth needs a lock on it," I said in Marathi before she could, making her laugh despite herself. "Hehehe." I flashed my devious smile, adding, "Yes, it *is* lots of fun to harass Mom. How do you say 'corrupt' in Marathi?"

"I'm not telling you."

"Okay, I'll ask Ramesh." The driver. "He'll tell me."

"Ha! He wouldn't dare. I've already warned him if he teaches you any curses or naughty words, he's fired."

Vivek and I were only now discovering our mother omitted several choice words from our Marathi instruction.

"Good thing my future hubby speaks Marathi like a native, huh?" I said.

She heaved another sigh, the ol' classic what's-a-poor-mother-to-do kind. "I suppose it's too late to call off the wedding . . . ?"

"Afraid so . . . Unless *you* want to tell *Giru-mama* to take back my ever-so-lovely Paithani *sari.*"

"No . . . I couldn't possibly do that," she said ruefully. "The *sari* shops don't accept returns on custom orders. Looks like I'm stuck—the Paithani and John-*baba* are a package deal." She chuckled, pleased with her joke. Who knew cancer would give—or did it *bring out*?—my mother's sense of humor? She sprinkled tidbits like this throughout the program, *"F.A.Q.s to Commit to Memory: Hindi is a language. Hindu is a religion/way of life. Mistaking the two is a common mistake for foreigners. Misspeaking is grounds for deportation."*

I perused her list, commenting, "I love this one . . . And that one . . . Oooh, *write a novel,* huh?"

"Umm-hmm. I love to read, and I always wanted to write a book one day, just never had the time. People say you have to make time, but there are only so many hours in a day. Anyway, I'm going to give it a try. I don't know if I'll be any good. Guess we'll find out. . . ."

"You'll be great. Your letters are masterpieces."

She cupped my cheek with her hand and made a kissing sound. "I'm glad *you* think so. That's the important thing.

You know, writing to you really warmed up that part of my brain. First I struggled to fill the page. Now I'm practically writing short stories. The length of a novel isn't so intimidating anymore."

"You can definitely do it. But, um, can I make one teeny, tiny request?" I clasped my hands. "*Please,* I beg of you, *not* another Life's-a-Bitch-and-Then-You-Die novel. I mean, I get that no one, present company included, wants to read four hundred pages of shiny, happy people who don't have any problems, but—"

"No? How come?" She yawned, laced her fingers together, and stretched, palms to the ceiling, making me laugh. "Don't worry, *pillu*. I'll leave the tragedies to others. Not my cup of tea, either. I'd prefer a story that's ultimately uplifting. Sure, there will be hardships, obstacles along the way, but I want to write about survivors. Resilience of the human spirit."

"*Now* you're talkin'... People who take a lickin' and keep on tickin'. *That* I love."

"Me, too," she said, and I snuggled up to her, laid my head on her lap, closed my eyes, and fell asleep.

"*Kuryat sada mangalam... shubha mangala savdhan...*" "Listen to the *sounds* of these sacred Sanskrit mantras," my mother said in her reading. "All of us here, at one time or another, have had the experience of not being able to explain ourselves in words, right?"

Western heads nodded, and Eastern heads wobbled agreement.

"Well, the seers who authored the verses in the Vedas

over four thousand years ago were very wise and insightful. They noted language has literal and sonic meaning. Beyond 'word-pictures,' painted by definitions, language creates 'sound-pictures,' evoked by vibrations. *Now, what does that mean, Meenal?* I know you're thinking. I'll give you an example, so you can experience for yourself *what I'm talking*..." Here she gave a coy smile. "Because you know *I can't explain you* with mere words."

This, a grammatical joke. Those with a foot in each camp—East and West—got it and chuckled.

"We define the Sanskrit *om* with words like *all that is,* or *the universe.* But the sound, the vibration when we chant *om* has additional meaning. *Repetition* of a mantra enables us to *focus.* On sound and vibration. On anything and everything. When we chant, in any language, we heighten our perception, awareness, *consciousness* that there is *more.* Out there." She pointed to the sky. "And, in here." She tapped a finger over her heart.

"Kuryat sada mangalam... shubha mangala savdhan..."

John has a new nickname. John-*baba.* So christened by *Aji,* it's analogous to Little Johnny.

Apparently, it's quite common for grown Indian men to be called by highly embarrassing pet names given to them as boys. Saroj Auntie told me about one of Sandeep Uncle's brothers, a strapping, larger-than-life, fierce colonel who's cut down to size when Mummy calls him Bunny in public.

John agreed a pet name like *Bunny* would decimate his manhood. (Sorry, Bunny!) *Baba,* however, works for him—pronounced like *bubba,* which he's heard a lot, being Texan.

John was so adorable at his fitting. He couldn't stop posturing in front of the mirror, showing off his new duds, cream *sherwani* with gold embroidery and burgundy *dupatta,* worn stolelike. "Wow! Look at me! I look Indian! Don't I look Indian?" With his blond hair and blue eyes? Um, *no*. But he sure looked smashing.

I wanted so badly to kiss him right there and then, but Mom kept admonishing us this was India, no "touchy-touchy" in public. "Doesn't the Hindu wedding ceremony have some kind of a 'you may kiss the bride' part?" I asked, making my aunts giggle and blush. No, no, heavens no. Even the tailor chuckled.

"Arré!" exclaimed my sweet little old granny, startling my snoring grandfather from his impromptu nap. *"Luvang-tod!"*

"Huh, huh, luvang-tod," Ajoba mumbled and fell back asleep.

Aji shared with John-*baba* and me a tradition from yesteryear called clove-breaking. After the wedding ceremony, before the lunch feast, there are various fun rituals comparable to Western linked-arms champagne toast, glass-tinkling, and kiss traditions. For the *luvang-tod,* the bride holds a clove between her front teeth, and the groom has to break it with *his* teeth. All the while, the audience eggs them on, relishing their discomfort.

Aji reminded us that back then, brides and grooms didn't have much prior contact—some were seeing each other *for the first time* at their wedding ceremony! This was a highly intimate and embarrassing act to perform in front of an audience. Imagine having Your First Kiss in front of your entire family, including distant relatives. Now add everyone else you know, plus another couple hundred, even *thousand* other guests!

Aji clapped, her gold bangles chiming like a tambourine. In an animated, teasing voice, she sang, *"Kai bai Punyachi tariff, lavanga nighalya bareek."* How much can you praise Pune, because the cloves from there are so small.

"Aji!" I laughed with the others. "Who knew you were such a wild woman?"

Ajoba didn't even open his eyes when he said, "What do you think, you get it from your mom? *Hut*, you get it from your *aji*!" *Aji* blushed ten shades of crimson and raised her *palloo* to cover her face.

"*Kuryat sada mangalam . . . shubha mangala savdhan . . .*"

My stomach growls. I'd kill for a smuggled *jalebi*! The golden, sticky sweet and other treats await—we scheduled our traditional Maharashtrian vegetarian lunch feast earlier, around brunchtime, so John and I can break our fasts, and everyone can rest before the Christian ceremony in late afternoon. (For that, John will change into a tux and I a pale pink gown embroidered with Swarovski crystals.) Our evening reception follows—non-veg—at a five-star hotel designed after a *maharaja*'s palace.

At the *mandap*, I'm dressed in traditional Maharashtrian bridal attire. My hair up in a chignon, decorated with *véni*, strings of fragrant tuberoses. Diamond *kudi*, custom-designed by my mother, adorn my ears. My *sari* is a regal, silk Paithani. Mustard yellow with a forest green *zari* border and signature peacocks on the *palloo*.

Did you know there are ninety-seven ways to drape a *sari*? I do now. That said, I don't know if I'll ever manage to tie even one style unassisted. Mom, *Aji*, aunts, and cousins attempted to teach me, but like French-braiding hair, I'm hopeless when doing my own. Luckily, I have a family of experts.

While Mom dressed me, *Aji* told a story about Lord Krishna cutting his finger while visiting his sister. "Immediately, his sister ripped the *sari* she was wearing—a beautiful Paithani—and tied the strip around his finger, saying, 'I have all the best *saris*, but Paithani, being best of the best, is most worthy to bandage my brother's bleeding finger.' "

Traditionally, Paithani *saris* were draped in a trouserlike style called *nauvari*, but Mom draped me in today's most popular *pachvari* style. As I stood in ankle-length petticoat and belly-baring blouse, she went to work, my lower half first.

Starting at one end of the *sari*, she tucked the corner into the waistband of my petticoat at my naval, instructed me to hold it there, circled behind me, and returned to my naval. One loop completed, she folded graceful pleats, clipped them at the top with a barrette—I tucked the cinched packet into my waistband—and safety-pinned the pleats midthigh, so they stayed nice and neat when I moved.

For the second round, she raised the *sari* higher, so it covered the small of my back, curved around my side with the fabric up to my armpit. Coming around the front, she draped diagonally across my chest, like a seatbelt's shoulder strap, covering my stomach, breasts, and left shoulder—with my long *palloo* cascading straight down behind it. Another safety pin inside my blouse at the shoulder, and I was good to go.

"Look at me," I said in wonder. "I look Indian!"

"Yes, you do," Mom said with pride.

Aji's eyes watered. *"Ai gha . . ."* She sucked in her breath—the same sound I make when I've eaten something spicy and need to cool my mouth. *"Kithi sundar, maji pakhru."* She cupped my face. *"Umchi gunachi mulgi."*

How beautiful, my butterfly. Our sweet, good girl.

At my *gadhagner* ceremony, where close relatives presented me with gifts, *Aji* gave me her *tanmani* jewelry set and her *patlia*—old-fashioned gold bangles. When I touched her feet, she had this same reaction: *"Ai gha . . ."* She sucked in her breath, laying a hand on my head while blessing me, *"Akhanda saubhagyavati raho."*

Stay married forever.

"Kuryat sada mangalam . . . shubha mangala savdhan . . ."

When I move my arms, my bangles *ting-ting-ting* with music. Traditional bridal green glass, interspersed with gold. Almost three dozen: six gold on each arm, ten *chuda* on my left, eleven *chuda* on my right—an odd number for luck.

Though *mehendi* and *chuda* ceremonies are supposed to be all-chick affairs, our visiting male guests, anxious to soak up the culture, wanted to come, too. We opened the party to everyone and had that much more fun—the guys even lined up for their own temporary henna tattoos! A shamrock. A cross. *MOM* in a heart.

Uma Auntie said, "A granny with a big red *bindi* declared it to be the best *mehendi* party she's ever attended!"

Saroj Auntie said, "Some uppity-nosed lady was passing not-so-nice comments when her husband declared *'chalta hai'* and put forth his hand."

John explained this Hindi expression is used when giving

advice. The rough translation: Whatcha gonna do? Let it go. Deal.

The next day at lunch, when the power went out, John's father raised his stainless steel tumbler in toast, saying, "*Chalta hai.*"

Glasses lifted with laughter and jubilant echoes of *chalta hai!* My father, too, joined in; but I could tell from the look on his face, he wasn't thinking of the blackout, even before he raised his gaze skyward.

"*Kuryat sada mangalam . . . shubha mangala savdhan . . .*"

Mom's strategic *sari*-draping technique gives me plenty of wiggle room. I can kick as high as a cheerleader without any worries that my *sari*'s going to fall down. I demonstrated to Preity and Rani.

"Way to go, Meenal Auntie," Preity said. "Now our lovely bride can dance until dawn."

Rani snickered. "Don't get your hopes up there, sparky."

"Oh, ye of little faith."

"Oh, me of mucho experience."

Preity laughed. "Hold on to your conch shell, Jaded One. Just when you think you have this one figured out," she said, tipping her head toward me, "she throws you for a loop." And sure enough, at the *sangeet* held on our exquisite mosaic-tiled rooftop terrace, Rani ate her words.

We couldn't have custom-ordered more perfect weather for the *sangeet*. Warm and dry with a fantastic breeze. Stars from every constellation R.S.V.P.'ed, and the crescent-shaped moon appeared close enough to jump and touch. Flower beds lining the *gachhi*'s perimeter brought the entire florist shop home, a riot of colors with intoxicating fragrance—*raat ki rani*, gardenia, hibiscus, roses, tuberoses, and marigolds. Strings of tiny white lights illuminated handmade, paper lanterns—red, orange, and yellow with star and moon cutouts. Musical notes of *filmi* songs, *bhangra*, and laughter floated in the air.

Preity, Rani, and I each dressed in pastel-colored, gauzy georgette *saris*. Together, we resembled three scoops of assorted melon sorbet: watcrmelon (me), honeydew (Preity), and cantaloupe (Rani).

Dancing with John, I smiled across the dance floor at Rani, shrugged, nonchalant. Later, I explained, "John loves all kinds of music, all kinds of dance. His passion's contagious."

Vivek lifted his collar and pretended to hide. "Borderline T.M.I. Please don't go there."

The Mrs., wearing a gorgeous salmon-and-turquoise *ghagara-choli*, playfully socked him. "Speak for yourself, Vivek."

"And me," Nikhil Tipnis backed him up. "Don't make us stick our fingers in our ears and start la-la-la'ing."

The first thing Nik said to me when he got to India for the wedding was, *Please don't take this the wrong way, but I'm* really *glad it didn't work out with us.* And I said, *Please don't take this the wrong way, but I* really *am, too.* He told me all their friends agreed: The life was back in John's eyes for the first time since Madelline died, and it had to take a pretty special person with an amazing heart to do that. When I heard that, I got all choked up and couldn't speak for the longest time, but when I finally pulled myself together, I told Nik that was the greatest compliment I ever received.

Rani and I went to sit, catch our breaths. "Kiran, Kiran, Kiran." She shook her head. "I always knew you had it in you, but if I didn't see it with my own eyes . . . Preity's going to be bummed she missed it." Rani gestured toward her, clear on the other side of the *gachhi,* sitting on the swing. "Hey, if Preity didn't actually *see* you dance, is she still entitled to bragging rights? You know, if a tree falls in the forest, and all that?"

"You're a nut," I said. "And I love you." Just saying it made my throat tight. "Damn it, I *don't* want to cry right here in front of everyone." I fanned myself with my napkin.

"No, you *don't.*" Rani started fanning me with *her* napkin. "The night's still young. And more importantly, I've only had one drink. So go fetch Little Miss Muffet from her tuffet and let's dance." She hugged-and-shoved me on my way.

The wooden swing, the size and shape of a picnic table top, hung from the concrete rafters. Preity wasn't on it by the time I got there, having been accosted by an auntie every fifth step. She stood by the marigolds, gazing up into the night. Nearing, I heard her talking. To herself? No. Under that minklike veil of hair, she had a cell phone in her hand, tucked to her ear.

"I know," she said, her voice soft and dreamy. "Me, too . . . But remember, whenever you miss me too much, just look up at the sky, and know that's what I'm doing, too. When I remind myself we're seeing the same view—the same sun, moon, and stars—then you don't seem so far away. The world isn't so big. I can be here, you can be there, and our hearts are still side by side." She kissed the air, disconnected. Dropped her head back, winded.

I shouldn't have still been there. I was mortified that I was. And I was stuck, because the second I moved, she'd hear me. I should have left when I realized she was on the phone, but my God, what human with a pulse could leave in the middle of *that*?

"Kids?" I asked, belatedly wondering if I should've coughed or cleared my throat first.

"Eric," she said, not the least startled, or embarrassed I heard her private conversation.

"Is that what I have to look forward to, I hope?"

Her lips curved, and with the milky moonlight bathing her up-tilted face, she looked ethereal as an angel. "If you want it . . . and you work at it . . . and you never take what you have for granted. It probably doesn't hurt to have a lucky star or two, either." She winked and escorted me back to the dance floor.

The priest calculated the precise time when the stars would align in our favor, the *muhurta*, to be 8:15 A.M.

"*Don't* be hung over," I told Vivek, plucking the drink from his hand before he took a sip. It didn't pass the sniff test. He protested he was a guy, he was allowed, this was India, yadda-yadda. I handed the cup to Rani. "Welcome to the Modern India."

"Now, don't pout, V," Rani said, just to get a rise out of him. "I'm an *artiste*. People expect me to be a lush. And wax poetic. And be eccentric. Talk about pressure. And with only one out of three, you can see why *I* need this drink more than—"

"No, you don't." Bryan took the drink and acted like it was his, smiling and nodding at Patrick Uncle and Uma Auntie, who were looking our way at that moment. "You triple-check the eccentric box, hon. That's the one that *really* counts."

"Honest? You're not just saying that because you love me?" Rani batted her eyelashes. "I just feel I could do better if I applied myself. You know there's *always room for improvement* with this overachieving crowd."

At that, we all cracked up.

I glanced past Vivek, did a double take, couldn't believe what I was seeing. "You guys! Check this out! Behind you!"

John-*baba* had the Hindi-Bindi Club—including *my* mother!—*his* mother, and Rani's Anandita-*mashi*, country line dancing in their *saris*!

"Good God!" Vivek laughed.

"For sure!" Bryan agreed.

"This guy's *definitely* a keeper!" Rani clapped her hands.

An auntie came up to me. "Where on earth did you find him, Kiran?"

I smiled. "My mother introduced us."

Preity sidled between Rani and me, linking her arms with ours. "So, shall we join in, then?"

Rani and I turned to her. Simultaneously, we said, "You bet!"

It was while we were dancing, all of my favorite people in one place, on a beautiful night under the stars, that I spotted my father on the sidelines, alone, looking like he would rather have been in surgery, or anyplace else that wasn't *there*.

And there it was again, a pinprick of sadness, reminding me of the hole in my heart only my father could fill.

Nearing the end of the *sangeet,* John and I managed to steal ten precious minutes alone. Vivek and Anisha kept guard for us while we necked in the shadows like two teenyboppers.

"How much longer?" I whined. "Are we almost there?"

"Soon." John lifted one of my *mehendi*-decorated palms to his lips. "Soon." He knew I was sad about my dad and trying hard not to be. Slowly, he traced the outline of my upper lip with the pad of his index finger, dipped his head so his mouth hovered over mine, and whispered exactly what I needed to hear, *"Kai bai Punyachi tariff, lavanga nighalya bareek . . ."*

We laughed—the low, intimate laughter of lovers who have a repository of inside jokes. That's what I love most about him. About us. He's strong when I'm weak, and I'm strong when he's weak. We balance each other on the two-person bicycle of life. And, we can always make each other laugh—life's best medicine.

We did it all backwards, this mating dance of ours, but it worked.

Amazingly, *it works. . . .*

"Kuryat sada mangalam . . . shubha mangala savdhan . . ."

"For my final words," my mother said in her reading, "I'd like to share a passage from Rudyard Kipling. Most of you know his often-quoted opening line from 'The Ballad of East and West.' "

She gave the relevant biographical information: The Nobel laureate was born in Mumbai, to English parents, in 1865. He left India when he was five, came back at sixteen—to Lahore, which is now part of Pakistan—and left again at twenty-three.

"For everyone who's ever felt misunderstood, take note. We're in excellent company." She then proceeded to read the stanza in its entirety:

Oh, East is East, and West is West,
and never the twain shall meet,
Till Earth and Sky stand presently
at God's great Judgment Seat;
But there is neither East nor West,
Border, nor Breed, nor Birth,
When two strong men stand face to face,
tho' they come from the ends of the earth!

"Now, I offer my humble take: '*East is East, and West is West; in Truth, the twain are One.*' "

John and I walked back to the *sangeet* with Vivek and Anisha for the finale. Saroj Auntie's powers of persuasion had worked, and we were concluding the festive night with a traditional weepy ballad, during which Indian brides and their parents cry their eyes out because she's grown up, leaving their house, going to join her husband's family. Why did my mother give in and allow this? John was playing sitar, and his friend Abhay was playing the *tabla*—hand drums.

They were amazing. They played to a spellbound audience. Even my father wasn't immune. Watching, his eyes glistened. In the middle, he leaned over, said something to Mom, then stood up and left. She didn't follow him. While it could have been that he had to use the Little Surgeon's Room, somehow, I doubted it. I excused myself and went after him.

I found him on the open staircase, alone in the shadows of the balcony landing one floor down, his profile in silhouette. Reluctant to intrude on his private moment—hadn't I done that enough tonight?—I turned away, then reconsidered, looking back over my shoulder. What was one more time? As unobtrusively as possible, I walked down the steps and stood beside him.

"Hi," he said.

"Hi."

"Nice night."

"Umm-hmm."

Neither of us looked at the other one, each staring straight ahead into the night.

I took a breath and prepared to say some kind of goodbye, but all I could think of was: *Okay, this was fun. Gotta run. Later much.* Before I could come up with anything better, my father said, "I was just thinking..."

Was he talking to me or himself? He definitely wasn't on a cell phone—that much I knew!—so it was one of the two.

"It's the stiff branch that easily snaps," he went on, "not the flexible branch.... And in the E.R., what do we see with car accident victims? It's the rigid, unyielding bodies that break, not the supple. . . ." He looked at me then, his eyes moist. "It's the same with the spirit, isn't it?"

I didn't move. I couldn't breathe.

Awkwardly, he shuffled his hand along the railing. Put it over mine. Patted. Stilled. Remained. A surgeon's hand. How many lives saved by this one hand? "Better late than never?" he asked.

I bobbed my head, turned my hand over, gripped his tightly. "Better late than never," I whispered, not bothering to wipe the tears gushing down my face because I didn't want to let go of my father's hand.

"*SHUBHA MANGALA SAVDHAN!!!*"

A final cry. A shower of rice. The *antarpath*'s pulled away. And there he is. My goldfish. At last. As *vajantri* music crescendos—*shehnai* and *choughada* played by John's pals—we're not the least bashful but feast our gazes on each other.

John wears a cream, boat-shaped *topi,* my head's uncovered. Matching *mundavalyas* frame our faces—two bands of dainty pearls tied across our foreheads, dangling from our temples, flower-and-bead tassels on the ends.

I rise onto my toes, hefting the thick garland of red roses, white lilies, pink and purple asters, assorted greenery, and threads of silver tinsel.

John doesn't playfully dodge my attempt, but lowers his head, making it easier. Grinning, he says, "I couldn't wait another second."

"You and me both," I say, smiling up at him. "Could you step it up with that garland?"

He holds my gaze, slipping a necklace more precious than gold or jewels over my head.

We are officially husband and wife.

Pandemonium uncorks. The music cranks, amplified to the highest decibels of the speakers. Deafening cheers soar sky-high, ricochet off the mountains. Rice arcs through the air, pours down like red rain. Giddy laughter bubbles from inside John and me, spilling over.

I glance over my shoulder to make sure my mother's back. She is, and beaming at us. She's obviously forgiven Giru-*mama* for forgetting to bring the mango leaves which we now require—his responsibility. Dad saved the day by scaling a retaining wall and plucking them off a tree minutes before the ceremony!

Now, between our foreheads, John holds the copper *kalash* containing holy water and a bouquet of mango leaves fringing a coconut. Smiling big, our gazes and hearts locked together, we lean in, touching our foreheads to the copper at the same time. And in that moment, with mayhem swirling around us, we two are standing in the calm eye of the hurricane.

Kuryat sada mangalam . . . shubha mangala savdhan . . .

The sacred mantras are still echoing in my head. Echoing. Echoing . . .

I feel a sense of connection, unlike any I've experienced. With history, with the universe, with my place in the continuum of time and space. With my parents. Grandparents. My husband. Our unborn children. Even grandchildren.

All that was. All that will be. *All that is.*

Om.

Zarkha's Gosht Ki Biryani
[Lamb & Rice Pilaf Casserole]

SERVES 10

LAMB:

3 pounds lean boneless lamb, washed and cubed

10 cloves fresh garlic, peeled

¼ cup fresh ginger root, peeled and chopped

4 fresh green chili peppers, chopped

½ cup fresh coriander (cilantro), chopped

½ cup fresh mint, chopped

1 teaspoon cayenne powder

½ tablespoon garam masala

1 teaspoon salt

½ teaspoon turmeric powder

1 cup plain yogurt

1. In a blender or food processor, whirl to a smooth paste: garlic, ginger, chilies, coriander, and mint. If needed, add 1–3 tablespoons water.
2. In a glass bowl, combine lamb, cayenne, garam masala, salt, and turmeric. Mix well.
3. Stir in yogurt and paste. Mix well, coating evenly.
4. Cover bowl with plastic wrap and refrigerate for 1–3 hours.

RICE PREP:

3 cups basmati rice

1 teaspoon salt

water

1. In a colander, rinse rice under tepid running water until water runs clear.
2. Transfer to a glass bowl. Add cold water until rice is submerged by 3 inches. Stir in salt. Soak 3 hours.

BIRYANI:

4½ cups cold water

1½ teaspoons saffron

¼ cup hot milk

2 tablespoons ghee or unsalted butter

2 bay leaves

4 black peppercorns

4 green cardamom pods

1 3-inch cinnamon stick

4 cloves

6 cups medium yellow onions, halved and thinly sliced into half-rings

2 teaspoons coriander powder

1 teaspoon cumin powder

½ cup dried apricots, coarsely chopped

¾ cup golden raisins

½ cup cashews

½ cup slivered almonds, divided ¼, ¼

1 cup canola oil, divided ¼, ¾

½ cup pistachios

¼ cup fresh coriander (cilantro), chopped

¼ cup fresh mint, chopped

1. Drain presoaked rice. In a medium-large pot over high heat, bring rice and cold water to a boil. Reduce heat to low. Cover and simmer until rice is almost cooked, about 15 minutes. Fluff rice with a fork. Set aside.
2. In a small bowl, combine saffron and hot milk. Set aside.
3. In a large, heavy skillet, heat 2 tablespoons ghee over medium heat. Add bay leaves, peppercorns, cardamom pods, cinnamon, and cloves. Sauté until color changes, about 2 minutes.

4. Add half the onions. Sauté until golden brown.
5. Carefully add the marinated lamb cubes. Stir in coriander powder and cumin powder. Sear cubes so they are brown on all sides. Reduce heat to medium-low. Cover and simmer until lamb is almost cooked, about 20 minutes, stirring every 5 minutes.
6. Add apricots, raisins, cashews, and ¼ cup almonds. Sauté about 5 minutes. Remove from heat.
7. Preheat oven to 300 degrees.
8. Grease a large casserole dish with nonstick cooking spray. First, layer ⅓ of the rice into the dish. Next, sprinkle ⅓ of the saffron milk. Then, layer ½ of the lamb mixture.
9. Repeat, adding another layer of rice, saffron milk, and lamb.
10. Top off with remaining rice, saffron milk, and pistachios.
11. Cover tightly with aluminum foil or lid. Bake until liquid evaporates and rice is tender, about 30 minutes. (Caution: don't overcook!)
12. Meanwhile, in a deep skillet, heat ¼ cup oil on medium. Add the remaining almonds. Stir-fry until they change color. Remove with slotted spoon. Drain on paper towels. Set aside.
13. To same skillet, add remaining oil. When hot, add the remaining onions. Stir-fry until brown and caramelized. Remove with slotted spoon. Drain on paper towels. Set aside.
14. When casserole has finished baking, remove from heat and transfer to a large serving platter or bowl. Remove

bay leaves, cardamom pods, cinnamon stick, peppercorns, and cloves.

15. Garnish with caramelized onions, toasted almonds, fresh coriander, and mint. Serve immediately.

Acknowledgments

From inception to completion, *The Hindi-Bindi Club* took four years, during which time I made three trips to India. I'm deeply indebted to innumerable people with whom I'm honored to have crossed paths. Dozens of Indians and Pakistanis graciously and candidly shared their experiences and insights. **To be clear: All mistakes and literary licenses in this novel are entirely my own.**

My heartfelt thanks to these off-the-chart kind, generous, and dear souls who truly went above and beyond with their time and expertise:

Deepali Adhikari
Usman Aijaz
Tarun & Pratishtha Durga
Avinash & Aruna Karnik
Sanchayita Ray
Javed & Farida Talat
Osama Tariq

Many, many thanks also to: Big T, Little Ani, Kumud B. Chitre (a.k.a. Kuma-maushi), Abhay-kaka, Varsha-kaki, Neela-atya, Ashu-maushi, Vilas-kaka, the Dighe family, the Sabnis family, the Savkar family, Swati Kaushal, Bela Kaul, Meenal Madhukar, and Seema Behl.

Dr. Paul McKendrick (a.k.a. Pei McKay of purple pen fame), my inimitably awesome high school journalism teacher who gave me these invaluable words of wisdom: "No matter what you write, someone won't like it."

Dr. John Collins, one of my favorite college professors, whose ethics class continues to influence and inspire me.

Wayne Dixon, self-professed "redneck chef," for testing recipes.

Kathryn Quay, one of the most intelligent women I've ever known, for cheerleading/gushing on demand and the greatest adventures via private Learjet.

Danielle Girard, for the terrific Bay Area run.

Melissa McClone, for "I'll take the guy next to him."

Roxanne Richardson, for "ting-ting-ting," "I want to die," and her gigantic left brain.

Valentina Plant, for "rainbows" and her gigantic right brain.

Marc MacYoung, for "silence between the notes."

Sean Bosquez, for "three wars."

Nicholas Tomashot, for "rinse and dry cycles."

Swati Kaushal, for "paper tiger."

For the past sixteen years, I've been blessed to be surrounded by extraordinary writers, many of whom I'm lucky to call friends. I especially wish to thank these precious gems for sharing the journey of this novel with me and boundless support/enthusiasm for my heritage studies: Pamela Bauer, Jean Brashear, Helen Brenna, Inglath Cooper, Jennifer Crusie, Debra Dixon, Kathleen Eagle, Lisa Gardner, Danielle Girard, Rosemary Heim, Lisa Hughey, Becky Klang, Christine Lashinski, Susan Kay Law, Melissa McClone, Malia Nahas, Tina Plant, Katie Quay, Rox Richardson, Barbara Samuel, Anna Seymour, Mary E. Strand, and Valerie Taylor.

Finally, the three godmothers of *Hindi-Bindi,* for whom no words can adequately express my profound gratitude:

Karen Solem, agent extraordinaire, who's made every recipe in this novel (and lived to tell!), and who had a *bindi* and threw a "Monsoon Wedding" party for her friends well before *Hindi-Bindi* was even a gleam in my eye. To think, I almost didn't tell you that day in Denver in 2002, it seemed *so* distant, such a stretch goal! Thank you for pushing me out of the nest and repeatedly assuring me I was ready to fly when I thought I was years away. (Most memorable line from Karen: "I've been screaming at you, screaming at my dog, and no one's listening!") You were right!

Micahlyn Whitt, dream editor, who cut her teeth on every Indian Diaspora novel ever written, and who was eagerly awaiting a novel like *Hindi-Bindi* many moons before it landed on her desk. I was meant to write this book; you were meant to edit it. Thank you for tirelessly championing and protecting the work, securing the extra time, wringing the best performance out of me, and letting me tell the story I wanted the way I wanted. Love you, chickpea!

Last but not least, the place where I started in this life, and I'm so happy to have returned: my mother. Culinary goddess and wise woman bar none. Mummyji, such a treat riding on the Hindi-Bindi Express with you, my fondest stop: when you said, floored, "*You* are teaching *me* Indian history?" Oh, the devilish pleasure, the smug satisfaction, I shall cherish it always, muahahaha! No adequate words for you; however, sonic vibrations when chanting this mantra come close: *Tu maji mummy ay . . . tu maji mummy aaaaay*!

Select Bibliography

Over the four years I spent writing and researching *The Hindi-Bindi Club,* I consulted hundreds of sources. I wish to acknowledge the following authors and their exceptional works that I found particularly helpful:

Blaise, Clark, and Bharati Mukherjee. *Days and Nights in Calcutta.* New York: Doubleday & Company, 1977.

Bumiller, Elisabeth. *May You Be the Mother of a Hundred Sons: A Journey Among the Women of India.* New Delhi: Penguin Books India, 1990.

Butalia, Urvashi. *The Other Side of Silence: Voices from the Partition of India.* Durham, NC: Duke University Press, 2000.

Chopra, Deepak. *Sacred Verses, Healing Sounds: The Bhagavad Gita, Hymns of the Rig Veda.* San Rafael, CA: New World Library/Amber-Allen Publishing, 1994.

Daniélou, Alain. *Music and the Power of Sound.* Rochester, VT: Inner Traditions International, 1995.

DasGupta, Sayantani, and Shamita Das Dasgupta. *The Demon Slayers and Other Stories: Bengali Folk Tales.* New York: Interlink Publishing Group, 1995.

Dutta, Krishna. *Calcutta, A Cultural and Literary History.* New Delhi: Roli Books, 2003.

Haeri, Shahla. *No Shame for the Sun: Lives of Professional Pakistani Women.* Syracuse, NY: Syracuse University Press, 2002.

Mehta, Ved. *The Ledge Between the Streams.* New York: W.W. Norton & Company, 1984.

Menon, Ritu, and Kamla Bhasin. *Borders & Boundaries: Women in India's Partition.* New Brunswick, NJ: Rutgers University Press, 1998.

Mitter, Sara S. *Dharma's Daughters, Contemporary Indian Women and Hindu Culture.* New Brunswick, NJ: Rutgers University Press, 1995.

Nagaswami, Vijay. *Courtship & Marriage: A Guide for Indian Couples.* New Delhi: Penguin Books India, 2002.

Nevile, Pran. *Lahore: A Sentimental Journey.* New Delhi: HarperCollins Publishers India, 1997.

Roy, Manisha. *Bengali Women.* Chicago: University of Chicago Press, 1992.

Salim, Ahmad. *Lahore 1947.* New Delhi: India Research Press, 2001.

A Note on the Author

Monica Pradhan's parents emigrated to the United States from Mumbai, India, in the 1960s. She was born in Pittsburgh, grew up in the Washington, D.C., area, and now lives in Minneapolis and Toronto with her husband.

Monica has a B.S. in managerial law and public policy from Syracuse University and an M.B.A. in finance from the University of Cincinnati. Prior to writing full-time, she worked in investments and management consulting. She was thrilled to trade frequent flying and power suits for the two-second commute and pajamas of a novelist, her lifelong dream.

Dear Reader,

My father fostered my love of books when I was growing up. Like Kiran's father, mine did not have a privileged childhood in Mumbai but studied extremely hard from an early age, eventually earning a full scholarship to the University of Pennsylvania.

My father always told me that when he was growing up, certain foods and all books were considered luxuries, and he always wanted me to have them, would never deny me those two things. This was his definition of "living the dream"—his dream that he wanted to gift me. So throughout my life, I have been indulged to my heart's content with food and books. My blessings, that my dad gave me, are what I want most to pass along to others . . .

In my research for The Hindi-Bindi Club, *I came across an on-line newspaper article about Aseema* (www.aseema.org), *a non-governmental education center for street children in Mumbai. They were seeking children's-book donations to build a library. I e-mailed them. Over the Internet, I was able to buy and ship children's books to the other side of the world. For the first time, these children had access to interesting and beautifully illustrated books. Thus began a beautiful friendship with this remarkable organization. Their focus is education and nutrition.*

Now, in addition to Aseema, I'm adopting a second charity, a fabulous organization called Room to Read (www.roomtoread.org) *in San Francisco. They partner with local communities in the developing world to establish schools and libraries. It costs $2,000 to create a children's library in an existing school, $8,000 to construct a stand-alone library, and $11,000-18,000 to build a school. I would like to fund all of these, and a portion of royalties from sales of* The Hindi-Bindi Club *will go toward this goal.*

I would have loved to keep working on this novel for another year or ten, but two years after going to contract, my editor and agent pried the manuscript out of my hands. My mom wanted more recipes, but I kept reminding her (and myself!): This is a novel, not a cookbook. I did promise to make it up to her, and anyone else with a hankering for more Indian recipes, on my web site: www.hindi-bindi.com.

I do hope you'll visit. There is a kinship among readers. When we read the same book, we travel to the same world. Though I am here living my life, and you are there living yours, we now share a community. And though our experiences may differ, we know the same people: Kiran, Preity, Rani, Meenal, Saroj, and Uma. I would love to hear what you think about them. And if your book club plans to read The Hindi-Bindi Club, *I would be honored to phone in and join your gathering via speakerphone. Please feel free to email me at: Hindi-Bindi@pobox.com*

From my heart,
Monica Pradhan